MIA EVERS

AND THE DEMON'S CURSE

ANGELA GUAJARDO

Gila Monster Press

Mia Evers and the Demon's Curse

Cover by Bukovero

Published in the United States by Gila Monster Press.

ISBN: 978-1-961815-01-8

To students everywhere

Chapter 1

"This school is probably not the best place for your daughter, Mr. Evers," the principal said with a slight frown. Mr. Redd sat behind a sprawling mahogany desk, his short, stocky frame visible from half his tie and up. He placed a hand on my leather-bound transcripts, as if trying to cover the truth about me.

I sank lower in my chair, willing Mr. Redd to say I could go to this dumb school. I didn't care where I went next. The sooner I stopped getting expelled, the sooner life could get back to normal. Dad got madder and madder as school after school kicked me out. For the past few years, he'd worn a glare through all of Mom's urgings to calm down and my little sister's crying. Today he buried the glare under anxiety etching deep lines in his clean-shaven face.

"But you'll still take her?" My dad leaned forward in his cushioned chair, sweat beading on his tanned forehead despite the cool air.

The principal crinkled his nose. "Only if you decide Toolena Mesa is the best place for her and her... needs, Mr. Evers." He leafed through the pages that were my education from three other schools, six long years that were anything but fun. "Based on Mia's transcripts, she'll do fine academically." He flipped to the last few pages, a list of comments left by my previous teachers. "Antisocial, reluctant to interact with peers, hardly talks, but testing shows she performs at grade level. Avid reader, always at the top of her class in reading comprehension and vocabulary. Yes, yes, that's all very well and good but—" He flipped to the last page, and his pale green eyes peered over the rim of his glasses at me.

I dug my fingertips into the armrests.

"She's aligned with Dark."

My insides squirmed. Those eyes held the same silent ridicule as everyone else's once they'd found out. Of the seven elemental alignments—Earth, Air, Fire, Water, Light, Dark, and Kindred—Dark was the only one people feared and hated. Why did my teachers have to put something like that my in records? I bowed my head so my hair hid my face from the world.

"Mia's never hurt anyone," Mom said. Lines of worry wrinkled her brow as she hugged my sister tighter. Bela fussed about wanting to go play outside. Mom shushed her. "She's only eleven."

The principal scanned the page. "Ghosts following her everywhere. Scares fellow students and makes them feel uncomfortable. Sometimes scares staff. This isn't the environment I want to create at this school."

"They're afraid of the ghosts, not her," Mom said,

edging closer. Dad placed a reassuring hand on Mom's knee.

Mr. Redd closed the notebook and gave Mom a look that said her words didn't fool him. "No, they're scared of both, unfortunately. I myself don't fully understand the powers of those aligned with Dark, but —"

"I swear to you she's never hurt anyone."

He put his hands up. "Relax, relax. I believe you."

Mom sucked in a breath. The room fell silent. She sank back into her chair, the wood creaking. "You do?" she said.

"Based on her determination to not look at any of us at the moment, I'm sure she's given a student or two a good fright on purpose, but the personality description in her records makes it hard to believe she'd readily cause anyone harm. The specific incidences don't give me cause for worry. Besides, I'm sure life hasn't been easy."

I peeked at the principal through a gap in my bangs. Did I hear him right?

"People don't always react kindly towards what they don't understand," he said.

He stood and I did a double-take. How could an adult be so short? Mr. Redd had been sitting when the lady at the front desk ushered us into his office. He'd been an island of graying red hair in a sea of mahogany desk. Standing made him mere inches taller, bringing my eyes level with his elbow. How could someone so short be a principal? Still, I had to admit he looked like the kind of adult that never smiled or laughed.

Mr. Redd stationed himself between his desk and a cabinet with a bunch of pictures standing on it. "I consider myself progressive when it comes to Darks. Times have changed. While most people are afraid, I refuse to be. I'm trying to shape this school into being open-minded."

"Trying?" Dad asked.

"I've been with this district for years. Instilling progressive ideals in a community takes time. That's why I'm hesitant to encourage you to enroll your daughter at the moment. I don't think they're ready to accept Darks again."

"Where else would we go?" Mom asked. "We're running out of schools to try. Everywhere we go, they end up expelling her because she's a Dark. Schools think we're putting her up to it." She gestured to her and Dad. "Light preserve us, that's absurd. We are not raising our daughter to terrorize children."

Mr. Redd gave Mom a thoughtful frown. "Have you considered homeschooling or a private tutor?"

"We don't have that kind of money," Dad said.

Mr. Redd nodded.

I did the Dad-like thing and looked away from everyone.

"What about a boarding school for Darks?" the principal said. "There are state-funded ones."

Mom started to say something when Dad said, "Why would the state fund such schools?" He sounded curious.

Mom leaned away from Dad, her mouth ajar.

I clenched the edges of my leather chair and mentally braced for another fight as guilt made my chest roil.

"Jay! Don't tell me you'd consider such a thing?"

"Babe, we're running out of options."

"We're not dumping our daughter off with a bunch of strangers like that."

Dad's pale-eyed gaze darted to me.

I must've sensed it coming or something. We made eye contact. Fear filled me like ice water. My heart beat faster. "What's boarding school?" Whatever it was, it wasn't good, and Dad was willing to dump me there. That look, as brief as it was, had said as much.

"Don't worry about it," Mom said with a sharp shake of her head. "You're not going to one."

Mr. Redd held his hands up in surrender. "I apologize for suggesting such a thing."

The principal didn't sound in the least bit sorry. His straight face with slightly puffy cheeks was equally indifferent. His tone sounded no different from a math teacher telling the class he was giving long division homework. Real apologies were the ones Mom and Dad exchanged after yelling at each other a lot. This meant Mr. Redd was as willing as Dad to send me to boarding school. I sat up a little straighter, like a decent student who knew how to behave. I had to get into this stupid school.

"Apology accepted," Mom said.

Mr. Redd turned to his photos, a collection of thin stone slabs with images expertly carved into them with Earth magic. The dyes soaked into the surface were done so well that I did a double-take to absorb the fact that those weren't real miniature people etched into stone. I half expected them to start moving, like paintings did in some of my favorite books.

Mr. Redd picked up a photo, studied it a moment, and then showed it to me. "Miss Evers, which one of these students died?"

5

This was the first time someone had asked me something like that. He looked totally serious. This had to be a joke, though. My mom's slight grimace told me to answer the principal's question. I met his gaze. Just because he said he refused to be afraid of people like me didn't mean he meant it. My parents were a constant reminder of that. At least they tried to hide their fear. They failed miserably, but they tried.

Well, it was either stay quiet and make Dad madder or answer the question, get rejected from this school, and make Dad madder. At least Mom would appreciate it if I cooperated.

Four high school boys in team uniforms with big numbers on the front and pads protecting their shoulders, elbows, and knees smiled at me. Two of them looked really cute and one really scary, like his nose had been broken. The boy on the right side was half a head shorter than everyone.

How was I supposed to know who had died by looking at a picture of them? "I don't—" A white orb shot out of the shortest boy and flew at my face. A flash of his face full of terror appeared in my mind, the mouth forming two words.

Get out!

I flinched, and a wave of cold air washed over me. My heartbeat quickened. For a moment, I shared the boy's terror. Chairs creaked. My parents must've jumped, too. Sure enough, Mom clutched Dad's arm. Bela's gaze was fixed on Mom.

"Mommy, why'd you jump?" Bela said.

My parents stared at me with open fear. Mr. Redd, however, wore an expectant expression. Guess he wanted an answer. I'd learned never to tell my parents anything about what I'd seen or heard that had to do with dead people. I pointed to the short, blonde boy. "That one."

Mr. Redd nodded. "Correct. May I ask what made you flinch?"

Mom's knuckles were bright white against Dad's reddening arm. Mom stared at me. Dad glared at the sunny view outside the window, his face hard. If only I could pretend I hadn't heard the question, maybe Mr. Redd would stop asking things and leave me alone. Why'd this matter? "A white orb flew out of the picture and right towards me." It was close enough to the whole truth. I'd also learned to not repeat mean messages from the dead. "Get out" was a common message, usually carrying the weight of anger. Ghosts knew I could see and hear them. Most of them wanted to be left alone. But this ghost was terrified.

Why? This was so not a good first impression of this school.

Putting the photo back, Mr. Redd smiled. "Very good. That young man was Orton Totes. He should be a senior this year, but he died from an illness three years ago." His smile vanished as he studied the photo. "It devastated all of us to lose one so young. His parents moved out of town shortly after."

"That's sad," Mom said.

"Why are you sad, Mommy?" Bela said.

"I'll explain it later." Mom adjusted Bela in her lap.

Mr. Redd shifted his gaze to me. "Maybe you can show people that your alignment can bring them closure. Can you connect with the dead on command?"

Okay, that was too much to ask for in front of my parents. I sat hiding from the rest of the world behind my hair once again.

"Maybe your alignment can help you." Footsteps shuffled away, and a leather chair creaked. Mr. Redd sat at his desk again. "And maybe not. The last time we had a Dark student was the year Orton died. He became the scapegoat. Long story short, the district was forced to expel the Dark student despite the lack of evidence. That's why I'm reluctant to enroll your daughter here. People may fear a repeat of history."

"Did that student cause the boy's death?" Mom said.

He shook his head. "I highly doubt it, but once a rumor spreads, it cannot be unsaid. Still, it's been three years. Maybe it's time for a fresh start if we do this the right way. Maybe it's the chance we need to help the community accept people like your daughter."

I didn't care about being accepted. I wanted to be left alone. Well, what I really wanted… I looked askance at my family and my stupid heart twisted. Would we ever be a real family again? Maybe if I made this school work.

"And of course, maybe it hasn't been long enough. I don't want to make your lives harder than they already are."

Mom paled. "What if we hide her alignment?"

Mr. Redd placed a hand on my academic records. "The teachers have to know. Part of a proper education is honing and strengthening their alignment. Darks deserve the same education as all the other elements, despite unpopular opinions. It's also why I suggested —" He searched for the right word. "—alternatives."

"Mia, take your sister and go wait in the hallway a moment." Mom stood and guided Bela to the doorway, a thick alphabet book in hand.

Even though my sister was only four, she already knew a handful of letters and numbers. And since she was four, she was too young for her alignment to manifest. She was blissfully free of having to grasp and harness magical powers until around age five. My alignment had manifested days after my fifth birthday.

"We'll only be a minute."

Accepting the book, Bela drifted into the hallway, identifying individual letters in the colorful title.

Not wanting to risk either parent getting angry or making the principal think I was a bad kid, I slid off my chair. Mom pointedly stared at the principal, making me feel like I was walking past a statue that would spring to life and attack if I stuck around too long. I hurried out into the hall and the door clicked shut behind me.

Bela plopped onto the wood floor and continued cheerfully blurting out letters, as if each one was an amazing discovery. I scrunched up next to her, placing an ear near the base of the door. There was a small enough gap to wedge my pinkie finger through, plenty of room for their voices to reach my ears.

Mom said, "Mr. Redd, we love Mia very much. We want what's best for her."

"And what do you think that is?" Mr. Redd said.

A moment of silence followed. "I'm not sure anymore," she said.

No. Mom couldn't possibly agree with Dad. I bent lower and pressed the back of my head to the wall, only to have a small hand pat my back.

"Mia, is this 'e' or three?"

I flinched. Her voice was annoyingly loud. "E," I whispered tersely. "The next one's F. Use your indoor voice."

"Don't tell me what to do. You're not Mom."

Sitting up, I planted both hands on the floor and gave Bela *the look*. "And what would Mom tell you if she heard you talking this loud?"

Bela tried to give me her own glare. With her big dark eyes, small mouth, and bangs pinned back with a pair of daisy bobby pins, it was an adorable pout. As annoying as my sister was, she was too cute for her own good.

Bela's eyes teared up and her lower lip trembled. "Don't smile." She popped to her feet, sending the book to the floor with a clatter, and burst into the principal's office. "Moooom, Mia's being mean."

My heart beat so hard that I barely heard anything over the thudding in my head. This was it. This was all the reason my parents and the principal needed to dump me at a boarding school. Never mind the problems I caused at school. I was a problem at home and my parents had to be sick of it. I slowly stood, my back sliding against the wall.

Dad came out into the hallway, carrying a sniffling Bela, and taking one slow, purposeful step at a time. His dusty boots thumped on wood. I took an involuntary step back as he closed the office door. "What happened?" he said.

Bela had Dad's t-shirt balled up in her fists, pulling the shirt tight against all his muscles. "She's being mean," Bela said.

I dropped my gaze to the floor. "I told her to use her indoor voice."

Dad sighed through his nose. Without saying a word, he picked up the book and carried Bela into the front office. He went through the pages with her.

Muffled voices from the principal's office convinced me to peel my gaze away. As much as I wanted to be lovingly held by Dad, and as much as I wanted to scrunch back up to better eavesdrop, I settled for pressing my ear to the wall.

Agonizing minutes ticked by before the door opened, making me jump a second time. Mom stepped into the hallway, a piece of paper in hand. For some crazy reason, she gave me a hug, tears in her eyes.

Dad's frame towered over us. "We good to go?"

Mom nodded. "He accepted her into Toolena Mesa."

Chapter 2

The same ghost that had shot out of the picture now huddled by the dining area windows, wringing his wispy hands as I tried to figure out how to get rid of him without getting caught doing Dark stuff. His pale, incomplete figure was barely visible against the white wall. White and gray lines hinted at short, messy hair, like he'd worn a helmet all day, and shadowed curves arched over the empty spots where his eyes should've been. Those blank eye sockets followed my dad and some friends of his as they made trip after trip inside the new house, carrying wood crates and furniture inside.

Well, new to us. The outside was bleached from years and years of desert sun, and the paint was badly chipped. The inside needed more paint, too, and the wood floors looked permanently dusty from years of being walked all over. At least the place looked sturdy enough to survive storm season.

Several wood boxes filled the center of the living room floor, an old recliner sat opposite a fireplace, and a table with four chairs was set up between where the living room and kitchen met. I sat on one of the boxes, lightly tapping my heels against the side, and breathed in its pine scent. Bela sat beside me, watching everything as intently as the ghost, and drummed her heels hard enough to make my box vibrate.

I stuffed down my desire to snap at her to stop. Both the sound and the vibration were annoying. My sister was annoying. However, the last thing I needed was to make her cry. I redirected my annoyance to our spectral visitor.

Go away, ghost. I don't know why you're here, but leave me and my family alone.

I silently willed it to leave, picturing it zooming off like a shooting star. Sometimes that was enough to make a ghost leave. But not this one. My will was stopped by a sensation of pushing against a wall. This ghost blocked my will as it watched in terror at everything getting unloaded.

A wave of dust swirled across the living room. Dad walked in backwards, watching over his shoulder as he stepped up and inside. He held an arm outstretched, face etched with concentration as he repeatedly rolled his other wrist. Air swirled around him and under the floating mattress that followed. He guided the mattress across the living room and into the kitchen as one of his buddies, also guiding the mattress with his Air alignment, followed on the other side. The house filled with blowing air, sending dust everywhere.

The ghost lunged for the mattress.

I dug my fingers and heels into the wood. In my mind, I saw the mattress go flying, Dad and his friend gaping at the empty space between them, and then both of them turning in my direction, livid.

The ghost shot through the mattress as if it weren't there.

Dad's friend shivered as he passed within arm's length of the ghost. "Hold on a sec." Both he and Dad stop rotating their wrists. The mattress sank to the floor and the wind died out. The friend rubbed his muscly arms as if cold.

Dad's brows drew together. "You alright?"

"Random chill. I'm good." He rubbed his hands and nodded to Dad, who arched an eyebrow at me.

Orton stood near Dad's friend, staring longingly at the mattress. Dad's eyes narrowed. I shrugged. If he didn't know what was going on, I sure wasn't going to admit to knowing.

Dad shook his head. Together, they willed the mattress back into the air and guided it out of sight.

I let out a frustrated sigh. Why did this stupid ghost have to follow me home? Why couldn't it make it easy to pretend to be normal?

A snarl from my mom sounded from the direction the mattress had gone. A large wave of air blew through the house, sending mine and Bela's hair across our faces. I swept my bangs aside.

Bela pushed her hair back, too. "Whee! Again, Mommy."

"You two couldn't just carry it?" Mom said. "It's not like it's heavy."

"It's big and awkward," Dad said. "Besides, this is more fun."

"Maybe for you."

Another blast of air filled the house. Dad and his friend hurried to the front door, giggling like naughty schoolboys as they shielded their faces. They passed the ghost again and both of them shivered.

Dad stiffened and his eyes widened. He slowly turned in my direction.

Oh, no. He recognized that shiver.

Mom stormed into the living room. "I already have a big enough mess to clean up. The previous tenants clearly didn't take care of this place and the owners clearly didn't try hard to clean up after—"

Dad jabbed a thumb in my direction and gave a slight shake his head.

Mom's eyes widened with a mix of shock and rage.

The ghost boy drifted to the doorway and stared out into the desert. Dad passed through it and swore as he shivered again. "Do something about it," he said.

Whether he spoke to me or Mom, I wasn't sure. Mom considered the doorway a moment before turning to me. She forced a smile to appear. "Mia, why don't you take your sister outside to play?" she said with fake lightness.

"I want to stay inside," Bela said.

"Go outside," Mom said, giving us both the look. When she wore that expression, things only got worse if we argued. Bela had already learned that at age four.

I slid off my box and held out my hand. "C'mon, let's go."

Bela considered Mom a moment before spotting my hand. She took it and I led us into the back yard— well, into the desert. Real yards had fences or bushes to make it obvious where one yard ended and another began. We had no fences and neither did any of the handful of neighbors. Everyone was so squishy back in the city, but out here, it was more bushes, cacti, and open desert than houses.

A covered porch sat against the back of the house, complete with a table and four dusty cushioned chairs. To both my frustration and relief, the ghost followed us, keeping several feet between us and his terror pressing against me. Better to bug me than the rest of my family.

I mentally pushed back, refusing to let his terror become mine. "Why do you want me to leave so bad?" I said under my breath.

"What?" Bela said. She climbed onto one of the chairs, smearing dust all over her legs and pink shorts.

"Nothing. Just thinking aloud." Bela was too young to understand much of anything about alignments beyond knowing that Mom and Dad could make air move. She was oblivious to the existence of ghosts and how they liked to follow me everywhere. She didn't understand why our parents got mad at me a lot or why we were no longer in the city. All this was a big adventure to her. All she cared about was playing and having fun. No fair. If only we could trade places now and then. I could've used a break from being me.

"This is comfy." Bela sat back in the chair, her little sneakers barely reaching the edge of the cushion.

I cringed at the thought of sitting on one of those things before Mom cleaned them. They were more brown than the dark blue they were supposed to be. I lifted the seat cushion off the chair next to Bela, spotted stains, and let it drop. The cushion slowly slid against the metal armrests and settled back into place. Nope, not any cleaner on the other side.

"Are you gonna sit?" Bela said.

"I'm gonna look around."

"I wanna come." She slid off the chair, smearing her backside to match her front.

I clenched my teeth. I needed some personal space, not an upset Bela running Mom and Dad, complaining about me refusing to explain why I was talking to myself again. That'd make Mom and Dad mad, probably trigger another fight, and then Dad would disappear for a while, and then Mom would start crying, and then so would Bela, and then I'd cry, and then—

I took a deep breath, picturing a ring of white light surrounding me and keeping bad energy out. I needed calm. I needed the ghost gone. Mentally shielding myself from its terror was tiring me out.

"I'm not really going anywhere," I said to Bela. "Go look around and tell me what's in our yard."

"Where's our yard?"

I snorted. "I dunno. Let's find out." I tasked Bela with scouting small sections of desert. She brought back the occasional pretty rock, screamed once, and came running to me when she found a stinger, a many-legged bug that had a long tail with a needle-like barb on the end. I helped her throw some rocks in the stinger's general vicinity until something else caught Bela's attention. She ran a few bushes into the desert, staying plenty close enough to spot her pink shorts through the brush. I approached our ghostly company.

The ghost boy—I forgot his name already—gave me a brief look before resuming staring through the living room window, his fear pressing on me like midsummer heat.

I stopped outside arm's reach, shivered, and took a step back. Being a Dark, I was far more sensitive to the presence of dead things. Dad and his friend hadn't sensed the ghost until they were on top of it, which was made possible by the ghost's intense emotional state. Normally non-Darks wouldn't sense anything. All I had to do was be in the same building as one and I knew if any were present. Somehow, this ghost's presence had hidden from me until he popped out of the photo.

"Why did you follow me home?"

An icy wave of emotion rippled around me as the boy grimaced. He shook his head. "You need to leave and never come back."

Okay, freaky. Most ghosts wanted to be left alone, hence the get out comment, but this boy's soul belonged somewhere else. Why would he bother telling me to leave a place he wasn't attached to? "Why?"

"It's…" He huffed. "It's…" He shook his head again. "Leave."

"It's okay. You can tell me. I won't hurt you." I couldn't even if I wanted to. I didn't know how, much less if it was possible.

The boy shook his head again. "Can't."

That was an unusual answer. Taking a deep breath, I opened my awareness to dead things a little. Any more and his terror would overwhelm me. It was like opening a window in my mind enough to stick my finger through the gap. It let a little energy in and a little out, but not too much all at once.

The boy turned away. "Don't."

I tilted my head, feeling out the fear. This boy wasn't afraid of me. He was afraid for me, afraid of something else. "What's got you all scared?"

"Can't."

"Can't what? You're not making any sense."

"Don't go back."

"Back where?"

He looked into the desert.

I followed his gaze. There was nothing but open desert, a few roofs, and my sister crouched beside a bush, drawing something in the dirt with a stick. Maybe he meant somewhere beyond. "The school?" He said nothing, but his energy shifted, making my gut swirl. That feeling meant I'd guessed right. I took a step closer. "Look, I have to make this school work. You're the one who needs to leave."

The ghost shook his head and resumed watching inside the house. His transparent body didn't so much as flinch at the glare I gave it. He was more annoying than my sister. Huffing, I stomped away. Fine. Be stupid and annoying. I wasn't going to freak out over every last ghost who told me to get out.

"Mia, come see what I drew." Bela waved me over and pointed to the ground.

I stood behind my sister and took in a terrible drawing of some blobby thing with front legs and two horns. "Nice job," I said. Rule number one of avoiding meltdowns: pretend to be proud of everything a four-year-old did. "What is it?"

"A bunny."

I did a double-take at what I realized were pointy ears. The rest of her bunny consisted of a smaller circle for a head and a blobby circle for the body, and a lumpy little blob for its tail. It had no back legs. Her drawing gave me an idea. "Good job. Why don't you draw me something else? Take your time." Beaming, Bela merrily agreed and crouched over a fresh patch of rocky dirt. I took one step back and then another. When my sister remained focused on her masterpiece, I took a few more steps back before turning around. I hunted around for something to draw with, locating a triangular rock near one corner of the house. I crouched a few feet behind the ghost and began drawing.

There were these things called power circles every alignment could use. I didn't know much about them beyond that they were supposed to help a person focus their alignment to do stuff, like a Water could redirect rivers, Earths could move and shape more rock, and Airs could create air barriers to protect an encircled spot. I had no idea what Darks could do with power circles. Maybe I could use one to get rid of this stubborn ghost.

I drew a sloppy outer ring and stopped. What was supposed to go inside? I wrote the words "go away" in the middle and studied my progress. Power circles were supposed to include runes or symbols. They helped focus an alignment's power and give it clear intent. The world was full of runes that were a part of our daily lives, from runes that turned lamps on and off, controlled the flow of water so we could shower and stuff, kept heat in and out of houses, and so on. We were taught how to read runes after learning the alphabet, and each alignment had its own specially designed set of runes. Of course, no teacher ever dared teach me Dark runes.

I made some lines and squiggles around the two words, gripping my rock harder with every stroke. I was making nonsense. This wouldn't work. I didn't know what I was doing. And if my parents ever caught me experimenting with power circles, they'd probably ground me until they found a boarding school to stuff me in.

I threw the rock at my circle and stood. It bounced a few times, landing near where the ghost's feet would've been if they were visible. The ghost continued to watch inside the house.

"Mia, whatcha drawing?"

I did a full-body flinch and hastily dug some zigzags with my sneaker and swiped at the nearest edge as little feet thumped closer. "Nothing. I'm just doodling." Her shadow fell over the edge of my circle.

She tilted her head. "What's doodling?"

"It means you draw stuff without really thinking about what you're doing."

"I wanna doodle."

I picked up the nearest rock and handed it to my sister. "Here. Have fun."

Beaming, Bela took it and sabotaged my circle. Thank the Light for small mercies. Mom and Dad would never know about the circle. Hopefully, they'd never find out about the ghost.

Mom rounded the corner of the house and stopped. The ghost took one look at her and vanished, taking his terror with him. The emotion pressing down on me lifted. I took the deepest breath I'd had in hours.

Mom's gaze darted to me before settling on Bela. She forced a pleasant smile. "They're done unpacking. You two can come inside now."

Bela ran over and held out her arms to be picked up.

Mom's mismatched eyes widened. She stopped my sister at arm's length. "And go straight into the bathtub.

What on Aardra were you two doing?"

"Exploring and doodling," Bela said. "Look." She pointed to my sabotaged circle. The outer ring was still visible.

My stomach clenched as Mom's brows drew together. "That's very nice, sweetie. What did you draw?"

"I dunno. Mia said it's doodling."

A corner of Mom's mouth crinkled in a slight grimace. She took in the mess, glanced at me, and then at the ground one more time. "Very good. Let's get you washed up." She delicately held one of my sister's wrists and I followed them both to the front of the house. A beat-up truck now sat empty by the front door.

Bela ran over to Dad in all her pink and dirty glory. "Daddy!"

Grinning, Dad scooped her into his muscly arms. "There's my little gremlin. How'd you get so dirty?" He caught sight of me and his gaze shifted to the doorway. His smile vanished. "Go get washed up, cutie." He set Bela on the ground. "Hal, we should get to work."

"Tonight? I'm tired. Aren't you tired?"

"Tonight."

Mom took a step closer. "What about dinner, Jay?"

"We'll grab something on the road. Today was an expensive day."

Mom stuck out her lower lip. "You're right. Be careful."

"Always. Love you, babe. See you later." Dad pecked Mom's forehead, mussed Bela's hair, and climbed into the truck's passenger seat.

Yup, still mad about the ghost.

Dust rippled out in all directions as the hover

charm raised the truck off the ground.

Mom and Bela watched the truck leave, longing on their faces. Mom sighed and led Bela inside the house.

I took one last look at the truck, tail lights glowing red as they reached the main dirt road, and headed inside as well.

Not only did I need to make this school work, I had to figure out how to keep the ghost away from my family.

Chapter 3

I found myself stuck with two chatty ladies and the same stupid ghost in the front office as Mom filled out an enrollment form, Bela holding onto the hem of Mom's white shirt as she took in the space. The front office looked nice enough with its vaulted ceiling and cabin-like walls and floor. The pine planks were bright but full of knots, like dark, unblinking eyes dotting every surface. As if to hide those eyes, student decorations celebrating autumn blanketed the walls, including sloppy leaf cutouts that spelled "welcome" in all capitals. Kindergarteners must have cut the leaf shapes. Some looked more like swords or bird feet than leaves. Now if only they could hide the ghost.

He huddled near the hallway leading deeper inside the office. Shadowed gaze fixed on the papers, he wrung his transparent hands as he emanated terror once again. A door opened behind us. The boy gasped and vanished, freeing me from having to mentally shield myself from his presence once again.

Mr. Redd sauntered by, giving us a polite nod. I nodded back and shifted, putting my mom between us. She never looked up from the form. The principal waved the short, chubby receptionist over. He whispered something into her ear and disappeared into his office.

Mom handed over a completed form and the receptionist accepted it with long-nailed fingers. Bright teal nail polish contrasted with her curly hair when she pushed it aside. Her hair was as dark as mine. The tight curls bounced with every slight head movement. She chewed on gum as she studied the first page. Her bright red lips formed a smile, revealing white teeth. "Welcome to Toolena Mesa, Mia. Mr. Redd assigned you everyone's favorite sixth-grade teacher. You'll really like Miss Wren."

I'm sure I would for the whole two seconds she wouldn't know I was aligned with Dark. Teachers tried just as hard to be polite as my parents after they found out, but their forced smiles looked like grimaces, and they stayed as far away from me as they could, even going so far as to have students hand me graded assignments or claim they mysteriously went missing.

"My name is Desi," the receptionist said. "You can come to me for anything, even if it's to complain about how much homework you have." She winked.

I nodded, wondering why she was being so nice. Did she know about my alignment? Is that what Mr. Redd whispered to her? An elbow nudged me.

Mom looked down at me, her face stern. "Show some manners and say 'thank you.'"

I drew back half my bangs and mumbled my thanks before my hair fell back in place.

"Mia!" Mom said.

"Oh, that's quite alright," Desi said, waving a dismissive hand. She faced a slanted stone slab behind her desk that sat above a limestone water basin and placed the form on the slanted part, face down. "I don't blame her for being shy. She's changing schools two months into the year. That's scary for a lot of kids." She flipped an attached stone slab atop the parchment, like she was closing a book. That slab was as thin as the photos.

I didn't care about when in the school year so much as I did that this was my fourth school in six years. My parents used to be so much happier when we never had to move, so what could I do differently to make that bearable? At least my weak words of gratitude hadn't counted against me in Desi's eyes.

"We see it a fair bit out here in the boonies. Some want to get out of the city and into a quieter life. Others think they want that quiet life but can't handle being so far away from everything and move back." She drew a few runes on the stone with a long fingernail and then placed her hands on it. Veins of green light shot down the sides of the slab and into the basin, turning the water green too. The glow was so bright that it turned the undersides of her arms green. Desi removed the paper and repeated the process with my transcripts. "So what brings you all the way out here? I saw your husband leave earlier. Did he find a job in the mines?"

It was true we were a family that had come from the city but this was a huge move even for us. I didn't know what Dad did for a living but I had a feeling it wasn't a day job like other dads had. Mom would always say "I'll tell you later" every time I asked. My only clues were the neat things he brought home in the night and the occasional periods when we all were hungry all the time. Mostly he brought things we needed, like clothes, food, and kitchen stuff, but he often came back with a toy for Bela or books for me and Mom. Every time this happened, too absorbed in the latest fairytale, I'd forget for a while.

"Yeah," Mom said offhandedly. "A job," she added as if an afterthought.

"Yay, more presents," Bela said loud enough to make me cringe.

Whatever job it was, I knew it wasn't the mines. I looked at her, but she didn't meet my gaze.

"That's great," Desi said, switching out pages. Mom and I tensed when she got to the final two pages, the ones that marked me as a problem child and a Dark, but she scanned them into the memory stone without so much as a hint of hesitation. Mom's shoulders relaxed as Desi bound my transcripts back up with a leather cord and I remained tense. "All right, Mia, you are officially in our system. Come stand over here so we can get a picture of you."

Desi acted like she hadn't read the transcript. Maybe she hadn't. Her smile was genuine this time, too. I'd learned to tell the difference between real and fake smiles. Real ones took up a person's whole face. Fake ones forgot to include the eyes.

Mom nudged me. "Let's go. I still have a lot of unpacking and cleaning to do."

I shuffled over to the chipped X painted on the wood floor and faced the pedestal Desi slid a hand-size stone slab into.

"Eyes on me, please, and hair away from your face." I forced my gaze from my shoes and tucked half my bangs behind one ear. "All of it, hon."

Mom walked over and fussed with my hair. She hesitated, but whatever she did to pretend to forget about my alignment won over. She finger-combed my hair and I closed my eyes, relishing her touch. It happened so rarely. She loved me. She was my mom. But she was afraid of me, too, and I didn't know what to do with that other than not take her fear personally. Her nails gliding along my scalp sent relaxing waves down my back and suddenly the world didn't seem like such a terrible place after all. She licked a thumb to tame the last stubborn strands into place and guided half my long cascade of hair to fall over the front and the other half down my back, exposing me to the world.

"That's better." She planted one hand on her hips.

"Oh, that is," Desi said. "She looks so pretty and just like you. Now, eyes on the stone and smile."

I opened my eyes and fought the urge to look anywhere but at the stone. I'd been through this too many times. This would be just another picture that marked the beginning of my stay in this jail, until the jailer saw it fit to throw me out. Sure, Desi was nice, but that would stop one day. Even the principal would turn once he realized how difficult it was having me in a school.

No. I couldn't keep thinking like this. I had to make Toolena Mesa work.

Not having a genuine smile in me, much less the desire to fake one, I settled for giving the stone a look of terror.

Desi stood with a hand ready to imprint my face on the stone. Her eyes widened. She leaned to the side, as if not believing what she saw. "Oh, wow, your eyes are two different colors. How cool." She looked at Mom as if for the first time. "You both do. I can't believe I missed that."

"It's heterochromia," Mom said. "We were both born with it. Mine aren't as pronounced as they were when I was her age."

The trait made me feel special and closer to Mom —at least it did when I was younger. Now it seemed like a giveaway that I was a Dark. Mismatched eyes weren't normal.

I suffered through a moment of stillness while Desi used her Earth magic to take a picture of me. Dust fell away, making it look like parts of the surface slowly rose like pancakes cooking on a pan. Black ink soaked into the front of the slab, filling out my hair, outlining my face and body, including the summer dress I wore and the strap of my shoulder bag. Within seconds, a miniature version of myself stared back at me.

"Oh, sweetie, I really wish you'd smile when getting your picture taken," Mom said.

I freed my hair from behind my ears.

"We can retake it another day," Desi said. "I once took a picture of a boy right before he threw up, puffy pale cheeks and all. That's a visual I wish I could forget. This is nothing." She added the slab to my records, some book-sized niche in the wall lined with hundreds of files.

"Take my picture. Take mine!" Bela jumped on the "x" and beamed at Desi.

Mom scooped my little sister up. "Next year. You need to leave the nice lady alone."

"Next year?" Desi said. "How old are you, hon?"

Bela held her chin a little higher. "Four."

"Ooh, one more year and we get to find out your alignment. How exciting."

Mom's smile waned and I inwardly cringed. Here's to hoping she didn't turn out to be a Dark, like me.

"I want to be a cat."

Desi snorted.

Mom said, "That's not one of the seven alignments, sweetie."

Desi stood under a canopy of hanging vines and lowered the end of a particular one to her ear while Mom and Bela chatted about alignments. The vine wrapped a leaf over Desi's ear and a tiny portion snaked out in front of her mouth and a thick leaf sprouted, blocking her lips from view. A blanket of water trickled along the stone slab behind the vines. Desi made a quick call to the teacher unfortunate enough to have me, then let the vine retract back into the canopy. She turned to my mom. "You're free to go, Mrs. Evers, unless you want to meet Miss Wren?"

Mom backed towards the entrance. "What would you like, sweetie?"

I shook my head, then, remembering my manners, said, "I'll be fine, Mom. Thank you."

She kneeled and fingers dug into my shoulders. They didn't hurt but it got my attention. "Do your best to get along," she whispered. "Remember to be kind to them even if they're not kind to you." She raised her voice and said, "I'll have your favorite dinner ready for when you get home." I thanked her again as she gave me a brief hug and kiss, then brought her mouth to my ear. "And please, please, please try to hide it."

***

Mom's last words whispered in my head over and over as some bouncy boy escorted me to Miss Wren's class. We followed a straight sidewalk made of stone slabs. The sidewalk guided us from the office building to an identical one marked 6-8 in one corner. I didn't take in much of my surroundings beyond the openness of the world out here in the desert, how gravel, instead of grass, blanketed the ground hugging the buildings, and the boy's shadow bounding along the sidewalk in front of us.

Please try to hide it.

I heard a voice. I looked up to check whether it came from a living or dead person. The boy skipped more than walked beside me, his eyes on me. Guess he was the one who spoke. He was the only other person in sight.

"What's your name?" he said.

"Mia." I took in his round face, short dark hair, and ears that stuck out like handles on teacups. Did he get picked on as much as I did? I shook my head. Where were my manners Mom always reminded me to use? The boy had been kind enough to ask me my name. I'm sure he'd told me his name when he'd shown up in the office. I'd been too distracted by keeping my senses open to wherever the ghost might be hiding. "I'm sorry. What's your name again?"

"Deren. How come you cover your face with your hair?" He sounded genuinely curious as he did half a jumping jack while hopping alongside me.

I made partial eye contact through my curtain of

hair. "I like it that way."

He thought a moment and then nodded. He hopped on a stone wall leading to double doors. "I like your hair. It's pretty."

I shuffled to the double doors and kept my gaze on the sidewalk. I mumbled thanks when he held the door open.

This building had a wood floor and walls like the office, but with little decoration. Gaps marked the walls on both sides at even intervals. Doors filled each one, all of them covered in cut-out letters welcoming students to class.

Deren led me to the second door on the left. As he reached for the handle a black mass manifested between his shoulder blades and rose like steam off boiling water. A wave of bad energy hit me and I stopped. That was energy no one wanted to go near. It came from Deren. He didn't seem to notice. He opened the door without faltering.

The polite thing was to walk into the classroom. My alignment instinctively told me that dark mass was bad and to stay away from it. I took a step back. The mass formed fingers and reached out. I threw a hand up and formed an invisible protective energy shield. Deren's round face scrunched with confusion. The black fingers broke away from the mass and came together like drops of water combining into a bigger drop. I took another step back, unsure my shield would do anything to stop it.

The mass flew into my shield, outlining its curve, and evaporated. The impact felt like someone had hit my head with a dodge ball. However, its touch caused the high-schooler's ghostly face to flash through my mind again. I heard no words at least, and my shield was intact. I peeled my gaze from the spot overhead where the mass had evaporated. Deren looked at me, craned his neck past the door to look inside the room, and then back at me. He held a hand to the side of his mouth as the other half of the black mass disappeared from his back. "It's okay," he whispered in a voice that might as well have been a regular indoor one. "Miss Wren is, like, the best teacher ever. Don't be scared."

How did people not sense this stuff? I understood not being able to see it, but not sense it? Still, that bad feeling had disappeared with the black mass, and Deren looked perfectly unharmed. In fact, he looked ready to burst into more jumping jacks. I took one cautious step and then another. I felt no negative energy so I tentatively walked into the classroom, Deren behind me.

I barely stepped inside, forcing Deren to squeeze past me. Everyone's gazes pinned me in place. An open classroom door got everyone's attention without fail. Their curious gazes followed me as I took a few stuttering steps to a cluttered desk sitting in the corner. Stacks of papers covered every last open space, minus a large desk calendar in the middle. It was scribbled all over with memos and times and a few birthday cake doodles.

Deren marched to his desk and took a seat on what looked like a wobbly wooden mushroom. He quietly rocked back and forth in his seat, leaving his classmates on either side undisturbed. Other classmates had the same odd chair. Most had the familiar seat with four legs and a chair back.

A melodic lady's voice said, "Oh, thank you,

Deren." That voice belonged to the only adult in the room, Miss Wren. She was tall and narrow like the little tree Mom had planted at our last house, and wore a flower pattern skirt and a white blouse with sleeves rolled up to the elbow. Sunlight coming in through the windows gave her light brown hair a golden sheen. She held a narrow arm out to me. "Class, I'd like you all to meet Miss Mia Evers. She's your new classmate. Everyone, please say hello."

Everyone waved as they drawled out a hello. I hid my face and forced myself to wave back. Ugh, why did teachers always do this? Why couldn't they point to where they wanted me to sit and leave it at that?

"Evers?" a girl said from the middle of the room. "That's a lowborn's name."

The teacher's smile shrank into a thin line and she glided over to the girl who spoke. She kneeled. "Gwen," she said in a low voice, "that wasn't a nice thing to say."

"But it's true," Gwen, some chestnut-haired girl in a pretty summer dress, said.

"What have I told you about keeping rude things to yourself?"

"How's that rude?"

"Were you trying to be nice when you said it?"

"I—"

Lowborn? What did that even mean? If it was something else to be made fun of for, I'd take it over for being Dark. Still, I didn't like the way she'd said it.

Gwen lowered her head. "I'm sorry, Miss Wren."

"Thank you, but you owe Mia the apology."

Her green eyes looked in my direction, somehow making me feel even more exposed. I wanted to shrink into the corner. I made myself hold my ground. "Sorry, I guess," she said.

Pursing her lips, Miss Wren sighed and stood. She put a gentle hand on my back, guiding me to an empty desk with a standard wooden chair. I'd be sitting next to Deren with our backs to the doorless closets. Light jackets and backpacks hung in two long rows with a shelf slightly taller than me lined with lunch boxes. Miss Wren instructed me to hang up my bag and take my seat, and then I felt the emptiness of her lack of company as she returned to the front of the room. She reminded me of my mom on her good days. Now that she wasn't near, I realized how much she felt like Mom during those moments when she wasn't scared of me.

I held the strap of my shoulder bag in both hands, faced the closet, and froze. A large clawed black shadow of a hand gripped the wood trim lining the top of the closet and a shadow passed over the many boxes lining the closet shelf high overhead. I gasped and cringed behind my bag. Good thing I'd left my energy shield up.

The clawed hand slid towards the ceiling and the shadow disappeared. Whispers reached my ears and my spine tingled.

"What's wrong?" Miss Wren asked.

Hi, I'm aligned with Dark and I think you might want to know there's a monster in your closet. What was wrong with this school? First the high schooler in the office, then the bad energy attached to Deren, and now this? I shrugged off my backpack and jammed it on a hook as fast as I could. I retreated to my desk a mere five steps away. It wasn't far enough to get my spine to stop tingling. I raised my hand.

"Yes, Mia?" Miss Wren said.

Lowering both my arm and head, I spoke in a voice I knew she couldn't hear. I didn't mean to talk so quietly. I really didn't want the whole class to hear me. That and I didn't want Miss Wren thinking I was trying to cause problems. My new teacher floated over and bent closer. I said, "May I please sit near the windows?"

Miss Wren studied me a moment. "Will it help you relax?"

I nodded.

She scanned the classroom. "Would anyone along the windows be willing to switch seats with Mia?" Several hands shot up. She pointed to my desk and instructed a girl over, then gently prodded my shoulder and told me to take the stack of books and settle down in the new spot. I hugged the stacks of books to my chest and silently made my way to the other side of the room. My new shoulder partners were some girl with a ponytail and—oh, no.

Gwen. She glared at me.

I crept closer and Gwen's glare darted to the girl who'd offered to change seats with me. The girl settled next to Deren, stuffing her backpack under her chair. Deren stopped wiggling and sat hunched. Once the girl settled down with an open notebook in front of her, flattening the spine, Deren looked at me, longing all over his face. Normally I would've looked away. I held his gaze, even pulling my hair back a little so he knew I was looking at him, and projected an apology.

I slid into my chair, books in hand, like I was about to sit next to a dog that would bite me for looking at it. I scooted my chair as far away from her as I could. It was maybe an extra inch, but it was better than nothing.

The girl on my other side helped me deposit my books in my desk and get me on the correct pages in my language textbook, and once Miss Wren confirmed that I was all settled and ready to learn, a lesson on context clues resumed.

Gwen never stopped giving me or the girl, Nonaya, who'd traded places with me mean looks throughout class. Any time Nonaya answered a question, Gwen made sure to answer the following question. And every time I wrote something in my notebook, I'd see her hair twist in the corner of my eye. I resisted the urge to snap at her to stop so I could concentrate better.

Deren looked at me a lot, too. His hurt slowly turned back into the open curiosity he'd shown me on the way to class. It was annoying, but I reminded myself to appreciate the kindness while it lasted. Those dark, curious eyes would look on me with hate eventually.

My own gaze kept darting back to the closet every time my spine tingled a little. However, every time I looked, there was nothing there. If it weren't for the scary energy coming from the closet, I would have assumed my own fears had created the shadow claws. I knew it was there, like I knew my lunchbox sat in my shoulder bag. I couldn't see either lunch or monster, even though they were both there.

I tried my best to pay attention. My parents expected good grades. They'd told me a zillion times they wanted me to have a better life than theirs, like always having enough money for food and even extra for buying all the books I could ever want to read—which was all of them—and that started with getting good grades. They'd go on about having money for a home, clothes, toys, and such, stopping only when they realized I didn't care about all that grownup stuff.

I dutifully circled a whopping two unknown words in a passage, read around the words for clues as to what they meant, and drew sloppy pictures in my notebook that would help me remember their meanings later. A quick look around at other people's notebooks confirmed I knew more words than any of them. Gwen "accidentally" bumped my elbow while drawing, causing me to slice my stick figure's head in half with a pencil stroke. I looked at her notebook and my stomach dropped.

She could draw far better than me. Her people had actual fingers and clothes. Mine had five lines for fingers and lopsided ovals for feet. My eyes stung with the realization that Gwen was better than me. I mentally released more energy into my shield, even though it would do nothing to protect me from the living.

School should have been out for the day by the time I finished my pathetic drawing. Instead, Miss Wren told us to line up at the door for lunch. I buried my notebook in my backpack and made sure I was the last person in line. It brought me uncomfortably close to the closet. No one noticed me cower near the end of the chalkboard. My classmates stared longingly out the windows as other middle schoolers filed outside, all of them headed to the cafeteria.

Miss Wren stood in front of the door with a finger over her lips, a hand on the knob. "The longer you take to quiet down, the less lunch time you have." Classmates shushed each other and slowly the line became quiet, some of them smiling with fingers over their mouths like kindergarteners. Miss Wren scanned the line one last time and light poured into the classroom as she opened the door.

My knees locked. A deep shadow filled the closet's ceiling. I turned, fists clenched at my sides. Sunlight should've filled half the space. The shadow sucked it into its blackness. Claws slinked out of the shadow and gripped the wood trim. Another, larger shape dipped lower. It looked like a snake lowering its head from tree branches. This snake was all black with an oval head and no face. And then one slanted red eye opened and stared at me.

I see you, child, the monster said. It had a deep voice, like a growling dog. Its head snaked closer.

I wanted to run and scream. I couldn't move.

I know what you are.

Another set of claws formed from within the closet as the monster's head stopped within a foot of my shield. The head alone had to be half as big as my entire body. Claws reached for my shield and all I could do was watch. The air grew cold. My breath appeared in puffs.

"Mia?" The voice sounded distant, familiar. "Mia!"

The monster regarded the voice with a slight turn of his head before focusing on me. It reached for me with one claw, as if to touch my head, and connected with my shield. Its touch filled my head with dizziness. Somehow my shield held. *Hmm, interesting.* It casually raked its claw along it and a burning sensation seared the side of my face. I reached for my cheek.

The monster laughed.

"Mia, what are you doing? Let's go." Miss Wren's voice sounded normal again.

I backed away from the monster. It watched me

with its one eye. It had no mouth, but I knew it was smiling. Its dangerous energy had a happy feeling mixed in with it. I jogged for the door.

Miss Wren guided me out the door with a hand on my back. "Goodness, you're cold. Go warm up."

I fast-walked over to the back of the line and kept my head down. The sun was so bright that I could barely see, and its warmth felt like burning on my skin. Webbed shadows of mesquite branches covered sections of the sidewalk as I took in everyone's shoes and listened to the elementary schoolers yelling and screaming all over the playground sitting between four buildings. Part of me wished I could forget about everything and be like the rest of my classmates. I couldn't muster the courage to greet anyone. It's what I should do. My parents had said as much at the last school I'd gone to.

I'd believed them, but I hadn't had the courage to at least try. I'd hid and stayed alone, like right now. That drew the attention of adults first, and then my classmates. I'd managed to keep my alignment secret for months while getting picked on for keeping to myself. My parents got mad and told me I should've acted like a normal kid.

Like normal was an option for a Dark.

Memory of their anger surfaced as I watched elementary students swish down the slide, one after the other, and then scurry up the jungle gym for another ride. I wanted to do the same. It looked like fun, even at my age. What was the point of turning recess into a class and calling it Physical Education anyway?

Another student rode the slide, merrily screaming all the way down, and popped to his feet at the bottom.

My class reached a painted brick building that was the cafeteria. It had a vaulted ceiling, tiled floors, and more painted bricks. Three different growing lines of students divided row upon row of circle tables. I made a beeline for a table in a lonely corner, someplace I could go invisible from the rest of the living. Sensing no dead wandering among the living, released my shield with a wave of my hand and began munching on a floppy sandwich Mom had packed me.

I was halfway through my sandwich when a wooden tray laden with colorful tacos slid closer to my paper bag. Deren. Why wasn't he sitting with anyone else?

"Hi, Mia," he said.

I looked around to make sure there wasn't another Mia he was talking to. I knew there wasn't. I had to make sure anyway. "Hi, Deren."

"May I join you?" He sat down without waiting for an answer. "Why are you sitting all alone?"

I gave him a noncommittal shrug. When he didn't probe harder for an answer, I took another bite of my sandwich. He looked at me with open curiosity, not one drop of fear in his dark eyes, and a part of me yearned to open up to him and make a quick friend. I'd been down this road so many times but—

No, don't go there. Not again. You'll get burned, Mia.

"So what's your alignment? I'm Earth."

My half-chewed bite cut my inhale short, killing any chance at earning cool points as I coughed it back up. My cheeks burned from both embarrassment and the coughing fit. As uncool as I was, Deren still slid his unopened carton of milk over. I nodded thanks as I dragged the carton closer. I didn't want the milk, but it was an easy excuse to avoid answering his question. I gulped it down between bouts of catching my breath.

The girl who'd switched seats with me, Nonaya, appeared behind Deren like a ghost walking out of a wall. Something about that girl didn't agree with me any more than Gwen had. Nonaya put her fists on her hips and stuck out her chin, pinning me with deep blue eyes in a face framed by soft blonde hair. I couldn't help feeling jealous of how pretty she was, along with her pretty summer dress.

I wanted to run and hide. My pale blue dress and black hair weren't good enough. It didn't help that Deren stared openly at Nonaya.

A small smile formed on Nonaya's face and her chin rose a little higher. "You shouldn't be hanging out with someone like him."

"Why?" I asked.

She grabbed one of Deren's arms and held it up. His eyes went wide and he froze. "See his skin?" Deren's skin was a light milk chocolate tone. "It means he's Dark. It's a dead giveaway."

My pale mocha skin looked almost white when compared to his. While my dad was white, I got my color from my mom's side. As far as I knew, skin color had nothing to do with a person's alignment. "How do you know that?"

"My mom said so," she said, dropping Deren's arm like she was trying to throw it on the ground. Deren clung to where Nonaya had grabbed his arm.

"I'm not a Dark," Deren said to the floor. "I'm an Earth."

"You're a Dark and a liar." Nonaya turned her

pretty face to me. "You should be friends with us instead. I'm Nonaya. Come over to our table." She walked off.

Deren and I watched her take a seat with three girls who took turns admiring Gwen's dress. She was the shortest of the group, yet everyone already seemed to look to her as the boss. Nonaya turned around and put her fists back on her hips. "Are you coming or what?"

If I pretended to be their friend, maybe it'd help me avoid the temptation of befriending Deren. There was even one last empty spot as if they needed me to complete their group.

I hesitated, though. There was something off about those girls. Something that I didn't want to be around. However, none of them had a dark mass clinging to them, or any mean spirits trying to keep me away. Deren did. Maybe that was another sign as well.

Deren looked at me, pleading all over his face. He was kind and polite, the type of friend I wanted. I didn't want to abandon him. I looked again at the girls and my stomach squirmed as I left Deren for Gwen and the others.

Chapter 4

The weight of Deren's gaze pressed down on me all the way to the table. It was wrong to leave him, dark mass or not, but safer to join Gwen and her friends. She patted the last empty seat and I sat. I half expected them all to laugh at me and to tell me to go away, that this was all a joke. I had no friends at Toolena Mesa. However, no one laughed after my weight settled on the worn wood.

Gwen straightened the lap of her green layered dress. It had cream-colored lace trim on the neck, short sleeves, and hem. Matching the dress were pretty green eyes and chestnut hair that fell halfway to her waist. Gwen carried herself like she thought she was the smartest, most important person in school, and she wanted to make sure everyone knew it. "Hello, Mia. I'm Gwen, and these are my friends." She gestured to the three girls. "Nonaya is the one who traded desks with you and called you over to my table. This is Sussi, and that's Chibya."

It'd probably take me a month to remember their names without confusion. I studied each of them. Nonaya had brown hair pulled back in a complex braid and a freckled face that looked like she was always daydreaming. Sussi was the tallest and, despite her plain yellow dress, looked like she could beat up an eighth-grader. Chibya was a plump girl with a pleasant smile.

Gwen said, "I'm aligned with Fire, Nonaya's Florakin, Sussi's Water, and Chibya is an Air. What's your alignment?"

My face went cold and the part of my turkey sandwich I'd eaten felt like it was about to come back up. Asking a person's alignment was like asking their name. Darks happened to hate answering that question. I took a few steadying breaths so words, instead of my sandwich, would come out. "Crystal."

They all snickered. Sussi said, "Have fun making song stones for the rest of your boring life."

Crystal was a sub-alignment of Earth, meaning they were aligned with Earth, but were super talented at working with crystal rocks. While useful, it wasn't a sub-alignment anyone bragged about. I nodded to my sandwich to hide my relief that they'd believed me.

"Anyway, we were all born and raised out here, as were our parents," Gwen said. "Everyone knows who we are."

"There aren't many people out here," Chibya said. "Everyone knows everyone in Toolena."

"Yeah, but we're the most well-known families out here," Gwen said.

That reminded me. "What's 'lowborn' mean?"

Gwen stared at me with a crinkled nose. "How do you not know?"

I shrugged. "No one ever called me that in the city."

"Well, then they must all be—" Her gaze focused on me. "Wait, you came from the city?"

I nodded.

"Like, Marohu?"

I nodded again. Marohu was the state's capital with over three million people. Toolena Mesa had more cacti than people.

"How did you end up out here in the middle of nowhere?"

The truth wanted to escape my lips. I mentally batted it away in time to allow this morning's conversation in the office to come to mind. "Work. My dad found work out here."

"In the mines?"

I nodded a third time. Let her make up her own story for me and my family.

"My dad owns the mines," she said, her air of superiority raising her chin again.

"He does?" The stupid question escaped before I could stop it.

"Yeah. Just about everyone's parents work for mine, even Sussi's and Nonaya's. I bet I'll see your parents if I ever visit Dad on the weekends."

I grimaced. I really didn't want to talk to any of them, but the best way to hide my alignment, as Mom asked, was to pretend to be normal. "So what is this school like?" It was the most innocent way I could think of asking if they knew anything about ghosts or

46

monsters lurking around.

Gwen said, "I don't know what you've had in Marohu, but this place has nice teachers who know a lot. They don't always let us do what we want. At least we get to go on lots of cool field trips."

That didn't come close to answering my question about the closet monster. "Is this place...safe, too?"

She shrugged. "Yeah." She sat up straighter. "Well, something happened three years ago over at the high school and someone died."

"Yeah, it was so scary," Nonaya said.

"I really don't remember what happened," Sussi said. "I remember my parents saying the high schooler died because some Dark used neh...neh-meny or whatever it's called."

"Necromancy," Gwen said.

The word necromancy sent the same chill up my spine as the closet monster. It sounded familiar, even though I had no idea what it was. The word had a dark ring to it.

"Anyway," Sussi said, rolling her eyes, "some Dark used necromancy and killed a classmate that had bullied him."

"That's not what I heard," Gwen said.

"Me neither," said Chibya. "I heard it was a Dark who used necromancy just to see what he could do. His friend was there to watch, something went wrong, and a monster killed his friend."

"No, the Dark used necromancy to scare off a teacher he didn't like," Gwen said, "but the monster ended up attacking and killing that student and the Dark."

"Either way, a Dark did something with

necromancy and a student died," I said to my sandwich. They all spoke agreement.

Sussi and Nonaya looked behind me and stiffened. I turned around. Deren stood near me, a ball tucked under one arm and holding a tray with stray shreds of lettuce on the parchment paper. He looked at each of us, saving me for last. His dark eyes burned with questions. He took one last look at Gwen's narrowed eyes and walked off.

"So yeah," Gwen said, "stay away from him if you don't want to die."

Deren swept the parchment paper into a garbage bin and stacked his tray on a counter before exiting the cafeteria.

"Has he hurt anyone?" I asked, the words feeling wrong in my mouth. I already felt bad for ditching him. Deren was all alone like me—well, like I normally was. He probably felt sad and lonely. He'd been so nice to me on the way to class. There didn't seem to be anything cruel about him. Sure, he had that black mass that'd come after me, but that energy had been bad, not him.

"No, but he gets in trouble all the time," Sussi said. "He's really annoying."

"What kind of trouble?"

"All sorts of stuff. He keeps trying to sneak out of the classroom," Chibya said. "Most teachers catch him."

Gwen said, "Everyone knows he's trying to sneak off to the restroom to do Dark magic. I don't understand why the school hasn't gotten rid of him yet."

"Has anyone ever seen him do any Dark magic?" I'd done Dark magic when forming and strengthening my energy shield. I'd learned that only Darks could sense anything dead or undead. Not even Miss Wren had seen or heard the closet monster speak. I didn't walk around with a dark mass clinging to me. I had at least a little control over what I knew I could do.

"I haven't, but other people said he put a ghost in the 6-8 building last year," Gwen said. "Now no one will swim in the pool."

Memory of the ghost flying out of the picture flashed through my mind. "What about the main office?"

Gwen's brows furrowed. "What about it?"

Why did I ask that? Oh, right. I was bad at fitting in. "Any ghosts in there?"

Her eyes narrowed. "No. Why?"

My cheeks burned. "Never mind."

All four girls considered me with equal annoyance. Gwen said, "You're weird."

I shrugged. Classmates took turns dumping wrappers and cartons in garbage cans and heading outside while I half-listened to Gwen and the others gossip about him. No one seemed to care that I wasn't looking at them. I didn't care what they said. None of them had seen Deren do anything. It gave me hope that he wasn't lying about being an Earth.

Still, that black mass clinging to him was troubling. Was he a Dark with no control over what he could do, a Wild? Such people existed. Mom and Dad complained about them every time the Wilds from all alignments were on the news. Such people caused small earthquakes, floods, fires, and strong winds. Children did it by accident. Adults did it to be mean. And Wild Darks? Death. Lots and lots of death. At least my parents had thoroughly convinced me I wasn't a Wild Dark. Mom said she would have put me up for adoption if it were true. I didn't know whether to hug her or cry when she said that.

The lunch bell snapped me back to the present. My classmates finished their meals, cleaned off tables under the watchful eyes of teachers, and headed off to our next classes. Gwen and the others ran ahead of me as I settled into my normal walking pace.

***

The rest of the day went by without further incident. Gwen stopped glaring, the closet monster didn't show up in any of the other classrooms, and Deren's black mass stayed hidden as well. I even learned some new math stuff, despite that being my worst subject. Gwen hadn't been kidding when she said the teachers were good here. I felt like I could learn anything these teachers taught me.

When the bell tolled at the end of school, I waited at my desk in Miss Wren's class, which was also my homeroom. My classmates scrambled to the closet, competing to grab their coats and backpacks until just a few bags remained. I crept over. I wouldn't let a closet monster ruin my day whether I saw it or not.

I swiped my shoulder bag as the last students hurried out the door. No claws, no one-eyed face appeared. No voice sounded in my head. I deposited my homework in my bag and turned for the door. Miss Wren waved to the stragglers in the hallway.

I see you, child.

I froze, my spine tingling over and over. Miss Wren's waving slowed to a standstill, face stuck in a big smile. What was going on? Had time stopped? The air grew cold and my breath came out in white puffs again. I waited for Miss Wren to move, but her waving hand stayed high overhead, eyes fixed down the hall. I slowly turned in place. What else was there to do besides face the closet monster?

I know what you are, Dark One, it said in its gravelly voice as claws gripped the edge of the closet's ceiling. *The master has sent you to me.*

Of all the people to find out, I didn't care that this monster knew. It seemed natural that it'd know, just like I knew it wasn't a kind creature. "Who are you?"

Ah, clever to ask my name. I'll never tell you, child. I know yours, though, Mia Evers.

A fresh wave of fear rippled through me upon hearing my name through its voice. I took a deep breath, steeling myself to stand up to this monster.

The monster's head snaked down and its front claws reached for the floor. I backed up as the monster set its front hand-shaped paws on the floor. Its head followed, the neck elongating to stop a mere foot from my face, and then the rest of its black body snaked after it. The neck shrank to its original length. Two more paws touched the floor. The monster looked like a human crouching on all-fours like a dog. It had an unnaturally long neck and nothing on its perfect oval face but one slanted red eye.

I stepped back as I realized its crouched body touched the ceiling. I willed more energy into my shield, strengthening it so much that air shimmered like a mirage and my legs grew wobbly. The monster reached for my shield. A stab of dizziness struck my mind. The monster recoiled, a wisp of smoke rising from where he'd touched my shield.

Hmm, we shall play first then.

I shot a glance at Miss Wren. She was still smiling, but her hand was a little lower than where I'd seen it last. What the heck was going on? "What did you do to my teacher?"

Nothing. Time merely bends in my presence. Its gaze wandered over to my teacher and long legs circled me like a bunch of really tall adults walking by—ones that emanated cold like an icebox. The monster reached for Miss Wren, passing a claw the size of her face through her hair. *Too soon to mark another*, it said.

For some crazy reason, I sidestepped, putting myself between them. It paused, snapping its gaze back on me.

Feeling protective already, are we? How noble. I assure you that'll change once they all know what you are. When that day comes, your true nature will be known. We'll create chaos together.

"Go away!" I swiped at it with both arms.

The monster flinched and backed towards the closet. *Remember, it's only a matter of time.* Its body backed into the ceiling, spreading shadow around it, and its front claws lifted from the floor and vanished. Its faceless head lingered for a moment before disappearing as well. *Remember.*

My spine stopped tingling and I found myself staring at a perfectly normal closet, empty of students' belongings. I could see the ceiling again. Unable to believe what I was seeing—or rather wasn't—I took another step closer. No fear filled me, no unusual shadows hid the ceiling. The room felt perfectly safe and normal.

For a person who could talk to dead people, even

this was really, really weird.

Chapter 5

Four place settings awaited the impending meal. A bowl of strawberries sat in the middle. Mom worked up a masterpiece in the kitchen. Bela stood on a chair, watching everything while chewing on a fingertip. The scent of ground beef, onion, and garlic poked at my appetite. A real dinner sounded great after spending all day moving.

I set my bag and shoes by the door and helped myself to some strawberries. "Hi, Mom. Hi, Bela."

Mom looked up from the stove. "Hi, sweetie. Dinner's almost ready. Just waiting for the potatoes to finish." Bela greeted me as well.

"Need any help?" I stood before the island stove. Mom kissed the top of my head and resumed stirring her ground meat concoction. I inhaled the spices as steam rose.

"Why don't you go wash your hands and pour

some water?"

Stuffing strawberries in my mouth, I washed my hands in the kitchen sink, and then fetched my apron. I could barely tie a bow with the strings anymore, but I kept wearing it. It was my strongest memory of Grandma. It felt right to wear it when I helped in the kitchen, even if it was to pour water.

I flung the metal door wide and hefted a ceramic jug into my arms. The jug was refreshingly cold to the touch. I poured us water. It was so cold that the glasses frosted up. I drew a smiley face on my glass and put the jug away.

"Is Dad going to be home in time for dinner?"

"He shouldn't be."

"When will he be home?" As distant as my dad could be, I still daydreamed of us being a happy family again, nothing wrong with our lives, and no one afraid of me because I had no alignment yet.

Her face grew pensive. "After you go to bed, sweetie. I'm sorry. He's really busy."

"Did get a job at the mines?"

She forced her mouth into a fake smile while the hesitation in her eyes warred with what she wanted to say. She shook her head. "He's trying to get a job there. It'd be good, honest work." She grated some cheddar cheese into a clay bowl, each stroke a rough jerk.

"Where's he working right now?"

"On the edge of Marohu."

"Doing what?" Maybe she'd tell me for once. I didn't know whether or not to believe he wanted to work at the mines. I wanted to, though.

Mom pressed her fingers to her temples. "Mia, I don't know."

I clutched my chair, pressing myself against it.

"We just moved here. Your dad's doing whatever he can to put food on the table and keep this roof over our heads." Air swirled in the kitchen, sending a curtain dancing. The pots and pans shifted away from Mom. She was losing control again. I dared not move to protect Bela. My little sister crouched behind the chair back as swirling winds sent her hair dancing. "*Please* stop asking about your father."

Two pans clacked against each other, snapping Mom out of her trance and back in control of her Air alignment. She hugged the air in front of her, tugging the cookware back in place, and the curtain settled. She stood there, head bowed, gazing over the rising steam.

"I'm sorry," I said in a small voice. Mom had been getting angry so easily for the past two years. I didn't know why. She yelled at me and Dad a lot, but—

"No, I'm sorry." Mom's shoulders slumped. "I shouldn't have snapped at you." Her face was red, but there were no tears. "I'm sorry, Mia. I'm really stressed out. I shouldn't have taken it out on you." She pulled me into a brief hug. "Please don't ever stop asking questions. Never lose your curiosity." She kissed the top of my head. "I just need a break from questions about your dad. Now, let's have an early dinner."

We ate a delicious meal of seasoned ground meat on a bed of shredded potatoes. Everything was topped with cheese, diced tomatoes, guacamole, and sour cream. Mom and I didn't speak. Bela made up for the both of us, telling us a story about some imaginary pony in the sky and how they'd played tag while Mom unpacked. Annoying as my little sister could be, I appreciated her ability to talk when the rest of us couldn't. Bela went on about stomping on beetles in the dirt. Mom pulled aside the curtains.

The sky was bright blue, uninterrupted like a bed sheet pulled tight without a single wrinkle. The land looked perfectly flat at first glance, but gentle rises and falls added texture to the cactus-covered landscape. Our house sat atop one of the rises, giving us a view for miles in every direction. Toolena Mesa sat in a giant bowl of a desert with a mix of smooth and jagged mountains lining the rim. It looked like it'd take days to reach any of them.

We left the dishes in the sink and a covered plate in the frost box, ready for Dad whenever he got home, deciding to tackle the final touches on my bedroom first.

My room sat at one end of the house. It was spacious enough. My bed sat opposite the closet. The room had one tall window, thick curtains hanging in front of it. Two sets of folded sheets sat at the foot of my bed. Mom and I made the bed together while Bela played with my stuffed animals.

"So how was school?" Mom sounded like she'd been wanting to ask ever since I got home, but had been afraid to ask.

I opened my mouth, my thoughts going straight to the closet monster. I stopped myself before I could ask about trying another school. "It's… good. I like it so far."

Mom's gaze darted from side to side, as if she were checking to see if anyone was listening. We were the only three people in the house, placed on our own parcel of nowhere. "Do they know? About you?"

"No, but—" I stopped myself. I wanted to ask

about boarding school. Her worried look stopped me.

"What?"

I looked at her, the image of the one slanted red eye peering at me from the darkness. I bowed my head, hiding my face. "Never mind. I'll deal with it."

"Please make this school work. I know it's hard. I wish it wasn't." She sat on the bed, her gaze full of pleading.

I sat opposite her. "I know. I'm trying." Lines creased her face. "I think I made some friends today," I said, hoping to pull her back towards happiness.

The change from brooding to delighted surprise happened in an instant. "Really?" she said.

"I'm not sure," I said, thinking back to the moment in the cafeteria. "Two of the girls weren't very nice, but they made me hang out with them and their friends."

"Maybe they'll be nicer with time. Do whatever you have to do to fit in, sweetie."

That seemed like the best plan. "There was also this boy who sat with me at lunch." That openly curious face and those ears. "I think he wants to be my friend."

"Wow, I'm so happy for you." Mom smiled with tears in her eyes.

Bed made, we tackled unpacking my clothes, along with getting Bela to stop impeding our progress by wearing a few of my dresses. We had little in the way of furniture at the moment after not being able to fit everything in one small moving truck. Hopefully, a dresser or at least some hangers would show up soon.

By the time the sun had gone to bed, I was ready to do the same. I'd done my homework, helped with the dishes and lots of unpacking, and topped it all off with some sweet bread and lavender tea.

Despite being old enough to put myself to bed, Mom thought it necessary to tuck me in. She dug out my old song crystal and set it under the window. The crystal was a chunk of clear quartz the size of my head.

"Which song would you like, sweetie?"

I wiggled my feet so the tucked sheets would loosen up and allow me to easily shift position. "Mountain Shadow, please." It was my favorite. It was a mix of eerie and relaxing, and it helped me fall asleep.

Placing her hands over the crystal, she nodded, brow knit with concentration. She pressed her hands together like she was praying, then tilted her head back and reached skyward. The air swirled as Mom used Air magic to pull a memory to her consciousness and share the song with the crystal. She spiraled her arms back, bowed, and brought her hands together in front of her knees, like she was holding out something for the crystal to take. Its core pulsed with a soft white glow and a song filled my bedroom.

Mom meandered over to the door and kept her head bowed. "Good night."

"Night, Mom." She shut the door behind her as the opening phrases rose and fell. The music sounded like metal or crystal clinking together to form notes, along with bells and something tapping out a beat on a small drum. A wolf-like voice sang a wordless song, making me picture a deer wandering along a foggy mountainside. Everything was calm and peaceful in the world.

I drifted off to sleep as the song ended and the glow faded from the crystal.

Chapter 6

Dad lay asleep in bed the next morning. Mom wouldn't let me wake him while I got ready for school. At least she was always happier when he was home. When she went to the restroom, I peeked at the long, snoring lump under the sheets. If I couldn't talk to him, I wanted to see him, if only for a moment. I watched and listened to him snore lightly until I heard water running. I tiptoed back to my breakfast. A squishy armchair had been added to the living room in the night. Bela sat in it, bouncing a pair of stuffed animals off the armrests.

After breakfast, Mom and Bela walked me to the bus stop. I said nothing while we waited by the mailboxes, warming in the rising sun's rays. It got a little colder out here in the boonies.

My bus turned out to be different from the ones in the city. They were painted yellow and had rounded glass windows that made it look like a spotted caterpillar. The ones in the city were so full of magic that they could drive themselves around without missing a stop or a late child chasing down his or her ride. I did a double-take. Some lady sat in the front, instead of standing and watching over everyone on board. This bus hovered closer to the ground. Air magic kept it high enough to require a few steep stairs to descend as double doors swung open.

I climbed aboard and gave my smiling bus driver a limp wave. The hum of magic and chatty children hit me like a gust of cold air. I took a seat behind the bus driver, hoping to ignore everyone, and read the latest book in a series about a young fairy princess named Yuna. In this book, she was trying to save a unicorn forest from a Wild Fire person. The bus arrived at school in the middle of Yuna's scary boat ride across the lake. I tried sinking into my chair so I could finish the chapter, but the bus driver gently shooed me off as Yuna came face-to-face with a water dragon.

I followed the flow of students out to the playground and tried to find a solitary spot to sit and read while we waited for the bell to ring. The swings were occupied, the benches loaded up with backpacks, and shaded spots under the mesquite trees already taken. Gwen and her friends occupied the bottom of the playscape. They could wait. I really wanted to find out what happened next to Yuna. I angled for one of the thick wood beams holding up the swings. I barely made it when Deren showed up, a ball at his feet.

"Hey, Mia," he said as if I'd never abandoned him yesterday.

"Hi, Deren," I said.

"Want to play with me?"

Make up for ditching him twice yesterday or continue reading? My mind was set on finding out if Yuna beat the water dragon or had to rush back to shore, but another part of me wanted to return Deren's kindness. The ball's bright colors said there was fun to be had.

I deposited the Yuna book in my bag and glanced over at Gwen and the others. They chatted away. Gwen's gaze shifted to me and her smile turned into a scowl. The rest of the girls turned as well, swishing their perfect hair.

"Mia?" Deren said.

Not wanting to ruin my chance at fitting in, I started towards Gwen and the others, but stopped when her eyes narrowed. Gwen tapped Sussi's knee and her lips moved as she pointed at me. The other girls drew their heads closer and gave me dirty looks. I took that as my clue that I'd messed up and headed towards the swings. Like anyone would want to hang out with me after ditching them a second time.

I barely made it to the swing set when Deren said, "Forget about them. They're mean to everyone."

I spun around, nearly tripping over the wood beam, and threw up my protective shield with a wave of my hand. He didn't have that black mass or any bad energy coming from him. Not wanting to waste energy or look even dumber, I disguised the hand gesture to look like I was rolling my wrist and dismissed my shield.

"So do you wanna play?" He held the ball between us.

"Are you really an Earth?"

He blinked. "Yeah. I'll show you." Setting the ball at my feet, he ran over to the 6-8 building and brought back one of the pebbles lining it. He held it out on his palm, concentrated with the tip of his tongue sticking out, and the grape-sized rock hovered over his hand. He made a twisting motion with his other hand and the rock spun in place for a moment before he lost control. It flew off to one side. "See?"

Yep, definitely an Earth.

"Come on. I'll show you where to put your bag." He ran off and I walked after him. He bounced around impatiently while I set my bag by Miss Wren's door, then he sprinted to a patch of grass and kicked the ball. As soon as I stopped it with my foot, I smiled. Someone had actually kicked a ball to me, not at me. I kicked the ball back. He had to chase after my terrible aim.

We kicked the ball back and forth, steadily spreading farther and farther apart. This was so much fun, even with all the kids we nearly hit.

Deren kicked the ball for like the hundredth time, sending it high over everyone's head. It bounced way over my head and I had to chase it down after it rebounded off the stone wall. I wound up for a big kick and sent the ball flying. It bounced in front of him, over his attempt to head-butt it, and hit the K-2 windows covered in children's art.

A spiderweb of cracks covered a few drawings. My stomach dropped to my feet. Deren stared in openmouthed horror. A teacher emerged from the classroom and it took her an instant to spot Deren. She wordlessly waved him over with a wiggle of one finger. He slumped his shoulders and walked over to his impending punishment.

Part of me wanted to let him take the blame. It'd save me from being hated by teachers for at least a little longer. Maybe Deren would tell on me anyway, though. The other part of me wanted to run over and take responsibility for what I'd done. I didn't want Deren to hate me for running and hiding.

A hand settled on my shoulder. I flinched and spun around. A tall lady in a sleeveless black dress stood over me. Her dress had a circle-shaped opening over her chest. The front of her dress ended at the knees. The back fell all the way to the ankles of her long black boots. Her boots were covered in buckles and she had a belt around her neck.

A stern face with deep red lips and framed in long, golden curls stared down a straight nose. "Mia Evers," she said in a stern voice, "come with me."

My body stiffened. She knew my name. That had to mean the school had been watching, waiting for me to make one mistake so they could get rid of me. They'd sent the scariest person to come remove me so I wouldn't put up any argument. I looked around for Deren, but he was nowhere in sight.

I retrieved my bag and was escorted past students, most of them quietly watching us. Anyone who hadn't already noticed got elbowed by friends. A beefy eighth-grader said, "Ooh! Someone's in trouble." The teacher escorting me shot him a glare and the boy lost his smirk, shuffling to cower behind his friends. No one else said a word as the lady and I walked up to the main office and into a room near the principal's office. Great. I was going to get an earful before she sat me in front of the principal, the only person who could officially expel me.

The lady gestured for me to sit on a chair by the door. Her office had no pictures. Her walls were painted silver with black patterns all over them. Some of it was writing and other parts like symbols or runes. I felt like I should understand all those markings, but their meanings escaped me.

The lady interlaced her fingers in front of her stomach, the black lacy material making her look as pale as me.

I wasn't sure what it was about the way she looked at me that caused courage to bubble up. "Please don't expel me."

Her brows rose. "Who said anything about getting expelled? Miss Evers, I'm your Dark tutor. My name is Lyra Weever. You may call me Ms. Weever. The principal informed me that you're in need of my services."

"Services?"

She tilted her head. "Have you never had a Dark tutor before?"

I shook my head.

"Speak when spoken to, Miss Evers," she said in a firm but calm voice. "This head wagging doesn't become a Dark."

"I haven't had a tutor before, Ms. Weever." I mustered the courage to look at her with one eye.

"Better. Now, why have all your previous schools failed to provide you with a tutor? Did they not understand how dangerous a Dark can become without proper training?"

I shook my head before I could stop myself. "No. All I know is that people hate me because I'm a Dark."

She grimaced. "This world is full of so much stupidity that breeds, I swear." She inhaled deeply through her nose and let it out slowly, controlled. "Miss

Evers, they were right to fear you, but it was their own lack of foresight that there was any reason to."

"What does that mean?" Ms. Weever seemed more and more like the type of teacher I never wanted angry with me.

"It means that if they'd trained you like they do the other elements, they would've had no reason to be afraid of you. How many elements are there that humans can be aligned with?"

"Seven," I said. We were taught about them as soon as we were able to count.

"Correct." She paced around her office. "And what are they?"

"Earth, Air, Fire, Water, Light, Dark, and Kindred."

"Correct again. Now how do these elements work with each other?"

"They balance each other." That's what I'd been told. If I was wrong, then at least it wasn't my fault.

"And which elements balance which?" She glanced at me, the belt around her neck creaking.

"Earth and Air, Fire and Water, Light, and Dark. And Kindred helps balance all of them."

"Very good. So far, your education hasn't been a complete waste. Can you tell me why Dark is the only alignment people are afraid of?"

I'd asked my mom. She'd said something about wars from over 200 years ago, but I hadn't understood, so she simplified it for me. "People are afraid of what they don't understand."

Ms. Weever gave me a half smile. "An interesting answer. What do you think that means?"

My parents loved and never feared me until I'd turned five, the year everyone's alignment began

66

developing. That was the first time Grandma had tried to talk to my dad through me. "They don't understand why dead people would want to talk to the living?"

She stopped behind her desk. "That's a fair start. Why would the living be afraid of talking to the dead?"

I didn't understand the fear. I wasn't afraid of ghosts. I wouldn't have been afraid of the closet monster either if it weren't for the negative energy that came from it. "They're afraid of dead people?"

"So close. It's partially correct. Try again."

What answer could that be close to? I filed through the precious few answers Mom'd been reluctant to give me. "I don't know."

"Then this is where we shall begin your education and training." She pushed a leather-bound notebook stamped with the symbol of the seven elements. The symbol consisted of a circle within a circle, the outer one a swirl of what would have been black and white—Light and Dark—if it had been colored in. The inner circle was divided into five sections with a symbol of the four main elements in each one. The different thing about the outer circle was that the two parts were snakes trying to chase and eat each other.

The leather was nice and soft, and effortlessly stayed open when I turned to the first blank page. I grabbed a pencil from my backpack.

Ms. Weever said, "People are afraid of death and dying. Darks bring humankind closer to death, as do Lights. There's a similar fear of Light people, but also a large degree of reverence."

"Reverence?"

She paused, as if she hadn't expected any interruptions. "It means that people love and worship them. Pure nonsense, if you ask me, but I'm not here to push my agenda on students. Anyway, Miss Evers, you've been born into an unfair world where those with our alignment are hated and feared mostly because of lies. The purpose of today's lesson is to start equipping you with the knowledge to fix those lies."

My limbs went limp. "How am I supposed to fix it all?"

She put her fists on her hips and gave me a stare like she thought I was being silly. "Don't be ridiculous. You're one person. It's up to you to bring what balance you can to your part of the world, not the whole world. One person can't change the whole world."

I nodded mutely before remembering my manners. "Yes, ma'am. I understand."

She resumed pacing. "In order to help people stop being afraid of death and dying, a Dark must first learn what he or she is dealing with. Now, mark the date on each page we begin on. Title today's 'Types of Demons.'"

I stared at her. Had I heard that last part right?

Ms. Weever turned. "Well, what did you expect to be learning about? Unicorns and rainbows? Write it down, girl."

Feeling my face heat, I scratched the words down as the smell of fresh parchment filled my nose. Ms. Weever organized demons into seven main types. All of them wanted to create chaos in one of five ways—physical illness, mental illness, spread lies, spread fear, or spread hate.

The world began to make more sense. Maybe if I learned how to use my alignment, I could show people there was no reason to be afraid of me and they'd actually like me. Maybe even my parents would love me like they used to.

"Almost all demons you'll come across are minor. They're the ones who are the most willing to do all the work. The higher-level demons have a certain passion for bossing others around, for controlling things. It's very rare they meddle with the living world and do things themselves."

I thought of what I now realized was a demon in my classroom. "Where do demons come from?"

"You mean like where do they live or like where babies come from?" She touched one of the black markings on the wall, tracing it with her fingers, as if my question didn't bother her in the least.

It was more of the former, but now that she'd asked... "Both."

"Most demons were once humans." Her hand drifted from the markings to a statue of an angel sitting on a narrow table. Beautiful and creepy creatures of various sizes sat around the angel, the biggest of all the pieces. "This wasn't always true, but that's a lesson for another day. What's good for you to know now is humans are the source of any demon's power. That's why they're always preying on us. While we're alive, demons feed on our energy and emotions. When we die, we can walk into the Light or into the Darkness. Both ways lead to judgment. The light leads to truth and the natural cycle of the way life works. The dark leads to deception and chaos."

"Why would anyone walk into the darkness?" It sounded terrible.

Ms. Weever sat at her desk and her golden curls framed her face. "It's quite simple, really. I don't think you'll fully understand it until you're older, but your hardships have made you wise beyond your years." She interlaced her fingers. "People sometimes fear the truth. Some people will do anything to avoid it both in life and in death."

"Like when my parents tell me not to say anything about the demons that talk to me?"

Ms. Weever gave me a serious look. "You have more than ghosts talking to you already? Goodness, child. Do they take shape or are they black masses?"

"Both."

She sat up straighter, her voice growing firm. "Describe them."

"One is my grandma. She—"

"Your actual grandmother?"

"Yes."

"Then she's a ghost, not a demon, unless there's something about her personality or energy that doesn't feel right."

"It's her, the real her." I knew it as plainly as looking at my hands and knowing they were mine. There had been this one time that something—a demon, I guessed—had tried to pretend to be my grandma. I'd known from the moment I'd felt its presence that it hadn't been her. I also somehow made it go away like I had the demon in the classroom.

Ms. Weever nodded. "We sense and see both ghosts and demons. Ghosts are souls existing in a limbo between the light and dark. They're people who either don't know they're dead or haven't decided to go to the Light or the Darkness. Darks can find the stuck ones. Only Lights can help them move towards truth. Now, what else have you seen besides your grandmother?"

Far more than I cared for. "There's a demon in Miss Wren's classroom."

She raised an eyebrow.

"It's really big, has a neck that it can make any length it wants, and it's spoken to me."

"And has really long arms and legs?"

I nodded.

"Oh, that thing? He's harmless. I'll teach you how to get rid of him some other day."

Oh...kay. Not the reaction I was expecting. The scratch he'd made on my cheek didn't fit her description. At least it'd faded before I got home.

"Now, where did we leave off with your notes?"

I scanned my tiny handwriting. "How most demons I'll come across are minor."

"Right. In order to protect yourself and others, you have to know what you're dealing with. I know this is a lot to take in all at once, but I want you to look at the world like it truly is, starting today. You're old enough to understand. You're old enough to do something about it."

It seemed like a lot to expect of me, but I feared what she'd say or do if I argued. I dutifully jotted down notes.

"Just like humans, demons have their own social structure and pecking order. Remember, they were once human, which is why they're so good at tricking us."

"Is there anything you can do to help them be human again?"

She gave me a sympathetic smile that seemed out of place on her otherwise serious face. "I wondered the same thing when I was a child. It's a fair question to ask. Maybe if we were powerful enough, knew the right incantations and whatnot, or possessed a stronger will than those who've chosen a death of damnation." Her face returned to its default sternness. "Don't waste your energy trying to save every last demon you come across. Save it for those who are still alive. Believe me when I tell you that." Pain and sadness filled the gaze that studied mine, as if she was searching for any part of me that refused to believe her.

I nodded.

"There's one last thing I wish to teach you before I send you off to your next class."

I held my pencil ready.

"Just like you students answer to your teacher, all demons do as well. There's one ruling them all, the one everyone knows about. Do you know his name?"

I knew it alright. Everyone did. We were all taught about him, and to never speak his true name. Fear of what might happen kept his name trapped on the tip of my tongue.

"Molech, the King of Demons," she said in a soft voice.

My stomach flopped as the room filled with static and grew darker. Either that or clouds passed in front of the sun.

"Be very careful if you ever choose to say his name," she continued in her soft voice, her eyes fixed on me. "I know I said it now. I see in your face that you've sensed the energy change in my office. I want to make it perfectly clear that the Demon King is no joke." She walked over to a small bronze gong. She whispered a few words and hit the gong with a mallet.

A round, metallic note filled the room, chasing away the darkness. Tension eased from my limbs. I took a steadying breath.

"Names are powerful things," she said in a normal voice. "Never give a demon your name and never say a demon's name unless you plan to use it in some way. Demons are not benevolent like ghosts. If you don't use them, they will use you. And they all serve the Demon King in the end."

The room spun. The demon already knew my name.

Chapter 7

Every step towards Miss Wren's room felt as if a bale of hay was tied to my ankles. Each step brought me closer to where I had to go and at the same time closer to the demon that knew my name. I didn't know what to expect. Ms. Weever had shooed me out before I finished another question. She'd glared when I'd whined.

An eternity passed by the time I made it to the 6-8 building, the door the weight of ten Belas that didn't want to move as I hefted it open. A familiar voice rooted me in place.

"Why didn't you tell me this yesterday?" Miss Wren said in a harsh whisper.

A wall with doorways on either side blocked my view from the rest of the hallway. I slid inside and slowly let the door swing closed. Its latch made the softest of clunks.

"We wanted you to get a good, unbiased first impression of her before anyone told you." The second voice sounded familiar, too. I chanced leaning forward. Miss Wren's willowy frame dwarfed Mr. Redd's short one. She glared at the principal like she wanted to slap him.

"I don't care about her alignment, but what if other children's parents find out? Then what?"

"She's separated every time they have elemental training," he said with a dismissive shake of his head. "We already have a tutor for her."

"They'll figure it out. They'll ask questions. If this is her fourth school, this tells us she can't keep it secret forever."

Unless some other girl had changed schools as many times as I had, they had to be talking about me. I put more wall between me and them, entirely blocking Mr. Redd from sight.

"If worse comes to worst, we'll move her into self-contained."

"According to her file she's not special needs. She doesn't qualify for self-contained."

"Unless she does something to get expelled or her parents choose to un-enroll her, the district is legally obligated to give her an education. We can't send her away because people are afraid of Darks. It'd be better than opening ourselves up to a lawsuit."

Closing her eyes, Miss Wren slowly let out an exhale. "Damien, you know I share your views. How fair would it be to Mia if we stuff her in self-contained? She needs to build social skills."

A teacher knew I was a Dark, yet she was sticking up for me? A teacher wanted me to make friends?

"She seemed awfully content to hide from the world when I had her and her parents in my office."

"She was surrounded by adults in an unfamiliar setting. Of course she was. Gwen and her clique drew Mia into their group already."

Mr. Redd sucked in air through his teeth.

Miss Wren said, "She's making friends."

"Do you know anything about the Volaire family?"

Miss Wren said. "They're wealthy and they own the mines in this part of the state. Why?"

"Her parents are some of the most backward-thinking people in Toolena County. Remember that incident three years ago?"

"You mean the tragedy at the high school?"

The high schooler that'd told me to get out popped into my mind. Had his ghost told me, a Dark, to get out of the room, or to get out of Toolena Mesa? Maybe Ms. Weever could teach me how to make ghosts talk and make sense.

Mr. Redd said, "Raina almost convinced the school board to have me fired for allowing a Dark to be enrolled in the district. The only thing that saved me was state law."

"Is that why you came down here from the high school?"

"Correct. Now, enough about me. What I'm getting at is if you want Mia to make friends, that's great. It needs to be anyone but those girls. If Gwen's parents find out, not only will my job be on the line, but so will yours. Raina is on the school board now. She has the other four members in her pocket."

"Great," Miss Wren said. She opened the classroom door and hushed voices drifted into the hallway. She firmly told Gwen and Deren to get back into their seats and reminded the rest of the class to keep reading before closing the door again. "I feel terrible for asking, but I have to know. Why did you accept her if it's such a risk?"

Mr. Redd paused. "To be honest, I'd forgotten their daughter was in sixth grade. I had it in my mind to sneak in a Dark without their knowing, have her successfully receive an education, and then reveal the truth after she received her high school diploma. Imagine the look on Raina's face once she realized a school could function just fine with Darks." He chuckled.

Miss Wren didn't smile. "I'd love Mia to succeed here. She needs some stability in her life. You do realize how full of holes your plan is, right? Schools aren't good at keeping secrets."

He waved a dismissive hand. "Don't you worry about the details. I'll take care of that. You keep doing your job. If you're ever worried, send Mia up to Lyra and she'll take care of things. Alright?"

Miss Wren stood there, lips pressed closed and eyes fixed on someplace farther down the hallway.

Mr. Redd put his hands in his pockets. "Do I need to start looking around to fill your position?" His casual tone had an edge to it.

Miss Wren went wide-eyed and her gaze snapped to the principal. I couldn't tell if that look was filled with guilt or shock. There was definitely fear. Her gaze shifted slightly and I froze when our eyes locked on each other. She shook her head, as if snapping herself out of staring, and stepped around the principal's small frame. "Morning, Mia," she said as if nothing was wrong. "Did you enjoy meeting Ms. Weever?"

My legs moved before I realized what I was doing. I wanted to hide until Mr. Redd was gone. My steps faltered when he turned around, but I was already well into the hallway. I was like the heroine in my book, halfway across the lake and faced with a dragon. I had just as far to run past the danger as I did to run away from it.

Whether she meant to or not, Miss Wren stood between me and the principal as she ushered me into class. Mr. Redd politely greeted me and I mumbled a reply.

He turned to Miss Wren. "We'll finish our chat later. Have a good day, Miss Wren." He strode off, taking the feeling of danger with him.

Miss Wren crouched before me, bringing her pale eyes level with my hidden face. She absently tucked my hair behind my ear. Normally, I'd freak out if anyone besides my mom touched me, but the act had been so casual and unthreatening.

"How long were you standing there?"

I shrugged. "I don't know, Miss Wren." Some of my hair fell back over my face and she gently brushed it aside.

"Regardless, let's get to class. You have some reading to catch up on." She ushered me inside. There was more talking than reading going on. Miss Wren's mere presence served as motivation enough to make everyone get back in their seats and hunch over their textbooks.

I hid my energy shield hand flick as I hung up my bag in the closet. My spine tingle had returned, meaning so had the demon. The closet ceiling loomed over me like a low storm cloud. I woodenly took my place next to Gwen and glanced over her arm to see which page I needed to find.

The hand holding the top corner of her textbook tightened into a fist. I chanced looking at Gwen's face. Her pretty features were set in a hard glare, as if my mere presence offended her. Her eyes narrowed.

My hands grew slack around my textbook. Memory of her and Deren being shooed away from the door replayed in my mind. Oh, no. How much of the conversation had my classmates heard?

Chapter 8

The day dragged by with Gwen fuming beside me. Miss Wren carried on as if nothing was wrong, the demon's shadow popped in and out of sight, and I learned nothing in any of my classes. I mouthed my way through reciting pronunciations, stared blankly at the pages, scribbled nonsense for math, and pretended to fill out my workbook. My stomach felt empty. It was going to happen again. Kids were going to hate me for being a Dark. The most painful part was that I hadn't even told anyone. The teacher accidentally had.

When the science teacher released us for PE, I didn't bother approaching Gwen. I mechanically changed into a pair of ugly black shorts and a grey t-shirt with our Miners mascot on it and curled up in one corner of the gymnasium. Our PE teacher, some mannish-looking woman name Mrs. Viro, didn't notice me as I hid by a mesh bag overloaded with orange bouncy balls, open book in hand. I'd rather find out if Yuna was able to defeat the water dragon than deal with the real world. Mrs. Viro led the class through a stretching routine.

The dragon spoke to Yuna when a circular shadow fell over one side of my book. Deren stood before me, ears sticking out.

Deren looked away the moment our eyes met. He fidgeted, toes pointed towards each other.

Guilt from the broken window stung my chest. An apology sat on my lips. He was probably here to tell me how much he hated me for being a Dark. What good would it do now?

"I'm sorry."

The tiny voice belonged to Deren. I looked up, unable to believe those two words came from him.

"Do you want to play with me?" When I said nothing, he added, "I need a passing partner." He hefted a ball as big as his head.

I closed my book with a papery thump. "You really want to hang out with me?"

"Yeah. Why?"

"You don't hate me?"

He stopped fidgeting and furrowed his brows. "No. Why?"

"Even after all you heard when Miss Wren and Mr. Redd talked about?" I wanted it to be true, but I didn't know how to trust it.

His brows drew even closer. "What did they say?"

"You really didn't hear them?"

"I tried to, but Miss Wren shooed us away."

A weight lifted off my shoulders. The muscles in my back relaxed and my lungs expanded to normal size.

He didn't know.

"What were they talking about?"

And there went the relaxed feeling. I took in the shiny wooden floor. "The broken window." I felt bad for lying to him. I just wanted him to like me.

His shoulders drooped. "Dang."

I let the moment draw out, relieved. Deren still liked me and wanted to be my friend. He wasn't even mad that I'd gotten him in trouble for a broken window. Well, there was one thing I could do—try to be a decent friend. "I'm sorry about the window. It was my fault."

"Thanks. The teacher said I'd get my ball back at the end of the day. What did that teacher in black do to you?"

Ms. Weever's stern face glaring down at me flashed through my mind. "Nothing. She didn't say anything about the window."

"Then what did she want?"

Again, my insides squirmed as the truth sat on my lips. "She's my elemental tutor."

"Cool. What's your alignment?"

Why did I have to bring up the ball? I stood to stall for time. Deren was shorter than me. For some reason, that gave me some courage—not nearly enough to tell him the truth, but enough to lie instead of run off. "Crystal," I said to his sneakers. No one would question it so long as no one pressed me to move crystal rocks around.

"Oh," he said. I felt his embarrassment for me.

The hairs on the back of my neck stood up, and I took an involuntary step back as the dark mass attached to his back manifested. It was small as a mouse. It slinked over his shoulder and reached for me. Deren paled and his face grew slack. The mass grew to the size of Deren's head. He pressed a hand to his stomach and turned in time to throw up on the floor. It splattered onto my shoes.

I backed farther away, hands over my stomach. At the same time, I wanted to slap away the black mass. It had to be what made Deren sick all of a sudden. My Dark instincts told me not to touch it. "Deren?"

He threw up several more times, attracting the attention of nearby classmates. The din of bouncing balls quieted. Mrs. Viro ran over and guided a hunched-over Deren towards the boys locker room. She glanced at me with all-too-familiar ridicule, silently telling me she believed I had made Deren sick.

"Not a good first impression, Miss Evers." Her voice was surprisingly feminine. It clashed with her square jaw and close-cropped hair. "You're getting a zero for the day."

Classmates came over to investigate the vomit splatter. It looked like pureed cereal with chunks of apricots dotting the milky mess. I backed away, bile rising in my throat.

A hand grabbed my arm. I nearly screamed as I spun around. A glaring Gwen with her three friends stared me down, all of them looking thoroughly pleased.

"I told you not to hang out with him." Gwen's chin rose slightly higher as she stood with her fists on her hips. Her PE uniform somehow looked good on her. No fair. Her friends said nothing, probably waiting for permission to pick on me. "Since you got what you deserved," she said, eyeing the vomit on my sneakers, "I'll give you one last chance."

I picked my book up off the floor. Why did she even want to be around me?

Gwen stood in the middle of them like she was their queen, and they her royal advisors. I felt like Yuna when she'd met the unicorn king before her trip across the lake. That visit had been equally terrifying. Hopefully, I'd come out of this meeting for the better, too.

"Since you're not from around here, someone needs to teach you how we do things in Toolena Mesa."

She probably wanted to boss me around and feel important. I kept the thought to myself. It'd be worth it if she bossed me around and no one picked on me.

"You're lucky that Dark didn't throw up on you. He would've marked you with his taint."

I doubted the vomit would have tainted me. I'm sure I would have also thrown up out of sheer disgust.

"Bad things happen to anyone who hangs out with him," Gwen said. "That's why no one plays with him. You already broke a window and got in trouble with that lady this morning."

"I didn't get in trouble," I said in a small voice.

Gwen stared open-mouthed as if she couldn't believe I'd dared contradict her.

"Then what did she do?" Sussi, the tall, tough girl said.

"Nothing. She's my elemental tutor."

"Crystals need elemental tutors?" Gwen said.

"Someone has to teach them how to make song stones," Sussi said. Nonaya and Chibya laughed.

"I'll just go." I turned to leave.

Gwen's voice held me in place. "I didn't say you could leave."

I held my book like a shield over my chest.

"You're an outsider with a stupid alignment. You need all the help you can get."

"Why do you even want me in your group?" Again, she glared at me. I should've kept my mouth shut.

"Do you want to end up like Deren?"

I then remembered Mr. Redd's reaction when Miss Wren told him about Gwen. She was dangerous for sure and I'd already walked into her den before realizing what I'd done. It was too late to back out. I had a feeling she'd spread rumors that Deren had tainted me or something. This school would end up being like all the others. Wouldn't hiding the truth while sitting at her side be safer? "No."

"Good." She glanced in Mrs. Viro's direction, who exited the boys locker room. Miss Wren entered the gymnasium, her steps gliding along the polished wood, and talked to Mrs. Viro before escorting Deren away. Miss Wren gave me a disapproving frown in passing. Deren clutched his stomach, the black mass gone.

Mrs. Viro said, "Everyone, go sit on the bleachers until this mess is cleaned up." The lot of us moved as one to the other side of the gymnasium as chatter filled the vaulted space.

Gwen roughly guided me to a top corner and made me sit against the wall. Glancing over a shoulder, she slipped a hand into a shorts pocket and produced a pair of tweezers with a bowl on the end. She held it out, revealing the tweezers were a fire starter.

That totally had to be against the rules to have in school. Gwen's friends circled her, blocking my view of our teacher. Yep, they knew it was wrong to have this, too.

Gwen squeezed the handle a few times, creating sparks in the bowl with every stroke. She caught one of the sparks in her palm. She concentrated and bloomed it into a flame over her hand. I sank a little lower, the flame's heat caressing me. As a Fire, Gwen was immune to its strength. She curled and uncurled her fingers like she stroked a kitten's chin, eyes filled with admiration. "There's a ritual to be accepted in Toolena Mesa," she said in a soft voice, as if mesmerized by her magic. She wore a slight smile on her lips. She had me and she knew it. "It'll hurt for only a moment, but it'll mark us as friends. Just know that if you ever break my trust or friendship, it'll hurt more, a lot more. So." She brought the fire closer to me, stinging my forearms. "Do you accept my friendship?"

I wanted to run. Everything about this was wrong. I was in no position to refuse. My back pressed against the stone bricks, which were as cold as death. Swallowing, I nodded.

"Say it out loud."

I swallowed again, my arms burning. I spread my fingers over the top of my book, hoping to keep it from catching fire. "I accept."

"Good. Hold out your hand and shake on it."

I clutched my book harder, my legs shaking. This was wrong. This wasn't what friends did to each other. I knew what friendship felt like before everyone turned on me eventually. This was something entirely new, entirely wrong.

"Just do it," Sussi said. The other two voiced agreement.

I loosened my grip on my book. My hand shook. Gwen seized my hand and squeezed. The fire seared my palm. I let out a cry and tried to break away. My hand felt like I'd grabbed a burning cactus.

Gwen leaned in and spoke in my ear. "Welcome to Toolena Mesa." Stepping back, she let go, and the four of them sat on the bench below me and chatted away as if nothing had happened.

Blood pounded in my ears as my hand continued to burn and shake. The book dropped to my feet. I didn't bother picking it up. A lone, spindly symbol of the Fire element glared a deep red at me with the shape of a distant mountain range reaching outward on either side.

Chapter 9

My hand burned all day. Thinking about it made it hurt. Trying not to think about it made it hurt. Looking at it made it hurt, and so did not looking at it. Nothing I tried to do or not do helped. I hid my aching hand palm-up on my leg as I failed miserably at writing with my left hand. I only bothered in order to avoid unwanted attention from my teachers.

Deren never returned. The demon in the closet left a constant shadow looming in the ceiling, dipping lower when a student stopped in and retrieved Deren's things. I sat upright, causing Gwen to raise an eyebrow at me. I mumbled something about accidentally bumping my palm on my desk. She smiled and went back to doing vocabulary work.

By the end of the day, my hand was numb and my entire palm was red. My fingers were swollen. The bell rang and Miss Wren dismissed us. The realization that I was about to go home brought some relief. I was that much closer to soothing the pain with one of the aloe plants growing outside the house.

"See you tomorrow, Mia," Gwen said with a pleasant smile as she passed.

"See you tomorrow," I said in a tight voice. She'd probably get mad if I didn't reply. I grabbed everything we'd worked on, figuring I'd get it done later when I could concentrate. Maybe even Mrs. Viro would like me more if I showed her I could be a good student.

My hand was numb enough to hold all my workbooks and one textbook in both hands. I pushed my chair in and turned to find Miss Wren's thick-soled shoes facing me. She wore another pretty floral skirt with a solid white blouse. When anyone heard the word "teacher" they'd easily be able to picture her.

"Mia, will you come see me at my desk after you collect your things?" she said in a teacher voice that told me she had something important to say when no one else was around.

My heart sank, drowning what hope I had. "Yes, ma'am." What had Mrs. Viro told her about PE class?

I headed over to the closet, shield up, like I was headed to a funeral. The only funeral I'd ever been to was my grandmother's. I'd made a silent promise to myself to never go to one again. Funeral homes had too much activity for Darks. The demon in the closet was nothing compared to that, but it was still dangerous.

I paused before the closet as claws stretched out of the portal like a cat flexing its paws.

I see you, child.

Oh, no.

Come closer, Mia Evers. The demon drew out the

"s."

Something tugged on my body. I closed the gap between me and the emptying closet as my classmates snatched up bags and light jackets, oblivious to me and the demon.

The demon's head separated from the darkness like a drop of water collecting and hanging off the edge of the closet. Its one red eye stared at me, delight coming off it in waves. *Just stay right there.* As its head stretched lower, it seemed like time sped up around me. My classmates moved faster with crisp, sudden motions, their walking gaits moving as fast as if they were running. Their voices moved too quickly to make anything out. They filed out the door in a fast march. I remained an unmoving statue when a classmate tugged on my arm three times and shrugged as fast as a hiccup before following everyone else out the door.

I tried to move my limbs, willing my arms towards my shoulder bag, teeth clenched, as the room emptied and Miss Wren hurried out of sight.

The demon tilted its head as its delight shifted to curiosity and annoyance. *Interesting. You are full of surprises, child. You shouldn't be able to move at all.*

I raised my hands enough to create a gap between my chest and books, and my hands continued creeping upwards.

You will fully bend to my will in time. As if the ceiling sucked up the black drop of water that was the demon's head, it disappeared, claws and all.

I nearly fell over as my weight shifted forwards. I snatched up my bag with my unburned hand and stuffed my books inside. Miss Wren sat at her desk, awaiting my presence, staring at me with a raised eyebrow.

"What?" I said, embarrassment twisting my chest.

Her gaze darted to the closet before settling back on me. "What was that all about?"

I stood before her cluttered desk, a stack of papers piled as high as my chin. "Nothing."

"Mia, that wasn't nothing," she said. "You stood there for a whole minute, staring at the ceiling."

I bowed my head, hiding my face.

"Please tell me what happened."

I shook my head. Why'd there have to be a demon in here? This was embarrassing enough. Silence followed. The classroom song stone had stopped playing. Maybe if I ran to the bus fast enough, I could avoid more questions.

"Mia, I don't know what happened at the other three schools, but I want you to know I'm not like your previous teachers. I don't know what you've been through. By the looks of it, it's been very unfair for you. I'll admit it's a little scary having a Dark in my classroom, but I'm willing to stop being scared and start understanding instead. Will you help me?"

The fact that Miss Wren was sitting was my first clue that she wasn't like my other teachers. None of them sat in my presence after discovering I was a Dark. It was like they wanted to be ready to run at the first sign of danger. No one understood me. My eyes stung. My teacher looked perfectly relaxed behind her desk. "Do you hate me?"

Miss Wren flinched as if the question surprised her. "Goodness no. Why would you think that?"

Her expression from PE class flashed through my mind again. The exact features were lost, but I remembered the look in her eyes. "The way you looked at me when you took Deren away."

She furrowed her brows. "I'm sorry, I don't remember. What kind of look did I give you?"

This was such unfamiliar territory. No one ever wanted to hear about Dark stuff, yet here was a teacher who asked for help with understanding. Did she really mean it? Would she be like Mom and Dad and become afraid after they'd heard too much? Maybe, just maybe, Miss Wren would be different. "You looked like you thought I was the one who made Deren sick." My heart pounded.

"Oh. I'm sorry, it did cross my mind." Her cheeks flushed. "Can you even do that?"

"No, only demons can do that." By the Light, she'd asked a question.

"I didn't know that. That's good to know," she said with a thoughtful nod. "What can you do?"

And another. She was different. "I don't know yet. Ms. Weever is the first person to teach me anything."

"Your parents haven't taught you anything?"

I shook my head. "They're afraid of me."

"Oh, no. I'm so sorry." Her voice sounded as small as mine.

"It's okay. I'm used to it."

"It's not okay," she said, shaking her head. "That's not fair to you. Think of how it's made you feel."

Hated, rejected, feared. My eyes stung even more. I took one slow, deep breath after another to keep calm. I heard distant laughter—or at least I thought I did. The closet ceiling lay in shadow. The demon had to be listening to the conversation.

"What is it?" Miss Wren said.

I studied her kind face, hunting for the least sign of

insincerity, and found none. "Do you really want to know?"

"Yes. I need to understand if I'm going to be a good enough teacher for you."

I didn't understand her explanation, but it sounded important. I swallowed the dry lump in my throat. "There's a demon in your closet."

Miss Wren stared in mute astonishment. Goosebumps appeared all over her arms. "Really?" she said.

"It's why I asked to change seats yesterday."

"I see. Should I move everyone else away, too?"

Wow, she'd asked me for advice. "I don't know. So far, it seems like it pays attention only to me."

"Maybe because you're a Dark," Miss Wren said, getting up. "Have you told Ms. Weever about it?" She crossed to the closet and looked at the ceiling.

"Yeah, but she said not to worry about it."

The darkness swirled like a low storm cloud. *Are you offering this one up to me, child?* Claws appeared again. *How thoughtful.*

I ran over and pulled Miss Wren away, sending a fresh wave of pain into my palm and up my arm. I bit my lip to stifle a scream.

Miss Wren put a hand over mine. "What's wrong?"

"It spoke. It's not nice." I glared at the shadow and claws, and poured more energy into my shield. I positioned myself between my teacher and the demon. "Go away."

And like yesterday, it disappeared, leaving not one trace behind. The tingling in my spine stopped and I felt completely safe so suddenly that I had to take a moment to absorb the fact.

"What'd you do?" Miss Wren said.

"I made it leave," I said, eyeing the perfectly normal ceiling. "It'll be back tomorrow, though. I don't know how to keep it from coming back."

"Thank you for doing that."

Thank you. Those two heartfelt words echoed in my head over and over. I didn't want this moment to end. I didn't even want to go home anymore. A teacher knew I was a Dark and didn't hate me.

"Now, I don't mean to sound like I'm trying to get rid of you. I don't want you to miss your bus." She glanced at the clock. "They should be here by now. We'll have to talk more tomorrow. I wanted to let you know that I know you're aligned with Dark and that I'm here for you. I don't plan on treating you differently from anyone else in my class. Also, I'm here if you ever need to talk."

I clutched the strap of my bag with my unburnt hand. "Thank you."

"And thank you, too, for opening up to me. I imagine that was hard for you." She guided me to the rows of students waiting for the gates to open.

I joined a line as the gates parted. Most students filed onto the floating buses. Others veered towards their parents awaiting them in the parking lot. Among the line of floating cars was a sleek and shiny one that stood out from the rest. The car was covered in silvery curves and lines, a bold black paint job, and tinted windows.

Gwen approached that car as a gentleman stepped out of the driver's seat. He wore a crisp black suit, had a large nose, and a neatly trimmed goatee. He opened a passenger door as he accepted Gwen's backpack, helped her into her seat, and deposited her backpack into the trunk.

I studied the circles and curves of the fire symbol on my burnt hand, and the jagged outline of the mountain range on either side. It was the same symbol on the passenger door. I'd been marked as a friend of the daughter of the richest family in the area. Were her parents in the car at the moment? Miss Wren and the principal feared what they might do if they found out I went to this school. What would they do if they found out their daughter had made friends with me?

Why did life have to be so complicated?

Chapter 10

Deren remained out sick for the rest of the week, and Gwen and her friends dragged me to their lunch table every day. I felt like a reluctant pet they wanted for no reason other than to have me nearby. They chatted about school, Gwen, boys, Gwen, the mines, and Gwen. I listened and said what I knew they wanted whenever their attention turned to me. They'd smile and giggle every time I spoke. Otherwise, they left me alone.

Everyone else left me alone, too. No one outside Gwen's circle tried to pair up with me for classwork or PE. It was strange. At the same time, I wasn't surprised. By being Gwen's friend, I was off-limits to everyone else. Part of me felt disappointed. This was what I'd wanted. No one but the teacher knew I was a Dark, no one was afraid of or mean to me, and I was mostly left alone. This was everything I wanted in a school.

So why did what I want suck?

My thoughts often drifted to Deren. That train of thought always led to confusion and guilt. I buried myself in schoolwork and books to distract myself.

My thoughts also drifted to that dead high schooler. Maybe it was my curiosity. Maybe it was my alignment drawing me to him. I didn't know how to tell the difference and Ms. Weever wouldn't let me distract her from my lessons with such things.

When I entered Ms. Weever's office on Friday, I stopped inside the doorway, needing a moment to take in all the stuff that hadn't been there yesterday.

A violin sat on a stand atop a piano, its lacquered wood looking so smooth that dust would roll off it. Next to the violin sat some oval-shaped object with a bunch of holes in it. A hollowed-out wood box with metal strips attached to the top half sat propped up next to the hole-filled object, along with a giant seashell. A painted log stood propped up in the corner next to the piano, and a row of drums of varying sizes and shapes lined the wall connected to the doorway.

What on Aardra was all this about?

"Ah, there you are." Ms. Weever waved me over from behind her desk. "Come in already. And close the door behind you."

I hesitated, torn between hurrying and doing as instructed, or leaving the door open like we normally did. I didn't like the idea of being shut inside while I learned how to use my Dark powers. What were we trying to keep secret?

She gave me a flat look. "We're going to be playing some music. Shut the door so we don't disturb anyone."

Or that. I shut the door and settled in my usual

chair, notebook out and pencil ready.

Ms. Weever gave me a studious look, like she was searching for something to criticize. "That's better." Hands clasped behind her back, she positioned herself before the piano.

This was my opening. "Ms. Weever, may I borrow your oak wand?"

Her brows drew together. "Whatever for?"

"I want to know what the demon in my classroom is doing."

"Miss Evers, I've already told you that one's harmless. Stop dwelling on it." She glared at me like she was waiting for me to challenge her. I lowered my gaze. "Don't slouch. That habit doesn't become a Dark either."

I sat up straight as I scribbled today's date on top of my blank page.

"I want to make it perfectly clear that I don't want to hear about that demon again until we cover banishing circles. You're in no danger from it." She carefully plucked the violin and its bow from the stand.

"It knows my name," I said.

Worry flashed across her face before her stern glare reasserted control. "And how did it learn your name?" She shouldered the violin, shrugging twice to get it right where she wanted it under her chin.

"I don't know. It's trying to control me."

"Of course. It's a demon. Why are you surprised?"

And now I felt stupid.

"Has it tried to hurt you?"

I studied her stern gaze, wondering whether I should speak. However, I had a feeling I'd get berated if I didn't answer her. "It scratched me."

Lowering the violin, she gave me a flat look. "A scratch?" It was more a statement than a question. "You're all worried because of a little scratch? Miss Evers, you need to stop being so afraid in its presence. You give it power by feeding it your fear." She shouldered the violin again. "Cowardice does not become a Dark either. If you can't handle a demon as weak as that one, then you won't be worth my time."

I felt the size of my pinky toe. I wanted to cry, but I felt too empty to produce tears. Maybe I should get up and leave, instead of keeping on making Ms. Weever mad.

"Are you going to sit there and feel sorry for yourself, or will you toughen up?" She played a note on each string, filling the room with its pure, round sound. The sound seeped into my bones, like it was filling me with its power. "Miss Evers, life only gets harder as you get older. It's not the end of the world because you failed to stand up to a lesser demon. Learn from the experience. You know what to do now."

"Yes, ma'am," I said, misery needling at my insides. I couldn't deny the truth in her words. I knew what to do now and I wanted to prove to her that I could stand up to the demon. I wanted her to be proud of me, needed her to be. "I'm ready for today's lesson."

"That's better." She played up and down a scale, again filling the room with powerful notes, and lowered the bow. "Every alignment can use music in one way other another. For Darks, it amplifies our powers, helping us banish stronger demons and even call them to us."

She played a slow tune that made me picture hooves carefully treading along a shadowed path in thick woods. The notes carried a heavy, steady beat. The room grew darker despite the sunlight outside. Ms. Weever either didn't notice or didn't care. When my spine tingled, I conjured my shield. She continued to play, her curled fingers dancing along the strings, face set in concentration.

The song drew to a conclusion and Ms. Weever appeared as a gray shadow in the dark room. Everything was shrouded in darkness, even the doorway. Her boots were lost in the darkness and her black dress looked like it had risen from it. A row of buckles faintly gleamed down the front of her black corset.

A hot breath doused the back of my neck.

Taking a sharp breath, I jumped off the chair and backed towards Ms. Weever. Something circled us.

"Don't enter the circle," Ms. Weever snapped. A pair of notes screeched from the violin.

I spun around. Symbols lit up with a purple glow around my tutor. I stood mere inches from the spindly outer circle that reminded me of spiderwebs.

"Go back to your seat. You're safer outside the circle." Her voice held the same power as when the demon had ordered me closer to the closet. I stood by my chair, my back to Ms. Weever. Something huge slithered in a circle where the walls should be.

Ms. Weever played a different song, this one uplifting like a sunrise. The notes were slow and purposeful, gently leading into each other like one long breath. The slithering halted and the darkness receded as if the sun rose in the room. Fear eased out of my limbs as the room reappeared. It looked untouched, untainted. I felt perfectly safe and at peace, so much so that I took my seat. A typically sunny desert day shone through the office window as Ms. Weever's song drew to a cheerful close.

The office door flung open. Desi, one of the chatty front desk ladies, stared at the both of us with such wide eyes I thought they would pop. "What on Aardra is going on in here?"

"Teaching," Ms. Weever said. "Please shut the door and don't disturb us."

Desi gave my tutor an incredulous look, but offered no argument. She eyed me with the fear I was so used to seeing in everyone. A pang of disappointment filled me as she closed the door.

Ms. Weever returned the violin to its stand. "So what did you think of that?" She faced me, hands clasped behind her back like nothing crazy had happened a moment ago. The power circle was gone.

"That was amazing—scary, but amazing."

She nodded. "I won't be teaching you anything of that level until high school, but I wanted to show you a glimpse of such abilities."

"What'd you do?"

"That beast was a minor demon, a fury, something far more powerful than that beast you have lurking in your classroom. I was careful not to expose you to too much of its presence. You'll be far more terrified the first time you summon your own demon." Placing her hand on the floor, she whispered a few words. Runes and symbols lifted off the wood floor like pieces of paper getting kicked up by a breeze and whisked into her awaiting palm. "They are very forceful creatures, as you saw with how dark the room got."

"What did Desi get all scared for?"

"She felt the same fear you did. It can't be helped. She'll live." She broke into a crooked smile. "Whether or not she forgives me is another matter. Anyway." She plucked the hollowed-out wooden box from atop the piano. "The violin is the signature instrument of a Dark. We can use the rest of the instruments in this room in one way or another. Ultimately, a violin will be your most powerful musical tool. For now, you're going to start with this." She handed me the box.

It was too large for my hands. The box itself reminded me of a birdhouse. The hole had been cut out in a corner and was only big enough to stick my pointer finger through. Two rows of metal strips lined up tightly along the top of the box. They reminded me of piano keys, little tiny ones, each a different length and width. The top row spread in a "v" and the bottom row slanted down to the right.

"It's called an mbira."

"Em-beer-ah?"

"Correct. It's more common for Lights to use this instrument. Its purpose is to help the living connect to their ancestors. Darks can use this to draw a lost soul to us, one that hasn't yet turned into a demon. We can also use them to connect to our ancestors, but they don't work for us in the same way as for a Light. You'll be perfectly safe learning and experimenting with this instrument. The only problem you might run into is luring a spirit and being unable to get it to leave."

That wasn't so bad. I could handle that. It's not like I had to play this thing at home.

Ms. Weever handed me a songbook and a case to put the mbira in. "You'll be taking the mbira home daily to practice, no excuses. I'll give you extra homework if I so much as suspect you aren't practicing."

The color drained from my face. Never mind.

***

I couldn't feel the tips of my thumbs by the end of the lesson. Playing an mbira required flicking the metal keys with either a downward or upward stroke of my thumbs and right pointer finger. I liked the instrument, though. It was easy enough to learn the names of the keys, and the resonant sound was pleasing to the ear. The notes remind me of deeper register wind chimes with a woody overtone that made me feel closer to nature. If I were Faunakin, I could charm all sorts of animals over to me.

Ms. Weever escorted me to the nurse to relieve my tender fingers. My tutor bid me farewell at the door. Instrument tucked away in its case and inside my shoulder bag, I walked over to a small counter separating students from the nurse. A row of vine-like plants lined the floor on either side of me, creating a short runway to the counter. The leaves shivered as I passed. Some twisted, reaching for me. The farthest vines stilled when I reached the counter. The nearest ones crept towards me like little green millipedes snaking their way to my shoes.

"Ms. Weever?" I called, my voice an octave higher than normal. I lifted a foot as vines touched my shoe. "Ms. Weever!"

"Don't panic," a voice said from the other side of the counter.

Balancing on one foot wrapped in thin vines, I searched for the source of the voice. A tall lady whisked around a hanging curtain hiding a sickbed from view. A peony sat in her hair above one ear. She had long, straight hair, striking eyes, and a studious gaze. She reminded me of an elf from one of my books—well, an elf in blue scrubs.

"The plants are telling me what ails you, if anything," the nurse said. "You'd be surprised how many students pretend to be sick." She stopped on the other side of the counter, head tilted, gaze on the vines.

Florakin. The nurse was a Florakin. She had power over plants. "May I have some ice for my fingers?" I held up my hands, three fingertips bright red.

The nurse seized my right hand and analyzed my palm. "What happened here?" She ran a finger along the swirls of fading scars. They were hardly visible and I had several blisters that hadn't popped.

"Nothing." It was the first thing that came out of my mouth. I wished I could take it back as soon as I said it. The nurse gave me a flat look. "It was an accident."

"What's your name?"

"Mia Evers."

"Miss Evers, you must be new here. I'm Trisha Kor. The students call me Miss Kor or Nurse Kor."

I really wished she'd let go of my hand. My elbow hurt from holding the awkward position.

"Whenever I ask you a question, it's safe to presume I already know the answer." She took my hand in both of hers and passed a hand over mine like she was trying to soothe the last of the pain, then let go. "It's been ages since I've seen one of those burns. Now, get in here, please." She waved me over.

The vines let me go and sat still like normal plants. I lifted my feet higher than necessary to step over them and followed Nurse Kor to an empty sickbed. She spread a clear ointment on my hand that smelled like aloe and a hint of arnica. It smelled relaxing. I held still as she wrapped my hand and one thumb in long, thin green leaves. She took my hands in both of hers again, closed her eyes, and sang in a whisper.

My hands felt like they'd been dipped in ice water, cooling my pain away. "Do you use singing to heal people?"

The nurse opened one eye. "Yes."

"I'm learning how to play music, too."

"To do what?"

Oh, why couldn't I keep my mouth shut sometimes? "Stuff."

Nurse Kor nodded and sang the final notes. Warmth seeped back into my fingers. She unwrapped my hands and ordered me to wash up.

"Thank you, Nurse Kor," I said as she handed me a note for my teacher.

"No problem, Miss Evers. I'll have a salve ready for you after every lesson, until your fingers get used to the mbira." She bade me good day and returned to the hidden sickbed.

She sang again in a whispery voice. I hadn't heard a sound from the bed the whole time. Who was there? Carefully stepping over the plants again, I snuck around the counter and to the curtain's edge. Nurse Kor's feet and the bed's legs showed through the gap between the curtain and the floor. She sat with her back to me at the foot of the bed. I crept closer, closer, finally close enough.

A student lay asleep on the bed, another one of my classmates. I recognized him, but didn't know his name. All I knew was that he sat next to Deren in language class. A black mass materialized over his chest, reaching for me like the vines had. I gasped.

Nurse Kor turned.

We locked eyes for a heartbeat. I bolted out of the room. I only made it to the hallway by the time I stopped myself, forcing myself to be brave and face the consequences of my actions. Besides, I'd rather get scolded alone than in front of the entire class. I clenched my pass.

The nurse cornered me, eyes livid. "Why did you do that? That was very rude."

I wanted to blurt "I don't know." I believed her when she told me she already knew the answer to any question she asked me. "I was curious."

"Let your curiosity run free outside my office. Do you want me to tell the whole school who burnt your hand?"

"No, ma'am."

"Then do we have an understanding?"

"Yes, ma'am," I said with a nod. I completely understood. However, I couldn't promise I'd listen the next time curiosity overcame me in a situation like that.

She eased the tension out of her arms and shoulders, and her expression softened. "Now, what made you gasp?"

"He's very sick." I didn't know if that was true. I figured it was because he lay asleep in the nurse's office and had the same black mass as Deren.

"How do you know? What's your alignment?"

I lowered my gaze, hiding behind my hair. "I'd rather not say."

Nurse Kor tilted her head and a silence stretched

out between us as I repeated the truth in my mind over and over again. "You know I can go look at your file, right?"

Dread filled me as the truth escaped my lips in a whisper. "Dark." I braced myself for angry words, for yelling, to be told to get out. However, another silence stretched out between us. I couldn't bring myself to look up.

Nurse Kor shifted her weight to her other foot. "What did you see?" she whispered, her voice strained.

I looked away. "A black mass attached to his chest."

"What is it?"

"I don't know."

"Is it what's making him sick?"

"I'm not sure."

The nurse considered my words for a long moment. I had no idea what was going through her mind. That made me even more nervous. Would she hate me like everyone else, or would she be more like Mr. Redd and Miss Wren?

Instead, she chose neither. She merely walked back into her office without saying another word.

I stood there in stunned silence, unsure of what to do next. I looked at my handwritten note on a now crumpled piece of parchment. Instead of heading back to class, like I knew I should, I headed deeper into the main office, specifically Ms. Weever's office. The door stood wide open. One look inside told me it was empty. In addition to the instruments, her office overflowed with magical trinkets and items, including the wand I had asked for earlier. I knew where it was, too. A row of wands sat behind her desk, propped up like the violin, ready for the taking.

Would she notice if I borrowed it? My heart pounded like it was trying to knock some sense into me. If I took the wand, then it'd be considered stealing, even though I had no intention of keeping it. I'd get into huge trouble if I got caught.

The image of the sleeping boy and his black mass flashed in my mind, and so did Deren. I had to borrow the wand. If Nurse Kor couldn't sense what I could with her Florakin alignment, then it was up to me to help. Maybe once I figured out what it was, I could tell Miss Wren, who could tell the nurse.

I checked the hallway again. It was empty. The receptionists chatted away up front, too far away for me to worry about. I took one step inside and a line of runes lit up with a purple glow. I hopped backwards. The runes vanished.

Apparently, Ms. Weever didn't want living people stepping into her office while she was out. It seemed extreme. She could've shut her door, so why leave it open and place a ward instead?

The row of wands lay tantalizingly close, but too far away to take one. That left me with one other option I'd been considering for a couple of days—the photo.

I moved several doors down to Mr. Redd's office and peeked inside. It was empty as well. I checked the hallway to make sure no one was there. It was empty, minus the receptionists' voices. I snuck up to the front of the office to make sure all the grownups weren't hanging out there. Desi and the other lady chatted away about some person's new baby and how adorable it was. No parents or students hung out in the lobby.

I slowly backed away and half expected to see

someone standing right behind me when I turned around. That's what happened in stories when characters snuck around. They always got caught sooner or later. To my huge relief, the hallway lay empty, no grownups suddenly appearing like ghosts. I double-checked the principal's office to make sure it was empty, which it was, and headed over to the cabinet covered in photos. In one swift movement, I stuffed the framed stone slab in my bag and rushed back into the hallway.

Right as I finished smoothing down my bag, Mr. Redd emerged into the hallway, blocking my escape. Behind him lay a bathroom door. He straightened his tie and stopped when I stopped.

"Good afternoon, Miss Evers. Shouldn't you be back in class by now?"

My legs stiffened as my heart hammered away. "I'm heading there now." Great, my voice shook.

He glanced at the entrance to Ms. Weever's office. We stood between his office and hers. There was no reason for me to be in this part of the main office. "Your lesson ended several minutes ago. What are you doing over here?"

Guilt burned in my chest like my hand had the day Gwen burned it. I wanted to clutch my bag and run. I held one of the principal's belongings. I felt like he could sense his property by being near it. Hopefully, my hair hid my terror.

"I saw Ms. Weever leave."

A thought struck me. "I was looking for you."

"Oh." His suspicion softened into curiosity. "What can I help you with?"

I wrung the strap of my bag and strangled my note

in my other hand. "I wanted to thank you for assigning Ms. Weever as my tutor. She's really good."

"That's good to hear." He guided me towards the door leading out to the rest of campus. "Now, next time, please save such visits for outside class hours. If it's an emergency, my door is always open. Right now, you should be off to your next class." He opened the door, momentarily blinding me with sunlight. "Enjoy your weekend, Miss Evers."

The scent of heated dirt and rock filled my nose as I hurried to class.

Chapter 11

Instead of the day's last bell bringing relief, my chest filled with dread at the thought of walking past the main office to get on the bus. Maybe he had already figured out what I'd done. Maybe he was waiting for me to try to get away with it and pluck me out of line before I could step foot on the bus.

Maybe I should leave my bag at school over the weekend. My feet led me to the closet as students darted back and forth in my path. Excited chatter filled my ears like a buzzing swarm of bees. All that energy, all those people would leave me alone if I kept looking down and left the rest of the world alone.

I stopped before the closet, the threat of the demon looming overhead. It said nothing, made no reach for me. My bag hung among the rapidly dwindling selection of belongings. No, I couldn't leave my bag. It'd be the only thing left in the closet. Miss Wren always checked to make sure no one forgot anything. She'd get suspicious if I tried to leave something there, even if I pretended to forget. I shouldered my bag, the contents weighing me down. I arched my back, stretching it, and walked as tall as my slight frame could manage as I followed the last of my classmates out the door.

I did a full-body flinch when Miss Wren touched my shoulder.

"Oh, I'm sorry. I didn't mean to startle you."

"It's okay." Part of me wondered if she was working with Mr. Redd to trap me in line. I knew that was ridiculous, but I couldn't help it—not with the evidence bumping my leg with every other step.

"Are you okay? Did you have a good day?" My teacher walked beside me with steady, long strides that matched the pace of my shorter legs.

"Yeah." We stepped out into the sun and heat, and more voices buzzed in my ears as grades four through eight came together to get on the buses. Thankfully, Miss Wren didn't push for more information. She slowly pulled ahead of me, watchful eyes scanning the sea of children and occasionally reminding some to walk instead of run. I felt safer without her next to me. I couldn't help but wonder if she only pretended to know nothing about my thieving ways.

The flow of students rounded a building and the buses and parking lot appeared before us. Parents awaited their children, buses hummed with magic, and teachers stood on either side of the final stretch of sidewalk like guards watching prisoners march to the buses. Their smiles masked fangs and glares. The waving and occasional hugging of students guided my footsteps to the middle of the pack, out of arm's reach. I felt like Yuna when she was escorted through the castle to meet the unicorn king. Guards had watched her every step and she'd wondered if she would get help from him or get thrown into the dungeons.

Miss Wren stopped at her usual spot and waved goodbye to all the students. I kept my head down and avoided waving back, hoping to avoid getting spotted. Mr. Redd stood near the outermost gate, the last obstacle between me and freedom. He didn't wave or smile. He never did. That didn't help my guilt. His eyes searched the students like they always did. I drifted towards the opposite side of the path and my limbs stiffened the moment I crossed in front of him. His gaze swung in my direction. It felt like when the demon had run a claw along my shield and scratched my cheek. I wrung the strap of my bag in both hands as I fought the urge to run.

My spine tingled once my back was to him. Was he following me? Fear kept my gaze locked on the steep steps leading up to freedom. I climbed them and automatically waved to the bus driver before taking a seat a few rows deep, and sunk my eyes below the window. I didn't dare take out my book. Yuna had been unable to pass the water dragon and returned to shore. I'd have to find out what happened next another time. For all I knew, they had informed the bus driver of my thievery and they wanted me trapped on the bus before taking me in. I clamped my eyelids shut and pressed my forehead to the glass.

I flinched and bolted upright when the bus lurched. The students sitting across from me turned. They went back to chatting as the bus slowly glided forward, its magical hum sounding like what I imagined a purring dragon would sound like. The campus drifted away as the bus turned onto the main road and the teachers, including Mr. Redd, watched the fleet depart.

I sank back in my seat as a wave of exhaustion came over my relaxing limbs. I'd gotten away with it—for now, at least.

**

Mom sat in bed reading when I got home. She didn't speak or look up when I stood in the bedroom doorway. She turned the page and kept reading as I stood there. Her face, sad and downcast, warned me not to greet her. She'd snap at me for reasons beyond my understanding. Dad wasn't home, as usual. I wish I knew where he was. Mom always cheered up when he was home. Bela played quietly with some alphabet blocks in the living room, ignoring me as well.

I carefully set my bag on one of the dining room chairs so I wouldn't make any noise, took my shoes off, and made dinner. Maybe bringing her some food would make her happy. At age eleven, I wasn't much of a cook. I could make some basic stuff. Mom had taught me many things before she started acting weird.

Homework and the mbira could wait.

I pounded some dough flat to make tortillas. I didn't know how my mom made perfectly round ones all the time. Mine were the right size, but they were hopelessly lopsided. I made enough for Dad, too. I chopped some vegetables, including an evil onion that made my eyes water, some chicken, and added everything to a cast iron skillet. The ingredients sizzled away and filled the kitchen with the aroma of seasoned meat and vegetables. I stirred often, pushing the meal around with a wooden spoon until everything was tender and slightly charred on the outside. It wasn't perfect. It looked close to what Mom made. It smelled good enough to make my stomach growl.

As I finished placing my last lopsided tortilla onto a warmed plate, Mom roughly yanked me away from the stove. "Mia, what are you doing?" She slapped the rune that turned off the burner and glared at me, her long hair a mess. "Are you trying to burn down the house?"

A mess of bowls, a cheese grater, and a cutting board were on the counter. No smoke filled the air, just the smell of fresh-made tortillas. I didn't see fires or anything in danger of burning down the house. I studied her pale face, searching for a hint of love in her hard, mismatched eyes. The longer I looked, the more I wanted to cry. Why was she so mad? "I wanted to make you dinner."

Mom blinked and took in the stovetop and counters a second time. The hardness melted away. She lifted the cast iron lid keeping the meat and vegetables warm, then set it down and studied my ugly tortillas critically before pulling the cloth back over them. She took a deep breath and sighed. "Next time ask first." Her voice was softer, gentler.

"I didn't want to bother you while you were reading."

"Don't argue with me."

"I'm sorry, Mom."

She stirred the meat and vegetables, took a bite, added more seasoning, and stirred again. She took another test bite and nodded.

The three of us settled down to dinner. Bela chatted

away about how much her stuffed ponies liked the block house she'd built and Mom absently commented on how nice or sweet things were as she stared out the window, slowly chewing every bite before swallowing and taking another. She gave no outward indication of whether or not she liked it.

I finished eating before she did, then sat quietly and waited to be dismissed. I wasn't in any rush to start on my homework. My thoughts kept drifting to the picture sitting in the bag at my feet. School hadn't called. I was finally beginning to believe I'd gotten away with it.

Mom got up, empty plate in hand. "Thank you, Mia. That was good." She ran her fingertips through my hair and kissed my head. She set her plate and silverware in the sink and returned to the bedroom. Not exactly the reaction I'd wanted. However, I'd take it over another confusing angry outburst. Bela hurried after her with her empty plate, pausing to pick up her fork after it clanged on the floor.

Setting aside the leftovers for Dad, I cleaned up the kitchen before finally starting on my homework.

***

My original plan to wait for Mom to fall asleep before practicing the mbira didn't work. I should've thought of that way sooner. I knew she didn't go to bed until long after I did. This created a new problem. I didn't know which I was more afraid of, Mom getting mad at me for doing "Dark stuff" or Ms. Weever's punishment, whatever that would be, if I didn't practice.

I set the instrument and palm-sized pyrite memory stone on my bed. The instrument was quiet without the wood bowl an mbira could be placed in.

I carefully shut my bedroom door without making a sound. Memory stone in hand, I took out my notebook and whispered the Stonespeak incantation that would wake the stone and guide me through my scales. The language sounded weird, like trying to say words by rubbing or tapping stones together. The words were better described as sounds. I thought I would have to try several times to get it right. The stone grew warm and glowed gold. The glow shrank into several runes on the shiny surface and I tapped the one Ms. Weever had instructed me to use, then touched the stone to the mbira, synchronizing it with my instrument. The keys glowed one at a time in rapid succession, and then the golden light settled on one key. The memory stone ticked like a metronome. I followed the glowing keys as I practiced my scales, slowly at first, and picking up the tempo as the movements became familiar, automatic.

Some time later, a gaze bore into my back. I nearly dropped the mbira. Mom stood with her head in the doorway, watching with fearful eyes. How long had she been there?

I tapped the memory stone to the mbira, ending the lesson. "Was I too loud? I'm sorry."

Mom pointed at the instrument. "What's that?"

"It's an instrument used mostly by Light people," I said softly, hoping not to anger or frighten her if I didn't speak too loud. "It's called an mbira. I'm practicing scales. I'm not playing any songs."

Mom didn't move or speak. Her gaze darted around my room, as if looking for ghosts she couldn't see even if she wanted to. "Don't play it if your father's home."

"I won't."

The walls vibrated as the front door shut hard. Mom gasped and the faintest of smiles touched her face. "Go to bed, sweetie. Good night." She pulled the door closed, but it never latched. It slowly swung open as her footsteps pattered away.

I stared at the darkened gap, torn between doing as told or getting up and greeting Dad. I hadn't seen him since the day I was enrolled at Toolena Mesa. I put away the mbira and stone, changed into my pajamas, and tried going to bed. I lay there and stared into the darkened kitchen. I didn't feel the least bit sleepy.

A distant light spread over the stone floor, lighting the path to my parents. A handful of steps and we'd all be together in one room. Something told me they didn't want me in their room. Part of me firmly believed they needed me to appear. Maybe it'd be like when I was younger, woken from a nightmare and tucked into bed between them. My head would be smushed between their pillows and they'd take turns tickling me until I calmed down. Dad would carry me back to bed and tuck me in right as I drifted back off to sleep.

The last time that happened was in kindergarten, before my alignment manifested.

I folded back the covers and quietly set my feet on the ground. I ran the soft threads of the small rug through my toes before tiptoeing to my doorway. I sidestepped through. My shoulder blades brushed the door frame with a muted rustle.

I crossed the kitchen and crouched by the dining table. Their bedroom door was wide open, and they argued in hushed voices.

"Baby, please stop crying," Dad said, kissing

Mom's forehead.

"Then stop being gone for so long. I don't know how much more of this I can take." She stood in Dad's arms, hands on his chest.

"We've been super careful."

"I worry about you every second you're gone."

"Don't."

"I keep waiting for the day you don't come home because you got caught. Or worse." She sobbed as fresh tears rolled down her face.

Dad hugged her tight. "Baby, I'm right here. You don't need to worry. I've got a present for you."

Sniffing, Mom wiped her tears as Dad fished something out of his pockets.

"It's not as beautiful as you, but..." He held out a gleaming necklace.

Mom gasped. "Jay." She cautiously touched jewels, mouth ajar. Three rows of gems hung off golden metal laced together in artful knots and curves. "Where did you get this?"

"Don't you worry about that." He placed the necklace on her and kissed her on the lips. "My desert queen. You're so beautiful, baby."

Leaning back, Mom smiled. They danced in a slow circle, rocking side to side. I was old enough to know they needed privacy, but I was afraid the slightest movement would make a noise and cause Dad to yell at me. They stopped rotating and stood there with their faces pressed together and Mom's back to me. Dad shrugged out of his flannel shirt, revealing a torso that looked like the men on Mom's books.

As wonderful as it was to see them happy together, I inched away, peeling one foot off the floor slow enough to not make a sound, then the other.

Dad stood up straight to admire Mom as he removed her shirt. He froze as it fell to the floor with a flutter, his eyes locked on me. Oh, no. I threw out my arms to keep my balance. This was it. I was about to get a very loud lecture.

Wrapping an arm around Mom's waist, he guided her backward and shut the bedroom door.

Chapter 12

I woke to the sun seeping around my window curtain. I snuck out of my room and stopped in the kitchen when I noticed the bedroom door stood ajar. One lump, not two, lay under the sheets. Dad was gone. A hint of his cologne hung in the air. I breathed in the spicy scent, embracing the scrap of proof that he'd been home.

Mom was asleep. I slipped back into my room to read.

***

Despite Dad being gone, Mom woke in a great mood for the first time in ages. She greeted, hugged, and kissed me. She wore no necklace, though. I wanted to ask about it, but I wasn't supposed to know. The last thing I wanted to do was ruin her good mood by asking about things I shouldn't. Instead, I put down my book and helped Mom make breakfast.

She sang while we made eggs, bacon, and chopped

121

cantaloupe, and we giggled over silly stories about her and Dad while making sweet bread dough from scratch. Mom's face shone with a rosy glow and she even wore clothes that showed off her figure. She normally wore baggy shirts. Today she wore a short-sleeved shirt with form-fitting pants.

This was how life was supposed to be. These moments were few and far between, and it would probably be gone by the end of the day. I savored every second Mom wore a smile, every kiss to the top of my head. I filed away every last word she said, every kind gesture she made. I'd need it to make it through the next storm of confusing emotions. Like Yuna, I was storing power to make it across my own lake and defeat my own water dragon. Yuna had made it on her second attempt. I would make it as well, thanks to days like this.

We unpacked the last crates and set up the living room around a gorgeous quartz sound stone half as big as me. The stone sat in a huge basin filled with water and a bed of pebbles. Mom dragged it to the center of the room and touched a rune on one of its many scale-like facets. Two foreign voices filled the room with the morning news about the latest events back in the city, recent and upcoming sporting events, and a weather report. Why anyone bothered to forecast the weather daily confused and annoyed me. The desert was almost always sunny, except during the rainy season. The people on the sound wave should've said, "Expect sun and heat until further notice," and left it at that.

After the stupid weather report, the newsman's voice returned. "My boss just placed a paper on my desk. We have a safety alert for you folks out on the west side of Marohu and nearby towns."

Mom stopped fluffing the couch pillows and faced the sound stone.

The concerned look on her face made me do a double-take. I paused in my placing of family photos over the fireplace. "Is that where we live?"

She shushed and waved sharply for me to be quiet.

"A string of robberies has law enforcement officials on high alert. Several stores were broken into and robbed. Weapons, furniture, and jewelry were stolen. There appears to be no connection between the incidents, but investigators haven't ruled out the possibility. Each store was broken into in the same way. Both Earth and Wind scans revealed little. Investigators don't know if this is a lone person or a group of persons committing these crimes."

Mom's face grew distant as a hand drifted to her neck, where the necklace had been. Her eyes glistened.

I tensed, my limbs ready to carry me to my room at the first sign that this happy morning was over. Questions raced through my mind. I feared my voice would shatter the moment like glass.

"If anyone sees anything, law enforcement asks you to contact them."

Expression hardening into a glare, Mom took a deep breath and jabbed another rune on the speaker stone. The announcer's voice cut off and was replaced by an acoustic guitar strumming an upbeat tune. Music filled our home. Mom stood before the stone as if waiting for it to switch back to the news wave. The guitar continued to play.

Was this the end of her good mood? Just an hour or two of feeling like a normal mother and daughter? I carefully set the photo on the mantle without so much as a tap.

Mom's glare slowly softened. Closing her eyes, she took a deep breath and her hands rose. As she exhaled, her hands sank back to her sides. "I will not let this ruin my day," she whispered. She took another long breath, opened her eyes, and then returned to unpacking furniture pillows. "So how was your first week at Toolena Mesa?"

First, I thought the voice had come from the stone. Then I realized it was Mom's voice. And then my brain registered what she'd said. I set the last picture on the mantle, completing the visual story of the three of us when we were all happy and carefree, completely unaware that I was a Dark. And no sister yet. "It was good," I said. It was close enough to the truth. "I made a few friends and the teachers are really nice."

"That's great." Mom popped a genuine smile, one far more uplifting than the guitar filling the background.

I filed away the shape of her smile, her white teeth and full lips, how the corners of her eyes crinkled, and how her mismatched eyes were full of love.

"So what makes these teachers really nice? You've never said much about the ones at your previous schools." She set the empty crate by the front door and hung nicknacks and other Wind-themed decorations on the living room walls, making the room feel like we were drifting along in the sky.

Well, if Mom was willing to talk about school, hopefully that meant it was safe to mention or at least hint at Dark stuff. "They still like me even after knowing the truth about me."

"Your alignment?" The words came out as if I'd told her what I'd eaten for lunch at school.

"Yeah." It really was safe. Mom was back in full happy mode. I joined her by the box and handed her stuff to hang up, gingerly handling the decorations so I wouldn't break anything. "They treat me like a normal person. I'm even being taught how to be safe and protect people. You won't have to be afraid of me anymore."

Mom's smile faltered. "Sweetie, we're not afraid of you."

Now I knew how I'd sounded to the nurse when I'd told her I didn't know why I'd snuck a look behind the curtain.

"How will you be able to protect people?"

We hadn't covered any specifics yet. "I'm not sure. Magic circles, music, and runes, I think. I'm being taught all the basics before I do any real stuff."

Mom nodded. "That's good."

We both lapsed into silence. I wanted to say something to bring things back to normal and happy, but I feared making it worse.

We unpacked the last few boxes and stacked them by the door, and I helped Mom carry extra sheets and towels to the bathroom closet while Bela made a racket in her room. We carefully folded all the sheets and towels, big and small, and stacked them in tidy piles on the shelves.

"So tell me about your new friends," Mom said.

Well, there was my opening for normal. "There's this boy named Deren who—"

"Ooh, a boy." She grinned as she placed another sheet high up on the shelves.

"Ew, no. That's gross, Mom. It's not like that."

"That's what we all say, but anyway, go on."

I huffed. Seeing Mom's smile encouraged me to relax and return to folding washcloths. "We haven't hung out much yet, but he's nice to me. He even said he likes my hair."

"I really wish you'd pull your hair back so people can see your face. You're really pretty. You should try a headband that keeps your bangs out of your face."

"I'll think about it," I said to the floor.

Thought about it. Nope, not happening.

"There's also Gwen and her friends. Gwen's the leader of the group. We all do whatever she wants and everyone else leaves us alone. It's—" I wanted to say "nice." I couldn't bring myself to say it. "They're different—not like me different, but another kind of different. I think I like them." I told Mom about how Gwen's dad owned all the mines in the area.

A crease formed between Mom's eyebrows as we put the last sheet on the shelves. "Be careful around her," she said.

Memory of the talk between Miss Wren and Mr. Redd cropped up in my mind. "Why?"

Mom hesitated. "Rich people have a lot of influence and connections with other people. Gwen doesn't know about your alignment, does she?"

I shook my head. "I don't want her to ever find out."

Mom nodded, her gaze distant. "Good. Let's go get the herb garden started."

We threw charmed stones on a patch of dirt, dust, and weeds to root out and kill pesky critters, including a bunch of stingers and beetles. As beautiful as the desert was, it hid lots of creepy crawlies that made me want to hide indoors most of the time. Charms would keep them away. Mom used some hand movements and a spoken spell to blow away the layer of dust hiding fertile soil underneath, and then we got down and pulled weeds, bracelets around our wrists to protect us from getting cut or stabbed by plants. I loved watching the tiny needles on the stalks of some dried-out weeds turn to dust between my fingers as they failed to prick me. Bela tried to help. She got more dirt all over us than anything else, until Mom suggested my sister go pile up the rocks we'd dug. Bela dutifully set to work on a sloppy masterpiece only a mom could be proud of.

Mom sang some more as we planted several rows of herbs along the front of the house. However, her happy and carefree mood wore off when we sat down to lunch, and by dinnertime, she mechanically made dinner and hid in her bedroom soon after. My heart sank with her mood. At least she was okay enough to kiss me on the head before putting Bela to bed and burying herself in the pages of a book.

I retreated to my room and read until I realized I'd been reading the same paragraph over and over. The last thing I remembered before falling asleep was that Yuna had gotten what she'd needed from the Water witch. The witch had trapped her on the island soon after.

***

I awoke in the middle of the night, sweat on my forehead. I bolted upright and drew up an energy shield with a wave. A ball of light hovered over the song crystal, like a dandelion tuft trying to decide whether or not to finish sinking to the ground. A familiar energy seeped through my shield.

I threw off my blankets and sat up. "Grandma?"

The ball expanded and formed an incomplete apparition of my grandmother. She had her head, shoulders, and torso. *Hello, Mia. I finally found you.* Unlike the demon, her voice was sweet and gentle in my mind.

"How'd you find me?"

I could see the window through her body as she drifted closer. *We're family. We're always connected.*

I didn't understand what the words meant, but I found comfort in the "always connected" part. It made me feel closer to Grandma than seeing her spirit in my room. "Grandma, do you hate me for being a Dark?"

She tilted her head as if she'd never considered the idea. *Never. They should love you all the more for it. There can be no balance without Darks.*

"What balance?" I pictured classmates trying to balance a seesaw so it stood parallel to the ground. That probably wasn't what Grandma meant.

The world is out of balance. By being aligned with Dark, you've been called upon to help bring balance to the world, one person at a time.

She stood close, her coldness emanating like an open frost box. I wanted to reach out and touch her, hug her. Not even my alignment could make that happen.

Grandma sat on the bed. The blankets formed a depression beneath her. Despite knowing what would happen, I tried to rest a hand on hers. My fingers touched only sheets and grew ice cold. Grandma rested her hand on mine as if she were solid. Whatever rules that surrounded interactions between the living and dead, she could touch me, but I couldn't touch her. It was so unfair.

"What do you mean by 'help bring balance'?"

You'll understand as you get older. For now, start with your father. Tell him he needs to let go. He still hasn't done that after all these years.

"Let go of what?"

She shook her head. *Those details are not for you. He'll know what you mean when you tell him.*

Tell my dad something Grandma told me to tell him? He'd flipped out the first time I'd told him about Grandma talking to me from the other side. He told me to never talk about her again. "I can't."

Yes, you can, she said.

"He'll get mad."

Let him get mad. It's not your fault. He's angry with himself, not you.

How did that make sense? When I spoke about Grandma, he got mad. That made it my fault. "I'm afraid to tell him."

That's okay. It's perfectly okay to be afraid so long as you don't let it stop you.

"How do I tell him?"

Walking up to him and saying, "Hi, Dad. Grandma wants you to let go of something, but she won't tell me what it is" wouldn't work.

You'll find a way. She stood and her form began to fade. *I'll be watching over you, helping you as I can. Remember your love for your father when all else fails.*

And like that, she was gone. Such was the way of ghosts.

***

I tossed and turned, Grandma's words speaking in my head over and over. I respected the fact that whatever she was talking about wasn't my business, but refusing to tell me filled me with the desire to know to the point where I felt like screaming in frustration. What did he need to let go of?

The only logical thing I could come up with was him needing to let go of his fear of me. We would be happier if no one feared me or my alignment. It'd make us, I guess, balanced, whatever that meant.

I rolled over for the zillionth time. My desk, meaning a slab of wood propped up on four wobbly stacks of books, sat mere feet away with my shoulder bag, Yuna book, and a half-full cup of water on it. Floating a ways above the center sat my clock. It was a stone sphere the size of my head with two stones the size of eyes magically attached to it. The sunstone sat on the upper righthand quadrant, telling me that maybe an hour had passed since Grandma's visit, and hours lay between now and dawn.

Throwing my sheets off with a huff, I fished the photo out of my bag and propped it up on my desk. Light from a waxing moon filled my room, casting everything in a silvery sheen. I snuck into the kitchen for some salt and drew a sloppy circle on a small blanket I threw on the floor. The circle probably wasn't necessary since I'd be dealing with a ghost, not a demon, but I didn't know the land. For all I knew, far more dangerous things lurked near our house. I returned the salt to its rightful place before I could forget. The last thing I needed was to get caught trying to sneak Dark stuff at night.

I set the photo on the floor and sat cross-legged inside my salt circle. I didn't know what exactly I was doing. I could figure it out. Tucking hair behind one ear,

I stared at the lifelike image magically carved into a thin stone slab. The coloring skill that had gone into it amazed me. Many Earths tried to achieve this level of detail.

I stared and stared at the student who'd died. Nothing happened. I hadn't touched the picture when Mr. Redd showed it, so I didn't see the point in holding it now. Maybe it was the salt circle. Maybe it blocked both ways.

I stepped outside it, planting my bare feet on the cold floor. Standing and looking down at the picture felt wrong, too distant from the person I was trying to contact.

Stepping back in my circle, I set the photo on the stool and sat down. This put my eyes level with the people in the photo. There we go.

I stared at the boy on the right as I took several deep breaths. I needed to calm myself before ghosts showed up or I'd reflexively put my shield up and banish any unwanted company. I needed answers out of this one. Hopefully, I could make him stay and give them to me.

My limbs relaxed, filling me with the sensation of floating in a warm pool. The world around me narrowed to the face of that one high schooler. What was his name? I'd heard it. I knew it. I couldn't—

"Orton Totes."

The voice was mine, but it sounded different. It almost made me lose my trance.

Nothing happened. However, the energy in the room shifted. Orton wasn't here. He was closer than a moment ago.

"*Orton Totes, I command you to me,*" I whispered

in an altered voice. It sounded heavier, powerful. Was this me, or something speaking through me? The question would have to wait. He was coming.

Orton silently popped out of the picture, rising like smoke from the last embers of a fire. Like Grandma, he wasn't a complete apparition. Instead of the wall behind him, I had to focus on the white wisps that formed his features. He had outlines of his shoulders and silvery threads hanging in the shape of wiry arms.

Holy crap, it worked. I stared in mute surprise as he took in my room. It then dawned on me that I had brought a boy into my room. Thank goodness he was dead. Still, sitting there in my pajamas with a high schooler in front of me was awkward.

His transparent eyes went wide. *Who are you and where are we?*

I stood and Orton towered over me. "I'm Mia. You're in my room." My voice sounded normal again.

He looked around a second time. *Send me back. I don't want to be here.*

"Where'd you come from?"

He opened his mouth with a ghostly inhale, then stopped, his gaze growing distant. He walked in a circle before facing me. *Everywhere*, he said in a faint voice. *Nowhere. I don't know. It's all so confusing. Please send me back.*

"I will." His answer made no sense. Maybe I could ask Ms. Weever, or even Grandma, if she visited again. "I have some questions first. Do you remember who you are?"

Yes.

"Do you know you're dead?"

He studied his incorporeal form. *Yes*, he whispered.

The way he said that one word made my eyes sting. This sudden surge of emotion had to be his, not mine. We were forced to share it through whatever link I'd created. "Did you just realize this?"

He nodded.

Unbidden tears, the tears he would have shed if he were alive, rolled down my cheeks. "Do you remember what happened—how you died?"

His gaze lowered. *Sickness. Terrible sickness. I got better before I got worse and died.*

My skin crawled. "Did a demon make you sick?" Deren and that boy in the nurse's office popped into my mind.

I don't know. Please, send me back. I don't want to answer any more questions.

One more question spilled from my mouth. "Are you at least at peace wherever you are now?"

He thought a moment. *No. There are...fragments of me left among the living. I don't know how to explain it. Please let me go.* He reached for me. Sparks shot out from where he tried to cross my salt circle. *Please.*

I wiped the tears from my eyes and picked up the picture. "*I release you, Orton Totes.*" Once again, my voice took on that heavier, powerful tone.

With a drawn-out sigh, his form thinned into a long, silvery line and sank back into the photo, the last wisp jolting the stone. His emotions lifted. I gulped in air as the tension eased out of my chest.

I thought he'd drift skyward and disappear. Something about his departure seemed off. I studied Orton's smiling face in the photo. It yielded no answers to my new questions.

Chapter 13

To both my great delight and horror, Deren returned to school the next day. Was this that calm period of getting better Orton had mentioned? Was he about to get way worse?

A scan of the quad confirmed that Gwen hadn't arrived yet. I ran over to Deren, who sat on a bench at one end of the playground. He looked a little tired and pale, instead of his usual bouncy self. I kept some distance between us in case the black mass reappeared.

"Hi, Deren." My voice came out small and awkward. I tucked half my hair behind one ear.

He gave me a tired smile. "Hey, Mia."

"How are you feeling?" I tried to look calm and happy on the outside while I cringed on the inside.

"Better. I'm sorry for almost throwing up on you."

"It's okay. We're still friends." I glanced at the playscape again. "I don't know how long I have. I don't want Gwen to see us hanging out together, but—"

"I understand." A hint of hurt tightened his lowered gaze. "Everyone's afraid of Gwen. Nobody tells her what to do."

"I'm—" I cringed at my attempt to lie about not being afraid of her. I'd known her for a handful of days and it was painfully obvious that I'd do anything to keep her from getting mad at me, even if I didn't like it.

"You're the only one who's brave enough to be my friend."

"Why is she so mean to you?"

"I dunno," he said with a shrug.

I believed him. Maybe Gwen didn't need a reason. Maybe she did whatever she felt at the time, which was reason enough. Whatever it was, we didn't have the time to get distracted from what I wanted to talk about. Sussi and Chibya stood at the edge of the playscape, chatting away. Why didn't they wait for Gwen on the bottom step? I should be, too. Were they afraid of her as well?

I shook my head, getting my thoughts back on track. I didn't have time to wonder about such things. "Deren, was there anything strange about your sickness?"

He wrung the swing chains in his small hands, digesting the question. "I don't think so." He thought a moment. "I did have a lot of nightmares. I don't think that had anything to do with being sick. I've had many nightmares lately."

I took a step closer. "About what?"

He checked to see if anyone was listening. "Promise not to tell anyone?"

"There's no one I could tell." The truth sank into

my chest with grim realization.

He leaned close and spoke in a low voice I barely heard above the din of the playground. "I keep seeing this monster with one eye. I keep trying to hide from it. It always finds me and tells me to tell him my name."

My skin crawled as if the demon had appeared beside us. "Is it all black and has a really long neck and arms?"

His eyes widened. "You dreamed about him, too?"

Why did I always have to do things like this to myself? Why couldn't I keep my mouth shut at times like this? Now I couldn't tell him the truth without raising suspicion. "Yeah."

"What does he say to you?"

"Mean things."

"Yeah, me, too."

"How long have you been dreaming about the demon?"

"I don't know. Since the beginning of the school year, I think."

I'd said "demon" instead of "monster." Deren either didn't notice or didn't care. He merely watched me with his tired gaze. "Well, I'm glad you feel better."

"Me, too."

Looks like I had my answer. The demon and the sickness were connected. There's no way it was a coincidence and now I had more questions for Orton, but should I bother him again? Our first visit had been stressful enough. His picture was in my bag. I'd planned on returning it today. I wanted to be rid of it before I got caught.

Deren's eyes went wide. "You better go."

I backed up, half expecting him to get sick again. I

followed his gaze.

Gwen had rounded the corner of a building. She wore a pale yellow dress with a matching flower in her hair. She walked with purpose and an air that said she didn't care what anyone thought of her. Classmates shied out of her path as she neared them, and the kindergarten teacher gave her a slight bow as she walked by.

I waved and bid Deren goodbye. I took one step before stopping. There was a dark spot in the sand at the edge of the swings. I redirected my course. Gwen could wait a few extra seconds, even if she spotted me. This would be worth getting yelled at.

The spot looked like a shadow from a small cloud. Closer inspection showed that the shadowing stained the sand like someone had splattered black paint on it. I pushed some clean sand over it with a foot. The blackness seeped back to the surface. At first, I thought it was my shadow, but it was too dark. On top of that, my shadow lay behind me. I kicked more sand over the black spot and waited.

Sure enough, the black splatter rose to the surface again. I took a step back. This had to be the demon's doing, too.

"Mia, get over here!"

There was nothing I could do at the moment. I'd have to tell Ms. Weever later. I headed on over to Gwen's designated bench.

***

Ms. Weever wasn't waiting for me when the class broke up into our respective alignments for training. The ladies at the front desk informed me that Ms. Weever had called, letting them know she was running late. I retreated to the hallway.

The hallway was quiet enough for me to pause and feel out the air with my alignment. It didn't feel like anything good or bad was watching. I held my hands out at my sides, fingers spread, and imagined my hands reaching out into the surrounding space. My mind braced for anything unexpected to brush up against it. The entire hallway and adjoining offices turned up nothing.

With an inhale, I brought my awareness back to me and returned to the front desk. The ladies were already chatting up a storm about some dreamy Light priest. I rang the bell to get them to notice me.

Desi turned, her wavy hair bouncing. "Oh, hey, Mia."

"Where's Mr. Redd?"

Desi paused before glancing at her wristwatch, a copper band forged to look like vines. "He should be back soon. He's out sweeping the campus for snakes. It's that time of year again."

"Thank you."

I hurried off and their chatter resumed. Sure enough, Mr. Redd's office lay empty. I paused on the threshold and unclipped the buckles to my bag, my heart pounding. This was it. This was the moment where I either got away with it, or got caught at the last second. A quick visual scan of the hallway confirmed it was empty. I stepped inside as I fished around for the picture from among workbooks and homework packets.

Either my guilt weighed me down or the air in the office was heavier. My lungs shrank as I whisked over to the cabinet on silent feet. An empty spot among the photos was there, like one empty desk in an otherwise full class. There was a faint line of dust marking where the photo had sat. My searching fingers closed on the granite slab and produced the photo. I carefully set it back in place, doing my best to match the dust line, and stepped back.

There was a slight smudge in the dust where I'd had to adjust one corner. Anyone would have to look closely to notice the difference. My gaze drifted to Orton's smiling face, the face of a big kid who'd gotten sick and died. It was about to happen again with Deren, and I didn't know how to stop it. I didn't want this to happen. I liked him.

Part of me wanted to summon Orton in Mr. Redd's office. The rational side of me knew I didn't have the time. "Orton, I still have questions for you, but I'll give you a break for now."

"A break from what?"

I gasped so loud that it almost turned into a scream. Mr. Redd stood inside the doorway, hands on his hips, blocking any escape attempts. I shrank under his glare, the heat so intense that I felt like I stood before the dragon Yuna had taken two tries to conquer. It had a giant maw big enough to swallow her and the boat. Mr. Redd looked ready to douse me with scalding water breath.

"Miss Evers, I asked you a question."

"I—" Would he care or dismiss it like Ms. Weever? If he'd shown me the picture on the day I'd enrolled at Toolena Mesa, then maybe Orton Totes was still on his mind. "I was wondering how Orton died." My voice came out as small as I felt.

He took a deep breath and exhaled heavily through his nose. I shrank out of his path when he stomped to the photos and glared at them. I sidestepped closer to the door. I didn't dare leave.

"We all thought he was going to be fine." His pained voice belied the anger on the surface. "He got better and stayed healthy long enough for us to forget, and then he got sick again and never recovered."

"What kind of sickness did he have?"

Mr. Redd narrowed his eyes ever so slightly. "If we knew that, the doctors probably could've saved him. Why are you asking?"

I decided on a half-truth. The whole truth and a complete lie were too dangerous. "I haven't been able to forget about him ever since the day he startled me."

Mr. Redd faced me with his entire body. "Did he speak to you?"

Something about the way he acted put me on guard. "Yes."

"What did he say?"

"He wanted me to leave him alone. I accidentally called him to me. I didn't know I could do that."

"Accidentally?"

"I looked at the picture and called his name. Ms. Weever has already taught me about the power of names. I didn't think it'd work, but it did."

"Miss Evers, the fact that you're a Dark should be reason enough to behave and not go experimenting with your alignment. You will be removed if you ever give me reason to believe you're a danger to this school. Do you understand?"

"Yes, sir," I said to the floor, my heart sinking.

He escorted me to Ms. Weever's office and ordered me to sit in my usual seat. I kept my eyes on the ground. He stood in the doorway, arms folded, face almost as red as some of his hair.

Ms. Weever arrived a minute later. It was one of the most agonizing minutes of my life. I kept waiting for Mr. Redd to yell at me like Dad. Instead, he tortured me with silence and uncertainty about how long it would last. Ms. Weever gave him a studious look as she passed, and then her hard blue eyes turned to me. The room grew colder.

"I caught her finishing up a conversation with a ghost. She's all yours, Ms. Weever," Mr. Redd said with an edge in his voice. "I heard you called the school. What held you up?"

She set a purse as large as my shoulder bag on her desk chair and redirected her icy gaze to the principal. "Family issues." When she offered no further explanation, he bid my angry tutor good day.

I sat, waiting to be told what to do. I was too afraid to move without permission.

Ms. Weever retrieved her mbira from atop the piano and planted her glossy black boots in front of me. She plucked out a scale that dispersed some of the tension, but the heat of anger came off her. There was something about the way she stood that warned me to keep my mouth shut.

"Miss Evers," she said in a silky voice, "clearly you need a lesson on controlling your curiosity. Snooping around the principal's office to talk to ghosts? I haven't seen Mr. Redd that angry in three years. I do *not* want to see him that angry with you again. You've earned yourself a lesson on Dark disciplines. I better not have to repeat this lesson or else it's all we will do for the rest of the school year." She kneeled so she was eye level with me. "Do I make myself clear? Now, get on your feet."

I hopped off the chair as if it had bitten me, and stood with my arms clamped to my sides.

"Chin up."

My gaze remained attached to the wood floor.

"Up."

I snapped my head up, bringing my gaze level with her elbow. My neck felt so exposed, the air colder, as if a ghost stood nearby.

"That's better." Ms. Weever walked in a slow circle around me. "The more you disobey, the more of these lessons we'll have. Darks require the most self-discipline out of any alignment. We will not move beyond the basics until I can trust you to use your alignment wisely. And you just lost all the trust you've built thus far."

Tear stung my eyes. The only other Dark I'd met, the first person who'd ever taught me how to use my powers, hated me. I wanted to go home.

"Chin up."

My eyes latched onto the violin as my hair fell away from my face, revealing every last thought and emotion I'd been trying to hide.

"Everyone fails and makes mistakes. You'll run into failure and continue to make mistakes. You must do so with your head held high. You're a Dark. You must always be in control of your emotions. You'll become a slave to them and the demon realm if you don't. And that's what makes us so dangerous." She paused before me. "Now, what do you think I just said?"

My voice cracked when I tried to speak. I cleared my throat and stiffened my neck when my chin drooped again. "I'm dangerous if I don't control myself and my emotions."

"Yes. Why?" She walked another slow lap around me.

Blank confusion filled my mind. The urge to cry stung even more, making the world blur under a watery film. It sounded like I should know the answer, but I didn't understand. "I'll become a slave if I don't." Hopefully, that's the answer she wanted to hear.

"There's the part where you may simply be too young to understand. It's not a strike against you, but it does mean that when I tell you to do or not do something, you need to obey whether or not you understand why. I'm trying to teach you how not to be a danger to yourself or anyone else, understand?"

"Yes, ma'am." I could do that, would do that. I'd do anything to not feel like this miserable waste of space.

"Let me try to explain this one more time. Let's use a visual to explain it." She walked over to the small chalkboard. "On your first day with me, we talked about the types of demons and what kind of chaos they inflict on the human realm. What are they and how do they inflict chaos?"

I rattled off the seven classes of demons and the five ways they inflicted chaos. And then it dawned on me. "Do all the lies and warring and stuff have to do with emotions?"

"Correct. What connection did you make?"

I studied Ms. Weever's blocky handwriting. "People don't fight, unless they're angry and hateful. We also feel sad when we're sick. And people don't lie unless they're afraid of something. And when you

143

talked about how demons attack humans' minds, you described all sorts of unpleasant emotions." It was like my mind was playing connect-the-dots. Ms. Weever had placed all the dots. I connected enough that I finally saw part of the picture.

"Very good. Now what's the connection between all that and why Darks must always be in control of their emotions?"

"I don't know."

"Think." She thumped a fist on the board. "You're young, but you need to understand as soon as possible. No, I don't expect you to fully understand this for years. However, the sooner you do, the sooner you'll be more trustworthy. So, why are Darks the most dangerous?"

"Because we can summon and banish demons?"

"That's also true, but it's not the answer I was looking for. It's not so much about what we can do as it is how our powers and the connection between humans and demons work. Try again."

"I don't know how our powers work. I've figured stuff out by accident."

Ms. Weever closed her eyes and her mouth pressed into a thin line. She hissed something about idiot schools before taking a deep breath and trapping me with her icy glare again. "What were you feeling when you learned what you did?"

I tried to recall when I'd called Orton to me. I remembered what happened and that was it. "I don't remember anymore. It just...happened."

"How often were you afraid when something happened?"

That was an easy question that I didn't want to

answer. My hair blocked my vision. I snapped my head back up. My tutor watched me, waiting for an answer. "A lot." Come to think of it, I was almost always scared, constantly worrying about what I should say or not say, do or not do.

"And how often were you angry?"

"Not a lot." Sure, I got angry from time to time. It took too much energy to stay that way. I'd gotten angry at the closet demon when it tried to get to Miss Wren and somehow made it go away.

"And sad?"

I shifted my gaze to the board, unable to look Ms. Weever in the eye. "Sometimes." Grandma had always shown up during my saddest moments, an exception being her most recent visit.

"Emotions aren't something to be ashamed of. They're what make us human, what separates us from demons. Never forget that." She drew a circle on the board, a stick figure near the curve of its bottom left, a stick figure with a pointed tail and horns near the bottom right, and a capital "E" atop the circle. "Now, I believe each emotion I named invoked a memory. Think about what happened and the emotions you felt at the time."

"I made different things happen when I felt different things."

"Correct. Why do you think that is?"

"Our powers are connected to our emotions?"

"There's the answer I'm looking for." She didn't smile, but I heard it in her voice. "All alignments' powers are linked to emotions in one way or another. Darks are the most dangerous because of our link to the demon realm. We are the portal between humans and demons. No one else can say that, not even Lights."

"They're the link to the afterlife and all that makes this world good." The words came out with the steady cadence of recited information. I'd heard it at least once a month at my other schools.

She nodded. "What have they taught you about Darks?"

"They're the link to death and all that's evil."

"Spoken like a true brainwashed student." She set her chalk down and interlaced her fingers in front of her stomach. "Lights and Darks are two sides of the same coin. They both deal with death and the afterlife. The difference is that one pulls and the other pushes. Lights work to pull people towards joy and happiness. Darks try to push people away from misery and suffering. The problem today is that Lights are pushing and Darks are pulling. Energy is flowing in the wrong direction."

"Lights and Darks are making people sad?"

"You're too young to fully understand what's going on across the nation, but yes, you are correct, sadly. Don't bother asking around, though. Any senseless adult will deny it. Besides, you have the basics to worry about, nothing more. Worry about your own life for now."

"Yes, ma'am." The words came out quickly, automatically. I probably didn't need to say them, but I needed to let her know I was paying attention.

"Your life and alignment are difficult because society thinks you exist merely to torment people and lead them to the Demon King. The truth is it's our duty as Darks to protect the living from evil and shepherd lost souls back to the Light."

"Then why are my parents so afraid of me?"

She looked away, thoughtful. "Demons can control humans. Darks are the only ones able to control demons. Some have thought controlling humanity with demons would be a good idea. A few succeeded for a while." She settled her gaze back on me. "Corrupt Darks have dug a daunting hole for us. These past few hundred years have made it hard to convince people we're not all like that, or destined to become like that. Humans have a tendency to latch onto moments, instead of the whole picture. Millennia of Darks working to keep the balance were thrown away hundreds of years ago, buried under memories of a demon horde unleashed on the world."

"They lost people's trust," I said, picturing a broken, fiery land swarming with demons and screaming humans.

"Just like you have lost mine and Mr. Redd's," she said with a nod. "Trust is a fragile thing that can be lost in an instant."

"I'm sorry," I said to the floor, then snapped my gaze back to the chalkboard. Why was it so hard to keep my head up? I hadn't realized how much I looked at the floor, until now.

"As you should be." She picked up the chalk. "You'll work on earning it back by practicing the basics of protection circles and ward runes, protection and peace songs, and perfect behavior everywhere you go. This includes your schoolwork. I expect top grades from you."

"Yes, ma'am." My insides squirmed like a demon was trying to claw its way out of my stomach. I'd never been a student with great grades. I was good at reading and writing, and did enough work in the other subjects to avoid having teachers call home, except that one time in third grade. I hadn't forgotten the look of horror and rage my dad had given me the day my teacher had called about my poor grades.

"Now, this circle here represents the flow of power between humans and demons. Emotions fuel the ebb and flow, as represented by the 'E.' The flow can go both ways. Balance is best achieved when humans push on demons. We maintain power and control when we control our emotions. We give up power and control when we let demons manipulate our emotions. You'll be nothing more than a puppet in the latter situation."

"Why are demons so mean?" I think I followed so far. I began to feel scared of my powers and how dangerous I could be. I could hurt a lot of people if I wasn't careful. At the same time, I didn't understand why there weren't any nice demons. "Are they all like that?"

"Do you remember what I said about where demons come from, how they are made?"

I pictured the pages of my leather-bound notebook, tiny lines of notes scribbled on the pages. "They all were once human."

"Correct." She drew an upside-down "Y" beside the circle. "When we die, we have a choice between peace or chaos. Lights preach it's more complicated than that, but it's our choice in the end. We either become demons or add our strength to the Light. Forces pull us in both directions. The forces of Darkness are all negativity, so yes, they're mean because they've shut out the good in themselves."

My mind drifted back to the demon in the classroom. "Can they be turned back into humans?"

"Theoretically, yes. There are powerful incantations, circles, and charms designed for that purpose. The chances of success are very slim. Very, very few demons ever escape the grasp of the Demon King." She erased the upside-down Y with the heel of her palm and traced the circle, making it bolder. "Anyway, you needn't worry about such things for years, possibly ever. I'm humble enough to know I'm not powerful enough to attempt such a feat. Get your notebook out. Today's lesson will be on protection circles, and then we will review the information until your mind goes numb."

By the end of the lesson, I could probably draw a perfect protection circle with my eyes closed, maybe even in my sleep. I pictured myself lying in bed and a ghost appearing. My thought-up self turned over as the ghost floated closer, mouth wide in a silent scream, and fingers curled like claws, ready to attack my face. Right as the ghost hovered within inches of my bed, one of my arms shot up on its own and drew a pattern with the appropriate rune in the middle. Sparks flew from the ghost when it touched my circle and winked out of existence. My thought-up self curled into a tighter ball and went on dreaming.

"Mia, are you listening?"

I blinked several times, Ms. Weever's office coming back into focus, more specifically my tutor's stern face.

"Discipline yourself, child. We're almost done for today." She retrieved a book from a shelf behind her desk and leafed through the beginning pages. The binding was old and worn, like someone had traced all the edges with a white pencil and rubbed patches of the cover's woven threads like a chalk rubbing. Ancient as it looked, it fit comfortably in Ms. Weever's hand, and the pages stayed open without her holding them down.

Ms. Weever set the book on her desk and placed a piece of paper the size of two student desks on the floor. She glanced at the page one more time before kneeling by the paper and drawing a tidy protection circle. Her arm moved in steady, sweeping strokes, and it took her mere seconds to create a masterpiece. She ordered me to grab another large piece of paper from her cabinet and lay it over the first piece. She secured the paper with some tape and handed me the charcoal stick. "Your turn."

I accepted the stick. The perfect curves of her circle faintly showed through the second paper. It looked so perfect, like she had to have traced it. My charcoal-holding arm went limp and my gaze lowered. "I can't draw."

"I don't care. That's an excuse, not a solution. Chin up. Excuses get you nowhere in life and rob you of control. I never want to hear 'I can't' from you ever again. From now on, you will start telling yourself 'I can.'"

"Yes, ma'am," I said, doubts flying through my head like tumbleweeds kicked up by a dust devil, "but —"

Her eyes narrowed and I could've sworn she was suddenly ten feet tall. "But what?"

I inwardly cringed, wishing I could take that one word back. "What if I—" I wanted to say "can't do it." That word would set her off. Maybe she'd even tear the roof off and breathe fire. I wracked my brain for safe words as that forbidden word kept dancing to the tip of my tongue. "What if I fail?"

"What about it?" She sounded annoyed, but she watched me with open interest.

"What if I try—" What example to use? The circle? I pointed to it. "What if I try a hundred times to get it right and I still don't?" Would she then finally accept the truth that I couldn't draw?

"Then you try a hundred and one times," she said. "You try a hundred more times." She waved to the circle. "You think I could do that on my first try, much less on my thousandth try?"

I admired the faint, perfect circle with a new level of appreciation. "I thought you could do that because you're an adult."

"No, Miss Evers. This has taken years of practice. I have failed more times than I can count. You'll fail countless times as well. Failure doesn't justify quitting or telling ourselves we can't do something. Failure means we must try again or try a different way." She stood and brushed off her black skirt. "Yes, you're only eleven years old. The sooner you develop good habits, the better. This is the level of skill I'm building you up to achieve." Closing her eyes, she brought her hands together like she was praying, then reached for the ceiling with one and the floor with the other. She took a deep breath and drew a circle with her hands, then wavy curves inside that, and traced runes in front of her face. She brought her hands together again, reached for the sky, and swung them to either side at the ground as she yelled the runes' names.

The energy of her circle pushed down on me, rushing downward like a gust of air. It was all energy, like two magnets pulling themselves together. The circle appeared on the floor in glowing purple lines that crackled to life like someone was drawing it, filling me with peace and safety. The crackle turned into a hum as the last of the lines connected.

Ms. Weever opened her eyes. "This is what I'm building you towards." The circle's glow cast a pale light on her boots and skirt. "It all starts right here." She pointed to the paper.

Tucking hair behind my ears, I bent over the paper and traced, my heart racing. That was super cool. I wanted to be able to do that. I would learn how to do that one day, one year.

The final product was terrible. It looked like an earthquake hit while I'd traced the protection circle. Ms. Weever said it was good enough for a start. It would work against the weakest of demons for a short time.

The lines faded the moment she walked out of her glowing circle. The wood flooring smoked where the lines had been. I felt exposed, like the walls were no longer around me. A jolt of primal fear hit me as the protective energy dissipated before my rational mind took back over. Ms. Weever stepped through the thin smoke and I half expected the circle to light back up. The smoke curled away from her boots. She held a pad of drawing paper as big as the pages on the floor. "You'll take this home and practice drawing the circle ten times per day. Tomorrow, under my supervision, we'll test your circle against a demon."

I stared in open horror. She might as well have told me I would have to juggle ten knives. I didn't know how to juggle.

"Don't gawk. You'll be in no danger. We have to

establish your starting point so you can set a goal for the end of the school year, provided you prove to be worth my time for that long."

"Yes, ma'am." If she was going to do that, I would have to practice more than ten times between now and then. Part of me wanted to protest, to beg for at least a week of practice. I kept my mouth shut. As much as she scared me, I wanted her to train me. She made the world make more sense.

This was crazy—cool and crazy, and totally unfair that I was being tested on it tomorrow. However, there was a demon in Miss Wren's room, and Deren and Orton to worry about. Maybe the circle test was a good thing.

Instead of heading to class, I watched Ms. Weever pack up and spruce her hair. She paused, fixing me with a flat stare. "What?"

Opening my mouth, I sucked in a breath.

"And no, I won't cancel testing your circle tomorrow, so don't bother asking."

"That's not it," I said with a shake of my head. "It's...I...I was wondering." What to say so she wouldn't dismiss me with a wave? "I was wondering if you were wondering why I was in Mr. Redd's office today?"

"Will the answer help earn back some of our trust?"

"I don't know," I admitted. "Maybe."

"Well, out with it then."

Talking about the demon in the classroom was too risky. I'd have to try a different angle, had to find out if she'd help in any way. "Ms. Weever, students are getting sick again."

She tilted her head. "This is hardly newsworthy.

Students get sick all the time."

"No, not that kind of sick. I mean, they're getting sick like three years ago."

It happened so fast that I thought I'd imagined it. Ms. Weever's eyes widened before she regained control of her emotions, masking her thoughts with her usual disinterested glare. "What do you mean?" The hint of fear in her voice assured me I hadn't imagined the flash of fear in her eyes.

"Orton, the boy in the picture, spoke about how he died. A friend of mine and I think another classmate have gotten sick the same way. My friend's better—for now. I don't know for how long."

Ms. Weever stared at me. Should I say more or wait for her to speak? Another hint of fear cracked her hard glare. She shook her head, as if trying to shake thoughts from her mind. "I wasn't here three years ago." She stormed out.

Chapter 14

I didn't know how my legs brought me to tutoring the next day. I'd drawn lousy circles twenty times last night, instead of ten, had barely slept, couldn't recall walking to my bus stop, much less the ride to school, and didn't hear a thing all morning while my teachers taught. Gwen and the others left me alone. Whatever Deren was doing, I was too preoccupied to notice more than my hair hanging in front of my face and the pounding in my chest that was my heart.

Gwen had asked what was bothering me during lunch.

"I have a test during elemental training today," I said to the table.

"Aha." Her knowing tone and all their voices told me they totally understood. After Sussi made a sarcastic comment about me failing at making my first song stone, they left me alone to the thoughts needling at my frayed nerves.

The weight of sleeplessness bore down on my eyelids and my legs shook all the way to Ms. Weever's office, which was closed. A note was taped to the door.

Mia-

Head to the recreation room next to the gymnasium in the high school building.

-Ms. Weever

Adjusting the strap to my bag, I asked the ladies at the front desk for directions to the recreation room. They assured me it was easy, then described a labyrinthine list of twists and turns to and inside a building I'd never been in, then waved like they were seeing me off on a grand voyage. I trudged off, dragging my feet. Maybe she'd cancel the test if I took too long to get there.

"Mia, it's faster if you go that way," Desi said, pointing to the door I'd avoided using.

"Why don't you go with her?" the other lady said. "I can watch the front. Pretend it's a bathroom break."

Before I knew it, Desi walked beside me, escorting me across a parking lot and to my doom. We headed down a sidewalk under the blazing sun. The high school's double doors loomed before us and we arrived without incident. Desi opened the doors without hesitation and waved for me to enter first.

Carpeted floors and walls decorated with art and math projects transformed into an endless dark cave. Desi guided me deeper inside as she continued rambling. A few high schoolers emerged from different rooms. After a few more twists and turns, we arrived at a plain door labeled "Recreation Room." It might as well have been a twenty-foot door covered in serpentine carvings, wards, and protective spells. Desi opened the door and gave Ms. Weever a quick wave. "Here you are, Mia. Have a good day." My babbling escort wandered off.

Grabbing the door, I went lightheaded. My feet carried me inside and I could've sworn the door closed behind me with a deep, echoing thunk.

Ms. Weever stood in the far corner, plucking away at an mbira. Gentle, metallic notes drifted to my ears like raindrops pattering on individual leaves of an overhanging branch. "Good day, Miss Evers," she said without looking up. "Do not take another step into this room until you get your emotions under control." More notes filled the room.

Taking a deep breath, I locked my knees, trying to make my legs stop shaking. Instead, the rest of my body shook. My curtain of hair closed before me, cuing me to raise my chin. Tucking hair behind one ear, I took in the room. The ceiling had a closed sun portal to let in light. Candles filled every corner of the room, along with four large candles placed in a square around the center. All the chairs were pushed to one side near a piano. Curtains hung bunched in two corners, revealing a mirror spanning the length of the room, making the whole place look larger. While the candles did anything but make the room bright, my reflection cowered by the door's reflection. Even though I held my chin up, I stood hunched a bit, clutching the strap of my bag for dear life.

I straightened my back and planted my feet a little farther apart.

"Breathe," Ms. Weever said. "Take long breaths in and slow breaths out. Whatever doubts and fears try to distract you, push them away and concentrate on feeling air fill and leave your lungs. Nothing else is important right now." She played a descending string of notes, concluding a song, and lowered the mbira.

Breath filled my lungs almost as fast as my heartbeat. I snatched my next inhale, filled my lungs to the point of bursting, and held it, then slowly let it out. The blood pounded in my throat and lungs and I let go. I grabbed another deep breath and slowly let out the entire thing.

Doubts and worries cropped up, telling me this whole breathing thing was stupid. It wouldn't work. I was wasting my time. I needed to hurry up and face whatever demon Ms. Weever summoned. I tried pushing the thoughts away as fear of facing an unknown demon wouldn't stop scaring me.

Fear aside, I managed to get my breathing under control. My heart slowed from a frantic pounding to an insistent beat. I calmed enough for blood to flow back into my fingers as I eased my death grip on the strap. My reflection looked taller.

"You're ready to stand in the center of the room."

My eyes stung with fear and frustration. I held myself back. I wasn't ready. "But I'm still scared."

"That's okay," Ms. Weever said in a soothing voice. "Go stand inside the four candles."

"No, it's not." My voice trembled and the room blurred. "I want to be able to do this. I want you to trust me." My throat tightened. I forced in a few breaths. "How can I do that if I feel so scared?"

Ms. Weever approached the center of the room. I braced for a berating. She looked calm. Candlelight flickered against her leather boots, making them look like they gleamed with an enchantment. "I would be worried if you didn't feel scared. You're right to feel so. Today's lesson is no trivial thing. Only fools claim to feel no fear."

"Then how is it a good thing?"

"Fear keeps you alert, your senses sharp, and ready to react to danger." She circled the candles. "However, too much fear will paralyze you with inaction." She put a reassuring hand on my shoulder. "You were ready for today's test the moment you'd calmed yourself. So long as calm focus dominates your mind, the rest of your emotions will be under control."

"Even if I still feel afraid?"

"Yes. It's not the absence of fear that means you're under control. It's when you don't let fear paralyze you. It's okay to feel afraid so long as it doesn't control you."

The sting of tears lifted. I blinked several times, clearing my vision. "It's okay to feel afraid?"

She nodded. "Remember the day I played the violin?"

Memory of the devouring darkness and an unseen monster coiling around us flashed in my mind. How could I forget? "Yes."

"I felt scared in that moment, but I didn't let my fear control me."

Ms. Weever had played the violin without faltering, stood straight and tall as the darkness clawed closer and closer. "Really?"

Her eyes narrowed and her expression flattened. "No, I'm saying this to paint a picture where life is full of rainbows and unicorns, and nothing bad ever happens to anyone." She took one look at me and let out a frustrated sigh. "I apologize, child. I know better than to use sarcasm on students as young as you." She headed back over to the four candles in the middle, the heels of her boots thumping on the wood with every step. "But yes, I still feel afraid, even as an adult. Our alignment and what we deal with are truly terrifying. It's up to you to choose whether you let that fear control you or learn to embrace it to help you focus. Do you understand?"

"I think so."

"Remember that calm you felt a minute ago while you focused on your breathing. You can do this. Now, get your emotions back under control, then stand in the center of the room."

Minus the whole unicorn part, what Ms. Weever said made sense. I used my breathing to get my fear back under control, and when my reflection looked tall and confident, I took off my bag and set it by the door. I stepped inside the four candles.

Nothing felt special about the space. I'd expected some surge of energy, maybe even static. It was as plain as the front office. A stick of white chalk lay by one candle. I picked it up and began drawing the protection circle from memory.

As I counted out the curves of the braided lines inside the main outer circle, Ms. Weever said, "Good, you practiced. I don't remember if I told you this yesterday, but I'll tell you again, just in case." Ms. Weever circled the candles, one purposeful step at a time. "Each stroke you use to draw your circle becomes part of it. It's best to lift your chalk as few times as possible."

This was new information. The outermost circle

was widest near the candles as I'd redirected my path closer to them, and dimpled where each plank of wood met with another. I might as well have drawn it with my eyes closed. At least Ms. Weever didn't tell me I had to start over.

"If you make a bunch of smaller strokes, you risk fraying the circle, meaning you weaken its power. You did the right thing by drawing the entire outer circle by holding your chalk in place every time you had to move. You can't see where you paused. If you could, then that means your circle would fray. All those frays make it harder to draw the power it invokes."

I wasn't entirely sure I understood everything she said. It sounded like I was doing this correctly, which only boosted my confidence and need for her approval. I wanted to rush the circle. I forced myself to keep a steady pace and connect all the braided lines. When I turned to the center of the circle to draw the rune, Ms. Weever stopped me.

"Face the green candle. This is something new and I'm going to walk you through it now. It's another layer of protection. You don't need it with me here, but its protective power will help your confidence."

Under her instruction, I drew the protection rune, filling up as much of the inner circle as my short arms could manage. I stepped out of the circle when I was done and together my tutor and I studied the final product.

"It'll suffice, sloppy as it is." She handed me a stick. When my fingers closed around it, I realized it was a wand. The gnarled wood vibrated faintly with magic, like it wanted to draw on its power and make things happen. Joy surged through me with a need to leap around the room like a dancer. Ms. Weever nudged me back into the circle. "If you ever fray your circle, be smart and start over. I thought I would have to do this with you several times. You seem to have a knack for this."

My chest swelled with pride.

"Don't get too confident, though. That was the easiest part. The rest falls on your strength of will and ability to control your emotions." Ms. Weever explained the candles, and how they were placed in line with the four cardinal directions—north, south, east, and west. The colors also represented earth, air, fire, and water. "You aren't using the other elements. You can't. You're a Dark. You're invoking their innate power, creating a balanced environment within your circle. This helps you concentrate and stay in control. It's always useful even at your most skilled. Anyway, I'm going to teach you parts of an incantation that draws on elemental balance and helps protect you." She explained how I'd start on the green candle and work my way clockwise, saying a portion to each cardinal direction as I pointed to it with my wand. "Alright, let's begin."

I faced the green candle and pointed with my wand. "Spirits of Earth, I call upon your balance and protection in this circle." The wand flinched and warmed in my grip. I turned to the white candle. "Spirits of Air, I call upon your voice and protection in this circle." The wand flinched again and air swirled around my hand. I turned to the red candle. "Spirits of Fire, I call upon your energy and protection in this circle." The wand flinched and a hum emanated from it. I turned to the last candle, a blue one. "Spirits of Water,

I call upon your purpose and protection in this circle." The wand flinched one last time and a cool air swirled around my hand. I faced the green candle again.

Ms. Weever held a large lizard's foot in one hand, with feathers hanging off a string. She closed her eyes and muttered a guttural incantation, making every last candle in the room flicker. A wave of fear rose inside my chest.

I took a deep breath and pushed it away with my exhale. Fear chilled the back of my mind, but I'd come too far to fall apart now. The candles flickered as darkness bled into the wood outside my circle. A growl rose from the floor, followed by a clawed hand large enough to crush my head. A second clawed hand appeared, like some huge beast gripping the edge of a hole.

Fresh blood.

The deep, resonant voice made the wood floor vibrate. More and more claws rose out of the darkness, connected to thick, spidery legs. A giant shadow of a body rose out of the floor. Where the head should've been were only two large feelers as long as my body. One swung over to my circle and showered me with sparks. Cowering behind my wand, I flinched.

Young blood. Feed me, morsel.

An undulating body spilled forth, filling the room with its massive black body. The faintest flickers of light danced the corners as the demon's sheer size coiled around me and my circle. Legs and claws were everywhere in a black spiderweb of limbs. The demon looked like a centipede twisted by evil and darkness. All those legs made my skin crawl. I wasn't the type of girl that freaked over bugs, but spiders did it for me.

And this monster's legs looked like spider legs. A primal fear surged through me as my eyes watered. This was too much.

"Banish it!" Ms. Weever's voice yelled in the darkness.

The serpentine carapace of the demon's body coiled around me, constantly testing my circle and sending sparks showering down. The wand pulsed with every hit and my head swam.

Take down your defenses.

Too many legs. There were too many legs, too many creepy crawly legs everywhere.

"Stay in control."

Let me eat you, morsel.

The circle thudded like thunder shaking a house as pincers clamped down on the invisible barrier. Claws propped themselves up on it, showering me in so many sparks it was like lightning going off in the room. A scream escaped my throat as I pointed the wand at the beast's maw.

The demon recoiled as if the barrier had burned it, and paced around me, steam coming off its claws. *I am hungry. Let me feed on your soul.*

"No." My voice came out small. "My soul is my own. You had your chance." Tears streamed down my cheeks and my legs shook.

"Breathe," Ms. Weever's voice said from some far-off place.

Taking a deep breath, I closed my eyes and wiped my tears. More replaced them. I let them be. Control my emotions. Be afraid but don't stop.

In and out.

This demon could swallow me whole and barely fit

in the room.

In and out.

It had far too many legs. There was nothing I could do about it.

In...and out.

My arms felt weightless. I opened my eyes. The wand thrummed with my heartbeat and the four candles surrounding my circle burned brighter. The demon tested my circle, jolting my mind with each stab. I accepted it was there and wouldn't go away until I did something about it. I raised my wand above my head. "In the name of the Light, I banish thee." A pulse emanated from the wand and the demon flinched.

Not strong enough, morsel. Let me eat you and we will grow stronger together.

No, I had to be strong enough. I turned and pointed at its giant pincers. "In the name of the Light, I banish thee." My voice shook and the demon recoiled, stunned. It faced me and reared up.

I braced for impact with the wand in both hands.

Feed me! Its voice shook the walls as pincers and claws slammed into the circle's barrier. It reared and clamped over and over, and soon the barrier developed cracks of white light. My circle was failing.

I felt disconnected from the moment, like watching the scene unfold from another room. A calm washed over me. All there was to the moment was breath and purpose. I was in control of the situation. The demon knew it. That's why it was trying so hard to scare me.

Breathe in.

I aimed at the center of the pincers clamping on my barrier mere inches from the wand's tip. The same voice that had summoned and released Orton Totes came out.

"*In the name of the Light, I banish thee.*" My throat grew raw. A huge pulse of white light shot out of the wand.

The demon reared and froze, and then cracks formed all over its body with glassy snaps. Light seeped back into the room until only a puddle of darkness remained. The demon sank into the darkness with what sounded like a large inhale. Maybe the Demon King was sucking it back into the demon realm.

As soon as the last claw tip sank into the darkness, the puddle shrank and vanished. The candlelit room returned to normal. Ms. Weever stood behind where the darkness had been, wand raised and eyes wide.

My heart sank. If she had a wand out, then that meant— "Did you help me?"

"No." Her voice was as shocked as her expression.

Chapter 15

I rode an emotional high during the following weeks. Ms. Weever pushed me hard to draw better circles and memorize protection spells. I met every challenge head-on. Mom had her ups and downs, but she seemed to feed off my joy, instead of how much Dad was absent. She smiled more and cooked more desserts. We finished up the herb garden and I helped her place charms around windows so they would redirect the worst of the desert sun away from the house. The last few days had been like living in an oven. With a bit of help from Mom's Air magic, the house finally felt pleasantly cool all the time, instead of only at night.

I spotted Dad's sleeping lump in the bed from time to time, and gratefully snatched up Yuna books he'd left on the dining table, which was good timing. I'd finally finished the latest one. Yuna broke out of the witch's trap, who then deemed her worthy of receiving a charmed bracelet that ended up helping her defeat the Wild Fire goblins attacking the unicorns. The book ended with a big party, only to be crashed by a panicked satyr begging Yuna to rescue his tribe from Crystal serpents.

Like the good hero she was, Yuna donned her armor, strapped on her sword, and rode off into the sunset with a satyr plodding along beside her horse.

I felt like Yuna. I'd conquered a demon with help from Ms. Weever's wand and knowledge, and while my party was more like studying hard, I felt just as accomplished. I'd proven to myself that I could do something, that I could conquer my fears and banish demons. The demon's days in the classroom were numbered.

***

Ms. Weever and I finished practicing a duet on mbiras placed in these giant wooden bowls called dezes. The dezes had shells strapped to them, creating a vibrating sound whenever we plucked certain notes. Listening to one mbira was hypnotic. Listening to two with their sound amplified by the bowls was magic. The song was called "Bangiza," some ancient spiritual song that originated on another continent and had survived the centuries somehow. The song made me feel like we watched water drip rapidly along a wall of rocks after a monsoon storm had passed. Every drop turned into a note when it hit the rocks, and the song wasn't over until the final drop found its resting place.

I usually felt relaxed after playing the mbira. Today I stiffly returned my instrument to its bag and set the deze back atop the piano. "Do we really have to play this for the All Souls Day talent show?" Banishing a demon was one thing. Standing on stage, in front of all my peers was far more terrifying.

"Why are you still asking me this? You know I'm not changing my answer."

"Are you sure they won't wonder if I'm a Dark?"

"No, they'll think it's a very fitting song for the holiday. 'Bangiza' was composed to honor ancestors, as is this holiday." She set her deze beside mine.

"Wait, what?" I slowly slung the strap of my bag over my shoulder. That wasn't what I'd been taught. "I thought it was a day about how Lights bring us closer to peace and all that's pure." She gave me a deadpan look. "I've been brainwashed again, haven't I?"

"Unfortunately." She stowed her mbira in a leather bag.

I let out a frustrated sigh. "Why is everything I've been taught all wrong?"

"Some of it is your previous schools' faults. They fed you lies, thinking they would keep you in line and out of trouble." She sat at her desk and threw her curly hair behind her shoulders.

"Because they're afraid of Darks?"

"Yes, and you need to stop worrying about hiding your alignment from the world. You need to be proud of being a Dark."

"I feel a lot better about it since meeting you." It was true. Sure, my parents were weird about it, but Mom had gone from not wanting to be reminded that Darks existed to being able to relax when I practiced my instrument, drawing circles, and other stuff. She'd even asked how my schooldays went when she wasn't buried in a book.

Ms. Weever's stern gaze softened. "I'm glad to

hear that. Now—"

"I still have to hide it at school, though."

She gave me a slow, knowing nod. "It's no accident that you're the only Dark at this school." Her glare turned towards Mr. Redd's office. "If I had my way, I'd give this town a piece of my mind." She turned back to me. "More stupidity requires you to hide a part of who you are. I'm sorry things are this way for you. It shouldn't be."

"It's okay," I said as my heart sank with the truth.

"No, it's not. This country's attitude towards Darks is all wrong. We're out of balance and won't return to it until we embrace all seven main elements again. But anyway, I could rant about that all day." She plucked a choice book from a shelf behind her desk. "All Souls Day." She leafed back and forth through the pages, wafting the scent of old parchment through the air. "*All souls.*" She turned to the opening pages and set the book on the desk, facing me. Like the cover of my notebook, it contained a circle with Earth, Air, Fire, and Water symbols in it, along with a swirl of a larger circle divided in two, surrounding the smaller circle. Light and Dark. A lone circle containing a leaf and paw for Kindred sat below the other symbols. "All Souls Day used to be about bringing all the elements together, not this glorified farce about how Lights are so great."

"Why'd it change?"

Ms. Weever absently flipped through a few pages. "Time passed. Change is a natural thing. However, some things should remain unchanged. Humanity has lost sight of what's important regarding this holiday."

"How do we change it back?" It all sounded so terrible. The way she frowned at her book told me the changes to All Souls Day were bad.

"Let more time pass and learn the truth." She closed the book and stood. "I'll teach you the truth so it may live on in you, and you may pass it on to those willing to listen." Taking a deep breath, she organized her thoughts. "All Souls Day originates from the legend of the Fyr, the first people to become aligned with the elements. It's said that the spirits of Aardra gathered those seven people and charged them with keeping balance and protecting the world, and they were each endowed with an element. When the spirits returned to their realm, they left behind a temple for the Fyr."

I pictured seven men in robes, long beards, and standing in a semicircle before seven giant, elemental creatures looming over them at the edge of a grassy cliff. The elementals were ghostly yet vibrated with energy, stunning the men into reverent silence. Each elemental touched the forehead of one man, and then all seven backed away, melding into one giant elemental creature that grew and spread into a pillar of light. When the light faded, a towering mountain sculpted to look like a castle stood in its place.

"From that day on, people from all over the world made pilgrimages to the temple. Each person—each soul—would be tested, and in the end, became aligned with the element that best matched the nature of their soul. Every soul serves a purpose in one way or another. We're all responsible for helping create balance."

I pictured a line of people as far as the eye could see traveling to the temple under a blue sky dotted with fluffy clouds. "So that's why it's called All Souls Day?"

"Correct. Every last soul is a part of the balance, responsible for keeping it."

"Then how did things get this way?"

She gave me a rare smile.

I almost gawked. I maintained enough control to not look stupid.

"That's a long, complicated answer best left for another day. You need to get to your next class." She slid her book back on the shelf.

That reminded me. "Can we banish the demon in my classroom?

"At the end of the year, yes. You're not ready yet."

"But—" First, I thought of Deren. I had no clue how long he had until he got sick again and died. Then I realized what Ms. Weever said. "Wait, I can?"

"When you're ready," she said with a nod. "Why else would I leave such a creature lurking around the school grounds?"

Why leave it around at all? The question remained unasked. I didn't want to make her mad for talking too much about the demon. The situation felt like I wasn't getting the whole truth.

"I've kept an eye on that demon ever since you mentioned it." She looked away. "It's too weak to leave your classroom. The worst it does is create fear and doubt, and lurks in its portal, pretending to be all big and scary when, in fact, it can't do much of anything."

Something about her tone coaxed more questions to the tip of my tongue. I mentally batted them away. I didn't have real proof it was the demon, but I had to be right.

She ushered me to the door and checked down the hall. Parents and children walked into the front office. Ms. Weever pulled me back into her office and bent forward so we were eye-to-eye.

The gesture surprised me—so much so that I tucked half my hair behind one ear. She'd given up on fighting me and my hair weeks ago, when she realized I paid attention no matter how little of my face she could see.

"Mia," she said in a hushed tone, "get all thoughts of banishing that demon out of your head. You're not ready."

My jaw grew slack, but I clamped my mouth shut. She'd never used my first name before. This had to be serious.

"As far as you've come in mere weeks, the circles I've taught you are too basic for that one. Your control has improved, but you can't slip for an instant. Trust me when I say you're not ready for that test, so put it out of your mind." A hint of that same fear when I mentioned Orton Totes and the sickness passed across her face. Her fingers dug into my shoulder, making me wince. I put a hand on hers. It felt ice cold. She eased her death grip. "Focus on keeping your defenses up while in its presence. Learn all you can about it. Even try to trick it into telling you its name. Don't try to banish it. Do I make myself clear?"

"Yes, ma'am."

She released my shoulder. "Good. Now, get to class."

Massaging my shoulder, I dutifully headed out of the main office, a hive of thoughts buzzing around in my head. Something was off about all this. That was twice now I'd seen Ms. Weever look scared, and twice it had disappeared as quickly as it came. What was she thinking? Why was she scared?

The lunchtime sun blazed down on me as I walked

between buildings. I had half a mind to shade my head with my bag. I settled for hiding behind my hair.

Maybe I was too young to understand everything going on. Maybe my imagination was playing tricks on me, making me see what I wanted to see so I could justify what I wanted to do. The thoughts bothered me like a piece of food stuck between my teeth.

I gratefully entered the 6-8 building, plunging myself in shade. I gulped cool air into my lungs.

I reluctantly pushed aside the idea of banishing the demon in the classroom. It felt like turning down my vegetables at dinner. I never really wanted them even though I knew they were good for me. I was scared of trying to banish it, but it couldn't stay in the classroom forever.

Miss Wren waited outside her classroom, holding the door open. She greeted everyone with a big smile and one by one, told us to get our language workbooks out. I followed my straggling classmates inside and conjured my protective shield. I hung my bag with only a mild pang of fear as the usual tingling settled in my spine. Learning to control my fear had taught me to accept that I couldn't control my spine tingling in the presence of a demon.

Miss Wren walked inside and redirected a few students back on the task of getting out notebooks, instead of goofing around with making leaves dance on their palms. My classmates darted to their desks as the leaves fluttered to the floor in swooping zigzags, forgotten.

The sense of feeling like something was off filled me again. I raised my hand.

Miss Wren floated over. "Yes, Mia?"

"Miss Wren, where's Deren?"

Her serene smile waned. "He went home sick."

My stomach dropped to the floor so fast I thought its thud would make the whole class turn and look at me. My legs might as well have been made of cooked spaghetti as they carried me to my desk.

The demon chuckled. *He'll be mine soon. More will follow.*

Oh, no. Deren couldn't wait until the end of the school year. I didn't care if I got in trouble, so long as I saved Deren. I had to be ready. Ms. Weever had to be wrong about me.

Tomorrow I would confront the demon.

Chapter 16

Tomorrow came and went without me so much as asking to borrow the oak wand. Deren's chair remained empty, and the rest of the school went on as normal, like they had no clue someone was about to die thanks to a demon. I fought a losing battle with fear and doubt. All my teachers constantly tried to redirect me to pay attention. My mind drifted back to the closet every time. Even the demon occasionally spoke, reminding me that Deren's time was running out.

Tick-tock, tick-tock.

Miss Wren pulled me aside at the end of the day while my classmates packed up and grabbed their stuff from the closet. She propped herself up against her desk and studied me with a slight frown. "Mia, you seem real distracted today."

My legs wanted to move, to run in circles, to do anything besides stand in place. My hands craved to hold a piece of chalk and start drawing a circle. Every second that ticked by put Deren a second closer to dying from whatever illness the demon had given him. "I'm sorry, Miss Wren," I said to her feet.

"What's on your mind? You seem worried about something." She leaned a little closer.

No one paid attention to us. However, a few students came over and asked Miss Wren about All Souls Day. She patiently answered them one by one. As I built the courage to say something, Gwen ran over and handed Miss Wren a piece of paper. She took it with a smile and studied the drawing.

"This is very good, Gwen. Thank you. I'll put it up on my wall." She set it aside on her desk. "Now please go line up with everyone else."

Beaming, Gwen tossed her perfect tawny hair and joined the back of the line.

Miss Wren turned her attention back to me. "I'll understand if you don't want to say anything. I wanted to let you know that I've noticed something's bothering you. I'm here for you if I can help in any way."

My traitorous gaze darted to the closet.

Her gaze followed mine. "Does this have anything to do with what we talked about a while back?" I nodded. "Okay. Let's get everyone on their way and we'll have a quick chat."

She directed the students into a straighter line and took her spot outside the classroom door. The bell rang. She bid everyone a cheerful farewell and gave out a few hugs. Gwen, the last in line as usual, gave me a curious look before hugging Miss Wren goodbye and disappearing into the hallway. Great. She knew something was up. Hopefully, also as usual, she was wrong. I didn't care what she thought so long as she didn't know the truth.

Miss Wren rejoined me by her desk, hands on her hips. She reminded me of Ms. Weever, but she was too kind and gentle to be as scary. "You've been doing pretty well lately. Your grades are solid, Gwen and her gang seem to be treating you well enough, and it looks like your alignment is still a secret from your peers. Ms. Weever says you'll perform a duet with her for All Souls Day. I'm looking forward to seeing you play."

"I'm not." Not only was our song a way of bringing truth back to the holiday, but it was another challenge with fear Ms. Weever wanted me to face— something about expanding my comfort zone.

"You won't be alone onstage. You'll be fine."

"I know," I said, responding more to the onstage part.

"Anyway, I'd like to know what's on your mind if you're willing to share."

"I'm worried about Deren." There. I said it. Maybe she would see the strangeness of the situation Ms. Weever didn't.

"He did get pretty sick this morning. He should be fine in time for All Souls Day."

"No, he won't," I said to her shoes and the bottom half of her peach skirt.

"What makes you say that?"

I shifted from foot to foot. "I don't know if you'll believe me."

"We won't find out if you don't tell me. I promise to keep my mind open."

I took a deep breath and slowly let it out, feeling my heart rate slow as I forced myself to calm down. I had to accept my fear and not let it stop me from acting. I met my teacher's gaze. "The demon made him sick. He's not going to get better ever again."

Miss Wren's face might as well have turned to stone. I couldn't tell whether or not she believed me. The silence stretched from seconds to an eternity.

This was it. She didn't believe me. She was thinking of a way to politely tell me I was being ridiculous, and that was all my imagination.

"How do you know it's the demon?"

Okay, not total dismissal. "He said something about Deren being his and that there'd be more."

"More students that'll get sick?"

"I think so." The demon had given me enough information to worry, but not enough to know how to act.

"Does Ms. Weever know?"

"She doesn't believe me. She wants me to banish the demon at the end of the year, when I'm ready. She keeps telling me it's harmless."

Miss Wren thought a moment. "Maybe it is. Maybe it wants you to think it's the one making people sick."

She's in denial, the demon said. *Do you really think I'd claim responsibility for another demon's handiwork? My king would not approve. Besides, are you sure you want to risk being wrong?*

The demon remained hidden, a mere shadow over the empty closet. Ms. Weever had made it very clear that demons lied. A lot. There was a way for Darks to detect when demons lied. I wasn't skilled or strong enough for such things. I wanted to believe Miss Wren, not the demon, but the weight of its gravelly words held truth.

"It has to be the demon." I meant to say, "It is the demon." A seed of doubt planted itself in my mind.

"I can go talk to Ms. Weever if you want."

"No." I held up a hand. "She'll just get mad." If I was right about a connection between the demon and Deren's sickness, I would have to do this alone. If I was wrong, it'd be that much more embarrassing if Ms. Weever found out I'd misled Miss Wren. "I'll figure it out."

"Are you sure?"

No. "Yeah. I'm sorry I let it distract me all day." I headed for the door.

"Thank you for telling me. I want to believe you, but I know Ms. Weever wouldn't leave that demon alone if it were dangerous. Do your best not to worry about Deren and go enjoy your weekend."

I headed for the buses with the demon's laughter following me.

***

The weekend went by agonizingly slow. I kept picturing everyone showing up for school on Monday, only to learn that Deren had died over the weekend. I used this fear to push myself to practice more advanced circles. After finding a few too hard to draw, I settled on the simplest one listed in the Advanced section of my circles book. I almost gave up a few times. It was a far more complicated pattern and had more runes in the middle. Every time I threw my charcoal stick down, I'd hear the demon's laughter, picture Deren lying sick in bed, and pick the charcoal back up. If I gave up, he was as good as dead.

Once I felt confident, I waited until well after bedtime and drew the circle in white charcoal on my bedroom floor, one ear trained on my door. I would bolt back under my sheets at the slightest sound. Even with Mom feeling more comfortable about my alignment, I didn't want to risk anything. It was so late at night that Mom was asleep and it was past the time Dad would usually show up. Hopefully, I would get through this with no one the wiser. I'd already memorized the circles I was supposed to be practicing. Ms. Weever would never know that I jumped ahead in my lessons.

My circle was sloppy, as usual, and frayed. I knew from experience that it'd work. It wouldn't be strong or last long. It was good enough to protect anyone inside.

Instead of a wand, I used my mbira and a choice string of notes to call upon the four elements for protection. I had no candles. Those were too crazy risky to sneak into the house. If Mom woke up to pee and caught the scent of a blown-out candle, I'd get in more trouble with her than with Ms. Weever. I didn't need candles or a wand to activate my circle. All I needed was focus and strength of will. The objects were only aids for concentration and confidence. The strongest Dark could conjure a protection circle with a mere thought.

Using the same incantation with the candles, I played an ascending string of notes in every cardinal direction. Each time, my mbira flinched as the wand had, and each time I almost lost concentration. I hadn't expected this to work. My circle lit up with purple-glowing lines, and the hum of energy tickled my bare feet.

Holding the instrument to my chest, I took in my handiwork, not quite sure I believed what I saw. Woven and overlapping lines glowed a reassuring purple around me. I barely saw my toes in the glow of the four runes in the middle, the lines looking like an incomplete spiderweb. The circle's energy put me completely at ease. I could announce to the whole school that I was a Dark and everything would be okay. No harm would be done. I could also feel the weak spots in my circle, like stray strands of hair tickling my neck. The protective energy swirled around me and leaked out of the frayed spots. It was power lost—only a small amount.

The circle would work. Considering the unknown amount of time I had left before the demon claimed Deren, I was as ready as I'd ever be to face the demon.

Chapter 17

The school was covered in decorations when the bus pulled in on Monday. I'd barely been able to read a page on the ride in because students were all excited. It was All Souls Day. Today would not be a regular school day for anyone. It would be more like a holiday where everyone came to school to celebrate. Everyone wanted to show up for once.

I did and didn't want to come to school. I did because I wanted to save Deren. And I didn't because I had to save Deren. I wanted more time to prepare, to practice. I wanted Ms. Weever to be there to help, to save me if I failed. I hardly worried when she was there. This time I'd be all alone.

White streamers lined every building. Dancing lights the size of fireflies glowed around every cactus and prickly bush. Streamers charmed into animal shapes drifted overhead like stringy clouds oblivious to the breeze. The animals made the sky look ghostly, but everyone embraced Light stuff.

Like Ms. Weever said, the decorations had no hint of the other elements. Everything was white, silver, and gold. Everyone dressed in those colors today, even me. I sported a silver sleeveless dress with gold lace trim and matching sandals. I felt more like a decoration than a person. I ached for my usual muted summer dresses.

The ladies at the front office handed out lollipops as students rolled in, creating a mob as some tried to double back for a second or third pop, only to be told to move on and stop being greedy. I wordlessly accepted my lollipop and slipped it into my bag. I'd try giving it to Mom at the end of the day. Hopefully, it'd cheer her up. If that didn't work, I'd give it to Bela.

I smoothed down the front of my bag and stopped, causing a few students to bump into me. They regarded me with confused looks before unwrapping their lollipops and moving on with their day. Ms. Weever stood at her usual corner to greet students coming in, although she more stared like she was waiting to pounce on someone for breaking a rule or misbehaving. Students usually quieted when they walked by her. Today, they gave her a wide berth.

She wore all black. Shiny black boots with three-inch heels, a layered black dress with a black corset, and black sleeve things that looped around her thumb and ran from palm to above her elbow. Blonde curls spilled on either side of her bare shoulders, and red lipstick lined her slight frown. A big black mark among the sea of white. She spotted me and her frown deepened. Her icy eyes stuck to me like a wolf staring down an intruder, waiting for the right time to attack.

Keeping my chin up, I tried to walk by.

"Good morning, Miss Evers," she said in a voice that was anything but light and cordial.

"Good morning, Ms. Weever." I kept walking.

"I'm disappointed in your attire. You blend in with the brainwashed."

I should've known that frown was a heavy hint that my hopes to keep walking were ridiculous. "I didn't know what else to wear. We didn't discuss it."

She tilted her head. "It's not up to me to discuss every little detail with you. It's up to you to learn to think for yourself."

So much for trying to make it her fault. I took in her clothes, mine, and everyone's around me. "I don't own any black dresses."

"We'll have to fix that one day." She spoke like she was thinking aloud to herself. She waved me off. "Away with you. We'll meet later for the talent show." Her gaze roved among the sea of students filling the sidewalks, hunting for trouble. She snapped at a pair of boys to stop pushing each other. I headed off to the playground, drawing the protection circle in my head over and over.

Deren was absent from his usual spot on the bench, which sent my heart racing. My imagination conjured up all types of horrible scenarios, including one where the principal led morning announcements with the fate of Deren's illness. The holiday would be canceled, everyone would gather to grieve and reflect on the loss of a student. I wouldn't have to get onstage and perform, but I'd also be too late to banish the demon.

Gwen touched my shoulder and I jumped.

"What's up with you?" She carefully sat in her

usual spot in the middle of the five of us and rearranged her layered dress to lay a particular, tidy way on her lap. I did a double-take. She looked like a queen or princess. She even wore a tiara. Her perfect hair was arranged so it ended in a bun in the back with little silver and gold butterflies and flowers dotting her head. Maybe a fairy princess. Gwen looked a little tired, too. Her hair must've taken hours.

I felt like such a pauper sitting next to her. And here I thought I looked like an ornament. Maybe I was Gwen's ornament, me, Sussi, Nonaya, and Chibya, her ladies in waiting, ready to direct any arriving prince to her. He wouldn't need our help, though. He would notice only her. Yuna had suffered through the advances of some flowery prince in the first book. She proved her point that she wasn't ready for all that icky kissy stuff after beating the prince in a formal duel.

Anyway, Gwen had spoken to me. Royalty didn't like being ignored. "I'm nervous about the talent show."

"Don't be," she said, her gaze distant, pensive. "You're performing for our ancestors, not for the crowd anyway. Our ancestors don't care if it's perfect, only that you honor them."

I stared. Was this the Gwen I'd come to know? Her words sounded rehearsed, maybe not her own. Whatever. Why was I questioning a moment of kindness from her? Setting my shock aside, I took a moment to absorb her words as children all around us played and got yelled at to be careful with their clothes.

Gwen was totally right. "Bangiza" was a song for ancestors, not for classmates. My classmates would be there, watching and listening. No amount of kind words could change that. "You're right. Thanks." All I could do was embrace my fear and keep moving.

Gwen stared off into space. "What are you doing in the show?"

I described the song to her, which led me to describe what an mbira was. Gwen and the others thought the performance would be cool and were looking forward to it. "What are you doing?"

Gwen said, "I'm doing a Fire dance. My mom'll be onstage with me. I wanted a full group of musicians, but my mom told me to keep it simple. She thinks I'll forget all about our ancestors if I try to be too flashy." She let out a huff of frustration and tried tossing back her hair, only to remember it was done up in a bun. "By the way, your tutor is weird. Why is she dressed in all black?"

There was the usual Gwen. I shrugged. "Maybe she forgot today is All Souls Day."

Gwen's face crinkled with disgust. "How could anyone forget? The school has been preparing for it for weeks." Her friends chimed their agreement.

"I dunno. My tutor is weird." It was the only thing I could think of without revealing our being aligned with Dark. Annoyed as my sort-of friends still looked, they seemed satisfied with my answer.

The morning bell chimed and students filed into their respective classrooms before being brought to the cafeteria in three separate waves. My class joined the second wave to a feast that stretched beyond school proportions. This wasn't the usual apple sauce in a cup with a side of toast and a sausage patty. This was something far better. I hurried to our assigned table with Gwen and the others, waiting our turn to be called up to the buffet lining one wall.

Gold, silver, and white decorated the lunch tables. More charmed streamer animals floated near the ceiling. A traditional bouquet of five pink and white flowers with a white rose in the middle were placed on every table. There was also a silver tray beneath the flowers, specks of food visible from the first wave's use.

Sweet, flowery scents mingled with fresh-cut fruits, scratch-made breads, and other traditional pastries. Everyone was instructed not to eat yet. We had to wait for the ceremonial poem to be read first. Mouths watered, fingers poked fluffy buns with flaky crusts, and the occasional morsel snuck between lips. I longingly eyed my plate of goodies as I respectfully waited with my hands in my lap.

As soon as the final student sat with a mound of food on his plate, Mr. Redd stood behind a podium, standing on a box to make himself taller, and read a poem in a language I didn't know. The words sounded rhythmic and used a lot of "a" vowels. The power in the words hushed the cafeteria to perfect stillness. Even the streamer animals fell still, the tails of the longest, thinnest strands the only thing that wavered.

A note that sounded like someone running a finger along the rim of a wine glass filled the room. Gasps whispered from all the tables, one escaping me when I felt Grandma's presence. My chest fluttered. Mr. Redd instructed us all to place our offerings on the silver trays. We all placed pieces of fruit, chunks of bread, fruit tarts, and other items on the tray, thus inviting our ancestors to dine with us.

An invisible hand placed itself on my shoulder as cool air wafted towards the silver tray. None of the food moved or changed in appearance, but our ancestors were eating it. I knew as surely as I felt Grandma's cold hand on my shoulder.

Thank you, Mia. Stay away from the darkness.

My mind raced across campus, through a few doors, and into Miss Wren's classroom, where the demon lurked. I'd forgotten all about it these past few minutes. After all that worrying and preparing, I'd been distracted by food. Guilt stole my appetite. I put my chunk of sweet bread down.

The coldness disappeared from my shoulder. *Stay away from it.*

Grandma had to be talking about the demon. I wanted to ask her about Deren. How could she expect me to sit around and do nothing, to let him die because my dead Grandma told me to? She wouldn't have to deal with his ghost. I probably would. How would I feel then with the ghost of a classmate angry at me for doing nothing to save him?

I eyed my plate again and picked up the bread. I needed all the energy I could to face the demon.

***

The rest of the morning was full of games and stories, games I pretended to participate in, and stories I half listened to as I mentally prepared myself to face the demon alone. Grandma's words echoed in my head over and over. I'd had my doubts. Now it felt like I was about to make a huge mistake. How could it be? All my classmates were blissfully ignorant of the demon. Miss Wren had doubts simply because Ms. Weever had done nothing about it. And now Grandma was telling me to leave the demon alone. Why couldn't the adults see things the way I saw them?

I kept trying to push aside doubt. It kept whispering in my ear and tapping me on the shoulder. Doubt was as dangerous to feel as fear when facing a demon. I tried accepting my doubts like I'd embraced my fear a zillion times. For some reason, this was way harder.

Maybe I was wrong about the demon. It was lying about making people sick. Maybe I wasn't ready. My circle wasn't good enough yet. I wasn't strong enough. I needed to back out for my safety. It wasn't my place to decide when to banish the demon. I was just a kid.

So then why was Ms. Weever evasive when talking about the demon?

That was the only thing that kept me—saved me—from giving in to doubt and giving up on my secret mission. There was something off about the whole situation. I had to be right about needing to banish the demon as soon as possible. I had to be right that it couldn't wait.

The school day progressed in a blur as we moved from Miss Wren's room to the gymnasium for some games, to another classroom, and finally to the dreaded auditorium once school was out.

We followed other classes inside as everyone converged on two sets of double doors like lines of ants returning to the colony to deliver food. I'd tried to purposely forget my mbira in the classroom so I'd have a valid excuse. Miss Wren had everyone place everything they needed on their desks before we packed up. It's like she knew how forgetful we could be.

My mbira case thudded against my leg, pounding out a rhythm to a funeral march. The lights were up to full brightness over the rows of folded chairs. We were herded into our assigned section and instructed to sit quietly and wait. Miss Wren stood watch over us all from the end of one row. She wore a silky white dress with a silver shawl and had her hair pulled back behind her ears so her annoyingly pretty hair spilled down the back of her neck.

Parents filed in as well. I sank deeper into my chair as Gwen waved to her parents. Even Sussi's, Nonaya's, and Chibya's parents showed up, all of them having to fill in the back while the students sat in front.

I knew my dad wouldn't show up. Mom wouldn't either. The most foolish part of me sat up and searched among the excited parents for a slender woman with long black hair like mine. I'd told her about it and my dreaded performance. "I'll think about it" was her polite way of saying, "No, thanks." As much as I didn't want to perform in front of the school, I wanted my family to act like everyone else's and show up, and embarrass me with kisses in front of my friends.

Thoughts of friends brought me back to thoughts of Deren. I couldn't forget about him in this moment. Daydreams of having a normal family would have to wait.

The house lights went down. The Kindergarteners sang—more like yelled—a song about the Fyr. Their teacher conducted the song, pointing to specific students to cue them to move into different places and do certain motions while a piano played in the opera pit. The song talked about how the other elements revered the first Light, named Lux, how he spread peace and happiness to the world, and how he became responsible for connecting the living with the souls of lost loved ones. It was a story everyone knew well. I knew it well. And now I wondered if it was true.

When the Kindergarteners finished, the auditorium burst into cheers, applause, and a few ear-splitting whistles. The students lined up and were supposed to bow in unison. Laughter rippled through the crowd as clumps of students bowed together. Their teacher tried to get them all to stop and do it together. Several of them got on tiptoes to hunt for the parents, then popped huge grins and waved. Their teacher gave up and ordered them off stage. Only one child fell because he tripped over the boy in front of him while waving to his parents.

As the Kindergarteners filed off, the third graders rose and headed backstage. The first graders took the stage and sang another song that their teacher, a tall man that towered over the class, performed with them. A flutist and drummer accompanied them, giving the performance a more traditional, ancient feel.

When the first graders finished, Miss Wren ushered us all backstage, where everything was black or painted black. One of the janitors, dressed in black so he'd blend in, grabbed a black rope and spoke a charm to it. The first graders' backdrop lifted into the air. Another person up in the flies adjusted one of the giant, cylindrical things so its light beam hit the right part of the stage.

My class broke off into groups to prepare for our respective performances. I trudged over to Ms. Weever in her black outfit and usual frown. I slowly removed the mbira case and plucked the old instrument from the velvet lining.

"Hurry up, girl. We're going to practice in the band room."

The auditorium, cafeteria, and band room were all clumped together in one building, leaving a huge gap between me and the 6-8 building. It might as well have been a desert wasteland that stretched for miles. I'd be spotted before I made a clean getaway.

Ms. Weever gave me my deze and I followed her out a side door. I winced after spending a few minutes under red lights backstage. I blinked rapidly to adjust my eyes and spotted a door with a picture of a female stick figure.

That gave me an idea, a scrap of hope.

I followed my tutor into the band room. Cloth-covered percussion instruments lined the back wall. Several signs had been taped to them at intervals, each reading "DO NOT TOUCH" in big red letters. Of course, a couple of my classmates took that as an invitation to go touch them. Ms. Weever snapped at them to get away.

She and I sat in one corner by a wall covered in cage-like lockers stuffed with instrument cases. The room smelled like leather and spit. Fifth, sixth, and some seventh graders filled the room, chatting away and rehearsing. I set my mbira in its deze. We played several notes and then a few scales to make sure our instruments were in tune. I adjusted a couple of keys, making our mbiras sound as one. Satisfied, Ms. Weever counted a measure of beats that matched the tempo of "Bangiza" and we played in earnest.

Our song filled the room, the metallic notes vibrating with ancient magic, an ancient message. The seashells vibrated in time with the notes, and soon I got carried away with the song. It was the two of us, our fingertips dancing along the edges of the elongated keys, paying tribute to our ancestors. If there was anyone else in the room, I didn't know anymore. My fingers plucked away inside a bowl that was a portal to another world, another time.

"Bangiza" steadily danced and drifted to its conclusion, the final notes humming as the seashells fell still. Ms. Weever looked at me with a straight face, instead of a frown, which I'd learned was her way of smiling.

"Very good. You'll do your ancestors proud today."

"Thank you." Eyes tickled my skin like a spider crawling up my bare arm. Everyone had stopped talking. They all stared at us—even the seventh graders. My stomach twisted, filling the back of my mouth with something acidic and unpleasant. I swallowed. "Ms. Weever, I don't feel so good." My original plan was to fake sick to get out of stepping onstage. Apparently I wouldn't have to. I swallowed again as color drained from my face, making it feel both hot and cold at the same time.

"Hurry up." Setting both our instruments down, she ushered me to the bathroom door. "I don't care how sick you get. You're not getting out of this performance. You have plenty of time for your stomach to settle." She pushed the door open for me. "I'll be waiting for you backstage. I will not come for you. You're responsible for facing your fears and getting yourself onstage. There'll be dire consequences if you don't." She marched off and the door shut, closing me off from the rest of the world.

The door's thud echoed and the sound of running water hit my ears. I wasn't alone in the bathroom. It had four stalls, the biggest one at the back. A few second and third-graders looked at me like I'd punch them if they spoke to me. I rushed into the biggest stall, latched the door, and stood before the toilet bowl as something stirred the contents inside my stomach. Eyes closed and head tilted back, I willed my breakfast to stay in my stomach as sweat beaded on my face. Why did I have to eat so much sweet bread? My breath came in ragged gasps and I swallowed repeatedly. I thought it was a lost battle, but soon my face settled on feeling warm and my stomach stopped churning.

Someone rattled my stall door. I focused on breathing as more girls popped in and out of the bathroom.

After what felt like an entire day had passed, silence filled the space. I was finally the only one in there. Heaving a sigh of relief, I leaned against the wall and wiped the sweat off my forehead. The agony of a tumultuous stomach became a memory. I was about to sit on the floor to give my shaky legs a break when the door opened again.

"Mia?"

I shut my eyes. It was Gwen. How did she know I was in here? I wanted to yell at her to go away. I said nothing, hoping she'd think I wasn't in here.

"I see your shoes and dress. I know you're in here."

"What do you want?" My weak voice echoed off the walls.

"Oh, nothing." She stepped closer, stopping before my door and peering between the crack. "How are you feeling?"

Eyeing the empty bowl, I reached over and flushed, then settled back against the wall.

Gwen laughed. "That good, huh?" She took a step back. "Look, I'm not here because I'm worried about you or anything. Ms. Weever sent me to check on you and tell you to hurry up. She said something about having a bucket onstage, just in case." She glanced over her shoulder. "I don't know about you, but she doesn't seem like the kind of teacher I'd want mad at me. You might want to hurry up and grab your stuff." She walked off. "Just sayin'." With that, she was gone and I was all alone again.

Taking in the refilled toilet, I heaved a sigh and willed my legs to carry me to the sink. I rinsed my face and drank water before returning to the band room. More seventh graders were in there now, switching into costumes. This had to mean that the fifth graders were performing.

My mbira waited where I'd left it. Scooping it up, I headed back out into the hall and stopped.

One way led to embarrassing myself in front of the entire school by puking onstage. Maybe I should've let myself get sick. The other way lay freedom, solitude. And, of course, whatever dire consequences Ms. Weever had in store if I chose not to show up.

The word dire reminded me of Deren and his dire situation. I had my mbira and my bag with chalk and the book of circles in it. Ms. Weever was nowhere in sight—or Miss Wren, or any adult for that matter. Sure, a seventh-grade teacher was back in the band room. She'd have no clue what I was doing, much less suspect anything, if I went back inside. This might be my only chance to take advantage of an empty classroom with no one nearby.

Whatever consequences Ms. Weever had for me

wouldn't be as bad as Deren dying. I returned for my shoulder bag and ran to Miss Wren's classroom.

Chapter 18

I sprinted across campus, bag in one hand and mbira in the other. Fear fueled my feet with extra speed and a thrill electrified my limbs. I was finally going to face the demon and save Deren. No one would know where to look for me. They'd all think I was in the bathroom, and if they didn't find me there, all sorts of rooms and corners could serve as hiding places all over campus. It's not like banishing took long. I had plenty of time to banish the demon and make it back in time to perform. I could save Deren and avoid the consequences of missing the talent show.

The realization gave me one last burst of speed right before I arrived at the 6-8 building. I darted inside the empty halls, stopping before the classroom door to catch my breath. As aware as I was of time slipping away for both me and Deren, I needed to focus before entering.

A few deep breaths and I breathed almost normally as my heart pounded away in my chest and ears. I reached for the handle and tugged, only to find it locked.

The world spun as my heart sank to the floor with a thud.

No, no, no. This couldn't be. After all this effort, I was stopped by a locked door? Setting my bag and instrument on the floor, I grabbed the handle with both hands and tugged over and over, only to feel that dreaded thud of a—

The handle swung downward and the door popped open.

The gap between the door and the frame widened enough to stick my hand inside. I wasn't a Metalmind, so I couldn't have willed the door unlocked. Even so, wards probably protected the locks from thieves. Maybe I'd only imagined the door locked or never tugged quite right.

A tiny voice in the back of my mind told me to close the door and walk away. Something was really off about the situation, something far more serious than Ms. Weever hiding the truth.

My fingers grew slack on the handle. It'd be better to face the terror that awaited me in the auditorium. Entering the classroom on my own was a bad idea.

Shaking my head, I gripped the handle and threw the door open. That tiny voice had to be doubt, not reason. Doubt wanted me to forget about Deren, to take the easy way out and let him die. I gathered my things, conjured my protective shield, and stepped inside.

Being only late afternoon, it should've been bright enough in the classroom to read without the lights charmed on. For some reason, I could barely see. The playground was a haze of straight lines through the windows. The groups of desks sat in a clump of shadows, Miss Wren's large desk a sleeping beast. I'd stepped into the demon's lair.

I drew the activation rune with my fingertip on the ceramic panel that controlled the lights. They shone like rows of giant fireflies, but their light brought little color back to the room. Taking a deep breath, I held my chin up and headed to the center of the room.

Welcome back, child, the demon said from somewhere in the closet. It stretched its front limbs and head into the classroom, and the rest of its body followed like a coiling snake. Its black mass reshaped into four giant limbs, an oval head attached to an elongated neck, and one slanted red eye opened. *Finally accepted the truth, have we?*

Putting on the best imitation of Ms. Weever's glare, I set my bag on the floor. "Yes. I'm banishing you back to where you belong." I fished around for my chalk and took out the circles book, looking at it one last time to make sure I knew it perfectly. My spine tingled in the demon's presence. I accepted it as I pushed my bag away.

You think you're ready for something like that? It stood on all its legs like a dog. Its shoulders and back touched the ceiling.

A scrap of fear cracked my hardened exterior. The demon barely fit inside the room. It could crush my head with its paw-like hands the size of student desks. It was awfully large for what was supposed to be the weakest type of demon. Or was that a scare tactic to hide how weak it was?

I couldn't think about that. I had a job to do. Taking another deep breath, I looked over the circle in the book. Sure enough, its lines and curves, and the runes in the middle had become as familiar as my mother's face. It looked exactly like I'd been practicing in my head all day. I could do this. I propped myself up on one hand and both knees.

The demon loomed close enough to chill the air and make my breath appear in small puffs. *That wasn't what I meant, child.*

I clenched my teeth as I outlined the circle on the carpet. The surface was tricky with how much it made my chalk bounce and catch on the lumpy surface. The carpet was so thin that I thought it would be smooth. It was smooth when I walked on it. For a piece of chalk, it was as lumpy as a mountain range. I slowed my strokes after I snapped my chalk in half. I'd come with a dozen sticks, but it was important to complete the circle in as few strokes as possible.

I meant the truth about my power and influence. Why go through all this trouble? Why not join me, instead, as others have done before you? It edged its way closer to my book.

This demon talked too much. Heaving a sigh, I straightened into a kneel and glared at the demon. This monster had once been human. Maybe that's why its back legs looked too long. It had similar proportions to a human. It'd been twisted and reshaped over the time spent as a demon. "Why not rejoin the human realm instead?"

It tilted its oval head at me. *You must be the first human to ask a demon such a ridiculous thing.*

"You were once human. Is being a demon really all

that great? Don't you miss being human?"

The demon laughed. *Why on Aardra would I want to go back to being something so weak? I offer a far better deal.*

"Not interested." I resumed scratching out my circle in far more short strokes than I would've liked. It couldn't be helped. The carpet was too lumpy for sweeping strokes.

Giant paws settled near my bag and the oval head dipped closer to the open book. Its one-eyed gaze snapped to me. *You dare try to banish me with this?* Turning, it slammed a paw on either side of my circle, making my protective shield crackle with static. *You have more gall than I gave you credit for, child. Stop this foolishness at once and we'll strike a deal.*

Chalk pressed in place, I looked up again. "The only deal I'll make with you is if you give up being a demon and go back to the Light."

You don't know what I can offer. Listen and you just might like it.

My fingertips numbed in the demon's chilling aura. The chalk dried out my skin. I continued with the outer portion of the circle. "My tutor taught me to never make deals with demons."

Having second thoughts, is she?

My hand slowed to a stop. "What do you mean?"

Oh, little Mia Evers, those words come from the one who summoned me.

I stiffened. My lips and ears felt like ice cubes. My voice came out in a whisper. "You..." I couldn't get the last word out. Everything fell into place. All the brushing off, the dismissal, the getting angry every time I asked. It all made sense at last.

The chalk slipped from my numb fingers.

Lie? Me? Never, it said. *But if you don't believe me, go ahead and ask her.*

I sat on my heels. "But she was going to have me banish you at the end of the school year."

Maybe a lie, or maybe more proof that she's having second thoughts. Which do you believe? Which one do you want to believe?

Tears stung my eyes as my resolve crumbled.

Yes, let's strike a deal. I'll give you power, make you even stronger than your precious tutor, and you'll let me continue to roam the mortal realm. It politely withdrew to one corner of the room, still close enough to claw me.

I didn't want power. I wanted the world to be how I'd envisioned it, a world where no one lied to or deceived me, a world where my mother was never sad, and my dad was always there at the end of every day, a world where I could freely be friends with Deren and—

Deren!

Sniffing, I wiped my eyes. "The only deal I'd make with you is you make Deren better, along with anyone else you've made sick."

No. Any deal I'd strike with you would only be between you and me. Our deal wouldn't concern anyone else.

Fresh tears formed. I glared through them. How could anyone or anything be so heartless, human or not? "Make him better."

The demon reached for my incomplete circle and rubbed at one of the bumpy lines. *I could give you the power to heal him if you give me something in return.*

A piece of my hard work disappeared. As much as I

wanted the power to cure Deren, something warned me it wouldn't be worth it. This went beyond everything Ms. Weever had taught me, trustworthy or not. Demons never gave something without gaining in return. They always walked away with the better deal. Why would it let me save Deren if it wasn't gaining something better instead?

Think about it. The demon erased another small portion of my circle as if scrubbing a stain.

Stay away from the darkness.

Grandma's words repeated themselves over and over in my head, drowning out the whirlwind of doubts and confusion surrounding Ms. Weever. Grandma was truth, a grounding force from pain and confusion. If I couldn't trust my tutor, I knew I could trust my family.

Picking up my chalk, I slowly stood, limbs stiff with cold. "I'll never make a deal with you. Go away."

I sensed the demon's mouthless smile, the energy of mirth coming off it in waves. Instead of being sucked back into its portal, the demon stretched its neck, bringing its oval face to the edge of my protective shield, making it crackle. It looked down on me as if deciding whether or not I would make a good meal. *No.*

I stood there in stunned silence as the demon continued scrubbing at my circle. Its gangly arms and massive legs remained before me, like a wolf scrunched into too small a dog house. I kept waiting for it to retreat. It remained as dark and solid as ever. "Why aren't you leaving?"

My power grows as the mortals I feed on weakened, child. Tick tock. Deren's time grows short. Strike a deal with me and save him, or stand there and let him die.

Stay away from the darkness.

Repeating the words in my head over and over to ground myself, I focused on my breathing to keep myself calm. My tears dried up, warmth seeped back into my limbs, and I finally realized what the demon was doing to my circle. This monster was not my friend. It had no interest in helping me. It also showed a hint of fear when it saw the circle in the book.

Holding out a hand, I raised my other and expanded my protective shield. It hit the demon with a flash, forcing it to retreat to the closet. I spread my shield further, until the strain pressed on my mind like a muscle strain from trying to lift too much weight. I pulled it back to the edge of my circle.

I snatched up the chalk and studied the damage. The demon had rubbed away a chunk of the circle so cleanly that it looked like I could replace what was lost, instead of start over. Restarting would be smarter, but the expanded shield drained my energy. Keeping a calm focus, I bent to my task, forcing myself not to rush.

My shield steadily shrank as I drew and the demon tried to pour doubts and fears in my ear with its words. I hadn't known I could expand it. Once again, my powers came through for me in a moment of need. Maybe this was how the first Darks figured out what they could do. They had to figure it out somehow. My arms shook as I finished the circle and all its curves and lines. I had to slow down even more to scratch the four runes in the middle, and my shield was barely big enough to protect the circle as I plucked the mbira from my bag. I faced the northern rune, instrument in hand.

You call that a banishing circle? The demon dragged claws along my shield.

Its attack stung my face. Three lines of fiery pain seared from hairline to chin. My body shook as the demon stepped onto my shield. It felt like gravity had suddenly grown ten times heavier. Smoke curled between the demon's claws as it crackled and tiny bolts of lightning danced all over my shield's surface. It roared in pain. I dropped to my knees and plucked out the notes that activated the circle.

Purple light shot upward as lines and curves lit up with power, nearly blinding me. The demon recoiled so hard that its massive bulk slammed into the wall, making the building shake. The muted lights flickered.

The demon growled and got back to its feet. *You better pray your circle is strong enough to keep me out.* It lunged and swiped at my shield.

It shattered with an electric jolt, making me cry out. Blood trickled down my face as cold soaked into my limbs. I played a string of notes that would help me concentrate. I had no wand to help me focus.

The demon didn't attack my circle like the centipede demon had. Instead, it groped around the edges as if searching for something. Sparks and smoke emitted from the circle's protective power everywhere the demon made contact. Facing the north rune, I played a string of notes. "Spirits of Earth, I call upon your balance and protection in this circle." The mbira jolted in my hand, letting me know the spirits had answered my call.

The demon touched a particular spot near the edge of my circle and slowly raised its head. *Call upon all the protection you want. You're mine, Mia Evers.*

I faced the east rune. "Spirits of Air, I call upon your voice and protection in this circle." The mbira jolted again and air swirled around my hands. I turned to the south rune.

The demon dropped to all-fours, its front paws smoking. *Yes, yes, child. Keep going.* It touched the edge of the circle with one claw. The circle's glow dulled around that one little spot. A black line leaked inside the outermost circle like water following the lines of a crack.

"Spirits of Fire, I call upon your energy and protection in this circle." The mbira hummed. I turned to the west as more black lines wove in with the glowing ones, like never-ending snakes searching for the exit through a labyrinth with alarming speed. The farther the lines spread, the duller my circle grew.

"Spirits of Water, I call upon your purpose and protection in this circle." The mbira flinched one last time and a cool air swirled around my hands. I faced the demon and its one red eye. The entire outer circle was dull and tainted with black lines. I held up my instrument like I'd held up the wand, the old wood thrumming away in my grip.

The dead calm I'd felt in the same moment I'd banished my first demon filled me. My legs stopped shaking and my breath came in and out so slowly that I thought time had slowed. I took one last breath, the inhale sounding like a roar of wind in my ears, and I spoke in a deep, rich voice that was not my own. *"In the name of the Light, I banish thee."*

The circle pulsed and, at the same time, cracked. It wasn't the demon stiffening up and cracking. It was my circle. Instead of light filling the room, it all went dark. Wind swirled around me so violently that I thought I'd been thrown into a dust devil. I lost my balance and tumbled through the air. I kept expecting to crash into chairs, desks, or even a wall. I flailed around in absolute nothingness, mbira in one hand, my empty hand clawing for anything to grab.

I did another midair cartwheel and landed with a thud on something hard and flat, knocking the wind out of me.

A muted light shone down from I didn't know where. Where there should've been the ceiling was a lot of black nothingness. I flexed each of my limbs before tentatively sitting up. Everything ached. Nothing was broken. Metal clinked to the black, featureless ground. Two of the mbira keys had broken off.

Oh, no. I hadn't heard the circle crack. I'd heard metal and wood. The mbira had split in two.

Laughter rumbled overhead. I turned and almost screamed. The demon stood not on four paws but two, like a human, its limbs now looking proportional. It towered over me, standing on clawed feet big enough to crush my body with one stomp. *Welcome to the demon realm, Mia Evers.*

Chapter 19

Not one scribble of the circle lay anywhere. Nothing separated me from the demon, not even my shield. I'd lost concentration during the tumble. Scooping up the broken instrument, I threw my shield back up. Its return filled my limbs with comfort, like gently slipping into a warm pool. At the same time, it felt strained, like I couldn't take a full breath. My shield barely spread beyond the top of my head and the soles of my feet. I hunched, feeling the need to put more space between me and the demon.

The demon's one eye crinkled with an invisible smile. *Hide behind your protection all you want. You can't keep it up forever.*

I took a few steps back so my neck wouldn't feel like it'd snap while trying to make eye contact with the demon.

By all means, try to run and hide. You've nowhere

to go that I can't find you. Shifting its weight, the demon wound up a leg.

I took one more step back and ran. The classroom materialized around us, with desks, walls, and all, but no ceiling. Everything was transparent and shadowed, looking like ghosts. I darted among the clumps of desks as fast as my heavy feet let me. It felt like a stretchy rope was tied around my waist and connected to wherever I'd landed. The farther I ran, the harder it got to keep moving forward. I ran to the transparent wall with drawings pinned to it and reached out to brace myself against it. My free hand groped empty air. I stumbled forward.

Something huge and dark collided with my energy shield, which sizzled and sent me somersaulting. Snippets of the inside of the 6-8 building spun around me. I rolled to a stop on a sidewalk, but my head continued tumbling. I closed my eyes and focused on my breathing.

There, I gave you a head start. Please do get back up and keep running. Chasing prey is such good sport.

The demon dropped to all-fours. It prowled closer, cutting through the walls as if they weren't there. The demon's head was fixed on me, floating closer with intense focus.

I held the mbira in both hands and tried to force both halves back together. The wood creaked and bent, and little snaps reached my ears, each one urging me to stop. The mbira let out a whiny groan, and then the wood snapped in two. I smacked both halves together with a discord of muted metal notes. More keys plinked to the ground.

At first, I thought I heard the rumble of a bus's Fire

engine trying to roar to life. Then I realized the rumble came from overhead. The demon was laughing at me.

Whatever will you do now, Little One? You. Are. Mine. The demon stiffened, then suddenly looked out into the distance.

A wreath of darkness blotted out the distant mountains. Shapes manifested. Some looked human, some like bugs and beasts, others had limbs twisted at angles that made my stomach squirm, and a few had shapes that looked like they should fall apart.

The demon charged on all-fours at several shapes and raked claw marks in the ground. *Back off. This one is mine.* The nearest ones retreated into the darkness as the demon charged the others and clawed the ground over and over. What I guessed were more demons steadily backed off and disappeared, taking the wreath of darkness with them. My least favorite demon trotted back over and did one more lap around me, eyes scanning the grey horizon for more intruders. None came. The distant mountains appeared again.

I slowly got back to my feet. The demon turned its head so sharply that I let out a squeak of a scream and my eyes stung with tears.

See? You are mine. Coldness came off it in waves.

Shivering, I clamped the broken halves of the mbira together, hoping to hide my discomfort and terror. All I managed was to make the wood rattle. I pressed them harder and plucked a few notes. I didn't know what I was trying to play. I didn't know what to play. I'd never had a lesson on how to escape the demon realm. I didn't even know a human could get sucked into it. "How did I get here?"

Its one red eye finished roving the horizon. *You*

succeeded at banishing me, but I'd dismantled enough of your protection circle to take your soul with me. You are truly mine now.

I should've cried. I didn't know how to process the information. Instead, a hollowness opened up in my chest. I couldn't imagine anything other than waking up from this or something, the holiday celebration would be over, I'd go home, and sleep in my bed. All this would be a bad memory. The other part of me acknowledged the very real danger I was in. And I had no clue how to free myself. Ms. Weever would know, wouldn't she? Even if she did, would she save me? I didn't want to believe what the demon had said about her, yet a tiny voice in the back of my mind said it was true.

I tossed the mbira on the ground. "What do you want with me?" A piece of hope broke away from my heart and fell to the ground with the broken instrument.

I already have what I want. Now the real fun begins.

"You wanted me in the demon realm with you?"

Oh, yes. What fun we'll have. Balancing on the balls of its feet, the demon settled into a crouch.

"What are you going to do to me?" I didn't want to ask the question. It came unbidden.

Oh, it's not what I'm going to do. It's what you'll do for me. It raised a giant, black claw and poked my stomach hard enough to make me fall. My protective shield burst, showering golden sparks that vanished when they touched the ground. *You're my puppet, now, child.*

I clutched my throbbing stomach, the pain driving home how helpless and defenseless I was. I got back to my feet. I wouldn't give this demon the satisfaction of facing me sitting down. I hugged myself, trying to stay warm.

The demon set its hand on its knee. *So, let's strike a bargain. If you agree to my terms, I'll return your soul to your body.*

"Return my soul?" The classroom closet popped into my mind, giving me an idea.

Oh, yes. The real fun begins when you carry out my will and shape the living realm to my vision. Some demons only destroy. It placed a clawed hand over its black chest. *I have more refined ambitions.* It stood, towering over me at its full height, my eyes level with its shins. *Let me switch to something less intimidating to show you how reasonable I can be.*

The one red eye closed and the demon bowed its head as it wrapped its arms around its emaciated waist. Its body writhed and shrank.

I ran for the classroom, more specifically the portal it used to enter and exit the human realm. The demon stayed put. In case I passed through again, I held out my hand as I ran for the door. I didn't slow down for one second, not even the last few feet between me and the door, and I nearly knocked myself senseless on something solid. My eyes rattled around in my head. The thump of my collision echoed out into the bleak grayness. The world stilled again and I spun around, expecting a giant monster to be chasing me down.

To my great surprise and relief, the demon stood where I'd left it, half as tall as before. It continued to shrink as I groped around behind me. A solid handle met my fingers. I gave the shrinking demon one last look before slipping inside.

The door thunked closed with a menacing rumble and my footsteps echoed off walls that sounded farther than the ones closing in on me. Maybe the walls were an illusion to match what my memory expected to see. I slowed down so I wouldn't slam into the door. I glanced over a shoulder to double-check to make sure the demon wasn't chasing me.

Nothing but the echo of my footsteps filled the darkened hall. I reached for Miss Wren's classroom door and took such a sharp intake of breath that the cold air stung my throat.

A man stood between me and the door, hands clasped behind his back. He wore a suit and tie, had shoulder-length golden hair swept back in the shape of a lion's mane, a friendly face, and piercing blue eyes with a tint of red in the irises. The man reached for the door, held it open and, bowing, gestured for me to go inside. "Please step inside, Little One, and we'll discuss the terms of our bargain." His voice was rich and melodic, like that of a storyteller.

I glanced in the direction where the demon had been, and then back at this man. "You're—?"

He nodded. "My demon name is Allosyr. As for my true name, that you'll never know." He brushed a sleeve. "As for this form, I use it only as necessary when striking bargains. It's shaped after my former human life." He held up a hand and acted like he was examining his nails. They looked perfectly human until black claws extended and retracted. "But with a few tweaks to make it more accommodating. I learned in my demonic youth that mortal souls are more open to bargaining when you give them a gentler face to look at. My preferred form is a bit much." He flashed a crooked smile, revealing a sharp white fang. "So, shall we?" He gestured towards the classroom again.

It was exactly where I wanted to go, and someplace the demon had no problem allowing me to enter. Could he read my mind in this realm? With all I didn't know, it was possible. Was he the type to be so confident that he didn't guard his exit?

I only had one chance to find out.

Darting inside, I dragged a desk to the closet and climbed onto it. I stood on my tiptoes and reached for the ceiling. Maybe it'd suck me up like it did the demon.

Nothing happened.

I jumped several times, arms reaching for the path to freedom. The closet had no boxes, books, or anything hanging on the hooks. The walls themselves stretched on into the endless gloom. The ceiling wasn't anywhere to be found. The desk wobbled when my feet hit it again. I caught myself on the shelf with one hand. I swung myself forward and hoisted myself onto my elbows. The shelf was so narrow that my forehead hit the inner wall.

I kicked my legs like a flailing swimmer. Any moment now, I'd feel clawed hands grab my legs and I'd be thrown to the ground. It was only a matter of time before the demon caught on to my plan. My heart pounded out an urgent beat as my vision narrowed on the shadowed space in front of me. My breathing sounded frantic in my ears.

Pain flared in my elbows as most of my body weight balanced on those two small, bony points. I scooted an arm forward. All my weight on one elbow made my arms give out.

The edge of the shelf dug into my underarms and my toes kicked the wall. I took a million frantic breaths as my body swung forwards and back, and then took a big gulp of air when I realized I wasn't about to fall any farther. I scraped my toes along the wall, unable to grip it. My foot kicked a coat hook. I searched around with both feet to confirm it was indeed one of those two-pronged hooks, not the demon's claws wrapping around my feet. I propped one foot on a hook and swung my other leg. My first try fell ridiculously short. I tried again with a little hop and scraped the shelf with a toe before it slid back off. Trying one more time, I swung with all my might and a girly grunt, and my entire foot thudded onto the wooden shelf.

My ankle bone dug into the wood with a sharp pain as I strained to get the rest of my leg up. I pushed aside the pain until I lay face down on the shelf, a little further out of the demon's immediate reach. I didn't dare chance a look around the room.

I scrambled to my feet and reached into the gloom.

Again, nothing happened.

I tried jumping as I reached and got the same result. Maybe I had to say something to make the portal open. "Send me back." I jumped and reached again, and my feet thudded on the wood with another failed attempt. "In the name of the Light, I command thee to send me back." It was my normal frightened voice. It lacked power. Not even I would obey if someone told me to do something in a voice like that.

My breath huffed in a high-pitched wheeze. I was too scared. My emotions were out of control. I only gave the demon more power over me in a state like this.

Closing my eyes, I took one deep breath after

another. I'd be too tempted to look around and scare myself anew if I kept them open. Soon, the thumping in my chest quieted to a steady drum. I wanted to run screaming or start clawing my way up the wall. I accepted my incurable fear as I focused on my breathing. My fear became this tiny little ball in the back of my mind as calm filled me. I opened my eyes and reached for the gloom. *"In the name of the Light, I command thee to send me back."* That powerful other voice escaped my lips.

I waited for the sensation of my body being lifted in the air. Nothing happened. My feet remained rooted to the shelf. A growing sense of dread filled my chest. My arms went limp. I let them drop to my sides.

A slow clap made me flinch.

The demon sat behind Miss Wren's desk, leaning back with one ankle propped up on a knee. He looked perfectly relaxed and in his element.

"You're getting good at controlling your emotions, especially for someone so young." He pressed his fingertips together. "You're going to make quite the fine Dark one day. Oh, the chaos we'll sow." He flashed a fanged grin, and then wore a mask of a welcoming, friendly face. However, from this distance, his eyes shone more red than blue, a predator fixated on his prey, waiting to pounce.

He could hide it all he wanted with human skin. He was clearly all demon.

"Are you done with this nonsense, now? You're a human trying to use a demon portal. You have to create your own portal before you enter this realm. You are irrefutably stuck here, child. The only way out is through me and my bargain." Allosyr gestured to the student desk in front of Miss Wren's. I could've sworn it hadn't been there a moment ago. "Come. Sit. Let's talk like civilized creatures do."

No wonder he hadn't attacked me. The weight of truth sank in like a giant rock in the pit of my stomach. My legs folded under the weight. I sat on the shelf, all hope gone.

The desk I'd dragged over stretched and rose, forming a flight of stairs leading to the ground. The topmost step slowly rose, stopping when my feet sat flat on it.

"Perhaps I should apologize for my earlier behavior. Spending century after century as a demon makes one lose one's grip on humanity. Your first impression of me has most certainly been anything but pleasant."

I wasn't stupid enough to miss the absence of sincerity in his voice. "You're not sorry."

He gave me an indifferent shrug. "I only act according to my nature. You cannot hate the coyote for killing a rabbit so it can eat. Do not hate the demon for sowing the terror it feeds off of."

Nature or not, I didn't care. He wasn't nice.

"Now, do you want to return to your realm or not?" Allosyr gestured to the chair again.

The empty desk looked perfectly normal, safe. Would he turn it into a cage the moment I sat down? He could do whatever he wanted in the demon realm. He could even be lying about sending me back. It made no difference whether or not I believed him.

I slowly descended the steps, each tier bringing me closer to my fate, my doom. I couldn't recall Yuna ever getting stuck in a situation this severe or scary. Sure, that water dragon had been scary, but she'd had two ways out of danger. I only had one, and that path lay through even more danger.

Arms clamped to my sides, I crossed the room and stiffly sat opposite the demon.

Allosyr's eyes crinkled with a far too delighted smile.

I narrowed my own. "That's my teacher's chair. You don't belong in it."

Wearing his closed-mouth smile, he tilted his head. The chair grew and morphed around him, stretching into a sinister throne with thorns on either side. Flames rose behind him, yet cast no warmth. "Where are we again, child?" His voice grew and deepened. A shadow passed over his face, covering everything but one glowing red eye.

I swallowed.

The demon leaned closer, bringing his face out of the shadow. "I suggest you don't forget your place. I like you and your spirit. However, don't get it in your head that you should start telling me what I should and shouldn't do. It'll sour our bargain."

I lowered my gaze to Miss Wren's cluttered desk. I wanted to yell at him for being so cruel and such a horrible monster. I didn't trust myself to say anything that wouldn't worsen my situation.

"I'm glad we're at an understanding on this detail. Now." Leaning back, he absently waved a hand. The heatless flames vanished and the chair shrank and softened to its normal leather padding.

I rubbed my arms. It was like I'd woken to a freezing bedroom in the dead of winter after having forgotten to close the window before I went to sleep.

"You want out of here and I want to send you back."

"Then please let me go."

A slight smile touched his fake human lips. "Why?"

I hadn't said that because I expected him to. I'd said it because...because...I didn't know. I wanted to leave that badly.

"I'd love to hear your rhetoric."

"What's rhetoric?"

"A logical argument. Try to persuade me to let you go, no strings attached. Give me good reasons."

I sat there with words lodged in my throat like a trapped cough. I didn't know what to say.

Smiling a little wider, he nodded. "Go on. Persuade me." When I said nothing, he said, "Here, I'll get you started. You should say, 'Allosyr, you should let me go because—'"

My tongue stuck to the roof of my mouth before I managed to lick my lips. I swallowed, pushing down the lump in my throat. "You should let—"

"*Allosyr*, you should let me go because...Don't forget your manners because I'm being nice."

I studied his gentle face, trying to picture the demon in its place. I knew what the real monster looked like, but that fair complexion, golden hair, and piercing dark eyes locked itself in place. This man—this monster—didn't deserve manners. I didn't want to say his name. I'd give him exactly what he wanted if I said it. I crinkled my nose. "Allosyr, you should let me go because..." My thoughts faltered as my belly-flopped. Even though it wasn't his true name, there was a power to it. He subtly pulled me closer, pulling me into his web. "Because I'm only eleven years old. I'm just a kid. It's mean and unfair of you to do this to me."

"Alright. Why else?"

More? My mind frantically sifted through ideas as I pictured myself over and over running back up into the closet and jumping through the portal. "Because I want to go home. I'm cold and scared. Please let me go."

Allosyr tilted his head to the other side. "So you want me to let you go because you're young, I'm being mean, you're cold, scared, and want to go home?"

"Yes."

"Alright. So what's in it for me?"

"What do you mean?"

"How do I benefit from letting you go because you're young and scared?"

This wasn't about him. This was about me. "It'll make you a nicer—" This man wasn't a person, not even a man. He was a demon. "Demon."

He raised an eyebrow. "Try again."

I huffed. What did he want me to say? "I don't know. Why do you care if you get anything out of letting me go?"

His deceptively inviting face grew serious. "It's quite simple. The rhetoric you're attempting to use is begging, not bargaining. We're here to bargain, not listen to you beg." Darkness curled around his shoulders.

That darkness reminded me of the dream I'd had last night. "My grandmother told me to stay away from the darkness, and that darkness means you."

Allosyr playfully pouted. "And you wouldn't be here right now if you'd listened to her. Your choices have rendered her advice invalid. You're in the demon realm. You need to listen to me now. If you want out, you're going to strike a proper bargain with me."

The truth of the demon's words sank in, making me feel smaller. I was a rabbit pleading with a wolf to spare my life and let me go. Taking a deep breath, I set my elbows on the desk and interlaced my fingers like I was praying to the Light. My voice probably couldn't reach the Light from here. I'd never made a habit of prayer. It wasn't something a Dark tried. Different beings responded to me—at least that's what I'd been led to believe.

Holding my chin up like Ms. Weever had taught me, I held the demon's red-tinted gaze. "Then let's bargain." If I had to be the rabbit, I wouldn't sit there and shake. I'd meet this with some pride.

The demon graced me with a flash of fangs. "There's the spirit I like about you, Little One. I've had grown, hardened men soil themselves in my presence. And here you are, a child of eleven years, facing me with the dignity of a queen." He paused. "Maybe I will make a queen out of you one day."

"I don't want to be a queen. I want to know what you want so I can get out of here."

"Yes, Your Grace," Allosyr said with a mocking smile. He steepled his hands. "What do I want with you?" He pointed skyward. "First, let's discuss what I have to offer you. This wouldn't be a bargain, after all, if you didn't gain something in return."

"I get to go back where I belong. That's all I want."

"You don't want the power to save your friend?" He gave me a studious look.

"I—"

Stay away from the darkness.

Making deals with demons was wrong. This was all wrong. But, Deren. If I said no to this, I was probably passing up my only chance to save him. "I don't want him to die."

"We all die one day, child. There's no way around that no matter how much power you have. However, I can give you the power to save him from a premature death. Would you like that?"

Don't say anything. One word burned on the tip of my tongue. Keep your mouth closed. My throat burned to release the thought. This was very dangerous territory. Was Deren the noble type that'd tell me to save myself and let him go, or was he too young to think of such things? Was he lying in bed, feeling horribly sick and scared, yearning to feel safe and secure again? "Yes," I whispered, then sucked in a breath as the pressure released from my throat. Had the demon forced the truth out of me?

The demon grinned. "Very good. That's half the bargain. Now for my half." He sucked in a breath and then stopped, his brows knitting with confusion, all cunning gone. He looked pure human. And then his gaze shifted over my shoulder, his eyes flashing a tint of red. "What is this?"

The surrounding energy changed from cold despair to frantic desperation. I turned around.

I did a double-take. In a realm dominated by grays and blacks, I hadn't expected the speck of white floating in the air in the middle of the classroom. That whiteness grew to the size of a hand and glowed. A voice whispered from within.

"Mia? Mia. Hurry! Come to the light."

That woman's voice sounded familiar. I should've known who it was. Like the demon had yanked the truth from my lips, it stole her name from my mind. I slowly stood, mesmerized by the light. It looked so warm, so inviting, and I was so cold.

"Mercurial wench," Allosyr said in a low snarl.

The white light grew until it was taller than the demon in his human form, narrow as a cracked-open doorway. What was this? My feet moved and I drifted closer.

"Where do you think you're going, child?" The demon stepped around the desk and his grip plunged my wrist in ice. There was no kindness left in his flat eyes and deep scowl. He looked ready to burst out of his human skin and take on his demon form.

"Mia." The woman's voice cracked with panic. A white-glowing hand shot out of the light. "Get away from him. Take my hand."

The moment felt surreal, like I watched myself stare at this hand while the demon held onto me. This couldn't be real.

"Don't listen to her," Allosyr said, tightening his grip on my frozen wrist.

The sudden pain snapped me back to reality. Someone had opened a portal to the demon realm, and Allosyr didn't want me to go through it. If he didn't want that, then that's exactly what I needed to do. I reached for the light.

"You step through that portal and our deal is off, and your friend dies. Think before you make your choice, child."

I wanted to turn and face him. Something compelled me to keep my gaze on the light. More of the arm forced its way into the demon realm, spreading more light into the classroom. Warmth touched my fingertips.

Warmth, life.

Stay away from the darkness.

"Hurry, Mia."

Leaning towards the light, I reached for the hand. My feet wouldn't move and the demon didn't let go. I tried to pull my arm free and failed. The distance between me and the portal bent and shrank, like the shape of the room was changing to bring me closer. The lady's fingertips brushed mine. Warmth filled my body, wrapped me in a soft, comforting blanket.

The demon snarled. "This one is mine."

"You cannot have this one," the woman said in a forceful, resonant voice. It was so familiar.

I pulled my gaze away from the light. Every fraction I turned took monumental effort and an eternity. I met the demon's fake human face. It was contorted with pain and fury. Smoke rose from where it held my wrist. "I reject your bargain. I'll find another way to save my friend."

A second white-glowing arm protectively wrapped around my shoulders and pulled.

The demon narrowed his eyes. "This is only one battle, child." He held on tight. His body darkened into black and expanded as I drifted backwards into the light. I let it take me like a current guiding me downriver. The distance between me and the demon grew and grew, stretching beyond the length of the classroom. His hand held my wrist as he swelled into his full demon form, complete with one red eye. His arm stretched into a thin rope as I drifted away.

His arm snapped in two, leaving his claws around my wrist while the rest of his body retreated into darkness. Light fully enveloped me.

You are mine, Mia Evers.

Chapter 20

Warmth enveloped me. I shivered and my teeth chattered. I lay propped up against my savior, eyes closed, legs stretched towards the sunlight hitting my eyelids. I was safe at last.

I cracked my eyes open. To my great surprise, it was dark out. I squinted at the classroom lights. They were overwhelmingly bright. My eyes must've adjusted to the demon realm's gloom. Dots of Water lights sprinkled the campus with silvery luminescence, turning the playscape into a shadowed, resting beast. How long had I been gone?

How long had people searched for me?

My eyes stung with tears of gratitude. Someone had come looking for and rescued me. I was out of there. I was safe. I placed a hand on my savior's forearm, my attempt at a hug and wordless thanks. She rocked me side to side like my mother used to.

"Oh, you stupid, stupid child," she said in a thick whisper.

My eyes went wide. I knew exactly who that voice belonged to. Shoving her arms off, I bolted upright and faced her. "You." I'd expected the ghost of my grandmother or even Miss Wren, but not her.

Ms. Weever stared at me in openmouthed surprise, black mascara lines outlining a trail of tears on her flushed face. "What?" She sat with her legs folded beside her, dress splayed out over the floor.

"You rescued me." After all the demon had said. "Why?"

"What do you mean?" She looked genuinely surprised, and how her blue eyes searched me conveyed confusion.

I didn't buy it for one second. Getting to my feet, I backed away from her. "Allosyr told me the truth." There. I'd used his stupid name. That ought to get her attention.

She closed her mouth as fresh tears pooled in her eyes. Her gaze fell to the floor and her golden curls partially covered her face, like my hair almost always did.

This was new. She'd told me countless times to keep my chin up, to carry myself with pride. Now my mentor hung her head in shame. This must've been proof that he hadn't been lying.

"Mia, whatever he told—"

"Tell me the truth. Don't lie to me again. It's not fair that you expect me to never lie to you when you've been lying all this time." I didn't know where I got this courage from. Maybe facing demons had that effect on me. I wanted to tear down everyone's posters, throw chairs around, stomp my feet, scream at the top of my lungs, and have a good, hard cry. The one person who'd mentored me, who'd instructed me to be proud of being a Dark, and take on the responsibility that came with our alignment, she'd lied to me and been irresponsible. She was the reason the demon was here. She was the reason Deren was sick and dying.

Taking a deep breath, Ms. Weever sighed and sat on her heels. She wiped her eyes and held her chin high again, looking as proud as ever. She sat with her shoulders square, hands in her lap. The icy detachedness in her eyes was gone. In its place radiated shame and hurt. "I'm sorry, Mia."

"Did you really summon him?"

"Yes."

Wow, a straight answer. I'd expected her to be evasive until I wore her down, like I often had to do with my mom. "Did you really strike a bargain with him?"

She hesitated. "That was a long time ago. I'd never —"

"Why?"

She held my gaze. "It's a long story."

"I don't care. I need to know."

"Not all of it is appropriate to explain to a child."

"I'm not like most people my age. I act more adult than a lot of them do."

Ms. Weever let out a weak laugh. "I do agree you're wise beyond your years, but you're too young to fully understand."

"Just tell me."

She took another deep breath and sighed through her nose. She interlaced her fingers in her lap and her gaze drifted away. "Remember how I've taught you to always stay in control of your emotions, especially around demons?"

"Yeah. Why?" Her eyes welled up anew and my own stung. This was genuine, raw emotion. It was too much. I had half a mind to tell her to stop, but I wanted to know the truth more than I wanted this emotional pain to stop.

"I hope you never know the agony of outliving your own child."

Silence stretched out between us. I didn't know what to say. What could I say? "I'm sorry." I wanted to yell and throw a tantrum, but I was definitely too old for that sort of thing. "What happened?" I took a sharp intake of breath. "That demon isn't your child, is it?"

"Goodness gracious, no. Thank the Light it's not."

That had to be true. Allosyr had said something about being a demon for a long time, so long that he had a hard time remembering what it was like to be human.

"Mia, I want you to learn from my mistakes."

"How can you expect me to trust you anymore?"

She met my gaze with a level, regal one. "I saved you from the demon realm, didn't I? If I were truly aligned with that demon, why would I do such a thing?"

"I don't know." The demon hadn't been happy. At the same time, he hadn't been surprised. Maybe many people regretted their bargains with him. Maybe everyone had.

She stood and straightened her dress. "I understand and accept that you may never fully trust me again. I ask you to at least listen to what I have to say. Whether or not you choose to believe me, that's up to you."

I stood where my circle used to be and waited for her to continue.

"Darks have the responsibility and burden of always having to stay in control of their emotions no matter what. Every alignment has its hazards when they lose control. None of them bear the same consequences as a Dark. Fires can accidentally set things ablaze, Earths split rock, and so on. Once their emotions are back under control, all is well again.

"When Darks lose control, they attract demons and whatnot like vultures to a carcass. Demons don't leave because you're feeling better again. They linger. They wait. They nurture your negative emotions as they attempt to smother anything positive." She gestured to the closet. "This one found me when I was lost in grief. He's very subtle. I gave in to his nudges, his whispers, even though I knew the signs to look for. He fed my desperation to get rid of my pain, and when the time was right, made me an offer I couldn't refuse." Looking away, she shook her head. "By the Light, I was so stupid," she whispered.

"What did he offer?"

She shook her head again, her cheeks flushing. "It doesn't matter. It was all a lie. I was too distraught to see it for the lie it was."

"I want to know. He tried to strike a bargain with me."

Her gaze snapped to me as if looking at me for the first time all night. "You didn't strike a bargain, did you?"

"You saved me in time."

Closing her eyes, she pressed a hand to her chest. "Good." Her chest flinched with a silent hiccup and she swallowed tears. "He offered to show me how to bring my baby boy back."

The memory hurt, shamed her. I didn't know how to empathize with it. "I'm sorry." Maybe it was like losing Grandma. That'd hurt so much. I'd cried a lot. All three of us had. It'd be better if she were still alive, but the thought of bringing her back from the dead had never occurred to me. It wasn't the way things worked. Mom had explained death to me. Then Grandma's ghost showed up and confused the heck out of me, and then explained something about limbo and how she watched over the three of us. I missed her, her cookies, and her hugs. At least I could see and talk to her whenever she visited me. Maybe Ms. Weever's son never visited her and that's why it hurt so much. "I'm sorry," I said again.

"Thank you." She took in what remained of my circle. It looked like a jigsaw puzzle with all the pieces in place without touching. The mbira lay in two pieces with several keys lying around it. "I can't believe you tried something so stupid. Why were you so intent on banishing it?"

"He's making people sick. Deren's close to dying."

She froze and stared at me in horror. And then she closed her eyes as the truth sank in. Fresh tears drew more lines of mascara down her cheeks. "I know you've warned me of this before, but it's like I'm hearing it for the first time." She looked at the circle. "Whatever you did must have weakened his hold over me. I'll do what I can to save Deren now."

"Good thing I banished the demon then. I don't know how much longer he has."

Ms. Weever slowly shook her head. "The demon

will be back."

"How? That's not fair."

"Life isn't fair. In order to get rid of a demon forever, you have to send it to the Light. What you accomplished is only temporary."

"How do I send it to the Light?"

"I don't know. Believe me, I've looked. I've pored over countless books, pamphlets, essays, you name it. It seems that dark forces have been doing a thorough job of erasing such knowledge."

"But there is a way?"

"Yes. Allosyr may be blocking me from finding the answer."

Flustered, I ran a hand through my hair and Ms. Weever took a sharp intake of breath.

"I thought you said you didn't strike a bargain."

"I didn't."

She seized my arm. A pair of curved black lines wrapped around my forearm, one below my elbow, the other above my wrist. A pinched oval lay in the center with lines forming a gradual spiral from the pinched ends out to the outer oval. Someone had given me a tattoo during my trip to the demon realm.

Ms. Weever slapped her forearm beside mine and the same tattoo appeared on her pale skin, rising like black blood seeping through a bandage. Now that it was bigger, I realized it was an outline of the demon's face and one eye. She peeled her arm away. Her tattoo vanished and mine began to fade, taking its merry little time.

"What bargain did you strike?"

Chapter 21

"I...I didn't." I reviewed the conversation between me and the demon. "I couldn't have." The mark was visible on my arm, like strokes of black paint I'd tried to wash off, but couldn't completely remove. "What does this mean?" I held my arm out.

"It's his mark. You two are connected now."

My stomach flopped as memory of the black mass attached to Deren surfaced. "It won't make me sick and die, will it?" I held my arm away from the rest of my body.

She glanced at mine before looking at her own arm. "What did you two talk about?"

"He offered me the power to cure Deren in exchange for something he wanted."

Ms. Weever's eyes locked on me, her tense posture like a cat ready to lash out at the slightest movement. "What did he demand in return?"

"He never said. You pulled me out before he got to that part."

A wave of cold air passed through, making the both of us turn. I couldn't sense the portal and my spine didn't tingle. The closet was darker than the rest of the classroom. Ms. Weever narrowed her eyes. "Come. We need some privacy."

Eager to leave, I followed her to the door, which she pushed aside. I touched the knob. It wiggled, instead of twisted. Something crunched under my shoes. Taking a step back, I lifted my foot. Shards of glass lay all over the ground. There wasn't a window in the door or any glass structures in the hall. Where had this come from?

I carefully hopped over the glass splatter and into the hallway. A patch of black caught my eye. The outer knob was bent and slightly melted. It was charred black. "What'd you do?"

Ms. Weever glanced over a shoulder as she walked. "Judging by the lack of sun outside, the show has to be over. Do you want your parents to worry while waiting by the auditorium?"

"They didn't show up." I looked away, chin up, as my tutor stopped. A short silence followed.

She turned around. "Do they know when to pick you up?" Ms. Weever's voice was gentle, apologetic.

I'd mentioned it. Mom remembering was another thing. I shrugged.

"Speak when spoken to, Miss Evers. Don't fall back on bad habits because of our complicated circumstances. You need to maintain self-discipline now more than ever. Don't ever get sloppy. Learn from my mistakes and don't ever, ever get sloppy." Looking away, her cheeks flushed.

"Yes, ma'am. I told my mom. I don't know if she'll remember. She gets...busy sometimes." I pictured Mom lost in another book, and then lying in bed, crying while she missed Dad.

"Come." She led the way, heels clacking along the floor, the echoes reverberating off the walls with a comforting certainty that they were there, that I was undoubtedly back among the living.

We headed to Ms. Weever's office and took our usual places, she behind her desk and me in the cushy chair opposite it. I sat not because I wanted to, but because I felt like I was supposed to have gone to bed three hours ago. I wedged myself in one corner and tucked my legs beside me.

Ms. Weever set a cast iron kettle on a portable burner and filled the air with the bitter whiff of propane before the lighter did its job and ignited the gas. Blue flames curled around the kettle's base, mesmerizing me with their light. I let out a loud yawn.

"Don't fall asleep." She shifted and struck a high-pitched bell with a silvery rod.

I popped my eyes wide open and my brain went on high alert, even though the rest of my body felt limp and tired. I scratched one ear with my pinky. "I didn't mean to. I suddenly felt so tired and sleepy."

"A trip to the demon realm will do that." She returned to the teapot and filled it with water from a ceramic jar. "All things dead feed off the energy of the living in one way or another. We are like power stones to them. We're a store of energy they can soak up. Our demon friend was feeding off you the whole time you were there. I'm sure he didn't rush into striking a bargain with you." She opened one small jar after another and added a pinch of a bunch of herbs, spices, and stuff.

"No, he didn't," I said, clenching my fists. That demon was so horrible and selfish. He'd been stealing from me the whole time.

She added several scoops of some powder as steam rose from the kettle's spout, carrying the scent of chocolate. She sealed the kettle with its cast iron lid. "That's an example of how subtly he works." She adjusted the flame a tad with the copper dial.

"I hate him." Impotent fury stung my eyes. He hadn't cared about me for one second. All he cared about was himself and what he wanted.

"Don't." She turned around. "Feel nothing. Don't feed him with your hate." She plucked an incense stick from a mug on her desk, lit it with the burner, and watched it momentarily before blowing out the flame. A tendril of sweet-smelling smoke rose like a snake slithering up an unseen tree trunk. She retrieved an owl feather as long as my arm and drew ovals in the air, slicing through the smoke and spreading the scent.

"What are you doing?"

"Taking precautions." She walked a slow circle around the room, filling it with a scent that reminded me of pine trees I'd seen and smelled up in some mountains a few years ago. It was beautiful. It wasn't something I experienced down in the desert. "Did you hear what I told you?" she said.

"Don't feed the demon any hate. How do I avoid that? I hate him. He's evil."

Ms. Weever returned the owl feather to a drawer and set the incense on a brass plate. She took a seat, her blue eyes full of pity. "A neutral detachedness is your best defense."

I sat up a little straighter. "What do you mean?"

"I wasn't planning on this lesson until at least seventh grade. Seeing how you're trying to get ahead, it would be better to teach you now." She paused, studying me.

"Go ahead," I said the words reluctantly. I wanted to keep learning so I'd never end up in a situation like the one I'd been rescued from. "I'll decide whether or not I believe you after."

She nodded. "A neutral approach to demons is safest for Darks. Leave the love and happy nonsense to the Lights. It works for them. For us, it's a distraction. Same goes for negative emotions, but those are exactly what demons try to draw out from you. You have to learn to accept it and concentrate on the task at hand, be it banishing, probing for information, placing protection, and so on. You'll feel anger and hate. Acknowledge the emotions, let them be, and do what you have to do."

Feel angry and don't feel angry? "I don't get it."

Ms. Weever's shoulders rose and fell with a gentle sigh. "This is why I intended to wait on this lesson. Maybe I should."

"No. I need to learn now. I have to save my friend."

She studied me a moment. "Let's try a different approach." She set a piece of parchment paper between us and scribbled away with a shiny pen. She drew a bumpy cloud on the top and a stick figure with a really big circle for a head below it. She filled the cloud with the names of emotions and flipped the paper around to face me. "This thought bubble represents all your emotions and this stick figure is you." She drew a circle in the air over the thought bubble. "All these emotions exist inside you all the time, yet you can only feel one at a time."

I opened my mouth to object. She held up a finger.

"It may seem like you're feeling ten things at once. That's your mind taking quick turns with each emotion. One will eventually dominate all others." She wrote "hate" inside the head. "Yes, you hate the demon we're both dealing with. I do, too. I set that hate aside when near him. I'm not telling you to feel nothing. That'll never happen. It's what makes us human, for better or worse. You have to learn to accept that you'll never stop hating him and let acceptance fill you instead." She flipped over the pen and drew an invisible circle around "hate," then tapped twice inside the thought bubble. The word "hate" had been removed from the head and set inside the thought bubble. She wrote "acceptance" inside the head. "Instead of having your emotions be one big storm cloud, you need to learn how to detach yourself from them at will. This is why I've taught you to focus on your breathing." She drew two lines, one on either side of the stick figure, stretching up through the bubble, dividing it into thirds. With the lines there, I realized the emotions had already been separated into good and bad.

It suddenly made a lot more sense. I pointed to the lines. "I think I get it. I need to protect myself from the demon and my emotions at the same time?"

Ms. Weever thought a moment. "That's one way to look at it, yes. Demons will always try to press you to feel negative emotions." She drew curved lines from emotions to the stick figure, pointing at the head. "You always have to be ready for them to do that. It's one reason why you have to place so much protection around you. Most of what Darks do is put protection in place so we can concentrate on what we came to do. Directly dealing with demons is the small part."

"That's why the circles are so important?"

"Yes," she said with a nod.

"I think I understand now."

The scent of chocolate permeated the air. Ms. Weever tended to the tea kettle. A moment later, she turned around with two steaming mugs and placed one in front of me. She sipped her own as she settled in her chair. "Drink up. It'll warm you up and give you back the energy you lost during your stay in the demon realm." She took another sip.

Sitting on the edge of the chair, I dragged the mug closer and inhaled the steam. Yep, definitely chocolate with a bouquet of herbs and spices. I took a tentative sip, letting the flavor wash over my tastebuds. Warmth filled me on its way down. I took another sip and smacked my lips. It was delicious. "Why chocolate?"

"Because no child in their right mind would willingly drink something that tasted awful. It also doesn't dilute the potency."

"What's 'dilute?'"

"It means 'to weaken.'" She settled back in her chair, mug in both hands. "Now, tell me everything that happened."

More warmth spread through me, making me feel relaxed. My eyes stopped feeling so heavy. Memories of my unscheduled trip to the demon realm burned my chest with guilt. I accepted it as I took a deep breath and described how Allosyr had toyed with me, then changed shape to appear as a man in a suit with golden hair. I did my best to recall our conversation. I remembered one thing very well. "And then he said, 'That's half the bargain. Now for my half.'"

Ms. Weever paled. "Oh, dear child, you've struck an incomplete bargain."

My current thought went poof. "What does that mean?"

She took a steadying breath. "It means he gave you the power to heal those he's made ill."

I hopped off the chair. "Then that's good. We need to hurry up and find out where Deren lives."

"Not so fast."

"But he's almost out of time."

Ms. Weever slowly stood. "Whatever 'gift' he gave you came at a price. We don't know what that price is."

"I don't care. Deren's my friend. If I can save him, then I want to. I have to. It's not fair that he became a part of this."

"Mia."

"I know life isn't fair, but I can make this fair again."

"Miss Evers," she said, "I won't help you save him without knowing the consequences."

"None of the consequences matter."

"I refuse to be a part of something neither of us fully understand. If you discover the price is more than you can bear, I won't take responsibility for allowing that to happen. Do I make myself clear?"

I had half a mind to tell her I wasn't interested in listening to her anymore. How did she not care about Deren and what little time he had left before the demon took his life? "No."

She opened her mouth to speak. She did a double-take. "There's a safer way to save your friend if you'd slow down and listen."

"Why should I believe you want to save him?"

"Because Deren is someone else's baby boy." Her eyes watered.

Okay, that gave me pause. I believed her. "Then what is it?" I stood there with the mug on the desk and held it in my hands.

Ms. Weever set her mug down and browsed the rows of books sitting opposite the doorway. "Since you haven't struck a complete bargain, you should be able to do it." She followed her finger as she read the titles, tucked a choice book under her arm, and kept searching.

"Able to do what?"

"Send Allosyr to the Light. Be rid of him for good."

"I thought you said you didn't know how to do that."

"I don't. You're going to find out." She plucked two more books from the shelf and tucked them with the first.

"How?"

"Research." She picked up two more books and, sandwiching them all together, dropped them on the desk with a thud, making my cocoa ripple.

All the covers were worn, the folds frayed, and corners bent. They had to be hundreds of years old. "You expect me to read all those?"

"What did you say about not being a child anymore?"

I scowled at her.

"Miss Evers, if I could shelter you from this situation, I would. However, you and other innocent lives are paying for my stupidity. It is up to you, now, to fix the situation and restore balance. I don't want to hear any whining about how you're too young or scared to do this. I don't care. You're a Dark. You're the only one with the proper alignment who can face demons."

I was scared of facing Allosyr again. I refused to whine about it. I wouldn't give him the satisfaction. "Why can't you do it?"

She pushed the books over. "One, I've already told you I can't seem to find the information. Our favorite demon is meddling with my mind. I'm sure of that now. Remember how I kept reacting oddly every time you brought up the subject of him and the sick students? And two, even if I could, I wouldn't. The price would be too high."

"What do you mean?"

Ms. Weever took a sip of cocoa and sat, her hands looking like they were hugging the mug for comfort. "There are dire consequences both ways for breaking a bargain as powerful as one between a human and demon. I should be all noble and say I'm willing to pay the price for all the harm my stupidity has caused. The truth is I'm too selfish. I want to remain whole."

"So if you banished the demon yourself, something bad'll happen to you?"

"It would break the bargain and I'd be free of it. However, it'd also break my mind. I could do what you've done today at any time, but I'm unwilling to pay the price."

"What does it mean to break your mind?"

Her gaze grew distant. "My mentor ruthlessly described all the details. She thought she was educating and motivating us to never strike a bargain. I'd thought so, too, at the time." She turned her gaze to me. "A broken mind is not a pretty thing. You wouldn't be you anymore. Your thoughts would be scattered like seeds in the wind. You could see your mother and not recognize her. You could walk over to a swing set and, instead of using them for their intended purpose, start trying to eat the chains or use your clothes to dress it up like a doll. Nothing you thought, said, or did would make sense anymore. You'd be alive, but not yourself or aware of much of anything to get any enjoyment out of life. You'd be broken."

"Like gone crazy?" It sounded worse than dying.

"Yes."

"Can anyone be cured of it?"

"There are theories pointing to both answers. Thankfully, there haven't been enough fools throughout history to establish a definitive answer. I won't help you find out."

I sat there, absorbing the information. Everything Ms. Weever said made sense. I believed it. There was one last puzzle piece I was missing. "Why did you save me?"

"Considering his meddling, it shouldn't have been possible. I should've been blocked from interfering, especially if he'd been planning to strike a bargain with you. Maybe he was distracted while he unraveled your circle, or maybe when he transformed from monster to human. Maybe he never intended to strike a bargain with you."

"I'm pretty sure he did. He wasn't happy when you

showed up."

She nodded. "He's very old and clever. For every one move we plan, he's already planned twenty moves. Even if you or I surprise him in some way, he'll think of ways to twist things to his advantage. However, I hope to surprise him with you learning how to send him to the Light before he suspects such a move."

"You really think I can?"

"I'm not arrogant enough to wholly believe you'll get one over on him, but I'm willing to try."

"What happens if I fail?"

"Nothing. Your mind won't break while your incomplete bargain and everything else remains in place. Nothing bad will happen to you and nothing will get fixed. However, all that won't matter once you learn how to send him to the Light."

"You seem so confident that it's possible."

"I could sound all dramatic and say no one's sent a demon to the Light in over a thousand years. For all I know, someone in some far corner of the world did it yesterday like it was nothing. The world is too big a place to paint an accurate picture. All I know is it's possible. And I know that information is being hidden from me. The power to permanently fix this and save your friend is in your hands, now."

I gave the stack of cruddy old books a baleful look. They didn't look anywhere near as fun to read as my Yuna books. There weren't even any pictures on the cover or spines. These were old people books. As boring as they probably were, I'd suffer through them if it meant saving Deren.

Ms. Weever finished the rest of her herb-infused cocoa. "Hurry up and finish your drink. We need to get you home."

Home? As good as curling up in my bed and forgetting about this day sounded, there were other more important things. "What about Deren?"

She brought a ley line vine close to her ear and stopped. "I know your trust in me is shaky right now, but trust me on this, if nothing else. Allosyr won't let him die now that he's struck an incomplete bargain with you." Water trickled down the wall behind the rest of the vines. "He's given you some power. He wants you to use it. He wants you to go cure Deren so you can see for yourself the power is real. It'll only make it all the more tempting to go back to him for more and complete the bargain."

I folded my arms and held my chin high. "I won't strike a bargain with him. I refuse to."

"Yet he struck an incomplete one with you without you realizing it."

Guilt burned in my chest again and my chin dropped a little.

"Give yourself time to recover over the weekend. I'll contact Deren's family and discuss our next course of action on Monday. Whatever action you take with this gift he gave you, he has something to gain out of it, or he would have never given it to you in the first place. And if you need a distraction, start practicing a huge apology for the principal when he finds out about your failed attempt at banishing the demon."

"You're not going to tell him, are you?"

"Miss Evers, we're both in trouble. You got sucked into the demon realm and I destroyed school property. On top of that, we're Darks. We've both got a lot of explaining to do."

Chapter 22

It took a couple of tries to reach Mom. When she finally picked up the vine, her congested voice answered. Ms. Weever, her mascara lines cleaned off, gave me a curious look as both adults exchanged maybe four sentences. The conversation felt like it lasted ages. Ms. Weever got a peek into the world I didn't want anyone to see.

The vine sprung back to the wall and curled up in its place above our heads. "Is your mother okay?"

I wanted to run out of the room. "She's sick." Maybe it sounded like a cold.

Ms. Weever gazed levelly at me. "You've expressed your outrage over me lying to you. Granted I have a demon meddling with my mind. You don't. I would appreciate the same honesty."

I looked away, chin up, hair blocking my peripheral. "I don't want to talk about it."

"That's fine. Next time just say so." Ms. Weever lowered her voice. "Do you feel safe at home?"

That was a strange question. "Yeah. There aren't any demons or ghosts bothering me there."

"I meant with the living. Do you feel safe among them?"

"Yeah. Things are just—" My thoughts curled back in on themselves, clamping my mouth closed. I set my mug on the desk and studied the closed door.

"It's fine. Say no more. Let's get you ready for your mother."

***

Waiting under a campus lamp with Ms. Weever was awkward. Instead of feeling scared or nervous in her presence, I felt just plain awkward. She knew of things she wasn't supposed to. She'd asked questions about things she wasn't supposed to. And now I knew she knew I didn't have a normal home life. I would've traded her for Gwen's company.

I was one of a handful of students left, all of us waiting for the same thing. At one point, I let Ms. Weever know she didn't have to wait with me. She said something about it being illegal to leave students unsupervised. There were other teachers present. I didn't press the issue.

Footsteps hurried closer and shuffled to a stop right behind me. Miss Wren, wearing her pretty white dress and silver shawl, looked like her eyes were about to shoot lightning in my tutor's direction. She crossed her arms over her chest and spoke in Ms. Weever's ear. "What happened to my door?"

Ms. Weever calmly faced Miss Wren. "I will tell you after the students have all been picked up."

"My classroom stinks like sulfur. I know it was you."

"You are correct. We'll discuss this in private."

Without making a sound, I inched my way around so Ms. Weever stood between me and Miss Wren, whose glare darted to me. I shouldn't have been surprised when it didn't soften. My heart rebounded off my spine, hip bones, and one knee on the way down to my feet. There was the look I'd known to anticipate all this time. There was the look I'd dared hope never to see on her face.

Taking a deep breath, Miss Wren leaned closer, only to be stopped by Ms. Weever's hand grabbing her upper arm. Miss Wren flinched so hard, her shawl slid off one shoulder.

"Don't," Ms. Weever whispered. "She tried to do the right thing. She's been through enough today."

Miss Wren's eyes bounced between the both of us.

A car rounded the loop and stopped before me, kicking up an embarrassing amount of dust. It made the three of us cough. Our car was old, the hovering charm wearing out. Instead of effortlessly keeping the car afloat, the charm strained, constantly kicking up dust. I darted into the back and curled up in the seat's crux and door, scrunched low so I couldn't see out. Bela greeted me from her car seat. I gave her a small wave.

Mom pulled out onto the main road and the old Fire engine made the car vibrate so bad that I had to sit up straight to make my brain stop rattling against the door. Mom's mismatched eyes met mine in the vibrating rearview mirror. The image was too blurry to make out what was on her mind. I did the safe thing and stayed quiet.

"Did you have fun today?"

Hi, Mom. I got sucked into the demon realm after trying to banish one. Now I've struck an incomplete bargain with it and I don't know the consequences. How was your day? "Yeah," I said as convincingly as I could manage. "There was good food and games and stuff."

"Good. Did they like your song? I enjoyed listening to you practice it."

Memory of everyone watching us in the band room cropped up. "Yeah. I was so nervous. I thought I was gonna throw up." Hopefully, that was enough detail to keep her from wondering if anything else went on.

"Glad to hear. Really glad. You finally seem to be enjoying a normal life at this school."

After all this, I had to hide my alignment the most from the very person who urged me to hide it. "Yeah. Finally."

"Your father was home for a bit today. He made a nice steak dinner. There's plenty of leftovers. Are you hungry?"

My stomach growled at the thought of eating one of Dad's signature steaks. "Yeah." I was starving. Something about that herb-infused cocoa had made me starving. Maybe I needed the food so I wouldn't grow weaker and open myself up to the demon. "Lunch feels like forever ago." That much was true.

"They're a special cut, super tasty."

"Is Dad still home?"

Mom let out a sad sigh. "No, sorry, sweetie. I know you haven't seen him in a while. He told me to tell you he loves and misses you. He's been working hard. He got us both more books, though."

"I love and miss him, too. Please tell him thank you for the steak and books."

"I will, sweetie."

We rode the rest of the way home in silence. Stars dotted the sky so much that it looked like someone had spilled glitter, and then swirled and drew lines in it with their fingers. A smudge of pale light lined part of the eastern horizon—the glow of the Marohu, the capital city.

***

The steak was so good that I had seconds. Mom sat with me and got whatever I asked for as she watched me eat. Her company was welcomed and mostly comforting, especially after all I'd been through, but she moved too slowly for me to risk making small talk. I couldn't read her faraway expression either. Instead, I appreciated her quiet company and kissed her cheek when she ushered me to bed.

I changed into my pajamas and tucked myself into bed, my head sinking deep into my pillow. Eating all that food made me sleepy. I turned my forearm this way and that. To my relief, I couldn't see any lines.

I shifted, settling deeper under my blankets, and let sleep take me.

"There you are, Little One."

Letting out a startled yelp, I bolted upright.

Allosyr sat in a large, spiky chair at the foot of my bed, ankle propped up on one knee and hands steepled.

I sucked in a huge breath. "*Mom!*" I didn't care what she found out, didn't care what she saw or how she reacted. All I cared about was not being alone with the demon.

He popped a crooked grin, showing one fang. "Cry

for Mommy all you want. You're dreaming, child—perhaps you'd call this a nightmare. She can't hear you."

Tears blurred my vision. I took several deep breaths to get my emotions under control. I was in the presence of a demon. I couldn't afford to let fear control me. Sight of him set my hate off. I felt like I should sprout fangs and claws. I stayed perfectly human in the presence of the one being I feared and hated the most. I knew and believed I shouldn't let my hate fill me like this. I couldn't stop it.

I drew up a protective shield with a gesture and slid to my feet. Hate wreathed me, making my skin hot. Allosyr sat there, completely relaxed and unbothered. I took one deep breath after another, trying to fill myself with cold calm. The way he smiled so smugly made it impossible to stop clenching my teeth.

"Such a brave child. Your age belies your true grit. You're going to be quite the force one day."

"What do you want?" I felt so heavy, like there'd be dents in the floor where I stood.

"What's the hurry? You've only begun to dream."

"You're stealing my energy again. Tell me what you want and then go away."

"Ah, dreams don't work that way for me. This isn't the demon realm."

"Then how are you here?"

He pointed to my forearm. "We're inseparable now. Your eyes and ears are now mine. I can drop in as I please."

My stomach did a flop as I tucked my arm at my side. "So you heard everything Ms. Weever and I talked about in her office?"

His smile waned enough to reveal his annoyance. "No, but I'm sure you both discussed how evil and cruel I am, and other such nonsense."

I slowly let out a sigh of relief. I would have to learn the protection spells if I was going to keep my special hunt a secret. "Why are you bothering me in my dreams?"

"I've given you a gift. Don't you wish to know how to use the power?"

"You're not going to kill D—my friend." Oh, that was close. "I know you won't. You want me to use the power you gave me."

Allosyr examined his nails. "Perhaps. Maybe I'll give you the time to save him, or maybe not." He looked at me. "You hardly know him. Why do you care so much if he lives or dies?"

I like your hair. It's pretty.

He'd been nice to me no matter how I treated him. I didn't deserve his kindness. "Because he was nice to me. He's my friend."

"Yet he doesn't know about your true alignment. You lied to him. That's not being a good friend now, is it?"

Guilt burned in my chest with a sting my hate lacked. He was right. Friends didn't lie to each other. Maybe I'd tell him the truth after all this.

"*Deren* aside, don't forget, there's one other classmate of yours that's just as ill. And I know his name, too."

I gave him a blank stare. Which classmate?

"Remember the day you got a peek at a sleeping child in the nurse's office?"

Memory of the nurse singing a healing song to a

boy flashed through my mind. A darkness had hovered over him. The nurse hadn't liked it when she'd found out about my alignment.

"Yes, that one. You've got two classmates to save. I might kill the other, just to make sure you know this isn't some child's game you're playing. Bad things happen to good people. What are you willing to do to protect innocent lives?"

My hate boiled again, searing away the guilt in my chest. "Why would you do such a thing?"

Allosyr tilted his head, popping me a crooked smile. "Don't you want to know how your gift works?"

If he wouldn't answer my question, then fine. I'd probably get more information on my fake gift anyway. "Ms. Weever said it'd come with a price."

"Oh, it does, a most ingenious one, if I may say so."

"I don't know what that means."

"The word ingenious, or the whole price thing?"

I started to say something, but stopped. The whole price thing didn't make any sense. No one had yet to mention any money. "Both."

Allosyr pushed off the armrests and the chair vanished. Clasping his hands behind his back, he stood before me, a tall, wiry man with a mane of golden hair and blue eyes tinted red. He looked like a rich businessman.

I stood my ground with only a scrap of fear buried under a mountain of open hate.

"I'll try to explain this as plainly as possible. I've given you a power with a twist I'm most pleased with. You have the power to heal the sickness I've spread. All you have to do is place your hand on the sick person and will the sickness out of his or her body."

"That's it?" That was, like, really easy.

"Only the half of it. The twist is you must will the sickness out of that person and into yourself."

I felt my face pale. "You mean I have to make myself sick instead?"

"Yes, you must take the sickness upon yourself, but you have a choice. Keep the sickness and eventually die from it, or release the sickness into a new victim and that person will eventually die instead."

"That's—"

"Not fair?" He raised both eyebrows. "You have so much to learn about the way the world works. So, what will you choose? Let your supposed friend die? A noble death for yourself? Or transfer the sickness to some random soul who means nothing to you? Your choice."

My eyes stung. I took a few deep breaths to get my emotions—minus the hate—under control. "You don't care if I die either?"

He studied me a long moment, as if carefully picking his next words. "You're a very interesting person. It'd be a sad waste to see you go, yet your death would still benefit me. Besides, there are a lot of interesting people in the world. I need only wait for another to open themselves up to me like you have."

Misery and heartbreak tried to swallow me. I latched onto my hate. "Take the power back."

"No. It's far—"

"I don't want it. I'm not using it."

"Don't be hasty with that decision. I'm in no rush. The more you learn about the power I've given you, the more likely you'll complete the bargain with me."

"No, I won't." I sounded childish. I didn't care.

"I'll find a way to beat you."

He raised an amused eyebrow. "Oh, child, you have no idea how many times mortals have told me that. By all means, try. I'll take great pleasure in watching you fail."

I'll find a way. I swear it. I didn't say the thoughts out loud, though. Not only would they be childish, he wouldn't believe me.

"Even if you do find a way, the odds are against you." He dropped to all-fours and his hair and face turned black, shadowed. "You're young and inexperienced." At first, I thought he was taking a deep breath as his shoulders rose. He was growing. Claws spiked out of his darkened fingertips. "I'm hundreds of years your senior and have been down this path before." He took a deep breath and swelled into the four-legged demon shape, hunched inside my room. The top of my head barely reached his chin. An oval-shaped head loomed over me, swallowing what little brightness my nightlight gave off.

I backed up, thumping into the wall. I braced myself against it as fear melted my rage.

Even if you do find a way, you lack the balance and power. Brace yourself for disappointment. A giant paw with claws bigger than my fingers rose over me. I held a hand up as I concentrated on my protective shield. It shimmered gold. *The next move is yours, Mia Evers. Choose wisely.*

The paw came down, passing through my shield as if it weren't there. I swiped at it as it suddenly got harder to breathe.

Something plopped on the floor. I sat up in bed, gasping for air. I brushed hair out of my face. I was awake. My nightlight shone next to the song stone with its gentle orange glow. I'd sent my pillow on a trip to my closet. It lay in an unceremonious heap, half in orange light, half a lumpy shadow.

No demons were present. No warning crawling up my spine. My shag rug had no dents where I'd stood in my dream. It was a tidy carpet of pink threads sticking up like grass.

Taking one last deep breath, I fought the urge to curl up in a ball under my blankets and hide there until the sun came up. Instead, I slid off the bed and retrieved my pillow, dusting off the underside for good measure.

That nightmare had felt so real. I half expected to see Allosyr's human form when I turned around. I was alone. Hugging my pillow, I tiptoed to my door and peered into the darkened house. Silvery moonlight poured in through the kitchen window, lighting up the sink and island stove. I chanced stepping farther out to discover my parents' bedroom door stood closed, barring me from them.

I wanted to curl up between them, take a break from dealing with all this Dark stuff alone. I hadn't slept with them in years, not even during storm season.

Knowing what anger and fear my intrusion would stir up, I backed into my room and closed the door. Setting my pillow back where it belonged, I grabbed an extra blanket from the closet and used that to wrap a few stuffed animals in it. I tugged the bunny doll out by the ears so the rolled-up lump would look like it had a face and lay down next to the lump. I pressed my back up against it and tugged one corner so it'd feel like I had an arm wrapped around me.

My vision went blurry before I closed my eyes

again.

Chapter 23

We should've had Tuesday off. I felt like a zombie who hadn't fed in days when the bells chimed inside my clock, telling me it was time to get ready for school. The rolled-up blanket full of stuffed animals lay pressed against my back. The sensation had soothed me a little, but not enough to help me fall asleep. I'd kept worrying the demon would show right back up. Every creak and bump in the night got my heart pounding. Every rustle of the bushes against the house in the windy night made me sink deeper and deeper under the blankets, until exhaustion finally made me sleep.

I lay there for an extra minute before dragging myself out of bed, a fuzzy cloud behind my heavy eyelids.

***

The day seemed perfectly normal for the rest of the world. Mom prepared me breakfast, like always, the bus ride was noisy, as always, and the teachers awaited our arrival in their usual spots. I took my spot beside Gwen's bench, replaying my trip to the demon realm over and over in my head, until Gwen showed up and sat in her usual seat between the five of us. Sussi and the others had been kind enough to leave me alone and talk amongst themselves. Gwen took one judgmental look at me.

"Where'd you go yesterday?"

Wouldn't you like to know? "I couldn't stop getting sick."

"Your weird tutor disappeared, too."

"She called home and made sure my mom got me."

Gwen popped a mischievous smile.

Isn't that an interesting expression?

I choked on a scream as I shot to my feet, kicking up sand, and cast my protective shield. I backed into the sunlight, searching for the source of that horrible, familiar voice. Gwen and the others stared as if I'd drawn a knife. Nothing dark and unnatural accompanied any of the playing and chatting students or any of the observant teachers. Everything was normal—except me.

No one can hear me but you, child. Relax.

Allosyr's voice sounded like it came from behind my shoulder. I turned. There was nothing there.

We're inseparable now, remember? I hear what you hear. I see what you see.

My forearm itched. I scratched. Faint tattoo lines appeared. I froze.

This was real. The dream had been real. The trip to the demon realm was more than a bad memory. I mean, I knew it all had happened, but now it was finally sinking in. This was bad.

I forced my posture to relax. I might as well have asked a rock to tie itself in a knot. I stood up straight, rigid, unmoving.

"What's up with you?" Gwen said.

I shook my head. I didn't feel like coming up with a lie, much less tell the truth. I did a full-body flinch when Allosyr spoke again.

You'll get used to this in time, don't worry. You may even come to like it.

I clenched my fists as the girls giggled at me. I was making an idiot out of myself.

Anyway, that child knows something, he said. *Why don't you find out?*

"You are so weird, Mia," Gwen said.

"I didn't sleep well last night. I don't feel well."

"I hope you feel better soon," Chibya said, a genuine look of concern on her round face.

"Thanks. What did I miss yesterday?"

The other girls all said, "Nothing."

Gwen said, "A lot" at the same time. They all looked at her and she at them. She wore her wicked smile again.

"My mom was up late last night, talking on the vine, and boy did she sound angry, so I snuck downstairs and listened. The other school board members joined in on the conversation. Mom got so loud that Dad came downstairs and snapped at her to be quieter."

Her friends dutifully covered their mouths and giggled.

"What was the school board talking about?" Sussi asked.

"The principal was on the vine, too. They're not happy with him." Gwen looked at me. "They're really mad at your tutor. She did something during the talent show, and now she's in trouble." She looked around and leaned closer. "And so is the principal."

My face chilled as blood drained from my face. I swallowed the writhing lump in my throat. "What did they do?"

"I don't know. My mom did a lot of yelling. But all that's not the most interesting thing I found out." She waved us closer. The other three leaned in, creating a semicircle of faces. I stood my ground. "Ms. Weever is aligned with Dark."

I didn't know if I would throw up or pass out. It was happening again, like at all the other schools. This was the end of having friends.

The other girls gasped, their mouths hanging open. Gwen continued smiling at me, ignoring the other girls, who eventually turned. They cringed, scrunching closer to hide at Gwen's side.

She calmly stood and lowered her voice. "You lied to me about your alignment."

"I'm sorry." The words came out automatically. I wasn't sorry about the lie. I was sorry anyone found out the truth.

"Apology accepted." She probably sounded like her mom when she said that. No one else had been so calm about learning my true alignment. "I understand why you lied, and you know what?"

"What?" I said to the ground.

"You've been good so far, so I'll give you one last chance to be my friend again."

"I thought you hated Darks."

"Gwen, you can't," Nonawa said.

Gwen sharply waved a hand and shushed her. "I'll let you be my friend so long as you do one thing."

"You don't want her as a friend," Sussi said. "We don't either."

"Oh, yes you do," she said, "because if she wants her alignment to remain a secret, she'll do everything we tell her."

The bell rang and I bolted for homeroom. I didn't need to ask them to know what this meant. I was their puppet, their slave, at the mercy of whether or not they could keep a secret. If the others liked bossing me around, my alignment would stay secret a little longer. It was a matter of time. Secrets became everyone's business in a hurry in schools.

It doesn't have to be this way, Allosyr said as I headed for the back of the line for Miss Wren's room.

"What else can I do?" I said.

Give them the sickness. Put them in a situation where they can't tell you what to do. All you have to do is touch them and will the sickness into them.

I stood there in silence as students filed into crooked lines outside their respective classrooms. Several doubled back for forgotten lunch boxes and backpacks.

"That's harsher than anything they'd make me do."

The student in front of me turned around, brows furrowed.

Is it? One swift solution to stop many more bad things from happening. How many mean things will that girl make you do before you see I'm right?

"I'm not going to make them sick."

If you say so.

263

The itchiness in my arm went away. I took it as a sign that I was alone again. I kept my gaze behind my curtain of hair as we filed into class. A hand touched my shoulder and I flinched.

"Sorry to scare you," Miss Wren said. "Please hang back a moment. I want to talk with you before class starts."

My insides squirmed. I was in trouble. Adults talked with you in private only when you were in trouble. The rest of my classmates passed me in a slow funeral march. Gwen popped a smile I didn't like, and Sussi and the others gave me a wide berth.

Miss Wren instructed my classmates to get our vocabulary workbooks out, then held the door open with her fingertips. She crouched so we were eye level and her knees made rounded dents in her flowery skirt. "Mia, I wanted to apologize for being mad at you last night."

My brain took a moment to absorb her words. My reflection shone in her pale eyes—eyes full of apology.

"Ms. Weever told me what happened, what you tried to do. That was very brave of you. She also says smudge sticks and owl feathers are waiting for you on her desk. I don't know what she's talking about. She said that's all she could safely tell me, other than to remind you to keep your emotions in check at all times."

I nodded as I filed the information away.

"Mia, can you tell me more about what's going on?" Miss Wren's brows creased with worry.

My forearm had no tattoo lines for the moment. That didn't mean he wasn't listening. "I better not."

She considered my words for a moment. "All right.

May I give you a hug? I still feel bad about last night."

I stood there, torn between wanting to run away and cry, or accepting her kind gesture. "Okay."

Slender arms wrapped around and pulled me into a gentle hug. Friendly, compassionate human contact. My brain drew a blank on how to react, so I defaulted by standing there, arms hanging at my sides.

Before I could build the courage to hug back, she let go and straightened up. "You both give me the impression that something serious is going on. If I can help in any, let me know." She opened the door.

A thought crossed my mind. "May I go get what Ms. Weever left me?"

"Right now?"

"Yeah."

Miss Wren ordered a few students back in their seats and to stop using Air magic to mess with a girl's hair. She waved me inside. I followed her to her desk, where she filled out a hall pass for me. "Come back quickly."

"Yes, ma'am." I hurried off.

"Walk."

Okay, walked. Once I was back outside the classroom, I took off running and didn't stop until I was inside the main office. I reached Ms. Weever's office, which was closed. I wrapped my hand around the knob.

"Miss Evers, I need to see you in my office." The principal stood in the hallway, hands on his narrow hips.

I inwardly groaned. Despite the positive talk this morning, it didn't wipe away a lifetime of being in trouble. "May I get something from Ms. Weever's office first?"

"You have no reason to go in there."

I kept my hand on the knob. "She left something for me."

"And how do I know you're not lying about that?"

My mouth fell slightly ajar. Had she not told him? I took his reddening face as a warning not to press the subject. My fingers slid off the knob and I followed him. He took his spot at his huge L-shaped desk, which made his short frame look smaller, and I sat opposite him, my chin barely higher than the desktop.

"Why's her door closed?"

"She won't be tutoring you anymore." He interlaced his fingers and set his elbows on the desk. "We need to talk about yesterday."

"I'm sorry. I didn't mean to cause trouble." Tears stung my eyes. I focused on my breathing as I put the strap of my shoulder bag in a death grip.

Mr. Redd's glare might as well have been chiseled from red stone. He didn't look in the least bit sympathetic. "You took off without telling anyone where you were going, performed Dark magic you had no permission to do, put yourself in a situation where Ms. Weever had to destroy school property to rescue you, and, if I understand correctly, potentially put the rest of the school in danger."

And now I felt the size of an ant. "I'm sorry."

"I understand this isn't what you intended, but you're a Dark. You can't run around and be irresponsible with your alignment."

"I'm sorry."

"I accepted you into Toolena Mesa because I wanted to prove others wrong about those with your alignment. And now you've gone and done something

266

that could very well prove me wrong."

"I'm sorry."

"Stop apologizing. That won't fix this." He paused, probably to see if I'd be dumb enough to apologize again. "I could easily expel you right now. The state would fully back the reasoning."

My throat tightened. "I'll just go then." His stern voice stopped me before I could slide off the chair.

"You sit right back down. You are not dismissed, nor did I say you were expelled. I only said that because I want you to understand the severity of your bad decisions."

Part of me felt relieved that my family and I wouldn't have to pack up and move again. Mom would get super upset, and Dad super angry. I wasn't ready to go through all that again so soon. However, part of me felt disappointed. Expulsion meant I wouldn't have to deal with Gwen and her friends.

"Part of a good education is learning from mistakes. You won't find that anywhere on a teacher's curriculum, even though it's a part of any school's daily life. Yesterday you made a big mistake. Now it's time for you to learn from it. Do you think you can do that?"

I nodded, not trusting myself to do anything but cry if I opened my mouth.

"Good. This is your last warning. I'll have no choice but to terminate your enrollment if you step out of line again, do you understand?"

"I understand."

"Good. Now get back to class."

I didn't move. This wasn't how these conversations ever ended. "What are you going to tell my parents?"

The redness in his face faded. He shifted in his

seat. "How about this? As a show of good faith, I won't tell them anything. You be the good Dark I know you can be and this little mess can stay between you and me. Part of this means staying on top of your grades, too. So, if you can behave and keep your grades up, this can all be a thing of the past. Sound good?"

My mouth fell ajar and this time tears of relief stung my eyes. No one had ever done such a thing for me. It was so strange—wait, why was I questioning something good happening to me? "Yes. Thank you. I promise to make you proud."

He slowly nodded.

I hurried out of his office, tears blurring my vision. I wiped my eyes with a forearm and nearly reached the exit when Nurse Kor stepped in my path. She wrung her hands together and worry lines creased her brow.

"Mia, I need to talk with you," she whispered.

Another adult needed to talk to me? Why couldn't they leave me alone already? I got that I'd messed up. I'd already decided not to do that again.

"It's about Deren. Hurry up." She waved me inside her office.

I did as I was told. Nurse Kor shut and locked the door, and vines crept up the frame, covering any gaps. The nurse stood there, framed by the writhing vines, looking every bit like an elf with her fair complexion and a white flower in her hair. She stood a healthy distance away from me.

"Lyra—I mean Ms. Weever—called me last night and told me everything she could, including that you can heal those two sick boys."

How many people had Ms. Weever talked to last night? Who had she talked to? "I can."

"She said there will be unwanted consequences."

"I know what they are," I said, my heart writhing its way into my throat.

"Please tell me you still want to save them. They're just children. They don't deserve this."

"I know. I want to."

She pressed a hand to her chest. "Good. Are you up for a trip to the hospital?"

I stood there in silence. "The hospital?" While Deren had been out sick, I'd imagined him lying in bed at home, not in some giant building with white walls with room after room of sick, injured, dead, or dying people. I barely remembered going to one in Marohu the year Grandma died. I remembered Grandma's spirit rising from her body and kissing a crying Dad on the forehead before vanishing into the ceiling. The room had been a swirl of heartbreak and peace.

"I called both their parents. Neither boy is doing well."

I flinched when Allosyr spoke. *Yes, yes, time is almost out for them, child. The nurse speaks the truth.*

"What's wrong?" Nurse Kor asked.

Mentally brushing off the tingle down my spine, I said, "Don't I need a permission slip?"

"There's no time. I know it's breaking the rules, so I won't push you if you don't feel comfortable."

This was weird. Teachers and school staff were supposed to enforce the rules, not ask students to break them. And after Mr. Redd's warning... "What happens if anyone finds out?"

"I'll take full responsibility and make sure you don't get in more trouble." She gave my shoulder a reassuring squeeze.

It wasn't the squeeze that finally pushed me to agree. It was the desperate look in Nurse Kor's eyes, how they glistened with barely contained tears. She cared about the boys and wanted to do everything she could to save them. This wasn't about my alignment or how she felt towards me. It wasn't about me at all. It was about Deren and what's-his-face. A part of me felt guilty for not knowing his name all this time. "Let's go."

A hiccup of a cry escaped her lips. "Thank you."

As good as both our intentions were, there'd be consequences. "Can you tell Miss Wren where we're going and get something for me from Ms. Weever's office? Mr. Redd wouldn't let me get it earlier."

She hurried over to her desk and held a vine to one ear while holding out her free hand. She twisted her wrist this way and that, as if she were stretching it out. The vines covering the doorway receded and the door opened. One vine wrapped around the threshold and snaked its way down the hall.

"Hi, Miss Wren. I've got Mia with me." Her voice lowered. "We're making a special trip to the hospital. I'll try to make it as quick as possible...Thanks. If anyone asks, say what you feel is best. I don't care what happens so long as we save those boys...Thanks again. Bye." The vine sprung back into the leafy canopy. "Mia, when I tell you to, run into Ms. Weever's office and grab whatever you need. Make it quick." A vine spiraled up her leg and wrapped around her hand.

"What if I get caught?" This sounded like a terrible idea. It was too close to Mr. Redd's office for my liking.

She closed her eyes. "You won't. Trust me."

We both fell silent and the rustle of leaves and

270

snaking vines filled the silence. It sounded like the plants were whispering to us. Maybe they were. Since I wasn't Florakin, I had no clue what they said.

"Go."

Clutching the strap to my shoulder bag, I bolted into the hall on silent feet, hurrying alongside a vine that looked like an endless snake with leaves sticking out its back. The leaves angled towards me as I passed. The vine crept over to Mr. Redd's closed door, fanned out along the wall, and grew thickly over the doorknob. The nurse had trapped the principal in his own office.

I stuffed the sage and feathers in my bag and rejoined Nurse Kor in her office, the vines retreating. Keys in hand, she led me to the staff parking lot, her heart probably pounding as much as mine. The morning sun shone down as if it were just another happy, pleasant day.

I couldn't believe we were doing this. What was even more unbelievable was sitting in her car, sleek and shiny like Gwen's, but smaller. She cranked the keys and the engine rumbled to life with a deep purr. The car gently rose into the air. In the next moment, the car beside us looked like it was drifting backwards as we moved forwards. Her car glided through the air like a canoe cutting through still water. I would've enjoyed the experience more if I didn't half expect Mr. Redd to come storming out of the front office and yell at us to stop.

"Buckle up."

Doing as told, I sank deeper into the seat, just in case. We drifted over to the metal gates, which parted. Nurse Kor eased onto the main road, and then my back got pinned to the chair as she floored it. I clutched my seat and door for dear life as my school shrank in the side-view mirror.

This was crazy. We were going to get in so much trouble.

Chapter 24

Neither of us spoke the whole way there. Flat desert passed us in a blur, until we reached the Marohu suburbs. The town looked tidy with its exit ramps decorated with a tricolor wave pattern, tidy dirt roads, and store upon store placed in neat rows. We navigated a few blocks towards the tallest building marked with a big blue "H" encircled by a crashing wave.

We found a parking spot a ways back and navigated the maze of parked cars together, she clutching onto my hand. I didn't complain, though, torn between wanting her to let go or keep holding on.

Nurse Kor stopped by the reception desk, clinging to my hand. The building smelled like flowery soap and aloe. "Hello, we're here to see Deren Sevine and Carlo Nacinto."

So that's what the other boy's name was. We were here to save Deren and Carlo.

"Are the families expecting you?" A female voice said from behind the towering curved desk. I stood on my tiptoes. A mug of pens and a silver bell sat between me and the voice. A mop of curly red hair lay beyond them.

"I'm their school nurse. I've stopped by before. You can send me with an escort if you wish."

"That shouldn't be necessary."

"Have they moved rooms over the weekend?"

"Let me check." Water cascaded over stone as the building communication system linked to the reception desk. Nurse Kor tapped a foot. The receptionist confirmed that the boys hadn't been moved from someplace named the "I see you." The nurse led us down some long hallways lined with pretty, calming paintings, doctors and nurses bustling to and fro, fellow visitors heading one way or another, and the occasional patient getting escorted around in wheelchairs or on fluffy beds on wheels. How did anyone get around this place without getting lost?

We took one last turn down another hall when the smell of food met my nose. Nurse Kor led us away from the yummy scents. I adjusted the strap to my bag and stopped outside a door labeled ICU 109. ICU. Oh. Not "I see you." ICU. The letters stood for something.

Nurse Kor stared at the wooden door, her head bowed. She pressed a hand to the door and vines crept out from inside her sleeve, fanning out over the door, searching. She closed her eyes. "He's still alive. His parents and some other person are in there, too." The vines disappeared back into her sleeve and she opened her eyes. "Ready?"

I nodded.

She knocked and a woman's voice told us it was okay to come in. I felt like Yuna again, as the door swung inward, revealing the final lair where the big bad guy hid. Salt lamps dotted the room's corners, sunlight bled through the closed curtains, and a line of vines ran the room's length. Three adults stood over an oval-shaped bed placed in the center of a pool of water. Flower petals floated in the swirling water, which cast a faint green glow. In that bed lay Deren, asleep and dying.

Hurry up, child. The window of opportunity is fading fast, Allosyr said, not one drop of worry or urgency in his silky voice.

My feet carried me to the circle of water, not quite believing I had made it in time. Deren's parents looked up, the water's green glow making their faces look sickly. The mom's face was red and puffy from crying, and the dad had dark rings around his eyes. Both stood with their shoulders hunched, hair disheveled, and hands on the edge of the bed.

"Who's this?" the mother said in a dry voice.

"Mia Evers, one of Deren's classmates," Nurse Kor said.

"I'm his friend," I said, un-shouldering my bag. I wouldn't need anything in there. My tattooed forearm itched. This was it. I was about to find out if I could pull this off.

The mother's face lit up with recognition and a ghost of a smile. "Deren's talked about you. He really likes you." She turned to her son. "Hear that, baby? Your friend Mia is here to see you."

Deren lay inert, unresponsive.

"I don't mean to be rude," the man at the foot of

the bed said, "but how did she get permission to visit during school hours?" He wore a white robe with gold and silver scarves hanging down the front. The Light symbol, an open hand with rays of light shining from behind it, was embroidered into the front of his robes. A Light priest. He gave off a calm, peaceful energy despite his question.

"She got special permission," Nurse Kor said.

"I can heal Deren," I said. "I can save him."

Tucking his hands in opposite sleeves so the material looked like one endless loop, the priest said, "Dear child, I wish it were true." Lines of pain and exhaustion creased his wrinkled face. "I've been trying everything I know for over a week."

I turned to his parents. "May I at least try?"

They looked at each other and had a silent conversation all parents seemed to have, one that only they seemed to understand while children waited and watched. The mother nodded and they both backed away.

I hopped over the ring of water and held onto the handle that ran the length of the bed. Deren lay there, eyes closed, his face covered in sweat, and vines burrowed into various parts of his body, delivering life-saving fluids and nutrients. The sight creeped me out, like a splinter sticking out of a finger. This wasn't normal. I wanted to yank them out even though I knew they needed to be there. I took a calming breath and tentatively reached for his chest as my tattoo itched. This was weird trying to make myself place my hand on a boy's chest. Boys were just eww like that.

A wrinkly hand appeared over mine and guided me to Deren's chest. I would've recoiled if it weren't for the calm energy spreading into me. This priest had a power and energy I'd never felt before. It was so comforting. It felt like his feet were connected to the ground in a way that he'd never fall over no matter how hard anyone tried to push him. I felt braver, more confident. I could do this.

"Whether or not you succeed isn't the issue, child," he said. His pale eyes had a deep wisdom from having lived for so long. He knew so many things I didn't. "The fact that you're willing to try is noble." He pressed my hand to Deren's chest, which was hot. Too hot. Definitely too hot.

His chest rose and fell so fast I felt like I had to take a deep breath for him.

"Go ahead and do what you came to do."

I took a calming breath. This was it. The parents watched me from one corner of the room, a desperate hope in their eyes. They probably knew they shouldn't get their hopes up over some random kid showing up and making bold claims.

Nurse Kor placed a hand on my shoulder. "Go ahead, Mia. I know you can do this."

Nodding, I closed my eyes and concentrated, slowing my breathing until something like a can of worms writhed against my hand. Recoiling, I let out a yelp and clutched my hand to my chest as invisible worms squirmed against my palm.

"What is it?" Nurse Kor said.

"The sickness," I whispered. "It feels squirmy. It's so gross."

Exquisite, isn't it, dear child? Now, don't give up. You're getting there.

Taking another deep breath, I placed my hand back

on Deren's chest, and the Light priest's calm energy seeped back into me, helping me keep my focus when the squirming intensified. The sickness was everywhere, most strongly rooted in Deren's heart and lungs. In my mind, I saw white light in the shape of a body with a black mass strangling the chest. I reached for that black mass and pulled on it, willing it to my hand. The writhing slithered all over my hand and up my arm.

This was bad. This was dangerous. There was no other way.

I willed every last drop of blackness into my hand, and when nothing but white light filled the body, my hand jerked upwards of its own accord, throwing the priest's hand aside. I gulped in air and stood there with my hand raised. The Light priest stared at me in open awe.

And then he placed a hand on Deren's chest. He took a sharp intake of breath. "I can't believe it." He looked at me. "We did it." He turned to the parents. "He's healed. We did it."

The parents stood there in mute surprise, unmoving. "Are you sure?" the mom said.

Deren coughed.

"Deren!" both parents exclaimed and rushed to the bed.

"We're here, baby, we're here," the mom said. She wrapped her arms around her son.

A sob escaped Deren. He rubbed his eyes, finally opened them, and then cried as the three hugged each other.

I stepped back and stood beside Nurse Kor. I didn't feel well, my joints stiff. It wasn't anything I couldn't handle. The nurse hugged me and whispered, "good job" in my ear.

The Light priest beamed. "Well done, child. Together, we did what I thought was impossible. I can tell that took a lot out of you. Are you ready to go help the other boy?"

Carlo. There was still Carlo. I nodded even though part of me wanted to stick around to greet Deren and let him know he would be okay.

The three of us headed several doors down to Carlo's room. The priest knocked and entered without waiting to be greeted, and then stopped so quickly that I bumped into him.

"Oh, no," he said in a hoarse whisper.

I stepped around him as a doctor pulled a sheet over Carlo's face. Both parents bawled from the far side of the bed.

Oh, that's right, Allosyr said in mock surprise. *This isn't some fairytale story where nothing bad ever happens.*

The floor spun out from under my feet as the hospital room darkened.

I stared. I couldn't help it. Carlo would wake up, tear the sheet off his face and tell us he was only joking about dying. It was a bad joke, but at least it would only be a joke. The medical assistant mutely stood by, downcast gaze bouncing between the lump under the sheet and the sobbing parents. She shuffled closer to the parents, keeping a respectable distance as she clutched a clipboard to her chest.

The Light priest gently guided me back out of the room and closed the door. His calm energy grew heavy with sorrow. I needed to sit down. I stood before him, waiting for him, someone, anyone, to tell me what to do.

"I'm so sorry, child," he said in a humble whisper. "Please let me know if I can do anything for you."

I nodded, my mind going blank. Carlo would wake up any moment. He wasn't old, like Grandma had been.

"Thank you, Sanctus...?" Nurse Kor said, her tone unsure.

"Bylan. I'm Sanctus Bylan, Light priest out of the Order of Leo." The adults shook hands, and then Bylan turned to me. "You performed a miracle today, child. What's your name?"

Questions. I could answer questions. "Mia. Mia Evers."

"Pretty. What's your alignment?"

That was a question I didn't want to answer.

"The opposite of yours, Sanctus Bylan," Nurse Kor said in a low voice.

His watery eyes locked on me. His flash of fear calmed into an unreadable mold of wrinkles zigzagging across his forehead. His hands disappeared into his sleeves as energy gently prodded me like a lazy breeze washing over my skin.

To my great amazement, a hint of a smile twitched a corner of his mouth. "Just like the olden days. Why hadn't I thought of that before?" He let out a small laugh. "Go see Deren, child. Focus on our success with him. I'll handle what transpired with the less fortunate."

I didn't know what transpired meant. "Yes, Sanctus Bylan," I said, using his formal title. I knew all the rules on how to speak to and behave around a Light priest. Now that Deren was no longer in danger of dying and Nurse Kor's etiquette had kicked in, years of schooling finally kicked in as well. "Go with the Light."

"You, too, dear child." Bylan disappeared into Carlo's room.

A rope of blackness snaked out of the room and collected in the hallway. The black mass sank to the floor and reshaped into a man in a suit leaning against the wall. Color filled in blonde hair, pale skin, and blue eyes with a hint of red. Tilting his head back, Allosyr took a deep breath and exhaled with a sigh. "Ah, what a lovely boost of energy."

"You!" I tried to shove him. My arms passed right through and thumped against the wall. My arms felt like I'd plunged them into an icebox. Gasping, I recoiled.

"Mia, what's wrong?" Nurse Kor said, guiding me away from the demon. "It's really cold all of a sudden."

"It's him," I said, pointing. Allosyr popped a one-fang grin.

The nurse stiffened. Fingertips dug into my shoulders. "Where?"

"Only you can see me, Little One," Allosyr said. "Point all you want. Anyone who isn't a Dark will only feel a chill crawling up their spine."

"Why are you here now? What do you want?"

"A moment of your time. Is that so much to ask?"

I spoke over my shoulder. "I need a minute. You don't need to stay."

"Are you sure?" She sounded like she was only trying to be polite. Her fingers dug a little deeper, making me wince.

When she realized I was saying "yes" she bolted for Deren's room.

I faced the demon, who watched Nurse Kor slip into ICU 109.

He smirked. "A loyal ally, that one," he said. "She left your side without so much as a moment's hesitation."

"What do you want?" Better to get to the point than let him eat up precious time. Without Deren or Carlo to worry about anymore, I wasn't sure whose time was being wasted. I didn't want to find out the hard way.

"I gave you a name, you know."

I thought of a better name I'd gotten in trouble with my dad for repeating at school. However, Allosyr would probably eat up more time if I didn't go along with what he wanted. "What do you want, Allosyr?"

"That's better, Little One." Pushing off the wall with his back, he stood up straight. "As for what I want, it's simple. Now that you've seen the price of hesitating to use my gift, I want to revisit completing the bargain between us."

"No," I said.

"Are you sure that's wise?"

"I don't want to end up like Ms. Weever."

"Do tell me how you plan to avoid completing your bargain with me for the rest of your life."

An invisible force tugged on my lips as my mind raced back to last night in Ms. Weever's office. Words pushed at the back of my throat, burned to get out. I pinched my lips shut. I tried to turn away, willed myself to move, to raise my arms, turn my head—anything, but —wait. I was moving. Slowly. Very slowly. Allosyr wasn't getting this information out of me.

I tensed my entire body and then willed myself to make one explosive movement. At first, my limbs continued their slow motion. And then freedom. I stumbled towards Deren's room. I hurried over to my bag and dug out a sage bundle. Everyone, including Deren, looked at me. I snatched the lighter by the incense sticks sitting in the corner. It took a few tries before the gray bundle gave off smoke. I scratched out more sparks until I had a little torch, then rushed back into the hallway.

Allosyr stood by the door, hands in his pockets. He recoiled when I stuck the burning bundle under his nose. He bared his fangs and the skin on his hands turned black as his claws extended.

"My final answer is no. I'm never going to say yes, so don't bother asking ever again. Now go away." I waved the bundle in his face.

He swiped at it. His clawed hand passed through and snuffed out the fire. A coldness swept through my hand. Smoke billowed out of the blackened end and the demon kept his distance, hands raised. "I've been at this game for far longer than you, child. I can assure you this isn't your final answer."

"Go away." I swung the bundle at him as if it were a sword. His arms relaxed at his sides as the bundle swung through his chest.

"Fiiiine, fine." Wherever the smoke touched, his body disappeared.

I waved the bundle as if it were an eraser and he the chalkboard. Soon I stood in a cloud of smoke that faintly smelled of tobacco, and no demon in sight. Some staff members were further down the hall, all staring at me.

I returned to Deren's room. Whatever those people were thinking, I wouldn't stick around to find out. Of course, entering the room caused a new set of people to stare at me. At least they were oblivious to what'd gone on in the hallway.

Deren's face lit up and a ball of butterflies took flight in my chest. He really was okay.

"Mia. Hi. What are you doing here?"

"Hi." A demon tried to kill you and I struck half a bargain with him to save your life. That wasn't entirely accurate, but that's what I wanted to blurt. "I figured out how to make you better."

"Oh."

"The Light priest helped her," his mom said, pinching his cheek.

Deren pushed her hand away. He had only two vines connected to him now. "Thank you so much. I feel so much better. I'm starving. What time is it?"

***

Deren's parents called the doctors in, a team of four that scanned with water, plants, their minds, and some wooden rod that was supposed to detect negative energy. I stood there with my white sage emitting a steady tendril of bitter smoke. I had half a mind to place the bundle in the corner with the incense. Holding onto it felt like the only way to keep Allosyr away.

The doctors scanned Deren repeatedly, unable to believe he was perfectly clean and healthy. The rod pointed towards me a few times and the lady holding it ended up pocketing it, assuming it needed to be recharged. Every time it pointed at me, it reminded me of how the sickness was in me now. I didn't know how long it'd take to make me as sick as Deren had been. I'd deal with it later. The baffled doctors finally removed the last two vines, bandaged Deren's arms, and released us to the cafeteria.

Deren and his family piled their plates with a

mound of food from the buffet. Nurse Kor and I served ourselves more reasonable portions, and then all five of us sat a few tables away from the window. The sun was too strong to sit in its rays. Palm tree trunks and a busy town lay on the other side of the glass.

Deren sat between his parents and almost literally buried his face in his food as he ate. His mom firmly told him to slow down and sit up, which he did. Pizza, tacos, cookies, and more steadily vanished.

I enjoyed my pair of pork tacos on corn tortillas. I'd put too much creamy jalapeño sauce on it and made my nose run. A return trip for a glass of milk doused the fire in my mouth. At least it all tasted good.

Deren pushed his plate away and leaned back in his chair, a satisfied smile on his face, framed by ears that stuck out too far. "That was good. I can't believe how much better I feel."

"I'm glad you feel better," I said. I didn't know whether to cry with relief, give Deren a big hug, or politely sit there. Carlo's death rolled around in the back of my mind.

"Me too. What did I miss at school?"

I shrugged. "Lots of stuff. All Souls Day." I shrank lower in my chair.

His mom tried to keep a straight face as a smile appeared. "Honey, we should make some calls and let the rest of the family know the good news. Let's give these two lovebirds some space."

I gaped in abject horror and so did Deren. "*Mo-om*! She's not my girlfriend. That's gross."

All three adults laughed, taking their trays with them as they stood, leaving me and Deren alone. Nurse Kor seated herself a few tables away and took a book out of her purse. As casual as she looked, I didn't miss the vines peeking out of one sleeve. She was keeping an eye on us—or a vine was, as it were.

Deren and I sat together in awkward silence. He looked like he wanted to say something. Maybe he didn't know what to say or lacked the courage to say it. I figured it was my job to be brave after all this. "Be my friend, Deren. And I mean a real friend."

"What about Gwen?"

"I don't care anymore. I don't like her."

"Me neither," he said. "Let's definitely be friends."

I smiled a real, genuine smile.

He returned the smile, which then faded. His brows slowly drew together.

"What?"

"I don't know. We've agreed to something. Isn't there something we're supposed to do?"

"I dunno." When my mom and dad agreed on something, they kissed or hugged on it, two things I would totally never do with Deren, like ever. "Maybe we shake hands."

"Like spit and shake?"

"Spit where?"

He shrugged. "I've seen people spit in their hands and shake before."

"Eww, no." I couldn't decide which was grosser— kissing or a spit-filled handshake. Maybe the spit was some sort of way to make things official. It sounded important. "How about on our plates?"

"Spit on our plates and shake hands?"

I nodded.

"Okay, that sounds good."

I sat up straighter. "So, from this day forward, we

are friends no matter what, not even Gwen. Deal?" I held out my hand.

"Deal," he said with a nod. We both spat on our empty plates and shook hands. Even this kind of contact felt awkward, but it made the start of our friendship official. We quickly let go and sat back down. I wiped my hand on my dress.

Nurse Kor must've read something hilarious in her book. She burst out laughing.

"Now that we're friends, I need to tell you something," I said, my eyes back on my plate. "I'd ask you to promise not to hate me, but I don't think that's fair."

"Why would I hate you? I think you're the best person in the whole world—after my mom and dad, of course."

"Right." With nice parents like that, I couldn't blame him. I was more than happy that he liked me so much. It made me feel obligated to be honest.

"So, what is it?"

I took a deep breath. Hopefully, he wouldn't hate me. "I lied to you about my alignment."

"Oh." His smile vanished, and he looked more sad than anything. "I think I know what your real alignment is." He looked away as if he were the one with an uncomfortable secret. "When I was sick, I had a lot of nightmares. Every time there was this big black monster with one red eye. He said mean things and kept telling me you were on your way to save me."

"He did?" It was a stupid question to ask. I couldn't help it.

"Yeah." His chair wobbled as he swung his legs. "He told me you were the only one who could. I didn't know if he was telling the truth—he said a lot of things I knew were lies, but they hurt. When I saw you after I woke up, I knew what he said about you was true."

My stomach tightened. "What did he say?"

"You're a Dark, aren't you?"

A curtain of hair covered my face. "I'm sorry."

"I don't care. I'm your friend. I know what it feels like to be you because of Gwen. I don't like how that feels. I don't want you to feel that way. We're friends."

I chanced looking at him with one eye. "You mean it?"

He nodded. "My parents have taught me to treat others the way I want to be treated. I don't like how getting picked on feels, and I don't like how people treat me because Gwen thinks I'm a Dark. I'm nice to you because I like it when people are nice to me."

I wanted to hug Deren, but I kept myself seated, unable to take my gaze off my plate. "You're the best person in the world to me."

"After your parents, too?"

I loved my parents, but they acted differently than Deren's parents did. "Yeah. Same here." I wasn't sure if it was a lie. I wasn't ready to let him know about my parents yet. Maybe not ever.

***

Nurse Kor raced back to Toolena Mesa, explaining that the sooner we returned, the less likely she would get in trouble. I didn't see the principal standing near the parking lot or on any sidewalks as the nurse escorted me back to my classroom. She put a hand on my shoulder.

"Mia, I want to thank you for what you did today. You saved a person's life. Not everyone gets to say that, and not everyone is brave enough. You're a brave kid. You deal with strange, scary things I'm not brave enough to face."

"I wish more people understood I don't ask for these scary things to happen." The words came out before I could stop myself. I hadn't forgotten how quickly she'd run off after Allosyr showed up. Even his words hurt. I hadn't acknowledged their sting until now.

She pulled me into a hug. "I understand a lot better now. I'll help you deal with your Dark stuff in any way I can."

I leaned into her, my arms dead weights hanging at my sides. "What do I do about Carlo?" Guilt squirmed in my chest.

Her chest rose and fell with a sigh. "There's nothing you could've done."

"What if I'd gotten to him faster?"

She held me at arm's length. "You weren't the one in control of the situation. You didn't make him sick. You didn't make him die. You did everything you could. Don't let anyone tell you differently."

"I still feel bad."

"That's okay. Give yourself time." Her eyes watered and her voice tightened. "Death is never easy to deal with." She let out a weak laugh. "And I said that to a Dark. I think I'm finally beginning to understand your alignment."

I nodded, not trusting myself to hold it together if I opened my mouth.

Nurse Kor gave me one more hug and headed off, leaving me no choice but to return to class. I slipped inside. The whole class, including the teacher, turned to see who arrived. Keeping my face hidden behind my hair, I slid into my chair beside Gwen.

Mr. Thanin, our math teacher, carried on as normal, all the way until the lunch bell. Instead of heading straight for the cafeteria, I walked laps around the quad. I turned off the main path, parting from the rest of the sixth-grade procession. Gwen and her friends did the same. I should've known avoiding her wouldn't work. I veered towards the cafeteria, hoping to get lost in the crowd.

Here they come, Allosyr said.

So much for that idea. I stopped and faced the four of them. "What do you want?"

Gwen jutted out her chin. "Where were you for half the morning?"

"I'm not feeling well. I think I'm getting sick like Deren and Carlo." At least all that was true. I had achy joints.

"You don't look sick."

Holding up a hand, I took a step closer. "Want to find out the hard way? I'm trying to be nice by staying away."

All four of them stepped back, leery gazes on my hand.

Chibya gasped and pointed. "She has black marks on her arm. Look." The other three gasped.

Nonaya said, "Get away from us."

Gwen scowled. "You better stay away. You'll be dealing with my mom if you make any of us sick." She led the other three into the cafeteria.

For a moment there, I thought you would make her sick, Allosyr said from behind my shoulder.

I didn't bother trying to turn around. He wouldn't be there. And to be honest, the thought had crossed my mind. It would be so easy to do, so easy to go on with my days without her constantly going after me. "I told you I never will."

You don't sound as sure as before.

"You're wrong."

If you say so.

A series of urgent notes played from the bell tower atop the main office. All the students stopped and looked in the bell's direction. Those notes were our cue to head inside because of an oncoming dust storm. There were no walls of dust darkening the horizon, but that didn't mean they weren't there. Teachers blew their whistles and everyone scrambled to get inside, until teachers yelled at us to walk. Giggle-filled chatter filled the air as students returned to their respective homerooms. Miss Wren calmly ushered my class back inside, confusion lining her face. This wasn't a practice drill.

Everyone took their seats. Gwen scooted as far away from me as she could, snapping at the person next to her to move over, who did without question. Gwen took one look at the space between us and raised her hand. Miss Wren's gaze zeroed in on the outstretched arm. A chime that sounded like someone running their finger along the rim of a wine glass filled the air. Our teacher put a finger to her lips. Gwen pouted and jerked her arm down.

The water inside a glass globe rippled as Mr. Redd's voice rang loud and clear. "Today is a somber day for all of Toolena Mesa. We received word from Buckeye Hospital that we lost one of our students earlier today." His voice sounded detached, not at all remorseful. "He was a sixth grader named Carlo

Nacinto." Everyone looked at his empty desk. "We'll be releasing students as soon as the buses arrive. The district will have Light priests and counseling services for those who need help coping. School is canceled for tomorrow in observance of Carlo's passing. We'll have a memorial assembly the following day."

Gwen looked at me again and shot her arm back into the air.

Chapter 25

Thankfully, Mom was home when the bus dropped me off. I surprised her, though. She'd rushed out of the bedroom with an Air whip in one hand, ready to lash out as soon as I closed the door. One look at me and she lowered the wooden grip and dismissed the coiled rope of swirling air attached to it. It had looked like a pencil-thin tornado all looped up. An Air whip could slice through stuff like a regular sword.

Mom tossed the grip on her bed. "Why are you home so early?"

I told her only about Carlo, leaving out my trip to the hospital and back.

"Oh. I'm sorry to hear. Did you know him?"

I shook my head. "We have tomorrow off as well."

"I have to go into town to run errands tomorrow, so you'll have to come with me."

But I had research to do. I needed all the time I

could get before I got too sick to do anything except complete the bargain with Allosyr. "May I stay home instead?"

"You're too young, no."

I deflated. Then a thought struck me. It'd be a long shot. "May I go over a friend's house instead?"

Mom stared in blank surprise. "Did you say what I think you said?"

I was about to speak. I closed my mouth. This was new territory to me, too.

She took a step closer, a hint of joy lifting the features of a face so much like my own. "You asked to go over a friend's house?" I nodded. "Sure thing, sweetie. I'll want to meet the parents first."

A wave of fear passed through me. I probably had enough hair blocking my face for it to go unnoticed. If Mom met Deren's parents, would they brag about my trip to the hospital? And if they did, how would she react? Would she get mad at me for withholding such information, or would she gloss over my secrecy and be as proud as them? She'd grow suspicious if I backed out.

We ended up calling the school and Mom talked to Miss Wren, who gladly agreed to speak to Deren's parents on our behalf. She wasn't allowed to give out ley line coordinates, so we had to wait for her to call back with Deren's affirmation that I could come visit. We got an address and directions, and I hugged and kissed Mom before skipping off to my room to search in the books. No amount of worrying could stop me from being happy about hanging out with Deren tomorrow. I fanned out the stack of books on my bed, then paused at the sight of a piece of parchment sitting in the bottom of my bag. I uncurled the note.

Mia-

Light a smudge stick before reading any of these books and fill your workspace with its smoke. Demons can't penetrate a sage cloud.

Good luck.

-Ms. Weever

P.S. I hope you were able to save those two boys. They didn't deserve any of this.

I cracked open my window, snuck into the kitchen to use a burner to light my sage, and waved the smudge stick all over the room before tackling the first book.

***

I felt like a zombie when Mom called me to dinner. All the books were boring. From what I could understand, they were full of big words and went on and on about safety and warnings to be careful. Most of the content was about raising demons, their names, what kind of chaos each demon liked to sow, and incantations to bind them so they couldn't slip out of your control.

I slowed my skimming over that last part, hoping I could find a way to keep Allosyr in one spot and leave me alone. There were hundreds of names listed. A warning in big print told me not to speak any of them aloud without placing adequate protection around me first. It seemed rather silly, despite what I'd learned so far. However, all the names made my chest tighten every time I read one. Allosyr's name wasn't anywhere in there. Maybe because it wasn't his real name. Part of me was relieved it wasn't there. There was something creepy and powerful surrounding demon names. This book would get no argument out of me over carelessly saying any of them aloud. What was it with names anyway?

I jumped to the part about finding a demon's true name in a separate book and slammed it shut after a few pages. The book made it perfectly clear it was dangerous. Many Darks and Lights had died while compiling the recorded names. I would have to focus on figuring out how to banish a demon without a name.

Now if only these books had any information on banishing.

Mom had cooked some cheese crisps loaded with shredded chicken and diced vegetables. The tomatoes gave the meal a sweet tang, and the sour cream a creaminess that made it hard to stop eating until I was stuffed. Mom asked question after question about Deren —how we met, how we became friends, and what we liked to do together. It made our whole friendship sound an awful lot like we were going out. Which we weren't. Definitely weren't. That would be gross and weird.

The questions annoyed me. I politely continued to make small talk as we set aside a plate for Dad and cleaned up the kitchen. Mom was in a good mood. It would be smart to enjoy it. Once everything was dried and put away, we sat on opposite ends of the couch with our respective books. Mom turned on the song stone in the living room and read on the couch while Bela played with her alphabet blocks and pretended to make dinner for her stuffed animals.

I spent the rest of the evening resisting the urge to throw books across my room as they yielded no results. Maybe Ms. Weever had made a mistake and gave me the wrong ones. Wrong or not, they were all I had to work with and at least had good information, dry as it was. I ended up falling asleep inside a wreath of old books and dreamed of smacking Allosyr across the face with one, and then making him eat all the books while in human form. I was half disappointed, half relieved when all the books lay intact the next morning. I'd knocked a couple on the ground. I made my bed, stacked the old books, and grabbed my latest Yuna tale.

She and the satyr who'd found her celebrating with the unicorn king and his people had finally reached a huge old forest full of giant trees. The ground was so covered in gnarly roots that Yuna had to get off her horse and lead it by the reins. And Mom had to call me out to get ready for Deren's house just when a pack of evil-looking dryads caught them by surprise and dragged them off to their lair. I packed my shoulder bag full of books, sage, and homework, and snuck a peek at Dad sleeping in bed before the three of us headed out to the car, which roared to life with prideful fury, startling our neighbor's goats. If Dad hadn't been awake a moment ago, he had to be now.

"I know, I know," Mom said. "This hunk of metal is awful." She puttered down the dirt road, leaving a cloud of dust in our wake. Mom glanced at the parchment she'd scribbled directions on and took off down a perfectly straight dirt road.

The road looked so long, like it never would end until it reached the distant mountains. I hugged my bag to my chest as I counted the roads we passed, memorized the turns we took along a grid of seemingly endless roads occasionally interrupted by stop signs. It was only fifteen minutes away. Another week of school might as well have passed by the time we pulled into a cul-de-sac with three houses.

Mom double-checked her parchment and cut off the engine in front of the shabbiest-looking one. "We're here."

My heart pounded—not because of two big white dogs trotting to the car—but because I was about to hang out with a friend for the first time since Kindergarten. I was also about to find out if Deren's parents would make a big deal about what I did at the hospital.

The dogs' big black noses sniffed at my window and barked, sounding the alarm that an intruder was here. Bela whimpered. I didn't blame her. Those dogs were almost as big as me. A tall man with a gut rounding out his flannel shirt burst out of the house with a bow-legged gait. Mr. Sevine yelled at the dogs. They continued to bark and sniff, leaving trails of snot on the glass, until the dad prodded one dog with his knee and smacked the rump of the other. Both scooted out of his way, panting.

"Go on. Get, you two useless lumps." He sharply waved them off.

The dogs lowered their heads and trotted back towards the house, tails up like two great white horse manes.

"Sorry about that," Mr. Sevine said, straightening his cowboy hat. "I'd say their bark is worse than their bite, but they like to nip my ankles now and then, like I'm some stupid goat. They're not the brightest beasts. At least they're good at keeping burglars away."

Mom stepped out of the car as I eyeballed the dogs marking a patch of tall weeds. Bela whined about wanting to leave. Mom gently shushed her and plucked her from her booster seat. My door swung open and Mr. Sevine held it wide, letting the desert heat rush in. I politely slid out and shouldered my bag as I took a few deep breaths to let my lungs acclimate to the heat. "Good morning, Mr. Sevine."

"Mornin', Mia. Nice to see you again."

"When did you two meet?" Mom said. She rounded the car and shook his hand. "I'm Brecca Evers, by the way, and this is my daughter, Bela. Nice to meet you." Bela clung to her hand, suspiciously eyeing the corner of the house.

I tensed as Mr. Sevine's gaze bounced between the both of us. I silently willed him to stay quiet, or at least not to go into any specifics.

"Josua Sevine. It's a pleasure to meet you. We met only yesterday, but our son's been talkin' about her for ages." He popped a knowing smile.

Mom laughed.

My face heated more without the help of the desert. "Mom, it's not like that."

"My, you two are a spittin' image of each other, mismatched eyes and all. That is somethin'." Turning, he waved for us to follow. "Come on in."

Bela clutched Mom's hand as we followed Mr. Sevine inside. The outer metal door groaned for oil to smooth its hinges and the inner wood door was all scratched up. Black smudges lined the edge of the door where child and adult hands had touched it repeatedly for years without washing.

Mom cringed at the smudges and stopped. "I really should get going. I have a lot of errands to run and I don't want to force you to watch after my daughter for too long."

"Nonsense. It's no trouble at all. Besides, I can't let you go without at least giving you something to eat or drink first. It's a bit of a drive into town." He held the door wide open, revealing a cluttered, homey interior.

Mom hesitated, taking in the mess she'd never tolerate in our home. She touched my shoulder and guided us inside, steering me away from the dirty door.

Mr. Sevine popped a guilty grin. "Yeah, my wife has her hands full with me and our three boys. She does the best she can."

The four of us walked into a kitchen painted in warm colors and decorated in a rooster and chicken theme. This was where family gathered to smile, laugh, and share a good meal, and snuck unwanted vegetables to a patient dog hiding under the table.

The kitchen centered around a giant, round wood table with bark attached to the edges. The tabletop sat atop a twisted trunk. Roots spread and seamlessly disappeared into the stone floor. A seated Mrs. Sevine looked up from her newspaper.

"Mia. So good to see you again. Welcome to our home. Deren and his brothers are playing out back." Setting the paper down, she hurried over to my mom. "Hi, I'm Mara. It's wonderful to meet you." She hugged Mom, who went rigid a moment before returning it, patting Mrs. Sevine's back for good measure. Mara held her arms out for Bela, who hid behind Mom.

"It's nice to meet you, too. I don't mean to sound rude, but are you always this friendly to everyone who comes in your door?"

"More or less. You and your daughters are a special case, though. Come. Sit." She gestured to the table and waded over to a stone ice box. "What would you like to drink?"

Mom led me to the table. I sat while she remained standing. "I wasn't planning on getting comfy. I do have a lot to do."

"Then let me get you something for the road." She opened double doors, which gently rumbled with the grind of stone on stone, and a puff of chilled air stretched out into the kitchen and curled around her. "We have water, lemonade, apple juice, iced tea—"

"Water's fine, thank you," Mom said. "Bela, would you like some apple juice?" My sister shook her head.

"Mia, would you like some water?"

"Yes, please," I said. I didn't care what I got so long as Mom hurried up and left before any awkward questions popped up.

"What do you mean by 'special case?'" Mom asked.

And there was one of them.

Mrs. Sevine plucked a ceramic jug in the shape of a gaping rooster from the icebox. "Didn't she tell you?" And there was another one. Deren's mom poured two glasses full of water, topping two glasses off with a straw and lid.

Mom's voice sounded louder as her attention turned to me. "Tell me what?" Her tone grew dangerously annoyed.

I sat quietly, my curtain of hair getting caught in the bark. I wished the rest of the world would forget I was there. Why did Mr. Sevine have to invite Mom inside?

"Aww, it's nothing to be bashful about, honey," Mrs. Sevine said. "Brecca, your daughter saved our son's life yesterday." She set a tall glass in front of me and handed the other to Mom.

Mom accepted the glass. "I'm not sure I follow. All she told me was that a student died."

Mrs. Sevine's round face grew somber. "One did. Carlo Nacinto. They had the same illness. We got to know the parents a bit, and worried and cried together. Nice family. Real stoic. Life is so unfair sometimes. Deren had been sick for weeks. Carlo came down with the same illness as our son. His death was so sudden." She shook her head.

"I'm sorry to hear," Mom said. "This happened yesterday?"

"Yes. A Light priest had been doing everything he could think of for days. And then in pops Mia, unannounced. She and the priest did something, and a moment later, it was like Deren had never been sick. We had our son back just like that."

Condensation gathered on my untouched glass and the room grew hotter.

"What did you do?" Mom asked, shocked.

Mom and Mrs. Sevine studied me, their faces open with curiosity and eagerness for an answer. I mumbled something and they both took a step closer. My achy joints stiffened.

"Say that again?"

"I healed him," I said to my glass, keeping my mouth as closed as possible.

"How?"

"Took the bad stuff out." I kept the rest of the truth secret.

"Maybe the Light acted through her," Mrs. Sevine said. "Yesterday was nothing short of a miracle. Maybe she doesn't know. She did what the Light told her to. It works in such mysterious ways."

Keeping my eyes on my water, I watched Mom in my peripheral. She scrutinized me with furrowed brows. "That it does," she finally said. "Well, I better get going. Thank you for the water and it was nice to meet you, Mara. Mia, I expect you to be on your best behavior."

"Yes, Mom," I said.

"I'll have a treat for you when we get back." She kissed me on the top of my head and Mrs. Sevine saw her to the door.

As soon as the front door closed, a back door opened. In rushed three boys in an earthquake of stomping feet. Mrs. Sevine's face hardened as she crossed the living room. Her voice switched from sweet and motherly to furious. "That is *not* how you enter the house." The thundering and quaking stopped. "Go back outside and reenter like gentlemen."

"Yes, Mom," said three boys of varying ages. An unseen door opened again and three pairs of feet calmly clomped along a stone floor and into the kitchen. The first boy to enter was taller than me, gangly, and had a messy mop of dark hair. He looked old enough to be in high school. Mrs. Sevine swept his bangs aside as he walked by. The second boy was slightly shorter, just as gangly, and wore a cowboy hat like his dad's.

"Hat off inside." Mrs. Sevine prodded his shoulder and the boy snatched his hat off.

Bringing up the rear was Deren, ears sticking out farther than any of them. All three boys stopped at the sight of me. And once again, that ball of butterflies took off in my belly when our eyes met. It was such a weird feeling. I liked it.

"Who's that?" the boy holding the cowboy hat said.

The eldest elbowed him. "Dude, don't be rude."

"That's my friend, Mia," Deren said. He ran up and placed his hands on the table. They were covered in dirt. "Hey."

"Hey." My voice came out small.

The middle boy, maybe a year older than Deren, smirked. "Oo. Someone's got a girlfriend." Both his brothers shoved him as he laughed. "I'm going back outside." He helped himself to some water from the icebox before disappearing out the back door.

Mrs. Sevine set his cup in the sink. "That knucklehead was Silden. We're working on his manners, or lack thereof."

"It's okay." If he stayed outside for the rest of my visit, I'd have no problem with that.

"No, it's not," she said, sighing. "Anyway, this is my eldest son, Alden."

He politely nodded and turned to Deren. "You found a pretty one, Deren."

At the same time as I exclaimed, "I'm not his girlfriend!" Deren exclaimed, "She's not my girlfriend!"

"Why does everyone keep thinking she is? Jeez." Deren scowled.

Alden laughed and playfully punched him in the shoulder, then helped himself to some water his mother set on the table. "Cool story, bro."

"Alden," their mother said warningly.

"What?"

"You know your brother's too young for that stuff. Now, go wash up and tackle that homework you're pretending not to have."

"But I don't have any."

"Mhm," she said, giving him an unconvinced stare and putting her fists on her hips. "I wonder what Mrs. Edna would say if I gave her a call."

Alden's shoulders slumped. "Fiiine." He mumbled something about the situation not being fair as he trudged off.

Rolling her eyes, Mrs. Sevine approached the table and tousled Deren's hair. "Boys. Deren, go wash up."

"Yes, Mom." He zoomed off in typical hyper Deren fashion.

Mrs. Sevine watched him, a serene smile on her face. "There's the baby boy I've been missing all this time." She turned to me. "Mia, I can't thank you enough for what you and Sanctus Bylan did." Her eyes watered.

"You're welcome." I didn't know what else to say. Had Deren let them know about my alignment yet?

"Now, how come your mom didn't know?" She slid into the chair next to me and the scent of fresh spring water filled my nose.

Run. Hide. Get away from unwanted questions.

Now, now, Allosyr said from behind my shoulder, *don't be bashful. Look at how much good you've accomplished with the gift I've given you.*

I flinched. Of all the places I'd expected him to talk through our link, this wasn't one of them. Mrs. Sevine sat, brows furrowed, unaware that a demon had spoken. Maybe if she looked hard enough, she could sense him, too.

How could I be proud of saving Deren when so much darkness followed me everywhere?

"I don't want to talk about it."

"I don't understand."

Deren and Mr. Sevine joined us at the table. "What's wrong?" the father said.

"I was talking about yesterday and how thankful I am. She's clamming up about it for some reason. I figured she'd be super happy and proud."

The father's brows drew together.

"I think I know why," Deren said. He said, "Mia, want me to tell them for you?"

"Are you sure they won't hate me?"

"They're not like that." He turned back to his parents. "Mom, Dad, Mia's aligned with Dark."

I swallowed the lump in my throat. Silence filled the kitchen. His parents leaned back ever so slightly and their arms stiffened. They looked at each other, Deren, and finally at me. "Is that right?" Mr. Sevine said, his tone cautiously polite.

I nodded. I didn't want to say more. However, like when Yuna had to face the dryads in the forest, I had to face Deren's parents and the truth about my alignment. No amount of hiding would make the dryads or parents go away. "I was able to save Deren because I'm a Dark."

"Oh," Mrs. Sevine said. "May I ask how come?"

"I don't think you want to know." I flinched when a hand gently touched my shoulder.

"You need to be proud of what you did yesterday, regardless of your alignment—especially because of your alignment. You showed us that not all Darks are as bad as their reputation has made them out to be. You saved a life—our son's life. You should be very proud. I'm proud of you."

"As am I," Mr. Sevine said.

And just like that, being brave and facing the truth had turned out okay. I tucked my hair behind my ears, not quite able to believe it. "I'm glad I saved his life."

"Good," Mrs. Sevine said.

Not everything was okay. "It's just that bad things had to happen first so I could do any good."

"But you didn't make those bad things happen," Mr. Sevine said.

Allosyr had been plaguing the school long before I'd ever showed up. "True."

"Do you know what's causing the bad things?"

I nodded.

"What is it?" Mrs. Sevine said.

"A demon," Deren said, causing us to turn.

"Is that true?" the mom asked me.

I nodded. "I'm trying to figure out how to—" I stopped, the plan to send him to the Light sitting on the tip of my tongue.

Yes, child. What's your plan?

My lips tingled. I retrieved a sage bundle from my bag. My mouth kept trying to form the words. I clenched my teeth.

Say it, child. Tell me your grand, useless plan.

I held up the sage in a trembling hand. The top of the bundle was blackened and charred. I focused on those burn lines. "Light."

Tell me everything.

Mrs. Sevine left the table and returned with a brass bowl of incense sticks and herbs. She bunched them to one side, lit my sage, and tried to take it from me. I held on tight.

Allosyr's voice faded with every word he spoke.

You'll tell me everything in time.

As the pressure on my mouth lifted, I got up and waved the burning bundle all over the kitchen, spreading its smoke and minty tobacco scent everywhere. I blew out the flames and set the smoldering bundle in the bowl. "Okay, now it's safe to talk."

"It smells kind of gross," Deren said. "What is it?"

"White sage. It keeps the demon from hearing us talk. We're safe, now."

"Are you sure?" She looked around the house.

"Yeah."

"What was it trying to do?"

"Trying to find out what I'm trying to do." That gave me an idea. I took the books out of my bag and spread them on the table. "I'm trying to send him to the Light so he can never harm anyone again. The problem is I don't know how, but it's possible." I explained the contents of the books, how they held the answers, and how hard they were for me to understand.

Mr. Sevine pulled a book over and leafed through the pages. "So, what are we looking for?"

"You really don't mind helping me?"

Mrs. Sevine grabbed a book as well. "It's the least we can do for you saving our son's life."

The four of us pored over the books. I took notes as they pointed stuff out and I came across useful stuff they helped me understand. The biggest breakthrough was when Mrs. Sevine found a power circle called the Crossover Ritual. I'd been so focused on finding a title or heading with the phrase "send to the light" that I hadn't considered other words used to describe the event.

"Listen to this," she said, "the Crossover Ritual is intended for sending a demon to the Light. This ritual must be performed with utmost care and thorough preparation. Once it is started, it cannot be stopped for any reason, or those involved risk losing the demon to the void. It is not known if a demon can ever be trapped a second time. They will most assuredly know the signs and avoid being tricked again."

My heart sank. Just when we finally found the ritual I was looking for, I might not even get a chance for it to work.

"What's wrong?"

"The demon said something about being really old. What if someone's already tried to send him to the Light before?"

"So what? You'll never know if you don't try, and if you don't, then you'll always wonder if it would've ever worked."

"What do I do if this doesn't work?" Doubts crept into my mind.

"Focus on the task at hand," Mr. Sevine said. "You can only wrestle one steer at a time."

I had no clue what a steer was.

"He means to focus on one problem at a time," Mrs. Sevine said. She bookmarked the page and I took down notes as she dictated them to me, starting with the warning to not stop once started. The Crossover Ritual led with a pile of warnings and mistakes to avoid before diving into the how-to. We all hunted for information in our books on said ritual. By lunchtime, I had quite the list of details jotted down, and I'd practiced drawing the circle several times before returning to the table.

I pressed a fingertip to the top of the page in my

notebook. "Okay, so we know I need the circle called the Crossover Ritual. I have a whole bunch of warnings written down. The lines must be drawn in a particular order and the runes added in order, along with being lined up with the four cardinal directions."

Mr. Sevine said, "That's some powerful stuff there."

"Candles are a must, as is some tobacco to lure the demon in, and St. John's Wort to trap it in place once lured inside." I skimmed the notes. "Then it goes on with the incantation and three herbs I need to send the demon to the Light." I skimmed again. "The best time to perform a crossover ritual is at dusk because that's when the forces pushing and pulling Light and Dark are most balanced. And then there are even more warnings." The last one written in the book nestled above my notebook snagged my attention. I reread it. "Both priests shouldn't have any ties or links to the demon targeted for this ritual. If they do, they risk fracturing their mind or, worse, sacrificing themselves to make sure every last remnant of the demon has been removed from the human realm." My heart sank a second time. I was linked. Ms. Weever had warned me about this. I wasn't sure if an incomplete bargain was enough.

"What do they mean by 'link'?" Mrs. Sevine said.

I slid my marked arm under the table even though the lines were invisible. "It means it's a real good thing I healed Deren." His mom placed a grateful hand over her chest and breathed a sigh of relief. I continued reviewing our notes, no longer wanting to think about this detail.

I'd underlined the beginning of the last section of

my notes three times because the book had stressed the information a million times. "Please note, do not perform this ritual alone. In order for it to work—" I sucked in a sharp breath. "I think I know what to do." My fingertip followed my scrawly handwriting, my hands shaking with excitement. "In order for it to work, balance must first be established."

"What does that mean?" Deren said.

My thoughts raced back to one of my first lessons with Ms. Weever. I flipped my notebook closed and showed them the cover. The circle was divided into the five main elements inside a circle representing Light and Dark. The three of them leaned in. "Each alignment, except Kindred, has an opposite. Earth and Air, Fire and Water."

"Light and Dark," Mrs. Sevine said.

Risky or not, the crossover ritual had to be better than completing the bargain. Hopefully. "Is there any way we could contact Sanctus Bylan?"

***

Mrs. Sevine made a couple of calls, first to the hospital, which told us to contact his Order. Then she called the Order of Leo. Whoever Mrs. Sevine spoke to had no clue where Sanctus Bylan was, and grew annoyed when she asked if he would collect select herbs.

"They're for the Crossover Ritual." She faced me, the vine wrapped around her ear and a leaf over her mouth. "No, it's not for an apparition. It's for a, um, uh, a demon. There's a demon at—" She paused with her mouth open. "I know, but—" Her brows rose and her eyes widened. "No, wait." The leaf curled away from her mouth, and the vine retreated to the wall near the kitchen window. Mrs. Sevine let out a frustrated sigh.

"What happened?" her husband asked.

"Stupid lady told me Light priests don't deal with demons and to go call a Dark priest." She sighed again. "I'm sorry, Mia. I don't know what else to do."

"A Light priest is coming to our school tomorrow," Deren said. "Wouldn't it be him?"

***

Tomorrow took forever to arrive, and when it did, I felt terrible. It hurt to move and it hurt to lay there. My limbs creaked and moaned as I touched the song stone to turn the alarm off, and the ground felt uneven as I made my way to the bathroom to wash up and brush my hair and teeth. I picked at the breakfast Mom prepared, forcing myself to take bite after bite of the burrito that didn't want to stay down.

"You feeling all right, sweetie?" Mom said. "You don't look well." She ran a hand through my hair.

That gentle touch made me close my eyes. Going back to sleep seemed like such a good idea. My eyes snapped open as soon as I tipped sideways. I sat up straight and forced the burrito to my mouth for the millionth time.

"Maybe you should stay home."

"I can't stay home." This had to be the first time in my life that I argued to go to school. The Light priest would be there. Sanctus Bylan or not, I needed to talk to him or her.

"Are you sure?"

"It's Carlo's memorial. I'd feel terrible if I missed it."

Mom studied me as she thought for a moment. "I understand. Go to the nurse after it's over. I don't think

312

you should go to school at all, but I'll let you go to the memorial. Okay?"

"Okay." Hopefully, I'd make it that far. I set the remaining half of my burrito down, which spilled some of its scrambled egg contents. I turned and swallowed the bile rising in my throat.

This was going to be a long day.

Chapter 26

Despite the lack of bumpiness, the bus ride made me feel worse. My stomach contents sloshed around with the constant stopping and starting. By the time we arrived at school, my hands trembled. I clutched the strap of my shoulder bag to hide it as I passed Mr. Redd in the sea of students. His eyes followed me. He said nothing, though, so I continued to the quad, the din of children's voices making my eardrums vibrate. They sounded so loud today.

"Morning, Mia." Miss Wren tugged me closer. "You don't look well."

"I'm fine." I gulped down my rising nausea.

"No, you aren't. You're as pale as ever and you've got lines under your eyes. Go to the nurse."

"I can't. I have to be in school today."

"No, you don't. You're not well and I don't want you getting other people sick."

"I have to talk to the Light priest."

"Why?"

Yes, do tell, child.

I flinched at Allosyr's voice and silently thanked him for reminding me to keep my motives secret. "It's important. I'll tell you more when it's safe. Besides, I don't want to miss Carlo's memorial. I still feel bad for not getting to him fast enough."

Miss Wren took a slow breath in and out. Was she about to get angry, like Mom, or did she understand? "I'll make sure you get to the memorial. For now, I think you should rest up in the nurse's office. I don't want you to get anyone else sick."

"It's not that kind of sick," I mumbled, and swallowed another bout of nausea.

She raised an eyebrow. "You're too young to be having...girl troubles."

I gave her a blank look. Did she mean something about Gwen? If so, she was totally wrong about that. Gwen was trouble.

"Okay, never mind about that. Mia, you remember being taught about germs, right?"

"This isn't from germs." I silently pleaded with her not to make me say it aloud.

She studied me for a long moment, confusion drawing her brows so close together that they almost touched. And then they rose. "Is this something to do with—?"

I nodded.

"That—" She looked around. "—thing in the closet?"

I nodded again and headed for the playground. A hand grabbed my shoulder.

"I want you to go to the nurse and rest. I promise I'll make sure you don't miss the memorial or the priest."

Sight of a small, gangly boy with ears sticking out too far caught my attention. "I wanna go say hi to Deren first. He's all better now."

"He's—?" She followed my gaze to the lone boy by the swing set. "Oh, wow. He's back. Definitely go say hi. I'll have a hall pass ready for you when the bell rings."

Butterflies wanted to take off in my belly. It settled for gurgling as I headed for the swings. He hopped off and grinned. When I got within arm's reach, that grin vanished.

"Mia, you don't look so good today."

"I'll be fine." Hopefully. "How are you feeling?"

"Great." He hopped back on the swing and kicked his legs, twisting himself from side to side. His gaze shifted behind me and his shoulders drooped. "Uh oh, I think you better go."

Gwen and her friends stood in a semicircle, she glaring and the others frowning.

"What do you want?" I said. I didn't want to deal with her today. I didn't care what she wanted. I wanted her to leave me alone. I had other things to deal with.

"You're not allowed to hang out with him. He's a Dark."

"No, he's not. Only I am."

Deren gasped. "You just—"

"Shut up. I already knew." She kicked some sand at him. He shielded his face too late and had to brush himself off from the nose down.

"Then why do you lie about me to everyone?" he

316

said in an injured tone.

"Because I don't like you."

"I don't like you either," I said to Gwen.

Her eyes widened. "What did you say to me?"

"I said I don't like you. Now go away and leave us alone."

If those aligned with Fire could light flames in their eyes, the look she gave me totally would have. "Don't tell me what to do." She shoved me with both hands.

The world spun as I tottered backwards and hit the ground. She kicked sand again. My hair blocked most of it from hitting my face. My stomach roiled. I shrugged out from under my bag's strap and got back up.

"You blew your chance to be my friend."

I never wanted to be your friend, I thought, and boy, did it feel freeing to finally acknowledge that. "Then go away and leave us alone."

She shoved me again. I shuffled my feet and stayed standing. "I told you not to tell me what to do."

"Hey, leave her alone." Deren stood between me and Gwen, fists clenched at his sides.

Gwen crinkled her nose. "You two are so stupid." Her gaze shifted to me and I did not like the smile that spread across her face. "I know. I'll teach you a lesson." She took a deep breath and yelled, "Hey, everyone, guess what—?"

Lunging, I covered her mouth. I was about to tell her to shut up as overwhelming nausea choked the words in my throat, and then traveled down my arm. Blood drained from it and traveled down my arm as well. All the pain, all the nausea, fatigue, and discomfort concentrated in the hand covering Gwen's mouth and left my body.

My hand fell away and I stood up straight, no longer feeling achy or weighed down by illness. My stomach settled. I felt hungry. I hadn't eaten enough for breakfast. I wasn't sick anymore. This was wonderful.

Gwen teetered on her feet, her face slack and pale. Sussi, the tall, strong-looking one, put a hand on Gwen's shoulder, steadying her.

"What did you do to her?" she said.

I held my hand out between us, the tattoo lines boldly defined on my skin. "The same thing to you if you don't leave us alone."

See? Power is meaningless unless you use it.

Allosyr's feeling of pride filled me. I glared at Sussi, daring her to give me a reason to make her sick. I was in control of the situation. There was nothing any of them could do to stop me. I felt ten feet tall. I smiled, hand ready to dish out more sickness.

"Oh, yeah?" Sussi raised her fists and Deren stood between us—not facing Sussi—facing me. Sussi lowered her fists, puzzled.

A part of me willed Deren to step aside and give these girls what they deserved. I could've easily moved around him. Something in his expression sucked me into making eye contact with him.

"Mia, this isn't right," he said. He sounded afraid. His brows drew together, his posture tense, as if afraid I'd hit him. He held his arms up defensively, my reflection in his dark eyes, but with the demon's face.

My tattooed arm dropped to my side, no longer pulsing with demonic energy.

"I'm sorry." I didn't know to whom I said it, be it to Deren or all of them. I ran off. I didn't look at Miss

Wren when she handed me the pass. I hurried over to the nurse, Deren's gaze needling my back. I had to get away.

Patch after patch of tortoise shell-shaped pathway took me closer and closer to the nurse's office as I reflected on what I'd done. I'd given Gwen the sickness. I'd put her in her place. I'd also been far meaner than she ever had. Or had I? She'd burned my hand to officially mark the beginning of our fake friendship. She'd bossed me around nonstop, telling me who I could and couldn't be friends with. It'd gotten people to leave me alone and helped keep my alignment secret for weeks. I'd made it over two months without anyone finding out—not a record, but it'd been the easiest two months of going to school without fear of hate or ridicule for my alignment.

Was that what she was about to shout right before I put my hand over her mouth? And gave her the sickness.

Guilt formed a lump in my throat. No matter how cruel Gwen was, I shouldn't have done that.

But it got her to stop. That moment made me feel so powerful. I'd put real fear in those I feared. There was nothing anyone could do to stop me.

Except for Deren's sad, scared face.

Oh, the swirl of emotions coming off you, child. If only I could read your mind. This is a most delicious moment.

"Shut up and leave me alone." My mouth wanted to form a smile as Allosyr's joy filled my chest.

As you wish, my queen.

"I'm not a queen. Don't call me that."

He said nothing, made no sound. I felt his joy as

easily as the desert sun heated up the day. I wrenched open the building door, the metal handle warm.

I entered the nurse's office and dumped the note on her desk without stopping. I caught a glimpse of her surprised, elvish face as my mind turned whatever she said into a buzz of syllables jumbled together. I located the cot farthest back, slipped between the blue curtains, and curled up in a ball, clutching my bag to my chest.

I'd barely stopped bouncing on the springy foam when wood beads slid along a track with a hiss. Light poured in between the curtains and around Nurse Kor's slender frame. "What's wrong, kiddo?"

I buried my face in the elevated portion of the bed that was supposed to be a pillow. "I'm a horrible person. Please go away."

She sat on the bed, making us both bounce. "What happened?"

This was the opposite of what I wanted. She was only trying to be nice. I had half a mind to snap at her to go away. A tiny shred somewhere deep inside wanted to give her the sickness so I could be left alone.

I bent my limbs, forming a smaller ball. This wasn't me. This couldn't be me. Harming people wasn't me. These bad things had to be what Allosyr wanted. Yes, I wanted to be left alone, but I didn't need to make people sick to get what I wanted. "I don't want to talk about it. Miss Wren gave me a note."

"I saw." A moment of silence followed, filled by the rustle of leaves. A vine crept out of the nurse's sleeve and brushed against my forehead. "You're not sick, but...you have this...squirminess about you. It doesn't feel pleasant to the touch."

"I know."

"Is it making you feel sick?"

"No. Please leave me alone."

"I'm worried about you. I want to help you in any way I can—and no, that doesn't involve leaving you alone to stress over whatever's bugging you."

Instead of saying exactly what she knew I was about to say, I took a deep breath, huffed, and then closed my eyes as another bout of guilt made my insides squirm. Maybe she'd finally leave me alone if I stayed quiet long enough. I didn't feel like being brave.

The air pressure dropped as the office door swung open with a metallic click. In walked Deren with a very pale Gwen. Why on Aardra was he with her? Nurse Kor hurried over. I sat up. Of all the people, these were the last two I ever expected to see together. The nurse produced a garbage bucket in time for Gwen's breakfast to be deposited in its metallic depths. Deren grimaced as he stayed by her side, growing pale himself. Gwen heaved several more times before wiping her mouth and gasping for air.

"Oh, honey. Let's get you in the bathroom and I'll call your parents." Nurse Kor and Gwen trudged past my cot.

Deren approached and stopped by the curtains.

"What were you doing with Gwen?"

He glanced towards the bathrooms. "Making sure she made it to the nurse's office. No one else would go."

I flinched. "Not even her friends?"

"No. They were all too scared."

"Some friends they are," I said. "Why'd you take her? She's not your friend."

He nervously tugged on his too-wide ears. "It's...I

felt bad for her."

I wanted to snap at him for being so ridiculous. Instead, I sat in my well of guilt. I didn't like her one bit. It felt so good to finally have some power over her. I hung my head. "Why?"

"I don't know. I can't help it. I just know being kind is right." He fidgeted in my peripheral and kicked an invisible rock. "It's something my mom taught me when people made fun of my ears."

So he did know his ears looked a little weird. I never wanted to make fun of him or anything for it, but I'd done my fair share of staring.

"The more I tried to be mean back, the more they picked on me. Mom told me to be nice and say silly things about my ears. They stopped picking on me once they thought it didn't bother me anymore. Mom says sometimes the meanest people are the ones who need the most kindness."

Nurse Kor reemerged and thanked Deren for his help before sending him back to class. She then faced me, fists on her hips, and spoke once the office door had closed. "Why on Aardra does Gwen think you made her sick?"

Bowing my head, I hid behind my hair.

The hands came off her slender hips. "You didn't, did you?"

"I didn't mean to."

Oh, yes you did, Allosyr said. *That moment was glorious.*

"That was an odd response," Nurse Kor said. She sat beside me, making us both bounce again.

"I'll take it back," I said to my shoes.

"What do you mean?"

"I can heal her, like I did Deren."

"So you really made her sick?"

I dug my fingers into the cot. "She wouldn't stop picking on me and Deren. I wanted her to stop. I never meant to go that far. I'll take it back." I couldn't recall Yuna ever making any mistakes like this. I knew she'd do the right thing if she did.

"You're not the first to complain about her social skills," Nurse Kor admitted. "As much as she might've deserved it, you shouldn't have done that."

"I know. I didn't mean to."

"Then why did you do it?"

I turned my head away. "Because I'm a bad person."

Nurse Kor let out a sympathetic laugh. "Oh, Mia. You're not a bad person for doing one wrong thing. Good people make bad decisions. It's part of life. Are you willing to fix your mistake?"

"Yes."

"Then that makes you a good person. Bad people don't try to fix mistakes."

I slowly faced my shoes again, not ready to make eye contact. What she said made sense. I wasn't as good as Deren. "I don't feel like a good person."

"Why not?" She sounded patient, curious.

For whatever reason, I was in a confessing mood. My chest rose and fell with a sigh. "Ms. Weever told me I need to show the world that not all Darks are bad, and then I went and did that." I pointed to the bathroom.

"You showed me that Darks can save lives."

"I felt so proud of myself for making Gwen sick. It made her shut up and leave us alone. I was so tired of

323

her bossing me around. I wanted to be left alone, but she kept coming after me. And she hates Deren for no reason. I wanted to make it stop. So I did. And now I feel bad." There. It was all out. I'd confessed everything.

A moment of silence followed as Nurse Kor digested my words. I didn't look at her for fear she'd found a reason to justify hating me, a Dark. However, when she spoke, she was perfectly calm. "Thank you for sharing all that. What you feel is perfectly understandable. Bullies don't bring out the best in any of us. It's perfectly normal to want to hurt them back when someone hurts you. You show a lot of maturity in feeling regret. Many kids your age wouldn't. You have wisdom beyond your years, Mia."

"People keep telling me that. I don't know what it means."

"It means you're growing up faster than adults expect. Instead of behaving like a child, you're behaving more like an adult."

"Is that a good thing?"

It's one reason why I picked you, Mia Evers.

"It depends on how you look at it," Nurse Kor said. "Being smart is always a good thing. But we're children only once."

"I'd rather be a grownup."

She smiled. "Such is what we all want when we're young. Anyway, Miss Wisdom, let's see if Gwen's stomach has settled enough. Do you need a Light priest to heal her?" She stood.

"I don't know." I stood, too. I might as well right my wrong sooner than later.

Nurse Kor retrieved Gwen from the bathroom,

guiding her by the elbows, and gingerly set her on an empty cot. Gwen shivered and her teeth chattered. The nurse placed a blanket over Gwen, who tugged it to her chin. My classmate gave me a hate-filled look.

"Why's she here?" she whispered. "Get her away from me."

Anger roiled its way up my chest and clenched my jaw. Maybe I should leave her sick a little longer to teach her a lesson. One look at Nurse Kor, though, and I knew better. It was time to make things right no matter how much I hated Gwen. "I'm taking the sickness back, so shut up."

"Don't touch me."

Nurse Kor stood beside me. "Gwen, you're being rude to someone trying to help."

"She's not trying to help me."

Nurse Kor placed her fists on her hips. "Excuse me. I wouldn't let her do anything bad to you, so when I tell you she's trying to help, she's trying to help." Gwen opened her mouth. The nurse said, "Don't argue with me. Mia knows she made a mistake. She wants to fix things even after how poorly you treated her and Deren."

Gwen twisted under the blanket with painstaking slowness. She reached for the empty side of the cot. Her arm dangled limply at her side. "They're all after me," she whispered hoarsely. "They're all jealous. They..." Her eyes slowly closed.

Nurse Kor and I looked at each other. She said, "I think you can heal her in peace now."

I stepped closer, half expecting Gwen to jump up and start shouting at the both of us. She remained perfectly still, minus the rise and fall of her chest. I held a hand over her forehead.

Ah, Little One. Allosyr manifested on the other side of the cot in his human form, a slight frown on his face. He switched to speaking aloud. "I didn't give you this gift so you could kill yourself with it. Every time you take the sickness back, it will make you worse and eventually kill you. Do you want to die because of a twisted soul such as hers?"

"I won't," I said, holding my chin up.

"Who are—is it him again?" Nurse Kor said, searching the room.

He shook his head. "You will. I've been around far longer than you. You need to complete the bargain with me if you want to live. You'll have days at most if you take the sickness back so quickly."

"You're a liar." For once, I didn't think he was. Or maybe he was that good of a pretender. No, this had to be another one of his tricks to get me to complete the bargain with him.

He held up his hands. "It would be very convenient for the both of us if I was. I assure you I'm not. Reconsider your decision, Little One."

"No."

"With a complete bargain, you can hurt and heal people as it pleases you, with no repercussions, and so much more."

"I said no. Now go away."

Allosyr fell silent. He watched on, eyes lined with worry.

"What's going on?" Nurse Kor said.

"He doesn't want me to heal her for some dumb reason." Closing my eyes, I pressed my hand to Gwen's burning forehead. It was slick with sweat.

Concentrating as best I could with a demon staring at me, I mentally searched around her body and felt squirming like I'd stuck my hand in a bowl of wiggling worms. Gritting my teeth, I tugged at the horrible sensation as it clung to Gwen. I tugged harder. It rose into my hand.

The sensation was too much. My whole body squirmed. The harder I tugged, the worse it felt. And when the invisible ball of worms squirmed in my mouth, I gagged and balled my hand in a fist, willing the squirming sensation to stop.

"It's too much. I need a Light priest."

Chapter 27

You still intend to save her, don't you? Allosyr said plainly from behind me as I headed back to class. The Light priest hadn't arrived yet. The nurse and I agreed I might as well return to class.

"Yep."

That isn't wise. You were already on your knees not too long ago.

"No, I wasn't."

I didn't mean that literally, he said. *I meant you were on the verge of losing what little breakfast you had and were about to be the one lying on the cot.*

"So?"

He let out a frustrated sigh. *Do you not see the consequences of the actions you wish to take?*

"I know the consequences if I don't do anything."

Why do you care if she lives or dies? She hasn't done anything for you.

My chest tightened. He didn't understand what it was like to be me, to be hated and feared for being a Dark, and having the whole world against you before you'd done anything wrong. I'd finally done something wrong to earn that hate. I rounded on the voice coming from behind me and faced only empty air. Of course, he wasn't there. He was speaking through the tattoo. I resumed heading back to class. "You wouldn't understand."

I beg to differ. Don't forget, I was human once.

"What does that have to do with anything?"

Think about it. His voice switched to somewhere behind my other shoulder. I turned to look, despite myself. Again, he wasn't there. *Long ago, when I died, I had a choice, a choice between going to the Light or getting sucked into the Darkness.* He manifested beside me, matching my stride. I did a double-take of his clean suit and golden hair. I saw through him, like a reflection on a windowpane. "It was entirely my choice which path I took."

"You chose Darkness. I know. I don't care."

He held up a finger. "Ah, but why? Surely the sensible thing would've been to choose the Light."

I stopped and took in his see-through face. "Why *did* you choose Darkness?"

A fanged grin widened. It slowly melted into a pensive frown. "It's a long story for another day, provided you don't kill yourself first, but anyway, I understand your actions better than you think."

I said nothing. I didn't believe him for one second.

"If I were human once, that meant I had an alignment."

My stomach twisted and my pulse quickened at the

thought of me having anything in common with a demon. He couldn't have been a Dark. Just couldn't. "You're lying again," I whispered.

"Oh, how I wish I could draw some power circles for you right now to prove you wrong." He faced me, hands in his pockets. "Little One, your noble battle is already lost. Don't waste energy trying to change the opinions of those who have no interest in changing them. This world will never accept you for who you are."

"I already have friends—a friend."

"Enjoy it while it lasts. Friends come and go." He took a step closer. "I can give you the power to find happiness in this cruel, twisted world."

I clenched my jaw. "You're trying to get me to bargain with you again, aren't you?"

"I'm trying to keep you alive. I can tell there's no point in trying to talk you out of taking the sickness back again, so yes, it's back to bargaining."

I stormed off, then sped up when he caught up. He effortlessly matched my pace with his much longer legs.

"I wish you'd think about it. People like her would sooner spit on your grave than thank you for saving their life. They see Darks as worthless vermin, good only for being wiped from the face of this world."

"Go away." I ran to the classroom door leading directly to the quad and knocked.

Allosyr stopped at the edge of the sidewalk. "You force my hand then."

"I'll never give you what you want, so go away." The door opened, revealing Miss Wren in the doorway.

"Mia. You look...well," she said, her face wide with

shock. "How are you feeling?"

"Fine," I said sharply as I stepped inside.

Allosyr said, "If this is the path you choose, then prepare for another memorial service."

I spun around, catching a glimpse of the demon before the door thudded closed. I shoved it back open. Allosyr had vanished. The sidewalk was empty in both directions. He wasn't anywhere in sight. My stomach dropped to my feet.

"What's wrong?" Miss Wren said.

"When is the Light priest supposed to get here?"

She glanced at the classroom clock. "Any minute."

"Will he come straight to our classroom?" I let the door close again.

"I don't believe so."

Everyone stared at us. The entire class had turned in our direction. Whatever. They could stare all they wanted. I lowered my voice. "Gwen needs me and the Light priest really bad. I—" Confession of what I'd done did a circle on the tip of my tongue before dashing away. "She's really, really sick." I wore my pouty begging face. "Please."

Miss Wren studied me a moment. "I'll give the front office a heads up that you're coming." She crossed to the bundle of vines near her desk.

I bolted to the main office and burst inside, stomping to a halt on the wood floor, feeling like all the knots in the wood were eyes on me. Some of those eyes were covered with ears of dried corn, husks and all. The school was already decorating for Feast Day, the next holiday, one Darks had no problem with. Desi's curly hair bounced when she turned around.

"My, you got here quick."

"Is he here yet?"

"Who, the—"

"Light priest," I said at the same time she did. "Yeah."

"He should be here any minute. The memorial doesn't start for another half hour, though."

I ran to the glass doors. The parking lot filled up with parents coming to pay their respects to Carlo Nacinto and his family. None of the vehicles looked big and flashy enough to belong to any of the Light Orders. I rapidly tapped my fingers on my leg as two more vehicles lazily floated into the parking lot. None of them had any clue that another student was on the verge of dying.

I ran to the front desk, gripping the lip. "I'll be in the nurse's office. Please let me know as soon as he arrives." I ran off as a confused Desi voiced her guarded consent.

Nurse Kor stood over Gwen. Vines had wrapped around the base of the bed and Gwen's legs and forehead. The veins in every leaf glowed a faint green. Nurse Kor opened her eyes at the sound of my feet shuffling to a halt beside her.

"Mia, thank goodness you're back. Her symptoms are progressing far faster than Deren's or Carlo's ever did. I don't know what's going on."

"It's him." I pointed to the other side of the bed, at Allosyr in his demon form. He sat coiled in the corner, filling the space from floor to ceiling, the walls and curtains showing through him. His slanted, red-glowing eye roved in my direction before returning to Gwen. "He's speeding the sickness along."

"Then you better heal her now."

I glanced at the giant demon. He said nothing, all his concentration on stealing Gwen's life from this world. For once, he spared me any of his usual taunts or aggravating commentaries. He really must be in a hurry. That meant as much as I wanted to wait for the Light priest, I couldn't afford to.

This meant I might die for someone I hated.

"Mia?" Nurse Kor said. The palms of her hands reflected the green glow.

"I know. I will." I needed a minute to come to terms with what I was about to do. I could walk away from this with no risk to myself. But what kind of Dark would that make me? If I could live without everyone fearing and hating me for no reason, I wanted to take it. But was there a chance? Was Allosyr right, or were his words as poisonous as his "gift?" I didn't know what the truth was anymore. Heck, I didn't even know if I could take the sickness back without the Light priest's help.

I had to try. I couldn't let the demon win because I didn't try. I'd wonder for the rest of my life what would've happened if I'd tried. So, even if I failed, I'd at least know I'd done everything I could. I retrieved a half-consumed sage bundle and set my bag on the floor.

The red eye shifted back to me, specifically to the white sage. *That won't stop me and my work, child. Walk away and live to see another day.*

I lit the sage with one of the match sticks Mrs. Sevine had given me and waved the bundle around, filling the air with smoke and erasing the demon's hunched frame from sight. He didn't so much as twitch as the curtains and ceiling appeared in full solid form, obscured by smoke. The darkness of his presence loomed over the room, though. He was here.

I stood at the head of the bed. Gwen lay asleep and covered in sweat, her breathing quick and face pale. She didn't look so pretty while sick and dying, which gave me jealous satisfaction. I pushed the thought aside. Regardless of whether or not she'd thank me, I had to do what I knew was right. I hoped I could do it.

I placed one hand on her forehead and the other over her racing heart. I'd used only one hand on Deren, so maybe both were what I needed this time. Closing my eyes, I searched around for the sickness. The squirming and writhing rose to meet me, pushing against me. Ants crawled all over my hands and up my arms. I yelped and retracted my hands, shaking out the tingling.

"What's wrong? Can you not heal her anymore?"

"I don't know. It feels worse." I eyed Gwen. Maybe this wasn't such a good idea. Maybe I was better off letting the demon win this fight.

"Want me to try to help you like Sanctus Bylan did?"

The tingling faded as my heart pounded. Nurse Kor placed a hand on my shoulder, sending a wave of calm through me. It wasn't the same calm as from Sanctus Bylan, but it was far more than I could manage alone. "Please." I placed my hands back on Gwen's forehead and chest, Nurse Kor's calm energy filling me.

The ants needled at me. I clenched my teeth as a coolness washed over my arms. The tingling grew muted. I searched deeper for the root of the sickness. I'd found Deren's in his chest. The core of it wasn't in the same spot in Gwen. I rooted around like I was looking in my bag for a pencil buried under books and loose papers, and found it in Gwen's mind. Once again, it felt like a squirming ball of worms. I took the sickness in both hands and pulled.

At first, nothing happened. I really, really didn't want to take the sickness back. I was scared and didn't know what would happen.

"You can do this, Mia," Nurse Kor's voice said from some distant place. It sounded like she stood in the hall, instead of beside me. The comforting heaviness of her hand remained on my physical shoulder.

I took a calming breath. And then another. Yes, I was scared. I couldn't change that. However, I could accept it and keep moving forward with the task at hand. Taking yet another deep breath, I grabbed the writhing sickness and pulled again, willing it to transfer to me. After the dryads, Yuna had faced a troll ten times her size guarding a bridge leading to the satyr island village. Yuna hadn't gone looking for another bridge. She'd taken it down with her sword and fairy magic.

The sickness didn't budge. I kept pulling. The squirming and writhing intensified to where my whole body was covered in ants crawling all over me, and worms filled my mouth again. I swallowed them down and kept pulling, willing the sickness into me. Even if Gwen never liked me, people like Nurse Kor and Miss Wren would know that not all Darks were bad.

The sickness's hold snapped, one worm at a time, and then it broke free. It traveled up my arms and into my chest so quickly that I fell backwards into Nurse Kor's arms. Using her as leverage, I straightened up and put a hand back on Gwen's forehead.

"She's healed."

"Oh, thank the Light."

I wasn't feeling particularly thankful. I dropped to my knees by the nearest garbage can. I puked up my breakfast, which felt like a ball of worms on its way up and out. With so little in my stomach in the first place, retching turned into dry heaving. Blood pounded in my cheeks and forehead like I'd been hanging upside-down on monkey bars for too long. As soon as the vomiting ceased, the pressure on my temples lessened. I gulped breath after breath, my mouth tasting like bile and mushy eggs.

A calm energy washed into the room, easing the nausea out of my stomach.

Sanctus Bylan stood in the doorway, his white robes looking like they gave off a light of their own. The vines and leaves populating the walls, floor, and ceiling drew closer to him. Every last leaf turned to him, quivering. I felt perfectly healthy and at ease for a moment, until reality settled back into achy limbs. He wore a slight frown on his wrinkly face.

"Welcome, Sanctus Bylan," Nurse Kor said.

He nodded. "What's going on here? I'd sensed the evil from the parking lot."

"I'm not entirely sure."

Hands hidden in his wide sleeves, he stood inside the blue curtains. "You again, dear child. You don't look well at all."

"She's having quite the rough morning." Nurse Kor guided me to my feet. She led me from the sage to a cot closer to where the demon crouched. The proximity made the aching worse. I lay on the cot, anyway. What more could he do to me?

You stupid, noble child, Allosyr said in his deep,

336

rumbly demon voice. *You may have very well killed yourself with your noble deed.* One large, slanted red eye loomed outside the ring of sage smoke.

Darkness crept closer on all sides. I wasn't sure if it was the demon's presence, the adults', or me on the verge of passing out. Whatever it was, my range of vision shrank. "Then take your stupid gift back."

The red eye hesitated, shifting around with one thought chasing after another before settling back on me. *No. Complete our bargain.*

"No."

"Who's she talking to?" Sanctus Bylan said.

"A demon," Nurse Kor said in a subdued voice.

The demon let out a growl so deep that my chest vibrated. I didn't have the energy to argue. I reached for my sage and pointed at it when Nurse Kor looked at my hand.

She plucked the sage from the bowl. "What do you need?"

"I need the demon to leave me alone." I pointed to where he lay coiled. The nurse hesitated before gearing up the courage to approach a demon she couldn't sense or see. She wafted the smoke in the darkest corner, erasing the demon from my sight and sense. Tension vanished from my limbs. I felt sick and dizzy. At least the demon's presence was no longer pressing down on me. "Sanctus Bylan, I need your help. I've figured out how to banish demons to the Light." He raised a skeptical eyebrow. I sat up, making my head spin. I shook my head and everything slowly wobbled back into focus. "Let me show you."

***

"I must confess I had no idea Darks have poured so

much work into protecting the living from demons and other evil forces. This is most fascinating. But enough of that for a moment." He gave me a measuring gaze, and then checked his watch. "I saw you two days ago. You were perfectly healthy. Now you're exhibiting the same symptoms as those two boys. Do you need my help to heal yourself?"

I shook my head. "It won't work."

Sanctus Bylan drew back his sleeves with great sweeping motions, which looked much practiced over the years. "Have faith, dear child." He placed a hand over my forehead.

I pointed to Gwen. "To cure her, I had to take the sickness into myself and be sick instead. I had to do the same thing with Deren."

Silence filled the room. Sanctus Bylan studied me with his watery eyes, his mouth curved in a slight frown. He slowly turned to Nurse Kor. "And you let her do that?"

Her eyes went wide. "I didn't know," she said in a small voice. "I honestly—"

"I would've healed her anyway," I said. "And Deren. None of this is fair. It's why we have to get rid of the demon for good."

Sanctus Bylan grabbed the old book and skimmed a few choice pages, holding the book close to his face. He double-checked the notes, and then turned to another page. "The power circle and accompanying ritual are sound, very powerful."

"How soon can you get the stuff we need?" I said.

"I have everything and more in my transport." He set the book down. "The materials aren't the hard part. Do you realize how dangerous this ritual is?"

Knowing I'd need to perform the ritual with a Light had made me feel unafraid. I wouldn't have to do things alone. I'd have help. "Not really."

"Dear child, you're asking me to risk my life and yours. I refuse to do such a thing."

I sat there, unsure of what to say. If we didn't do the Crossover Ritual, I might have to complete the bargain with Allosyr after all. Being a Dark, I understood death far better than others my age. While I acted all stubborn and unafraid around Allosyr, I wasn't sure I was brave enough to stop myself from making the same mistake as Ms. Weever. That and me dying wouldn't stop the demon from doing more bad things. "I don't know what else to do." My eyes welled with tears. I hurriedly brushed them away as more and more snuck out. A hiccup of a sob escaped my throat.

Bylan placed a hand on my shoulder. "I'm sorry to disappoint you, child. The Crossover Ritual was—"

"I don't have that kind of time." I rubbed my eyes again.

"What do you mean?" Nurse Kor said.

The hand jolted off my shoulder. "Oh, no," he said in a horrified whisper. This time a hand settled on each shoulder with a comforting weight.

For a moment, I wished he'd pull me into a hug, like Dad used to. I wanted the reality of my situation to go away, for life to be all safe and happy.

"Mia, tell me everything that's happened between you and the demon."

More tears burned lines down my cheeks and dripped onto my dress, making darker spots on the blue material. I kept my face hidden as I explained how the demon had been at the school before I got here, how the

339

sickness had affected people before I knew what was going on, my failed attempt to banish him, and the incomplete bargain binding us. The only thing I didn't tell him was Ms. Weever's involvement in all this. No one else needed to know.

When I finished telling him about when I'd given Gwen the sickness and then taken it back, I lapsed into silence, tears no longer flowing. The confession had somehow made me feel lighter, despite the heaviness behind my eyes.

"Why didn't you ever tell anyone?" Nurse Kor said, and then sniffed. She had tears in her eyes.

"Who could she tell?" Sanctus Bylan said, standing up. He hid his hands in his sleeves once more, his face serious. He picked up the sage and wafted it, spreading a fresh wave of bitter pine aroma. "Get her to the hospital. It'll buy her some time."

Chapter 28

I sat in mute disbelief as Sanctus Bylan headed to the memorial service and Nurse Kor looked up my home ley line coordinates. This was it. I'd failed to get help from the only Light priest I knew. Now, I had a choice between dying, completing the bargain, or seeing what would happen if I performed the ritual alone. I read through the list of ingredients in my notes.

When water cascaded down the wall under the vines, I surged to my feet and ripped the vine from Nurse Kor's hand.

"Mia, what are you doing?"

"I'm not going to the hospital."

"You need to. You look worse now that Sanctus Bylan left."

I held up my notebook. "Do you have any of these things?"

She read through the list, then pushed it aside. "We

don't have time for this. Let me call your parents and take you to the hospital." She pulled down another vine.

"The demon's portal is in Miss Wren's room. If I don't get rid of him, he'll make more people sick and die. It's up to me to stop him."

"But…" She wrung her hands.

"I'll die and so will others if I don't do something. I have some ideas." I hated all of them. They were better than doing nothing. The satyr had hid, forcing Yuna to face the giant troll alone. She'd beaten the monster—not without getting badly hurt. I had to beat my demon monster. "So do you have any of these things or not?"

Nurse Kor took the notebook and read through the list. She turned to the empty doorway. "I bet I know someone who does. Let's hurry."

Hurrying was more like a slow crawl as Nurse Kor guided me to the biggest car in the lot. Desi took over, keeping an eye on Gwen. It hurt to move. I put one foot in front of the other.

Nurse Kor swung open a shiny white door to Santus Bylan's limo and the smell of leather washed over us. Tiny globes of Water lights winked on along the roof, bathing the black interior with pale blue light. It was like stepping into a wondrous cave as I led the way with the sage. The interior was almost big enough for me to stand up straight. Nurse Kor had to hunch as she made her way to cabinets with silver handles shaped like curved feathers. I said, "Why's it all black? I thought Light priests surrounded themselves in white."

"I don't know. Maybe it's to add to the air of mystery that surrounds Light orders, or maybe black leather is cheaper than white."

"Everything looks expensive." I brushed my fingers along one of the leather cushions that ran the length of the car, soft and smooth.

Nurse Kor opened the cabinets and more lights turned on within, illuminating shelf after glass shelf of herbs, branches, powders, vials, and more. The nurse kneeled before it all, mouth ajar. "Indeed it does." Using my notebook as a guide, the nurse deposited one herb after another in my bag, and then gently shut the doors. She brushed her fingertips along one of the silvery handles. "I need one of these." She gripped the handle like she was about to open it again, then shook her head, as if snapping out of a daydream. "All right, that's everything. Let's go. Everyone should be at the memorial by now."

"Isn't this stealing?"

"Yep."

The campus seemed deserted and unusually quiet. Well, maybe it was normally this quiet when everyone was in class. Schools weren't supposed to be quiet. Walking slow enough to make sure we stayed within the protection of the sage smoke, we made our way to Miss Wren's classroom. We approached the front door, instead of the back one that opened to the playground. I stopped before the repaired door, taking in the new, shiny, and clean metal handle, and the splatter marks from whatever Ms. Weever had done to break in. The memory of getting sucked into the demon realm swirled to the forefront of my thoughts.

"What's wrong?" Nurse Kor asked.

"This is really it," I said. "After all everyone's been through, it's finally going to end. It's all so sudden. It doesn't feel real for some reason."

"Some things take time for our brains to absorb. I'll stay with you."

Part of me wanted her to. This was scary. "No. It's not safe. Thank you, though. I appreciate your kindness and all the help you've given me."

She pulled me into a hug.

As much as I wanted to reciprocate the gesture, my heart raced as my arms hung limp at my sides.

"And I appreciate your big heart and courage. Sanctus Bylan is such a coward." She squeezed a little tighter before letting go. "I'll be right outside."

"Thank you." I willed the shock out of my achy limbs and opened the door.

"Good luck, Mia. I know you can do this."

The door swung closed between us and secured itself with a heavy, metallic click. I was alone again. This was it.

The classroom lay empty, chairs neatly tucked under every desk. Modest sunlight spilled in through the windows. Most of it got sucked up by the darkness emanating from the closet. Taking a deep breath, I stepped deeper inside and spread the smoke everywhere, especially near the closet. I set the bundle in a bowl and moved desks around so I'd have a space to draw the circle. Since it hurt to move, it took longer than I'd liked. None of that mattered once I had my bag settled on the floor, book open, and all my tools laid out. I picked up some chalk and scratched out the circle's perimeter.

I wished I'd had months to practice this. It was more complicated than Pre-Algebra. I carefully and lightly scratched out the basic shapes before going back over it in heavier lines. There were so many lines. It was like drawing all the bars to a circular prison, with runes scattered at specific points to strengthen them. I made a ton of mistakes along the way. I carefully erased them so as not to fray the circle's power. Yes, I was taking a risk by not starting over, but I didn't have the time or energy for that. I'd probably fall asleep in five seconds if I closed my eyes.

More lines, curves, and runes were added inside, guided by a giant swirl of exactly seven rings. Once the circle was drawn, I placed all the candles and herbs in line with the cardinal directions under the guidance of a compass, sprinkled other stuff on the circle itself, and placed a handful of rolled tobacco leaves in the exact center. The swirl effect made me feel like it was trying to suck me in as I stood back up. And as soon as I'd brushed off my hands, I bolted over to a garbage can and threw up the water I'd drank.

I sat up against the cold metal of Miss Wren's desk and caught my breath. My eyes closed, burning with fatigue. It felt so good to finally close them for a few moments. After a handful of breaths, I forced them back open. My eyelids were two great slabs of stone that unwillingly cracked upwards, revealing the dark, clouded classroom.

I retrieved matches from my bag and lurched to my feet. The circle looked miles away. I dragged one foot in front of the other on my path to redemption, then carefully tiptoed to the center of the circle, as if touching any of the lines would crack open a hole and I'd fall to my death. I carefully set my feet between swirl lines as I put out the sage and lit the tobacco. When its sweet herbal scent hit my nose, I felt like I had no legs. The ground rose to meet my face. I turned in time to hit it, shoulder first.

I stayed put for fear of smudging the lines if I moved. I lay curled around the smoking tobacco, facing the closet. Well, this was it. All I had to do now was wait for Allosyr.

Tears welled in my eyes. I closed them as the memory of Sanctus Bylan dismissing me to the hospital replayed in my mind. All that hard work just to fail at getting the help I needed.

It could've been days or it could've been seconds by the time my spine tingled. My eyes popped open. A giant black paw reached down from the closet and touched the ground. The rest of the black mass dropped out of the ceiling. It shrank and morphed into Allosyr's crouched human form. He stood up and straightened his crisp suit.

"Oh, Little One," he said in a pained voice, "look at what you've done. You're near death. Please complete the bargain with me. This isn't fun anymore."

This was it. Balance established or not, this was my only chance. Carefully peeling my hand away from the lines, I raised it towards him.

He visibly sagged with relief. "Finally. You've come to your senses." He took a step forward, holding out a hand.

I slapped the ground. *"Ard, thu, bennet,"* I rasped in that other, deeper voice. The lines exploded with purple light. Flinching, Allosyr shielded his face with his arms and backed up. He hit the circle's edge with a sharp crackle and jumped back towards the center. He took in the lines, the runes, and me, and his blue eyes flashed red.

"What've you done?" he shouted. His pale hands morphed and darkened into claws. He slashed at the edge of the circle. Each strike made my head pound. I clenched my teeth, silently praying to whatever answered a Dark's prayers to let my circle hold.

His claws transformed back into human hands. Blood ran down his fingers. Torso rising and falling with heavy breaths, he glared at the purple light, then took a deep breath and swelled into his demon form. The outer edge of the circle crackled and contained his form, blazing a deep purple all around him. His deep voice roared with pain and defiance. My vision exploded with purple and white stars as his will squeezed my head.

The circle blazed a brilliant white that swirled with purple, lighting the classroom as if the very sun shone down without a roof to block it. The pressure on my head lifted. Allosyr's roar turned into an agonizing scream that made my stomach flop. That was pure pain. I clenched my teeth. I'd never meant to hurt him like this. I just wanted to send him to the Light.

Allosyr shrunk back into his human form. He stood there with his head tilted back, mouth wide in a silent scream. Smoke rose off his now-tattered suit soaked with blood. Droplets fell from his fingers, sizzling on the ground with each plop. He dropped to his knees, gasping for breath.

"So this is the creature that's been causing so much trouble," said a voice behind me.

Allosyr's bleeding chin drew level with the ground. His eyes filled with a mix of rage and terror.

Sanctus Bylan stood outside the circle, book in hand. He glanced at the pages, and then stepped inside the circle and helped me to my feet. The circle glowed a swirl of purple and white. Holding tight, he poured energy into me, helping my legs stop shaking. I felt achy and sick. At least I could face the demon one last time while standing.

Sanctus Bylan wavered on his feet before steadying himself. "I must remind you of the price we could pay, child. Are you sure you're willing to risk your life?"

I squeezed his hand, thinking of my one true friend, Deren, and how Carlo's parents had reacted when he'd died, how Ms. Weever had reacted after saving me from the demon realm. All that pain started and ended with Allosyr. "Yes."

"Then so be it. I wouldn't be worth my salt as a Light if I ignored you and let you die." The priest read a part of the book again, then took a deep breath. His voice came out deeper, forceful, as if the power of a god fueled his words. "In the name of the Light, I command thee to tell me thy true name."

Allosyr let out a choking gurgle, then swallowed and said, "Vergo Aaron...Weever." He gasped for breath.

Weever. He was related to Ms. Weever. I forced my shock aside as Sanctus Bylan held the book in front of me. I skimmed through the curly handwriting, located the spot he'd left off at, and let emotionless calm wash over me. I wouldn't let this revelation distract me from my task. "Vergo Aaron Weever, I hereby break the chains enslaving you to Molech's will and free your soul." The demon's bleeding body jolted. He sat on his heels, arms hanging limply at his sides.

"I call forth—" The ground rumbled and the classroom grew completely black outside the circle—

not dark like a cloud had passed in front of the sun, but the pure black darkness of a storm cloud enveloping the sky. I thought Allosyr making my spine tingle had been bad. This darkness made my whole body tremble.

"Stay brave, Mia," Sanctus Bylan yelled over the rumbling.

"I call—" My eyes welled with tears as the priest's hand shook in my grip. Allosyr's eyes had gone wide, his chest frozen between gasps.

What's this? Two mortals dare steal one of my own from my clutches? The voice was as deep as thunder, and my chest vibrated with every syllable. Cold terror froze my limbs. I was a mouse waiting for the tiger to pounce. This voice dwarfed Allosyr's demon form. *And one of them a child, no less.* The darkness swirled where the light touched it, unseen eyes on me. *Such blasphemy. Such a creature has proved himself unworthy of my protection and caring.*

An arrow of darkness slashed across Alloysr's face. Flinching, he cried out in pain.

What have you to say for yourself?

A hiccup of a sob escaped Allosyr. Black lines dripped down his cheeks. Demon tears? "Please, Master. Forgive me. Please save me from the Light. I don't want to leave your side."

The Demon King let out a thoughtful hmm that sounded like a thunderous growl. My chest vibrated with its power. *Your words lack conviction.*

More black tears ran down his face. "Please. I swear it's true."

If Sanctus Bylan hadn't held my hand, I would've buckled under the sheer force of the Demon King's sudden rage. Even the air tried to squish me.

YOU DARE TRY TO LIE TO ME?

The building shook and stone cracked all around us. Dust tickled my cheeks. I dared not wipe my face.

I am the Lord of Lies, the Master of Deceit. Your soul has been laid bare. There isn't one thought in your mind I don't already know.

"I'm sorry, Master. Please give me another chance."

Why?

Allosyr hesitated before closing his eyes and bowing his head. "I'm afraid."

Good.

The darkness swirled and pressure of the Demon King's attention pushed down on me.

Second chances are not the kinds of gifts I give. Even better, you have come with a gift for me. I'll let you have this one in exchange for another.

"You will not have either of us this day," Santcus Bylan said, his voice trembling.

Oh, not you. Not either of you. The pressure of his attention lifted, and it was like coming up for a huge gulp of air.

Allosyr begged for a second chance. The Demon King said, *Do not dare cross paths with me again, mortals. You have been warned.*

The darkness swirled like a tornado, kicking up a wind inside the room. Desks and chairs thudded around us until the air pressed down, sucking the darkness. Bloodied as he was, Allosyr looked like any other man kneeling before us.

Sanctus Bylan squeezed my hand, sending warmth back into my body. I gulped in air as my brain thawed and I could form intelligent thoughts. I had a job to do.

"I call forth the Light to pass judgment on all your deeds and protect your soul from the darkness."

"No," the demon said weakly.

Sanctus Bylan held the book in front of both of us. We both said, "In the name of the Light, we banish the Darkness from thy soul and deliver thee to the Light."

There were no screams of terror, no screams of agony, just white light. So much white light. My head spun. My body tilted. I had no idea which way was up. And there was so much light. I was falling—no, lying down on the classroom floor.

The world around me stilled and the light eased off to reveal an open space dominated by white and distant puffy clouds lined in silver and gold, like a sunrise shone all around me. Whispers emanated from the clouds. I felt a serene calm. Everything was going to be okay.

Allosyr—Vergo—whatever his name was, stood before me, holding my tattooed forearm. His suit jacket, shirt, and tie had been burned away, revealing a lean, bare torso covered in blood. His arms and shoulders burnt and smoking. He stood there as if he felt no pain.

"The heroine awakes at last," he said. His voice echoed in the open space.

A confusing mix of fear and calm filled me. I wanted to be rid of the demon, yet here we were in this strange place. Maybe I was dreaming or something. Whispers urged me to be calm and serene. "Where are we?"

"With the Light, Little One. You succeeded at your task."

"You mean I'm dead, too?"

"Yes," he said, "but it's my choice to decide

whether or not you stay this way."

"What do you mean?"

He smiled. "You're such a brave little soul. I admire that. You've also done what I could not do centuries ago. It's quite humbling. Maybe I'm growing soft in the presence of the Light. Maybe not." He traced the tattoo lines on my arm, turning them white. "Your death was never what I wanted." He finished tracing the lines, then let go and stepped back. "Consider this my parting gift, this time no strings attached. Farewell, Little One."

White light engulfed us both and the whispering grew louder. There were too many voices. I tried concentrating on one voice. It felt like I'd been thrown into a river and was speeding off somewhere.

Rest, child. Rest at last.

I didn't recognize the voice, but I didn't care. I succumbed to the river's flow and drifted off to a much-needed sleep.

Chapter 29

At some point, I awoke to gentle prodding. I felt so light, like I had no body. It was a nice feeling after all the aches and pains I'd suffered. I was free of pain.

Some twilight space surrounded me and the two young faces looked down on me. A blushing sky filled my vision and everything surrounded the two figures. This wasn't the classroom. Where on Aardra was I?

I sat up. Nothing but flat ground blanketed in clouds bathed in peach light. What was this place? The two boys straightened up, both of them smiling. This was all so bizarre. I should've felt scared, but I felt as at peace as I had in that cloud place. Maybe this was a dream.

"You did it, Mia," the shorter boy said with an otherworldly echo. He looked about my age, had dark eyes and short hair. He reminded me a bit of Deren. He was more filled out and had normal-sized ears.

"Thank you," the other boy said in a vaguely familiar voice, also echoing. He was of average height and had a lean build. Something about his face, also familiar, made me picture him with a sports uniform on, big shoulder pads, and all.

My eyes widened. "Orton?"

He nodded and smiled wider. "You freed our souls. All of ours." He swept an arm out. Shapes manifested themselves as boys and girls, men and women of a wide range of ages, most of them adults.

"We're all at peace, now," the little boy said.

He had to be— "Carlo Nacinto?" The only time I'd ever seen him was lying on one of the cots in the nurse's office.

"That's me."

I lowered my gaze. "I'm sorry."

"For what?"

"I didn't get to you in time."

Little hands wrapped around ankles that appeared beyond my shoes. The thin layer of fog billowed in all directions. "It's okay. I'm not mad. Those things were out of your control." He sounded like he spoke with a wisdom that wasn't his own. "Besides, I get to be with my parents and watch over them for a little while." He gestured to both of us. "There are plans for me, even on this side. Everything's going to be okay."

"How do you know?" I said.

Carlo smiled.

"No one will ever be drawn into that demon's web again," Orton said. "You and Sanctus Bylan successfully sent him before the Light to be judged. All of us have been freed at last." Carlo straightened up.

"But there are more demons out there."

354

"And there are people like you who can do something about that." Orton's form faded.

Carlo said, "You have a difficult road ahead, Mia Evers." He faded as well, as did all the people beyond him. "You can do it. I know you can."

"What do you mean by difficult road?"

Everyone vanished like someone had drawn curtains closed. It was just me and the clouds.

Carlo's voice dropped to a whisper. "That's not our place to say."

"Whose is it?" I said, standing up. He sounded like Grandma when I tried asking her questions.

A giggle drifted to my ears. "You'll see. Get some rest."

I didn't want to rest. I wanted answers. However, the world around me grew dark. My eyes closed without my permission. I willed them to open at least a crack. I kept trying, determined to make at least one ghost give me some answers.

My eyes popped open and gentle orange light filled my vision. Bolting upright, I yelled Carlo's name. And that's when I realized I wasn't in that cloudy other place. I was sitting in a hospital bed with a bunch of people sitting or standing nearby. This was so not the classroom. How did I get here?

Mom hopped to her feet from one corner of the room. "Mia. You're awake." She wrapped her arms around me, hugging tight.

"Mom," I said, trying to absorb my surroundings. Confusion slowly gave way to the firm warmth enveloping me, letting me know I was back among the living and truly okay. I wrapped my arms around her, and then gasped. "Dad."

Dad crossed the room and stood behind Mom. "Baby girl, you scared us something fierce." He kissed the top of my head.

That bit of loving contact from a dad I hardly saw made my eyes sting. Dad kissed me maybe once a year on my birthday. I didn't know if he did that simply because Mom put him up to it, or if he was trying to be the good dad he used to be.

Dad stroked Mom's hair. He kept his eyes on me, though. The way he looked at me reminded me of all our bedtime stories, the loving cadence of Mom's voice on one side while Dad watched on from the foot of my bed. He was tall, even when sitting, and a full head taller than Mom.

Mom let go. "Don't ever scare us like that again."

"What happened?" I said.

"You tell us."

I took in my parents, at a loss for what to say. Another pair of eyes on me drew my attention. Sanctus Bylan stood a polite distance away in one corner of the room, hands hidden in his voluminous sleeves. His wrinkled face grew serious. "I know she's just woken, but may I have a moment of confidence with your daughter?"

Dad looked at the priest before heading out the door, hands tucked into his jeans pockets. Mom longingly stared after Dad before turning to me, eyes welling with fresh tears. "We'll be right back." She kissed me again and hurried after Dad.

They both walked past someone waiting in the darkened corner. At first, I thought it was the demon in human form, but the blonde hair was too wavy and he didn't wear thick heels. I gasped. Ms. Weever walked over, wearing her usual intense, serious gaze and one of her many layered black dresses. Once the door closed, she said, "It's good to see you again, Miss Evers. I hear congratulations are in order."

"Ms. Weever." Part of me wanted her to hug me like Mom had. I knew she wouldn't. While she had once, something about how she held herself told me she wouldn't again. "Where have you been?"

"Elsewhere," she said. "I hope to be back soon. Look." She held out her arm.

I pressed my tattooed arm to hers. No lines showed up on her skin. Faint white ones showed up on mine. "Yours is gone."

"Thanks to you." She straightened back up and interlaced her fingers in front of her stomach.

"How come I still have one?"

She turned to the priest. "You have any idea, Sanctus?"

He approached the foot of the bed. "Oh, several theories, each more of a stretch than the other. This is new territory for any Light order." His eyes met mine. "Mia, what happened?"

Memory of Allosyr bidding me farewell replayed in my mind.

"One moment, you were standing, and the next moment, you'd slumped to the ground. You had no pulse, no life in you."

I stared in disbelief. "Wait, I really died?"

"For a handful of minutes. Nothing I did to revive you worked. It's like you returned to life by your own choice."

I sat there a moment, absorbing the truth. I'd really died. Allosyr had decided not to take me with him.

I'd...I'd really died. I didn't know how to feel. I was alive now, so the experience might as well have been a dream. That moment felt fuzzier and less real with each passing moment, like a dream being slowly wiped from memory. But it'd happened. I knew it had. My now pale white tattoo was proof. "Allosyr said he had the choice to take me with him. He let me know he wasn't going to. Why would a demon do anything nice?"

Both adults looked at each other, their eyes wide. Ms. Weever said, "Miss Evers, I thought my lessons would stick better. Now, where did I say demons come from?"

"They're all once human. I know. But why?"

She pursed her lips. "I'm not sure. Maybe, since the Demon King's hold over him was finally broken, he could make different choices. Or maybe, since he knew the Light would judge him at last, he selfishly did it in hopes of less severe punishment."

The latter made more sense. I hoped it was the first thing. As much as I hated him, I couldn't help but want him to be a better person—demon—whatever he was now.

"That's one of those questions we'll never know the answer to," Sanctus Bylan said. "You'll find that life slowly fills with unanswered questions. One has to accept that in order to be at peace."

There was one question Ms. Weever should be able to answer. "We learned the demon's name. I thought you said he wasn't your son."

Ms. Weever's brows furrowed. "He couldn't have been. What was his name?"

The priest said, "Vergo Aaron Weever."

"My son's name was Sean. I'll have to look into my family tree. I don't believe I had any great-grandfathers named Vergo. This explains some things, though."

"Explains what?" I said.

She gave me a dismissive wave. "Things for me, not for you. But I will say that demons don't randomly pick their targets. A lot of cold calculation went into creating this chaos that is finally at an end."

"So what happens now?"

"I'll be returning to my Order to report these events." Sanctus Bylan inclined his head. "Thanks to you, I believe big changes are coming, changes for the better."

"I hope your Order is ready for them," Ms. Weever said.

He smiled. "Oh ye of little faith. Just wait and see." He gave her a slight bow as well, then placed a hand on my head. Go with the Light, my child." He bid us both a pleasant farewell and exited the room.

His warm, pleasant energy lingered after he left. Carlo had said everything was going to be okay. I wanted to believe it. I didn't know how. "So does this mean you get to come back and be my tutor again?"

"Actually, yes." She graced me with one of her rare smiles. "A lot happened while you were unconscious. You left quite the impression on Sanctus Bylan. He came to both our defenses. However, we do need to make sure nothing like this happens again for the remainder of your education at Toolena Mesa."

"That's easy enough."

She raised an eyebrow. "What does your student profile say? Ghosts following her everywhere, scares fellow students and makes them feel uncomfortable, sometimes scares staff, etcetera, etcetera." Taking a deep breath, she sighed through her nose. "Miss Evers, we're aligned with Dark. Things will find us. That's just how it is."

Chapter 30

Dad treated the four of us to breakfast at a popular pancake restaurant. Mom and Bela did most of the talking. Dad sat quietly, methodically clearing his plate. He wasn't looking at any of us while Mom went on and on about Sanctus Bylan and all the nice things he said about me. The way Dad kept his gaze down and head tilted indicated he was listening to every word. I felt like Yuna celebrating with the unicorns. She'd defeated a dragon. I'd defeated a demon. Now here was the grand feast. Instead of waiting for a satyr to crash the party with dire news, I waited for the day some other dark force crossed my path.

I tried pushing those worries out of my mind so I could enjoy sitting together as a complete family. Dad was quiet, but he was here. This was my first meal with him in months. And Mom was in a great mood. It wouldn't last forever. I had to enjoy it before Dad disappeared and Mom returned to being sad and strange again.

We headed home, Dad driving, Mom smiling away in the passenger seat, and Bela next to me in the roomy back seat. She tried to sing along with the music coming from the song stone and ended up making her own tune. The new car was great. It made only a pleasant hum, kicked up minimal dust as we flew down the dirt road, and the black leather seats reminded me of the Light Order's car. I stroked the soft leather and traced the white stitching. Despite Bela's off-key little voice, I drifted to sleep before we got off the highway.

When the car stilled and the pleasant hum fell silent, I became dully aware of my surroundings. Doors opened and closed, and then the door near me opened a moment later, engulfing me in warmer air. Someone undid my seatbelt and big, strong arms lifted me. I started at the sudden shift. Someone gently shushed me.

"Go back to sleep, baby girl."

It was Dad. I settled my face in his arm. His steady stride swayed me with every step as he carried me into the house.

"She's getting big," he whispered.

"I know. She's growing up so fast," Mom whispered back.

A moment later, Dad gently placed me on my bed and Mom pulled my shoes off. Sheets enveloped my body. I tucked the end under my chin and settled in place, sleep beckoning me once more.

"I want to be tucked in, too," Bela said and Mom shushed her.

I didn't understand why I was so tired. I didn't care. I felt so relaxed and at peace. All four of us were together without any fear of me and my alignment. This was all I ever wanted.

"You're missing our daughters' childhoods."

"I know. I'm trying to find honest work."

"I know. I hope it's soon. I want to be with you. I love you."

"I love you, too, baby." Feet shuffled, followed by the sound of a kiss. "I don't like being away from you so much." They kissed again. "I'll see what I can do." More kissing followed, and then three pairs of feet exited my room, shutting the door behind them. I fell asleep with a smile on my face.

***

I awoke to sunlight coaxing my eyelids open, along with a light weight on my stomach. Figuring it was one of my stuffed animals, I stretched and rubbed my eyes, dispelling sleep from my limbs. Then that light weight adjusted its position. I stopped mid-stretch, my arms posing like a flexing bodybuilder. A black cat sat on my stomach, a splotch of white on one set of toes. It calmly stared at me with golden eyes.

Letting out a scream, I dashed out of bed, clutching a pillow.

"Oh, stop that, Little One," the cat said.

By the Light, the cat talked. Either I was dreaming or this was a ghost cat or something. "Go away. I need a break from dead things talking to me." I gave the pillow a mighty swing.

The cat hopped out of range and settled on the foot of my bed, curling its tail around its paws. "Trust me. This wasn't my idea. I wouldn't be here if I had a choice." The cat had a distinctly male voice.

"Then why are you here?"

"Because the Light sent me," he said unhappily. "So here I am."

My room didn't have that fuzzy feeling of not being awake. "Is this a dream?"

The cat's eyes narrowed. "No, you're finally awake after quite the lengthy nap."

"Are you sure you've come to the right person? I'm a Dark, not a Light."

"Oh, I'm quite sure."

"Then why are you here?"

"You are my atonement, Mia Evers."

I held the pillow between us. "What's atonement?"

"It means to right your wrongs. I've done many wrong things. Now I must make them right by helping you."

"Help me how?"

The cat absently licked the paw that had white toes. "Oh, I could be all cliché and dramatic, and warn you about all the challenges that lie before you, which is true, but let's say we'll see. Let's take things one day at a time." He groomed himself behind the ears.

I slowly lowered my pillow. "You don't sound like you want to help me."

He paused with one paw up. "Not really, no. This is an unintended consequence of my one good deed. An eternity of damnation probably would've been a better choice." He set his paw down. "But here I am."

"Who are you?"

The cat looked straight at me, then tilted his head. "You don't recognize me? I'm hurt."

"I never had a pet cat," I said.

He stomped a paw. "I am most certainly not the spirit of some beloved little fur ball. I have more dignity than that. However, I forgive your confusion. I was a lot bigger the last time we crossed paths. And human. It's me, Vergo."

Blood drained from my face. "I sent you to the Light. You shouldn't be here."

"You most certainly did. I don't know whether or not to thank or hate you for it."

I took a step away. "How are you back? I don't want anything to do with you. I'm never completing the bargain with you." I held up the pillow.

He held up a paw. "There is no more bargain, Little One. I'm not a demon anymore."

"How do I know you're telling the truth?"

"Do you really think, with an ego as big as mine, I'd appear before you as some minuscule creature capable of hacking up hairballs?"

Something about his annoyed tone gave me pause. He honestly didn't want to be here anymore than I wanted him around.

"Besides, your change of tattoo should be proof enough."

"Can't you go back to the Light?"

"Not until I properly atone for my sins." Looking away, his little shoulders drooped. "And for that, I have many. We're stuck together, you and I, whether we like it or not."

"Why me?"

"That's a question we all ask ourselves in life and death. This time the answer is quite simple. The Light has assigned me to you because of my choice to spare you when I could've easily taken you with me. No good deed goes unpunished. Anyway, returning to the dark embrace of the Demon King is no longer an option.

Even he has rejected me. And walking into the embrace of the Light is not yet an option until I earn it. So here I am, stuck in this limbo of atonement, until I'm worthy of the Light's embrace."

I set my pillow on the bed. "So, in order to completely cross over, you have to earn it?"

"Correct." He lowered to his belly and kneaded my comforter. After a moment, he stopped and looked at his paws. He let out a kitty growl. "Bah. I'm even acting like this lowly creature. This truly is punishment." He curled up, tucking his paws under him.

Seeing this as an opportunity, I snatched up my pillow and hammered the cat.

Vergo shook his head, cross-eyed. "Ow. What was that for?"

"For trying to strike a bargain with an eleven-year-old."

"I already told you I'm not a demon anymore."

Whump. I smacked him again and he shook his head a second time, his fur bristling and ears flattened. "That was for killing Carlo." *Whump.* "That was for trying to kill Deren." *Whump.* "And that's for all the lies you told Ms. Weever." *Whump.* "And that one was for Orton."

Vergo sat there, fur helter-skelter and head drawing unsteady circles. "Are you sure there isn't one more for that last girl I tried to hurry up and kill?"

I considered it for a moment. "No, we're not friends. I don't like her."

"But you saved her life."

"Because it was the right thing to do."

He gave his head another shake and stopped

wobbling. "Oh, this is going to be so much fun."

Join the Mailing List

Get informed on the next book release without worrying about spam or filler. Keep an eye out for updates and chances to become a beta reader.

Sign up at AngelaGuajardo.com

Acknowledgments

I have so much to be thankful for. So many people have cheered me on over the years. Every last one of you helped me see this through to publication. A big thanks to my mother, cousins Jessie, Jennie, Jon, and my late grandmother for being my biggest fans of even the first chapters I dared call writing. You gave me the gumption to keep learning and growing.

Thank you to the WANA Tribe for all your support as well, for being my sounding board when I needed it, for all the help with the dreaded blurb, for helping me get unstuck on the rare occasion, and for just being there day after day, especially through the pandemic. We were not alone.

And, of course, thank you to my husband, who keeps me grounded and, for some reason, is willing to put up with my crazy. Well, I do put up with his stupid, so that makes us even.

About the Author

Angela Guajardo is an award-winning author, blogger, sports journalist, and editor whose heart lies with young adult fantasy. She currently lives in the Phoenix metro with her husband and fur babies. When not writing or editing, she nerds it out on various video games, walks her dog, binges on various paranormal programs, or watches lots of sports.